"QUARK, ROM.
YOU ARE UNDER ARREST . . ."

. . . the Bajoran officer said, "for violating the law that prohibits Ferengi from being within Bajoran space. You will now be taken into custody." She raised her hands, displaying the restraints. Quickly she manacled Quark's wrists, then Rom's. . . .

PNU

PROTEIN NITROGEN
UNIT

For information on how individual consumers can place orders, please write to Mail Order Department, Simon & Schuster Inc., 200 Old Tappan Road, Old Tappan, NJ 07675.

STAR TREK
DEEP SPACE NINE®

THE 34TH RULE

A Novel by
Armin Shimerman and David George
Based on the story by **Armin Shimerman
& David George & Eric Stillwell**

POCKET BOOKS
New York   London   Toronto   Sydney   Tokyo   Singapore

This book is a work of fiction. Names, characters, places and incidents are products of the author's imagination or are used fictitiously. Any resemblance to actual events or locales or persons, living or dead, is entirely coincidental.

An *Original* Publication of POCKET BOOKS

POCKET BOOKS, a division of Simon & Schuster Inc.
1230 Avenue of the Americas, New York, NY 10020

Copyright © 1999 by Paramount Pictures. All Rights Reserved.

STAR TREK is a Registered Trademark of
Paramount Pictures.

A VIACOM COMPANY

This book is published by Pocket Books, a division of Simon & Schuster Inc., under exclusive license from Paramount Pictures.

ISBN: 0-671-00793-9

First Pocket Books printing January 1999

10 9 8 7 6 5 4 3 2 1

POCKET and colophon are registered trademarks of Simon & Schuster Inc.

Printed in the U.S.A.

To my darling wife, Kitty,
my life's muse,
whom I can never thank
nor praise enough.

Armin

To my darling wife, Karen,
my earthbound star,
in whose orbit
I shall forever dance.

David

Acknowledgments

Armin and David together wish to thank several people for their generous assistance during the writing of this novel. First and foremost, they gratefully acknowledge the tremendous contribution of Eric A. Stillwell, without whose creative influences this book might never have come to be. Thanks also to Bob Gillan for cheerfully and expeditiously answering a number of questions, and to Lolita Fatjo for providing a list of the known Rules of Acquisition that she and Bob had compiled for the show. Mark Gemello graciously gave the benefit of his business knowledge, and Dave "Doggie" Denham was the veritable fountain of information when it came to the game of darts; Michael Simon was a similar source for baseball-related data. And when the resident *Deep Space Nine* actor and his trusty coauthor could not answer questions about the STAR TREK universe, Larry Nemecek could and did. And finally, they send their combined thanks to their editor, John J. Ordover, for being so easy to work with, and for his genuinely helpful suggestions.

Armin would also like to thank the "godfather" of all things STAR TREK, Rick Berman, who gave him a chance to be a part of history, and without whose help this book certainly would never have existed. The same thanks must go to Michael Piller, who first created Quark, and who then graciously took a liking to the actor who plays him. Armin's loving gratitude goes to Ira Behr and the staff of *Deep Space Nine,* who keep making the show the best adventure in the universe. Lastly, Armin thanks Max Grodénchik (Rom), who is truly his "brother," and who will star with him when this book becomes a major motion picture.

David would like to thank Pat, Jennifer, and Anita for their unwavering enthusiasm and support. And most of all, he thanks Karen, without whose support and love not only would this book not have been written, it would not have been worth writing.

Authors' Note

For those of you scoring at home, this novel fits into the *Star Trek: Deep Space Nine* chronology somewhere in the latter part of the fourth season. More specifically, *The 34th Rule* takes place sometime after the events depicted in the episode "Bar Association," and sometime before the events of the episode "Body Parts."

PRELUDE

The 62nd Rule

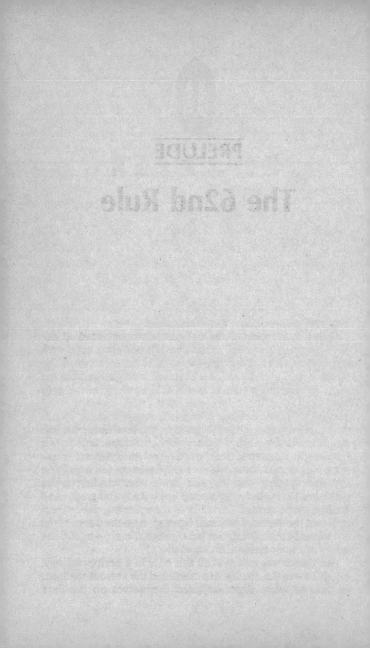

CHAPTER
1

THE UNIVERSE was about to make sense.

Quark stood behind the bar and anxiously studied the display screen above the replicator. His body was rigid with tension, motionless but for his eyes as he scrutinized the data before him. He held his arms folded tightly across his chest, as though trying to insulate himself against a cold wind.

Gripped by both expectation and apprehension, Quark felt isolated, although all about him, his establishment was awash in the sounds and sights and scents characteristic of a busy night. Conversations overlapped everywhere, glassware rang as customers were served, footsteps fell noisily on the deck plating and up and down the winding metal staircases that rose to the second level. Reds and greens and indigos gyred around the walls as the spinning dabo wheel reflected the ambient artificial lighting. And the odors of the occasional exotic drink floated through the air—as did the odors of the occasional exotic alien.

But Quark was aware of all this only in a peripheral way; his focus was the display. He examined the various readouts as tiers of white digits adjusted themselves on the dark

3

screen, as costs and prices fluctuated according to innumerous and often unpredictable economic factors, as months of his intricate planning and manipulation advanced toward a conclusion. Every few seconds, one complicated set of matrices replaced another, causing the display to emit a soft electronic hum, and Quark's mind hummed along with it.

It's going to happen, he thought: monetary values would slide the way he had foreseen, he would arrange the final transactions in this elaborate financial dance, and it would be done. Soon, he would be one step closer—one *significant* step closer—to being able to purchase the moon he had long dreamed of owning.

On the display, one of the numbers brightened, its hue shifting from white to a vibrant orange as it jumped past a threshold Quark had earlier defined. The value decreased for an instant, but then climbed once more, causing a staccato color change: orange, white, orange again.

If it did come, Quark knew, this would be one of those moments that rarely happened by chance. In truth, at least in his own experience, it would be the type of moment that seldom occurred even when painstakingly planned. How many times had he attempted a gambit such as this? How often had he scoured the business world for just the right set of circumstances upon which to found his financial future? Uncounted times, too many times, to be sure. True, there had periodically been a measure of accomplishment—Quark certainly felt justified in considering himself a successful businessman—and yet the level of his achievement had never attained the scope of his ambition. By Ferengi standards—and by his own as well—Quark knew that he so far had been only a marginal player in the thoroughly capitalistic system in which he had been raised. But now, at last, after months of labored and complex machinations, and after a lifetime of effort, lines of communication and intention—*his* intention—threatened to converge.

Quark's mind devoured the ever-changing numbers on the screen in front of him, willing them to achieve the values necessary for the fulfillment of his plans. He remained fixed in place, waiting nervously, until the heavy shuffling of feet directly behind him prompted him to move. In a single swift motion, his hand darted up to touch a control on the smooth surface of the display, blanking the data, and he turned to find out who had come within eyeshot of his work.

It was only Morn, Quark was relieved to see. He watched as the lumbering figure dropped onto a seat on the other side of the bar and set down a tall, cobalt-blue glass. The sole menace Morn posed, Quark mused, would be if he were to end his patronage here; because Morn had been a regular in the bar for almost as long as the place had been open, Quark had come to regard the monthly payment of his tab as a long-term business asset.

"You need a refill," Quark said, nodding toward the glass, and he was surprised to find that he felt momentarily unburdened as the simplicity of bartending replaced the relentlessness of his high-risk dealmaking. He reached for the glass, but Morn pulled it away and pointed a finger inside. Quark peered over the rim and saw a small amount of a bright-yellow liquid. "Oh, you don't want that," Quark said in a tone he had cultivated over the years to imply sincerity. "There's no flavor left in it." He reached forward again, more quickly this time, and took hold of the glass just above Morn's gloved hand. Quark tugged, and after a moment, Morn relented.

"You're really going through this stuff," Quark commented. He bent down behind the bar and quickly found the right bottle: short and bulbous, transparent, not even a quarter filled with what Morn had been drinking. An import hologram decorated with the circular ensign of the First Federation was wrapped about its squat neck. "I'm going to have to order another case of *tranya* from my supplier," Quark added as he stood and emptied the bottle into Morn's glass. He placed the exhausted container on a shelf, adding it to a motley collection of other discards. Later, he or one of his employees would dispose of these using the replicator, recycling their matter into stored energy.

While Morn picked up his glass and sampled his replenished drink, Quark took the time to scan the rest of the bar; after all, his vigilance at the display had left him standing in a manner he ordinarily avoided—with his back to the rest of his establishment. When filled with people, Quark's demanded attention. *Ears open, eyes wide,* went an old Ferengi saying, reflective of the wisdom that taught that customers should be trusted precisely as much as employees should be—which is to say, not at all.

Quark gazed about, concentrating on picking out individual sounds amid the clamor of the bar. He heard the odd admixture of sibilant and rasping speech of a pair of Gorn huddled somewhere on the upper level; the voices sounded to him like air escaping the station into space while somebody complained angrily about it. A lone Otevrel—evidently an outcast to be this far from home and in no apparent hurry to return—sat quietly in a far corner, one slim tendril tracing the lip of his glass with a slight, silky tone. Closer to the bar, Lieutenant Commander Dax was down from Ops to provide her amusing, sometimes biting commentary of the weekly dart match between Chief O'Brien and Dr. Bashir. Intermittent flashes of light and bursts of high-pitched peals also emanated from that direction, produced by the board as darts struck it and points were scored.

And somewhere, Quark was fairly sure, Odo lurked.

Upstairs, he thought. *Perhaps near the entrance to Holosuite Three.* If the station's constable was still in the bar, he was stationary at present, but earlier, Quark had heard the shapeshifter come in, had heard the strange liquid rushing sound Odo made whenever he moved quickly, no matter his form. The sound, though nearly subaudible, was unmistakable to Ferengi ears. Quark had never let on to Odo that he could sometimes hear the internal flow of the changeling's fluidal anatomy. Having taken advantage of the ability on a couple of occasions, though, he thought it likely that the constable suspected the truth; of late, it appeared to him that Odo was careful to move more slowly whenever he wished to go undetected.

Quark strained for a moment to listen specifically for Odo, without result. He was about to return to monitoring the status of his deal, but the sudden cry of "dabo" stopped him. He looked past Morn and over at the gaming table; it was ringed with people, many of them smiling and laughing.

Quark glanced up at a pair of inconspicuous convex mirrors strategically positioned to allow him to observe the entire surface of the dabo table. The ample quantities of gold-pressed latinum in the house's coffers were evidence that the house had been winning tonight, but the dabo girl—a lithe Bajoran named M'Pella—was now disbursing some of those funds to one of the players. The victor was a young Starfleet officer, Quark saw, one of those on leave from the *U.S.S. Ad Astra*, which was presently docked here at *Deep Space Nine*.

"Starfleet," Quark grumbled to himself. "Worthless. *Value-less*." He looked at Morn. "They're always more than willing to take my money at the dabo table," Quark said, as though the two had been in midconversation, "but they never want to drink anything." Quark briefly considered this, then added, "And when they do drink, it's usually only synth-ehol."

Beside M'Pella, the young officer took two handfuls of latinum and held them up as though they were trophies. The lustrous ingots caught the light and scattered golden reflections throughout the room.

"Of course, what should I expect from *customers?*" Quark complained. There were fifty-seven separate words for *customer* in the Ferengi language; the one playing through his mind right now had the secondary definition "river sludge."

"I'll tell you what I should do," Quark said. "I should close this place to Starfleet officers." Even though he was looking directly at Morn, Quark was really talking to himself. He did this out of habit, knowing that Morn was a talker, not a listener.

As if to confirm this, Morn shrugged—as best Quark could tell, his answer for everything that did not directly involve him—and went back to his drink. Absently, Quark began to clear the empty bottles from the shelf and place them in the replicator. He had grabbed the *tranya* bottle in one hand, and the curving, tapered neck of an amber Saurian brandy bottle in the other, when another thought occurred to him. He looked back over at Morn.

"You know, what I should do is just close the entire place down." The idea probably did not sound like a genuine suggestion, Quark suspected, certainly no more than it had any of the times in his beleaguered past when he had voiced similar notions. On those other occasions, though, the words had merely been a means of venting his frustrations about some unsatisfactory aspect of his life. But now . . . now he found that the idea suddenly held real appeal.

"I could do it," Quark told Morn earnestly, talking *to* him now, his hands waving the empty bottles about as he spoke. "If the deal I'm working on right now proceeds the way I designed it to, I should have enough assets to make a successful transition to a new business." Quark felt a flash of heat reach up his neck and across the back of his bare head at his own mere mention of the deal. Disquiet and fear mixed together in the four lobes of his brain. Before now, Quark had not told anyone anything about the deal he had been trying to engineer, not even of its existence. He had spoken of it only to the principals involved— discretion had been required from the outset—and even they were only aware of their isolated roles. Quark had diligently avoided doing anything that might even remotely jeopardize this potential masterpiece of his financial acumen.

"I could do it," Quark said. He put the bottles down in the replicator and pressed a control; they dematerialized in a coruscation of red light. "I could start a new business," Quark continued telling Morn. "It would take some time to prepare, and I'd have to find the right situation, but I could do it." It was a revelation: the profits he hoped to earn today would create not just a single opportunity for him, but many. For the first time in a long time, abandoning the bar for another, better venture would be an actual option. He would no longer be trapped by circumstance in this often troublesome corner of the universe.

Morn raised his glass, threw his head back, and downed his drink in one massive gulp. The movement seemed unrelated to anything Quark had been saying. It was difficult to know if Morn had even been listening; he had such small ears.

Morn brought his empty glass down and pushed it forward; it left two thin trails of liquid behind as it moved through a tiny puddle on the bar. Quark automatically took the glass, grabbed a rag, and wiped down the wet surface. Then he bent beneath the bar and exchanged the rag for another bottle of *tranya*. He broke the seal with the edge of one blue fingernail and removed the stopper.

"Why don't I just leave this here," Quark suggested as he poured another drink. He corked the bottle and placed it on the bar. Morn smiled and nodded his agreement, then lifted his glass in a mock toast.

"As I was saying," Quark went on, undeterred, "what do I need this place for anymore? It's always been more trouble than profit." Morn gazed askance over the rim of his glass.

"What?" Quark asked, reading the doubt in Morn's expression. "You don't think I would do it? You think I need this place?" Quark swept his arm out in an arc to take in his entire establishment. "I don't need this. Not for much longer, anyway."

Quark's voice was beginning to rise in volume, his words beginning to come faster. It was not what he was saying, he realized, but the anxiety and concern he felt about his deal that were surfacing. He was very worried that this business would not take place, even after all of his efforts—or worse, that the deal would transpire, but not in the way he had planned. Still, apart from all that, who was Morn to tell him that he couldn't move on from here to a better livelihood?

"I'm not just a bartender, you know. I'm not even just a bar owner." Quark leaned forward over the bar—palms flat on its surface, his elbows akimbo—to emphasize his point. "I'm a *businessman*. There *is* a difference."

Morn continued to regard him without saying anything.

"Fine," Quark told him. "Keep staring at me like that. It won't change things, won't—" Quark gestured broadly again with his arm. This time, his hand struck the bottle of *tranya,* sending it skidding toward the edge of the bar.

Quark lunged. So did the usually sluggish Morn, who somehow managed to get there first; Quark's hands landed atop his, which in turn had wrapped around the bottle and prevented it from crashing to the floor. The gloves Morn wore on his hands felt papery and rough.

"You must really love this stuff," Quark said, looking up

from where his upper body was stretched across the width of the bar. "I don't think I've ever seen you move that fast." Morn opened his mouth to reply, but before he could, a sound drew Quark's attention. Quark straightened quickly and spun toward the display screen.

The sound was a repeating pattern of tones, pitched so low that it was beyond the abilities of most humanoid races to hear. Quark stepped over to the screen and touched a finger to the control section. The alarm ceased.

Quark glanced around and saw Morn still holding the bottle of *tranya*. Out on the floor, several of Quark's employees were looking in the direction of the bar, evidently curious about what they had heard. Quark gestured to them with both hands, his fingers moving in an outward sweeping motion, an obvious signal that they should get back to work.

"Morn," Quark said, "why don't you sit back down and enjoy your *tranya*. I've got work to do."

As Morn eased onto his chair, Quark returned to the display and brought the arrays of data back up on the screen. In the background, he heard a dart thump into the board, causing a raucous electronic siren to play. From the disappointed words of Chief O'Brien, the winning dart must have been thrown by Dr. Bashir. Quark pushed those and all the other sounds around him away, once again immersing himself in the business at hand.

He scanned the readouts. Symbols representing dozens of different currencies—Ferengi, Bajoran, Bolian, Yridian, and others—decorated the screen. Latinum conversion factors competed with production assessments for importance. Treasury inventory quantities, pecuniary exchange rates, and tallies of monies in circulation aligned themselves in rows and columns. As before, numbers were spelled out in white digits and changed values several times a minute, some with even greater frequency. But now, five numbers were displayed in bright orange instead of just one; having attained specific values, it had been these which had prompted the alarm to sound. Quark had instructed the computer to emit the tones should all of the financial conditions he required finally develop.

For a short time, the reality of the situation failed to

impress itself upon Quark's awareness, even though he only moments before had been anticipating this very event. Initially, there was no joy as he surveyed the numbers and applied to them only the general fiscal meaning he normally would. But by degrees, the significance of what he was reading crept into his mind. His mouth opened in prelude to a smile, revealing his sharp and irregular teeth, but a cynical disbelief born of experience prevented it from fully materializing. Cautiously, he allowed himself to recognize that the successful culmination of his labyrinthine scheme might possibly be at hand. A slight tingling began in his earlobes.

Quark glanced furtively around to assure himself that he was not being watched. Even though the bar was filled with people, nobody seemed to be paying him any attention. He listened for any movement by Odo, but he heard nothing.

Quark's fingers skittered across the controls. He entered a command protocol and one of the readouts changed to produce a directory of his personal files. He keyed in an access code and retrieved a file he had set up previously; it was his confirmation of the individual transactions composing the overall deal. He reread the file while his hand hovered above the TRANSMIT button.

Quark hesitated. Once he approved the transactions, there would be no turning back. Everything would have to proceed, and if he had failed to consider some hidden aspect of the deal, or if he had erred in any of his assumptions or mistimed any one of the many actions he had initiated, he would wind up insolvent. That thought alone made him draw back his hand.

No, Quark insisted to himself. *This is your best chance, the best deal you've ever put together. It will work.* He repeated the 62nd Rule of Acquisition in his head: *The riskier the road, the greater the profit.* He jabbed the button, transmitting the file to a financial institution located on Bajor through which he had filtered all of the arrangements in this enterprise.

He waited. He felt incapable of moving his body. His eyes locked on the display. He was so intent on his own actions that he felt physically segregated from everybody and everything that formed his surroundings. The many voices and sounds of the bar did not remain distinct as they reached his ears, but blended together in an incomprehensible cacophony.

Failure now would destroy him, Quark knew that, and not just financially. When he had first conceived this plan and then devised its blueprint, he had told himself that victory was not only possible, but inevitable. He discerned now, though, that he had never truly believed his grand design would climax as it now appeared it might, in what was nearly the deal of a lifetime for him. Nearly, because the ultimate deal would be the one that provided him the ability to acquire the moon for which he had so long yearned.

The moon, Quark thought, and very specific images were conjured in his mind. His cousin Gaila owned his own moon, and Quark's memories of visits there provided a basis for his fantasizing. He recalled the luxurious estate from which Gaila ruled his natural satellite, the ultramodern façade of the structure contrasting both with the lush countryside in which it was set and with its more traditional Ferengi furnishings. The only contemporary section of the interior was the office, where sophisticated equipment allowed inspection and control of the mining operations on the moon; a communications console also permitted monitoring of three different financial exchanges. Standing in that office, Quark recalled, had felt like being at the hub of a personal commercial empire.

For years, Quark had privately aspired to Gaila's standard of achievement. Even in public, he had revealed the purchase of his own moon to be a long-term goal of great moment to him. But his inner voice, speaking to nobody but himself, identified ambitions surpassing more than just the possession of some inconsequential rock in space.

Over time, Quark's brother had come to share in his vision, or in what he must have believed that vision to be, anyway. Whenever the subject arose, Rom would visibly take delight in discussing it, frequently entreating Quark to describe the moon and the home he intended to have constructed on its surface. Rom would even offer his own details of life there, talking about "his room" and about what he would do there, mentioning such activities as raising small animals—cotton-tailed *jebrets* and *treni* cats and the like—and planting a garden. It was never clear to Quark whether his brother proposed to take up permanent residence on the moon, but he assumed that would be the case; after all, Quark knew that Rom was not fully capable of taking care of himself without his help.

But the tranquil picture Rom painted of life on the moon bespoke his view that Quark would retire there. And whenever Quark verbalized his desire for his own moon to anybody else, they always appeared to infer that he wanted to settle there in order to live in leisure. But Quark had no intention of dwelling in retirement. The moon was an objective, but it was not an end in itself. Quark was, at this point in his life, to one extent or another, what he had always wanted to be: a businessman. Business was not only his livelihood, it was his recreation as well. Success in the world of commerce would not motivate him to leave that world, but to climb to another stratum within it. What reason would there be to excel in a way of life you enjoyed if, in doing so, you were forced to abandon that way of life? Had Zek attained the office of grand nagus for the sake of the office itself? No, of course not: money begets money, and power begets money, and the nagus, while serving in his official role, also used the influence and resources of his position to continue engaging, with great success, in his own business ventures. On his moon, Quark would do the same.

Gaila's survey of the financial exchanges and his mining operation merely hinted at what Quark planned for himself. Quark's communications center would not simply track the three most important indexes, but all the interstellar financial data available in the Alpha Quadrant. Utilizing his connections on *Deep Space Nine,* on Bajor, and on the other side of the wormhole, he would also keep abreast of business opportunities in the Gamma Quadrant. He would not build and manage mining facilities, which would necessarily incur high overhead, but would instead peddle the rights to mine his moon to the highest bidders. He also envisioned endless rows of cheaply constructed warehouses sitting on the horizon of his little world, storage installations for rent to the traders near whose routes he would settle. He would also provide landing rights for the many ships that would use Quark's as a way station. Maybe he would even open up a bar.

Quark could not refrain from smiling at the irony of that last thought. As he did so, two words began to flash on the display: INCOMING TRANSMISSION. The thoughts of the moon in his future were eclipsed by the business in his present. He thumbed a control and the brief contents of the incoming message spread across the readout. There were acknowledgments of all but one of the separate pieces of his confirmation file, which meant that only a single transaction remained to complete the deal.

Quark felt exhilarated and terrified at the same time. His lobes buzzed now as though with an electric charge. Contracts had been written and agreed to, monies had been spent and received, inventories had been purchased and sold, all as a result of his foresight and maneuvering. Like the proverbial wise man, Quark could hear profit in the wind; it sounded sweet.

Barely able to curb his excitement, he manipulated the display controls to gain access to his primary account on Bajor. Numbers danced across the screen. His gaze traveled to the bottom line of the report. A long string of digits, representing his net worth, was displayed there in red.

Right now, Quark was deeper in debt than any individual in the quadrant.

The ninety-seven minutes following Quark's financial ruin were among the most difficult to live through in his life. He struggled to act normally, struggled not to entertain thoughts of bankruptcy, of the forfeiture of all his property, of a future plagued by litigation and garnishment. But walking through the bar, taking orders and serving drinks, he remained distracted by all of these fears, so much so that he found himself deaf to many of the conversations taking place around him. He interacted with customers, entered their orders and accepted their payments on the personal-access display device he carried with him, but it was as though he were watching and listening to somebody else performing these tasks. In his mind, there were great patches of silence that simply overwhelmed his abilities to process the input of his senses on anything more than a superficial level.

It will work out, Quark tried to convince himself. *Everything is happening just the way you planned it.* Except he did not really know whether that was true. Apart from the final transaction, yes, everything Quark had done had concluded successfully, producing exactly the results he had expected. But without the successful completion of that final transaction, he would gain nothing. More than that, he would lose everything.

The image of the red number denoting Quark's net worth haunted him. His debts not only surpassed his assets, they dwarfed them. He had known this would happen, had prepared for it, but still, it was painful to actually experience it. He had to continue to remind himself that this was really the foundation upon which his entire plot had been built.

The great sums Quark owed—to financial institutions, to governments, as recompense for monetary maneuvers he had orchestrated in the exchanges—all of that had gone to fund a single purchase. The commodity was one not typically available to individuals, both because of the nature of the merchandise and because of its immense price. But Quark had been in the right place at the right time, hearing early rumors of the impending sale. He had immediately understood the potential to reap substantial profits by setting himself up as a middleman, by buying and reselling the merchandise himself. But the amount of cash necessary as earnest money, let alone for the full purchase, had far exceeded Quark's resources.

That was when Grand Nagus Zek had docked his new vessel, *Wealth,* at *Deep Space Nine.*

The nagus spent three days on the station preparing for a trade expedition to the Gamma Quadrant, and Quark took advantage of his proximity to the fiscal leader by doing what he always did in like circumstances: he spied on him. Quark's intimate knowledge of *DS9*'s internal systems, coupled with his copious supply of security-defeating hardware and software, permitted him entry to many otherwise protected areas of the station's computer. In that way, he was able to access the companel in Zek's quarters and monitor his on-line activities during his stay.

Unfortunately, as Quark would have expected of any good Ferengi businessman, the nagus erected barriers against such surveillance. When he did not require *Deep Space Nine*'s superior computing facilities or its communications link to the other side of the wormhole, Zek conducted his business aboard *Wealth*. And whenever he did need to use *DS9*'s computer, every bit of information he entered or accessed was encrypted. All of his work also carried a destabilizing virus to prevent recording, a virus Quark was unable to neutralize in the short time the nagus was on the station; Quark therefore had to perform his observations in real time.

For two and a half days, Quark tracked each use of the comm panel in Zek's quarters. He forsook sleep as needed. He kept the bar open, but left it in the hands of his new manager, Broc, whenever the low-frequency alarm sounded, signifying that the nagus was using the station's communications or computer functions. In his own quarters, Quark stared at the comm panel for hours, studying Zek's handiwork as it was echoed there. The elegant, branching structures of the Ferengi language cascaded across the screen, its beautiful symbols and rich vocabulary rendered unintelligible by ciphering. Quark ran decryption algorithms, visually searched for patterns, pored over the notes he took.

His break came during the final fourteen hours of Zek's stay. Weary from his efforts, Quark was debating whether or not to continue when something in the scrambled data swimming across the comm panel drew his attention. He stared at the screen, but whatever it was had already been swept away in the currents of Zek's activities.

If only I could have recorded it, Quark thought, frustrated. Confident that it had been the key, he tried to replay the sequence in his mind, then sought to reproduce it on his padd, but he could not quite grasp what it was he had seen. All he could do was wait and watch and hope that it would happen again.

Forty minutes later, it did.

It was nonspecific, not exactly a pattern in the code, more a motif. Quark adjusted his decryption programs and put them back to work. The strings of characters transformed into something more recognizable, but not fully deciphered. Quark nudged his procedures and set them running again. Suddenly, the account codes and financial endeavors of the grand nagus were completely revealed. What he saw was unbelievable: Zek was losing money at an incredible rate.

Quark felt his eyes widen as the sense of that thought penetrated his awareness. He was unsure how to proceed. The financial leader of the Ferengi, the acknowledged authority of all commerce, the man after whom Quark had patterned his business life, was failing miserably, the deterioration of his business skills making itself plain. Just in the brief span he had been on *DS9*, the nagus had incurred astronomical debts.

It took more than ten hours of rigorous effort for Quark to assemble a sketch of what Zek had done. It was astounding. The methods, the decisions, the strategies, were far too complex for Quark to completely understand, especially since he had only been able to observe a portion of the entire plan. But he eventually understood enough of the broad strokes of the design: the nagus had floated obligations in currencies other than those in which they had been covenanted; had borrowed on time; had bought and sold on margin; had hedged his already considerable financial situation; and had promised, although he could not actually have done so, to be able to monetize vast debts at any time within a one-day period. It was impressive, it was brilliant, and it was even legal, though just barely.

But more was involved than that, Quark was certain. Even though he realized that there were subtleties he had doubtless overlooked, there also seemed to be something vital missing, the bargain or the piece of knowledge or the contact that allowed Zek the opportunity to do what he had done.

Basically, the nagus had re-created more than half of his personal fortune—and far more than all of his liquid assets—out of essentially nothing. That money—or more accurately, that *illusion* of money—had been invented at the expense of tremendous debt, and the debt was a time bomb armed to detonate in one day if the nagus was unable to clear it. Even using the influence of Zek's office, what had been done could not be undone without hard currency to make good on the money he owed.

The nagus departed *Deep Space Nine* and took *Wealth* to the Gamma Quadrant. Quark awaited the ship's reappearance with a growing sense of unease. He tapped into the station's sensors so that he would be alerted as soon as *Wealth* emerged on this side of the wormhole. Within a day, the ship returned, but it bypassed *DS9* and headed directly for Ferenginar. Quark attempted to view the accounts of the nagus, hoping that the access codes he had purloined had not yet been changed. They had not, and Quark marveled at what he saw: pure profit. The nagus had constructed an apparition of value, had utilized it to fund a deal, and then had recovered his imaginary investment quickly enough to dissolve the monetary ghost before anybody had a chance to uncover its want of substance. And he had produced a net gain for himself. An *ample* net gain.

Quark studied what he knew of Zek's audacious plan for weeks. He constructed time lines and business plans, checked and rechecked the financial exchanges, ran simulations. The genius of the nagus became more and more apparent as Quark was forced to admit that what he had witnessed was on the borders of his knowledge and abilities. Even if he entertained the idea of imitating the nagus's plan, he still did not fully understand the circumstances under which it had been made to happen; such circumstances, he was convinced, were not only rare, but unlikely to present themselves when they did occur.

Quark was wrong.

As he sat at the comm panel in his quarters day after day and studied the tactics and strategies the nagus had employed, he was led repeatedly to the Bolian Credit Exchange. Finally, he saw it: a flaw in the trade rules of the Exchange, a crack so slight that it was nearly undetectable. The crux of Zek's bold work, the fault had probably been virtually invisible prior to his actions, which had widened it; if others exploited the weakness, it would widen further.

Before long, the fissure would be as great as Terekol Chasm on Ferenginar, and as easy to see. When that happened, the Bolian regulators would seal the loophole.

Until that time, Quark could act. He recalled the upcoming sale, its demand for massive monetary commitments, and its potential for producing large profits. He began devising his strategy and then executing it. Unlike Zek, whose personal fortune buttressed his financial credentials, Quark had relatively little to reinforce himself. In the end, what his maneuvers obtained for him was a two-hour window in which he could resell the commodity he had bought. If he was able to close the deal, he would be able to cover his debts; if not, he would be destitute.

In one regard, the value currently representing Quark's net worth was erroneous, since Quark now owned merchandise which, if he was able to sell it, would offset his obligations and provide him with a handsome profit. But because Quark's purchase had been clandestine, and because the merchandise was practically unsalable, it retained no value whatsoever without a buyer.

The list of potential customers was a short one. The black market, a usually reliable outlet for almost any commodity, was not an option: few would be able to pay at cost, much less at a reasonable price. If the buyer Quark had lined up reneged—very much a possibility with this type of deal— he would probably be unable to move the goods within the two-hour time span. His creditors would not be understanding.

Trying to keep his emotions level and his thoughts positive, Quark continued to wait on customers in his establishment, snaking through the tables in a practiced but mindless way. Each time he returned to the bar to make drinks, he checked the display. There was nothing. He probably should have set another alarm to sound when a transmission did arrive, but he could not bring himself to do so; he was hoping for good news, but he was dreading bad.

Back to the bar again, this time to mix a Finagle's Folly for Dr. Bashir, Quark saw the words INCOMING TRANSMISSION flashing on the display. His earlobes grew cold from fear, heat slipping from them like water spilling down a drain. He punched the RECEIVE button and the message printed on the screen. Quark read it twice, then a third time, just to be sure he did not miss or misread any details. He checked the chronometer: ninety-seven minutes since he had received the first set of confirmations. He had another twenty-three minutes yet to make good on his debt.

Twenty-three minutes. He smiled. It had not even been dramatic.

Quark worked quickly at the display. He made the necessary transfers of funds and confirmed them. It would be several minutes before the transactions would be posted to his account on Bajor.

While he waited for that to take place, he turned back to the bar, which now suddenly came alive to him. The din became a mixture of discernible voices once more, the crowd a set of recognizable individuals. Quark noticed Dr. Bashir gazing in his direction. He motioned that he would be right there, then took out a glass and began preparing the drink the doctor had ordered. A shot from this bottle, a splash from that one; Quark's arms flew vigorously about, a frenzy of mixological élan. He felt thoroughly energized.

Quark delivered the drink to the table where Dr. Bashir sat between turns in his dart match with Chief O'Brien. The doctor thanked him and sipped from the glass. A startled look materialized on his face, accompanied by a throaty cough.

"Is it my imagination, Quark," he asked in his distinctive British accent—*Kwahk,* he pronounced it—"or is there more alcohol in this than usual?"

"Don't be ridiculous," Quark responded, but he did not stay to debate the matter. Time enough had passed. He headed back to the display behind the bar.

Nervous, Quark failed at first to accurately specify his account information. The second time, his fingers played more carefully across the controls and he gained access to his account on Bajor. His net worth came up in black; it did not have as many digits as when it had been drawn in red, but there were enough to indicate that the deal had been very profitable.

He had done it. He had completed the most lucrative deal of his life, had managed to navigate the complexities in making a deal with the Ferengi Alliance itself. Now, finally, Quark had seed money. From here, he could really start to deal, really begin to build up his finances to the point where he could afford the moon and its accoutrements.

A pleasant rush of heat suffused Quark's lobes, and he smiled broadly. He turned to face the rest of the bar, raised his arms above his head, and said loudly, "Everybody, drinks are on—"

—*the house,* he had been about to say. But he was interrupted by the financial planner in his head, who wanted to know why, just because he had successfully concluded a deal, he was about to behave so foolishly. About half of the people in the bar looked at him, waiting for him to finish. Morn sat straight up in his seat and gazed at Quark with an expression of what could only be interpreted as joyful expectation.

"—sale," Quark said. "Drinks are half-price for the next quarter-hour." There was a murmur among some of the customers, and several either held up their glasses or moved toward the bar. Morn slumped back down in his chair, his body language conveying his obvious disappointment that free drinks would not be forthcoming. Still, he picked up the bottle of *tranya* and held it up for Quark to see, indicating that he too would take advantage of the transient bargain.

Nobody said anything directly to Quark, though. The smile left his face, and under his breath, more to himself than to anybody else, he said, "Don't bother to thank me." And he thought: *I really* should *give up this place.*

But as Quark considered just how he could leave *Deep Space Nine,* about how the realization of his deal actually made that possible, he found that his resolve could not stand on its own. Leaving this place—and these people—would be nice, and Quark eventually would.

But not yet.

Being here at the mouth of the wormhole, on the very edge of the frontier, had permitted him to make this first sizable deal, and with his newly acquired wealth, being on *DS9* would now provide him with many more opportunities to make such deals. Quark had lived unappreciated—and even disdained—by the Starfleet and Bajoran officers on the space station for years now. For the sake of profits—for the sake of his moon—he could take this place and these people just a little bit longer.

Turning once more to the display, Quark reexamined the number spelling out his net worth. The smile returned to his face: the figure was still black, still sizable, and he knew it would remain that way. He closed the access to his account.

This makes sense, Quark thought. *This is how the universe is supposed to work.*

22

CHAPTER
2

THE CONFLUENCE OF space and time and thought sat inside a small box atop a table in the anteroom.

The box—unlike the object it contained—was unremarkable: a rounded, truncated pyramid, barely a meter around at its base. Simple designs had been fashioned in the dark wood that composed its exterior. A pair of hinged doors, closed at the moment, were set into one side. Even illuminated by a single, narrow shaft of light, as it currently was, the box did little to draw the attention of the eye.

In a corner of the octagonal room, Grand Nagus Zek stood leaning on his cane, his ancient, gnarled hands clasped around the great ornamental knob that decorated one end. Zek used the walking stick to get around, but it was also a conceit: he had long ago had the knob crafted in his own likeness from gold-pressed latinum. Such a wanton and ostentatious exhibition of ego and wealth was just one symbol of his great success as the ranking officer of Ferengi commerce.

From his vantage across the room, the nagus regarded the old wooden box. He had chosen the plain case because of its contrast with what it contained. Sealed up as it was, the box hardly seemed impressive, but Zek smiled widely as he contemplated how much profit he estimated its contents would bring him.

The nagus gazed around, verifying that arrangements were complete. Devoid of people but for himself, the room was quiet and still. Furniture of a decidedly Bajoran design currently lined its eight-sided periphery, and complementary artwork decorated the walls. The entrance to the room—a single-paneled door that slid horizontally into the wall to allow access and egress—stood closed on one side. A second door, also closed, was set opposite the first; it led into a large meeting chamber adjacent to the anteroom.

There were no windows here, although there appeared to be one. It was in a side wall, two meters wide and half as tall, divided into four identically sized panes. Beyond it, seemingly, lay a tranquil scene: the tree-covered hills of Zhentu Province sloping away to an open meadow, a blue sky above beginning to fade into the striated reds and pinks of a Bajoran sunset. But the vista was no more real than the window itself.

Zek walked across the room, leaning only lightly on his cane. The grating scrape of his shoes shuffling along the wooden flooring alternated with the thin tap of his cane. He sat down in a stuffed chair that would have been comfortable had its seat been lower, but Ferengi and Bajoran anatomies being what they were, the nagus's feet dangled above the floor. *Never believe anybody taller than you,* his father had once warned him, and it had proven to be judicious counsel, given that the average Ferengi tended to be shorter than the members of most humanoid races.

Zek surveyed his surroundings from his new point of view in the chair, wanting to be sure of every detail. As always, he had ordered the room prepared to specifications he had researched himself, but he usually found it necessary to make adjustments once things had actually been set up. He started to see that some minor changes would be required now.

For his own tastes, the environment that had been re-created here was lackluster: there were no sounds to speak of, the colors were too muted, the air too stagnant. And yet, even now, Zek loved this room, this and the seven others like it that surrounded the meeting chamber. The anterooms demonstrated a clever synthesis of business and technology. Environmental controls made it possible to adjust the temperature, the gravity, even the composition of the atmosphere, to comfortably support members of virtually any species. By means of holographic imaging and a transporter system, furniture could be modified to accommodate any type of physiology, and artwork—and myriad other accoutrements, such as windows—could be made to reflect countless styles and tastes.

The ostensible purpose of the anterooms was to provide people with a place to wait before entering the meeting chamber, where business would then be conducted. In practice, though, the rooms served a business tactic: to force potential customers and trade partners to tarry in whatever setting would best bend them in the direction of completing a deal. The rooms and their furnishings could be molded in such ways as to soften people, or disarm them, or even make them uncomfortable, if that was what was needed.

The chameleon-like rooms had been Zek's innovation, one facet of a minor revolution he had introduced into Ferengi trade practices. The prevailing and seldom-questioned sentiment of his predecessors had been *not* to conduct business with outworlders on Ferenginar itself. Previously, when attempts to transact business on Ferenginar had been made, they had generally been unsuccessful. The inconvenience of the planet's location, combined with its intemperately wet climate, had apparently poisoned the spirits of potential customers and partners. The programmable anterooms had proven to be at least a partial cure in some circumstances. While doing business on Ferenginar with outworlders was still not widely practiced, there were occasions when it was not only done, but it was an asset.

This occasion, Zek believed, was such a time.

"Computer," he said into the stillness of the room. He detected a slight echo, obviously the result of a floor that was uncarpeted, and walls that were bare but for a few small paintings. "Eliminate the glass from the window." There was a shimmer in the space on the wall where the window was being simulated, though it was impossible to tell from where Zek sat that the glass was no longer there. "Now, I want a light breeze. Warm. And sweeten it with the scent of some popular native flowers." At first, there seemed to be no change in the room, but then the air began to circulate gently. Zek felt the thick hairs in the centers of his ears quiver in the shifting currents.

That's better, thought the nagus, believing that the breeze would have a calming effect on the people who would soon be passing through here. The anteroom had been configured for the imminent arrival of a delegation from Bajor led by their minister of religious artifacts, a vedek named Pralon. The Bajorans were vigorously seeking to obtain the object that now sat in this room, in the box sitting on the pedestal table: an Orb of the Prophets.

The Orb was one of only nine such objects known to exist. Each had been discovered in or about the Bajoran star system during the past hundred centuries. At one time, every known Orb had been kept on Bajor; they had been public objects of worship and spiritual contemplation, enshrined in ornately jeweled cases and cared for by Bajoran monks. But when the decades-long Cardassian Occupation of Bajor had ended, several years ago, all but one of the objects had been seized by the departing conquerors.

Zek had come into possession of his Orb—the Ninth Orb, the so-called Orb of Wisdom—through a contact on Cardassia III. The Bajorans were currently negotiating with the civilian arm of the Cardassian government, the Detapa Council, for the return of the Orbs. The Ninth Orb, though, had somehow slipped away from the Council during the recent unrest in the Cardassian Union, and Zek had taken advantage of the rare opportunity and purchased it himself on the black market.

The nagus stood up and walked over to where the Ninth Orb sat. He reached forward to open its case, but then pulled his hand back sharply, as though he had touched something that had burned his flesh. The nagus had once experienced a powerful vision while inspecting his Orb, a vision that had temporarily altered his mind, and he had no wish for a recurrence of that incident.

The Orbs were curious artifacts. Hourglass-shaped and a vibrant green in color, they glowed from within and had been known to defy gravity. Other, more spiritual powers had long been rumored—to which Zek could testify—but as far as Zek knew, they had largely gone undocumented. Examination of the nagus's Orb by his scientists revealed only that it appeared to be an energy vortex of some kind, drawing in spatial, temporal, and mental forces. If the Bajorans or Cardassians had studied the Orbs—and the nagus was sure that they had—whatever they had learned remained a mystery. Zek suspected, though, that they had been able to uncover nothing more than his scientists had. No, the nature of the Orbs was unknown, and perhaps unknowable.

Despite their enigmatic nature—perhaps even because of it—the Orbs were a vivid symbol of the deeply held religious beliefs of the Bajorans. The strange objects were accepted by them to be manifestations of their gods, sent to teach them and guide their lives; they were thought to have originated in the Celestial Temple. The discovery of the wormhole, along with the aliens who had constructed it and lived within it, had not shaken the faith of the Bajorans, but had instead served to strengthen it. That the Celestial Temple could be explained scientifically as a wormhole, that the Prophets could be identified as alien beings, only underscored the plausibility of their beliefs. Could the Bajorans construct a wormhole themselves, they reasoned? Could the Federation, or the Cardassians, or anybody else? No; only the Prophets could. And like the Orbs, the aliens who lived within the wormhole—the Prophets residing in the Celestial Temple—were fundamentally unknown, and perhaps unknowable.

The Orb was the type of commodity that the nagus loved to peddle, because many factions were compelled by different reasons to possess it. There were those who sought it because of its intractable and potentially powerful nature. Others pursued it for its scientific mystery, still others for the political weight it would lend them with the Bajorans. And of course, there were the Bajorans themselves, whose campaign to acquire the object was born of possibly the most compelling reason: its great religious significance to them, a significance heightened even more now with the possibility of the return of all the Orbs but this one.

Zek had initially thought that he would merely sell the Orb directly to the Bajorans, but after some other business dealings, he had seen that there was another way to maximize his profit. After bringing it back to Ferenginar, he had made his ownership of the Orb known in all quarters, although he had not immediately accepted any offers for it. Rather, he had let demand build.

As Zek had anticipated, for no group did that demand increase as much as it did for the Bajorans. For months, they launched one diplomatic sally after another. In a series of unprecedented visits, various functionaries of the Bajoran government—from the ambassador-at-large to the second minister—met with the nagus on Ferenginar. Bajoran religious leaders, including several vedeks, journeyed to Ferenginar as well. They asked, cajoled, demanded. Zek put them off, maintaining that there was other business he needed to conduct before he could even concern himself with the sale of the Orb. He knew that they did not believe him, even though there had been at least some truth in his words.

Eventually, the nagus had received an impassioned letter signed by both the Bajorans' highest governmental official and their religious leader. In the letter, the first minister and the kai argued that because the Orb had originally been found in their star system, and also because of its revered place in their religion, it truly belonged to the Bajoran people. Recognizing the role of the nagus as the current possessor of the Orb, though, they pledged to pay a reasonable price for it. Further, the subtext suggested that they might even be willing to pay an *unreasonable* price, if that was what was required of them. Simply stated, they had to have the Orb.

Zek had expected the letter, or something very much like it, and he used it as the impetus to begin the process—an auction—that would lead to the eventual sale of the Orb. He solicited secret offers from many potential buyers. The Bajorans objected to the auction through official channels, renewing their claim that the Orb legally belonged to them. But Zek categorically denied that claim. With no other recourse, the Bajorans had entered the bidding.

What else could they have done? Zek thought now.

The nagus stepped away from the encased Orb and headed for one of the doors, which glided open to reveal the meeting chamber beyond it. He turned in the doorway and scanned the room a final time. It was too quiet, he decided, even for people such as the Bajorans, whose sense of hearing was not nearly as sensitive as that of the Ferengi.

"Computer," Zek said, "generate some background noise consistent with a meadow on Bajor. Leaves rustling in the breeze, birds singing, that sort of thing." Immediately, he heard the lilting chirps of several birds, underscored by the sough of a mild wind slipping through trees and grasses.

Zek looked over at the box in which the Orb sat. During the past several months, the nagus had reviewed a considerable number of tenders for the inscrutable object. He had narrowed the field of bidders in stages. From scores of initial offerers, only seven now remained. With the arrival today of those seven on Ferenginar, that number would ultimately be reduced to three, after what the nagus knew would be several weeks of his drawn-out consideration about the relative worths of the offers.

Zek wondered what the Bajorans would bid for it today. There seemed little question that the amount would be sizable. It might even be a sum that would strain the financial reserves of their world.

In the empty waiting room, Zek burst into a reedy cackle. Sometimes, he was taken with his own brilliance. Whatever amount the Bajorans bid, he knew it would not be enough.

PART I

The 2nd Rule

CHAPTER 3

MAJOR KIRA NERYS strode into Quark's near closing time. Because of the lateness of the hour, only a handful of customers remained in the bar. A few sat scattered at tables, pulling slowly at their drinks. Two older Bajoran gentlemen huddled about the dabo table, intermittently squawking their displeasure as their long night of gaming dwindled along with their reserves of latinum. And perched upon his customary seat, as if he had been born there and would likely die there, was Morn.

Quark usually hated this time of night in the bar; it was a time when revenue faded, but overhead did not. For that reason, he had already sent all of his employees home, but for one of the dabo girls—Leeta—and Broc. And if he could have fully trusted Broc to close up, Quark would himself have headed for his own quarters. With so few customers, he was not only failing to make much of a profit, he was also thoroughly bored.

Occasionally, on a night such as this one, Quark would be able to dispatch the nocturnal doldrums by picking up some valuable morsel of information. As the night deepened and closing time approached, some customers would grow tired or intoxicated—or both—and lips would be loosened. A crumb of useful rumor might be given voice, or a succulent tip let slip. It happened only rarely, but it did happen.

The possibilities tonight had seemed limited to a pair of Frunalian traders sitting at a table on the upper level. They were second-rate peddlers who had stopped on the station before, whose wares had never seemed worth enough even to pay for their travels, but the two had somehow stayed in business together for several years. They had been discussing their impending trip to the Gamma Quadrant and drinking *kiriliona*—a strong Frunalian liquor—since the middle part of the evening.

Quark had attempted to eavesdrop on the traders' conversation for hours, but he had been unable to do so effectively from his position on the lower level. He had picked up provocative words like *delivery* and *latinum* and *profit*, but nothing more than that. At first, it had been because the rough voices of the pair had dropped frequently into whispers, and Quark had patiently waited for the alcohol they were drinking to become his ally. But as their states of inebriation had deepened and their voices had risen, the traders' speech had become slurred and difficult to understand. Still, if they possessed information of any value, there would have been no better opportunity to uncover it.

Quark had climbed the winding stairway at the end of the bar, carrying a small handheld sterilizer as his only cover. Once on the upper level, he had pressed the power switch on the device, which had clicked beneath his touch. The device had beeped once and then begun operating with a soft whir. He had set to wiping down tables, his arm sweeping out across their surfaces in wide circles.

As he moved from one table to another, Quark's proximity to the traders had rendered everything they said, even drunkenly articulated, plainly understandable. The details of their plan had rapidly grown clear.

It was as Quark cleaned a table next to the railing that he noticed Kira enter from the Promenade. Quark always noticed Kira. He had done so when she had first arrived on *Deep Space Nine* as a Cardassian slave worker—her formfitting outfit had been particularly flattering that day, he recalled—and he had continued to notice her, albeit in a less conspicuous manner, even after she had rebuffed his advances.

"You want something, Quark?"

Quark turned from peering down at Kira. Both of the Frunalians were looking at him. Quark recognized the voice as that of Crimmon, the taller—and less friendly—of the two traders.

"Me?" Quark answered. "No. I'm just getting ready for closing time." The sterilizer in his hand continued its electronic purr, although Quark had for the moment stopped moving it across the tabletop.

"'Closing time'?" asked the other trader, Wyra. He checked a timepiece. "But it's only—"

"Sorry," Quark interrupted. "Captain Sisko enforces a strict curfew on all the businesses on the Promenade."

Wyra looked disappointed, but Crimmon's expression was clearly one of disbelief—and with good reason, Quark knew, since he had been lying about Sisko's rules. But Quark had no desire to stay open past 0300 for the paltry number of customers still in the bar. Nor did he need to ingratiate himself with these two; he had already gathered enough from them. The speculative venture for which they were taking their freighter into the Gamma Quadrant had been orchestrated based on hearsay, second- and thirdhand data, the origin of which was itself in doubt. Everything Quark had so far learned was either something he already knew, or something he knew to be untrue. There was no use in pressing Crimmon and Wyra for more information; he could not hope to strengthen his knowledge of commerce and opportunity in the Gamma Quadrant—and he certainly could not possibly hope to find his own next deal—based upon anything this pair knew.

Quark glanced over the railing and saw Kira standing at the bar, talking to Broc. She had entered the bar by herself, Quark realized. That was uncharacteristic; she almost never came in unaccompanied by at least one of her friends.

"There must be time enough for one more drink," Wyra commented, even though the glass sitting before him was nearly full.

"Of course," Quark said, turning to the two traders. "What can I get the two of you? Another pair of *kirilionas?*"

As he waited for their answers, Quark looked downstairs again. Broc was pointing up toward the second level, he saw. Kira followed the gesture until she spotted Quark. She made eye contact with him and then, unaccountably, she smiled. Quark shivered involuntarily; he was only slightly less wary of people who smiled than he was of people who made promises.

"Yeah, a *kiriliona,*" replied Wyra, evidently after some thought—or at least after an attempt at thought. His eyes were glassy.

"I want a margarita." Crimmon seemed to offer this as more of a challenge than a request.

"A margarita?" Quark asked, shifting his gaze away from Kira. "We don't get call for many of those. Let me see how much tequila I've got on hand."

Quark turned off the sterilizer with a click and set it down on the table, then drew a padd from an inside breast pocket in his jacket. He stole a glance back down at the bar, but Kira was no longer in sight. He quickly worked the controls of the padd and consulted the readout.

"Here we go," he said. "Plenty of tequila. Ice? Salt?"

"Yeah, ice. No salt."

"All right then. One margarita and one more *kiriliona,* coming right up."

Crimmon grunted his acknowledgment.

Quark keyed in the order and returned the padd to his pocket. He retrieved the sterilizer, then headed for the stairway. As he did so, he heard the ringing sound of boots on the metal stairs. Since the narrow staircase could accommodate only one person comfortably, Quark waited for the person coming up to reach the second level: it was Kira.

"Hello, Quark," Kira said, and there was that smile once more. Even worse than a smile in general, Quark thought, was a smile on the face of somebody who never even so much as grinned. Well, who never even so much as grinned at him, anyway.

"Major. What can I do for you?"

"How are you?"

Quark blinked.

"How am I?" he asked, unable to keep a note of shock from his voice. This was going to be worse than he thought. "Major, what do you want from me?"

"What makes you think I want something from you?" Kira evaded. Her tone made her sound anxious.

"Call it 'Ferengi intuition,'" Quark explained, sidling past Kira and starting down the stairs. "We always know when our pockets are about to be picked," he finished over his shoulder. Behind him came the hollow sound of Kira's footfalls as she followed him back down to the first level.

"I heard you completed an amazing deal not too long ago," Kira offered as she trailed him toward the bar.

So that was it. Quark had completed the deal seventeen days ago, and while he had not divulged the precise details of his business to anybody—for several reasons, including that he knew that the Starfleet personnel would not approve—he had still managed to tell several of the station's residents a rousing tale about it. So it was hardly surprising that Kira had learned of it. If she had mentioned it without some ulterior purpose, that would have been surprising. But Kira's undeclared motive seemed clear to Quark. He stopped and turned to face her.

"Yes. I made a wondrous deal a while ago," Quark told her. "It was masterful, and lucrative, and just barely legal." Quark held up his hand, thumb and forefinger only a centimeter or so apart to demonstrate just how close to unlawful his actions had been. "But you know what, Major? I *didn't* break any laws. I didn't cheat anybody. So go back to Odo and tell him you couldn't find out anything from me because there isn't anything to find out." His voice had become louder as he spoke, easily filling the nearly empty bar. Quark glanced around and saw that everybody in the place was looking at him; even Crimmon and Wyra were eyeing him from upstairs.

"Last call," Quark announced. Morn produced a sour look when he heard this; it was the same sour look he always put on his face when the bar was about to close. Quark paid him no attention. Instead, he moved behind the bar—Kira following slowly in his wake until she was standing across from him—took out his padd, and set both it and the sterilizer down. He consulted the readout of the padd, but only in a cursory fashion; he knew what the Frunalians had ordered. He opened a compartment beneath the bar and moved some bottles around, but he could not find the one he needed.

"Broc." Broc was leaning one elbow on the bar, his chin resting in his hand, listening to Morn.

"Yes, sir?"

"Go get a bottle of tequila from the storeroom."

"Tequila?" Broc seemed uncertain.

"Tequila," Quark repeated. "A human alcohol." He pronounced the word *hyoo-mon*, distinctly separating the two syllables. Quark punched up the inventory on his padd and held the device out so that Broc could see it. "There should be three bottles of it down there," Quark explained as Broc came over to peer at the display.

"Yes, sir." Broc took the padd and moved out from behind the bar, passed Kira, and made his way toward the stockroom.

Kira? Why was she still here?

"Something to drink for you, Major?" Quark asked.

"No," Kira said. Her mouth only approximated a smile this time.

"Is there something else on your mind then?" he asked. "Because if there's not, I'm getting ready to close for the night."

"Actually, there is something," she said.

"Imagine my surprise."

"I was wondering," she started, but then she hesitated. She looked tired and troubled to Quark. She sat down at the bar before continuing. "I was wondering if you would do something for me."

That *was* a surprise.

I can't believe my ears, Quark thought. *And that's saying something.*

Kira behaved in many ways Quark did not appreciate—she was rigid, strident, thoroughly Bajoran—but she was not hypocritical, which meant that she did not typically ask for favors—acts of friendship—from people she did not like. And although she had become less vocal over the years regarding her feelings of antipathy for Quark, she nevertheless left no doubt about how she felt toward him. If she was seeking his assistance in some matter, then that matter must be very serious, and Kira very desperate.

"That would depend on what the something is you want me to do," Quark said. "So what is it?"

"How well do you know Grand Nagus Zek?"

Quark felt the fleshy ridge that ran from ear to ear above his eyes involuntarily raise high on his forehead. He was nonplussed by Kira's question. The nagus was a well-known figure outside of the Ferengi Alliance, in the same way that the president of the Federation and the first minister of Bajor were known to Quark. And like all the inhabitants of *DS9*, Kira must have known that Zek had visited the station on several occasions, and that he had had dealings with Quark during those visits. On one of the more memorable of his stays, the nagus had named Quark to be his successor; although Zek had done this in order to subsequently fake his own death and test the mettle of his son, Krax, it still demonstrated a relationship of some sort between Zek and Quark.

But why would Kira want to know about that relationship?

"The nagus?" Quark asked her. While he was suspicious of Kira's motives—it was in his nature to be suspicious of everybody's motives—he saw no reason not to answer her question. "Well, I'd have to say we have a rapport."

"What does that mean, exactly?"

"It means he likes me," Quark further explained. His brother maintained the reverse, that Zek actually despised Quark, but what did Rom know?

"He likes you," Kira repeated. "Are you certain? Because I really need to know." Her tone was imploring.

"Why, Major? Why do you need to know?"

"I thought you would have guessed."

Quark thought this over. Absently, he picked up the sterilizer, activated it, and began cleaning the top of the bar. He wondered what he could have possibly known that would interest Kira. What could have provoked her to pursue his aid? He did not know.

"I'm deaf to whatever it is you're saying."

"The Orb."

"The Orb of the Prophets? Which one? The one the nagus is auctioning off?"

Kira's eyes grew suddenly cold. It was a look with which Quark was not unfamiliar.

"Yes," she responded, her voice dropping portentously. "The Ninth Orb, the one he won't sell to Bajor."

Finally, Quark understood. Kira was deeply committed to her religious beliefs, the greatest tangible symbols of which were the Orbs of the Prophets. If she believed that the nagus would not sell the Orb he possessed to her people, she would have been roused to action, to do whatever was within her abilities to see that the mystic item was returned to what she felt was its rightful place. But Quark knew of no reason why the nagus would not sell to the Bajorans for the right price.

"Of course he'll sell the Orb to your people. All they have to do is make a high enough bid. Surely the people of Bajor are willing to pay for something they so desperately want."

"We *are* willing to pay," Kira barked at him. "But that doesn't seem to matter."

"Paying *always* matters," Quark insisted. He flicked the sterilizer off and put it down on the bar. "In fact, that ought to be a Rule of—"

An unexpected thud drew Quark's attention away from Kira. She also turned her head toward the sound: Broc had returned from the stockroom and placed an unopened bottle of tequila on the bar. Quark had been so focused on Kira that he had not heard Broc come back.

"There's still one more bottle in stock," Broc said.

"Did you adjust the inventory accordingly?" Quark asked, turning off the sterilizer and sticking it beneath the bar.

"Yes, I did." Broc smiled broadly at what he must have considered an achievement for himself.

"Good. Now get on that order." Quark hiked his thumb up toward the second level. "Those two Frunalians up there are waiting for their drinks."

"Yes, sir." Broc's smile faded. He rechecked the drink order Quark had entered on the padd.

Quark turned back to face Kira.

"Now then, as I was saying, I'm sure that if the Bajorans just commit enough of their resources—"

"The nagus expelled Bajor from the bidding for the Orb earlier today."

Quark had not heard that. If it was true, then it explained why Kira was here talking with him. What it did not explain was why Quark had not heard about it. He thought his ears were always open for such information; it was vital to his future business interests that he keep himself constantly well-informed.

"Why would they be expelled from the bidding?" he asked.

The sounds of glass against glass, of liquids being poured, drifted to Quark's ears from where Broc was mixing drinks for the Frunalians.

"Seven factions bid," Kira explained. "Four were supposed to be eliminated, leaving three to bid in the final round."

"And Bajor didn't make the cut," Quark concluded. Kira's only visible response was the setting of her jaw as she clenched her teeth. Quark could easily see a fierce anger in her eyes, an emotion she was evidently attempting to hold in check. "I'd heard about the multiple rounds in the auction, and the lengthy periods between the rounds," Quark continued. "Very unusual, particularly in Ferengi commerce. Of course, I'm certain the nagus has his reasons." Quark considered this for a moment, but could not immediately determine what any such reasons might be.

"There was no justification not to sell the Orb to Bajor." Kira's words were delivered through her still-clenched teeth, her voice sounding like the growl of a dangerous animal.

"Well, there was obviously one reason," Quark said. "One *good* reason. Why didn't the Bajorans bid enough?"

"We bid all that we could," Kira snapped back, rising from her seat, her temper flaring. She glanced over at Broc and Morn, who were now staring back at her, then took a breath and settled herself back down onto her seat. She proceeded in a level voice. "Our treasury would have been gutted to pay for the return of the Orb."

That did not sound quite right to Quark. The Bajorans

were certainly not the best businessmen in the galaxy, but they were also not that bad. As important as the Orbs of the Prophets were to them, he could not believe that they would bankrupt their world simply so that they could possess one of them; after all, they had lived without all but one of the Orbs ever since the Cardassians had withdrawn from their occupation of Bajor. Still, Quark had expected that the Bajorans would have tendered a handsome offer for their lost artifact; with their planetary resources and the increased commercial base the wormhole provided, it had seemed reasonable to conclude that Bajor would win the auction with ease.

Quark looked over at Broc, who was just finishing mixing the margarita for Crimmon. He had already prepared Wyra's *kiriliona*. Broc started to put away the bottles from which he had been pouring, but Quark stopped him.

"Broc, forget about cleaning up right now; get those drinks out. Our Frunalian friends have been waiting long enough."

"Oh, yes, right away." Broc put down the bottles and lifted the two drinks onto a tray. A very light gas emanated from the *kiriliona*, dissipating just above the rim of the glass. Broc picked up the tray with both hands and headed for the two traders on the second level.

Quark walked over and started to shelve the bottles on the bar. Without looking back at Kira, he knew she was watching him; he heard the slight sound of the skin of her neck scraping against her uniform collar as she swiveled her head to do so.

"Well, Major, this is all very interesting," he told her, "but I'm not exactly sure why you're telling me. Clearly there's nothing I can do about it."

"Are you sure about that?"

The question stopped Quark. He was holding the bottle of *kiriliona* in one hand, the bottle of tequila in the other. He turned to Kira, who returned his gaze without blinking.

Remarkable, Quark thought. *She really thinks I can help her.* But he had been serious when he had told her there was nothing he could do. Quark put the *kiriliona* and the tequila in their places beneath the bar before answering.

"Actually, I'm quite sure about this." He picked up the

other two bottles on the bar. "If the nagus has made a decision—"

"—Then you can speak to him," Kira interrupted.

Quark walked over to Kira, the bottles still in his hands. "Speak to the nagus?" he asked.

"He likes you," Kira reminded him.

Quark found that he could not stop from smiling. She grinned back at him. It was all very disconcerting.

"And what is it you think I can do?" Quark asked. He moved away from Kira again and shelved the last of the bottles, then came out from behind the bar and sat down next to her. "You can't possibly believe I could change the nagus's mind?"

"Why not?" Kira wanted to know. "You can be very persuasive."

"Yes," he agreed. "Yes, I can be. But should I be in this case?"

Kira jerked her head back as though she had been slapped.

"All I want you to do is urge him to reinstate us in the bidding."

"Grand Nagus Zek is the highest financial officer in the Ferengi Alliance. For me to try to change his mind . . ."

"I would try to change Shakaar's mind about something important like this," Kira argued.

"Yes, well, I'd say your relationship with the first minister is considerably different than mine is with the nagus." Kira had fought by Shakaar's side in the Resistance during the Occupation, and when they had recently been reunited, the two had entered into a romantic relationship.

"It doesn't matter, Quark. You can still talk to the nagus."

"Yes, I can. But *should* I talk to him?"

"Of course you should: it's the right thing to do."

"That's *your* opinion, Major; it's not necessarily a *Ferengi* opinion."

"You mean it isn't *your* opinion, don't you, Quark?" Kira accused.

"I don't know," Quark admitted. He stood from the seat and paced slowly back and forth beside Kira. "You haven't given me enough time to think about this."

"You don't need to think about this," Kira said gently. When Quark continued to pace, she stopped him by saying: "Quark. Look at me."

Quark stopped and met Kira's eyes.

"You do not need to think about this," she told him again. "I am asking this favor of you." It seemed to Quark as if the effort Kira was making in treating him like this— like an equal, if not like a friend—was costing her. And for some reason, he wanted to help her. He was not sure why; he had lusted after Kira, but he did not really feel that he liked or respected her. Perhaps he simply appreciated being treated by her as if he possessed at least some degree of value. But he was fairly certain that Kira did not know the difficulties involved in what she was asking of him.

"Major, we—the Ferengi—we have rules about these sorts of situations." He sat back down on the seat, facing Kira.

"Yes, I know that."

"And the second Rule of Acquisition is: 'The best deal is the one that brings the most profit.'"

Kira fixed him with what she must have believed to be her most earnest look. It was definitely the most earnest look Quark had ever seen on her face.

"The Orbs of the Prophets are religious artifacts, Quark, religious symbols. They are extremely important to us as a people . . . historically, socially, spiritually. Allowing the Bajorans to purchase the Ninth Orb so that we can bring it back to our world is the right thing to do. We're not demanding that the Orb be given to us; we're willing to pay for it. We're willing to pay well."

"I understand your perspective. Try to understand mine."

"I don't." She paused, looking for other words, Quark was sure. "Quark, I know that you and I have never really gotten along." She looked almost apologetically at him. Quark supposed it was easy to see the error of your ways when you wanted something.

"On the contrary, Major: I have always gotten along with you."

"Yes, well . . . we are not friends, but I'm nevertheless asking a favor of you. I'll ask more plainly. Will you please try to convince the nagus to reinstate the Bajorans in the bidding for the Orb of the Prophets?"

Quark wanted to say yes, wanted to tell Kira that he would gladly be on her side and do what he could to help. But as best he could tell, the nagus had acted properly. Even if Quark could convince the nagus to grant him an audience, how could he possibly hope to get him to reverse a perfectly executed business transaction? At the same time, how could he possibly make Kira understand the situation she was asking him to face?

"Major, would you ever attempt to get Kai Winn to change her beliefs?"

"I've argued loudly and often with the kai."

"Would you try to change her *religious* beliefs?"

"What I'm asking of you has nothing to do with religious beliefs."

"You're wrong. What you're talking about concerns the tenets of business, and business is the most important thing to the Ferengi. The acquisition of profit is as meaningful to us as the spiritual life is to the Bajorans."

"I know the point you're trying to make, but if I thought the kai was wrong, if she had somehow misinterpreted our sacred beliefs—"

"And what if you believed the kai was right? Would it be possible for anybody to coax you into changing her mind then?"

"Are you saying that the nagus is right in refusing to sell the Orb to Bajor?"

"For just a moment, think like a businessman. What goal drives business?"

"Profit?"

"Profit. This is true in business in general, but it is true most especially for Grand Nagus Zek. The nagus is not merely a businessman; he is also a symbol, virtually a religious symbol—" Kira opened her mouth, apparently to protest Quark's use of the word *religious,* but he continued to speak, not allowing her to interrupt. "—of financial acumen for the Ferengi. As you've explained the situation to me, the offer the Bajorans made for the Orb was not one of the three highest tendered. Since the rules of the auction declared that only the three highest bidders would be permitted in the final round, the nagus's only option was to eliminate Bajor from the auction. There were no other alternatives open to him. And for me to attempt to change his mind about that, to even suggest that he should consider reversing his decision and taking some other course of action, well, I would be inviting censure and a fine. And I would be wrong to do it."

Kira simmered.

"Can't you at least try to understand what I'm saying?" Quark asked.

"Oh, I understand: Your people are greedy. *You* are greedy." Kira stood from her seat and stared down at Quark. "Profit is more important to the Ferengi—to *you,* Quark—than the spiritual needs of an entire population."

"Major Kira, you want me to help Bajor, and to get me to do that, you're trying to get me to see your point of view, to understand and even agree with your beliefs. But you're not even considering my beliefs. Perhaps if you could do that—"

"I don't want to do that," Kira interrupted. "I would never want to do that." Kira turned and slammed into Broc, who had returned from delivering the drinks to the Frunalians. Both stayed on their feet, but the tray Broc was carrying—and the empty glass on it—flew through the air. Broc looked stunned, but Kira still looked angry; the sound of the glass shattering as it struck the floor seemed to Quark the perfect accompaniment for her mood. He watched her as she strode quickly around Broc and out of the bar.

CHAPTER
4

KIRA WAS IN HER QUARTERS when the Bajorans retaliated.

She was sitting on the floor, with her back against an outer bulkhead, her head just below a window. A large book was propped open on her knees. The volume was old and worn: its textured, crimson cover was faded, its spine cracked, its gold-inlay title almost completely rubbed away. A sour but not unpleasant scent drifted up from the dried, yellowing pages; it was the smell of age.

The book had been a gift to Kira many years ago, given to her in her childhood by a woman she had barely known. Kira remembered only the given name of the woman—Klyta—and she was unsure even of that. She recalled the woman's plain face, her short brown hair, and the way her eyes had filled with tears when she had presented the book to Kira, but all other details had faded with the years.

Later in her life, it was explained to Kira by her father that the great crimson tome had been passed on from one generation of Klyta's family to the next, from mother to eldest daughter. But Klyta had had no children of her own, nor any siblings, and after she had suffered a serious injury while on a raid against a Cardassian garrison, it had become apparent that her family's lineage would likely end with her. Determined to preserve her heritage in some fashion, she had chosen to give the heirloom to her closest friend's only daughter: Kira.

As Kira opened the book now, its often-handled cover smooth against her fingertips, she thought of Klyta, and she regretted that the family name of her father's friend had not fixed in her little-girl's mind. She felt it unbefitting that such a gift did not carry along with it the surname of the people to whom it had so long belonged. Kira would have liked to have researched the archives on Bajor to learn more about Klyta and her kin. Perhaps she might even have been able to identify surviving relatives, if there were any. Still, despite the paucity of Kira's knowledge about Klyta, she had always treasured the book as the profoundly meaningful gift it had been.

Kira turned to the table of contents, the brittle pages crackling beneath her touch, the sound like that of flames consuming dead wood. She ran her hand across the familiar chapter headings—"Home in the Firmament," "Bajor Rises," "Prophecy," and others—and found consolation in the simple contact with this most treasured and important of her possessions. The text was one of Kira's favorites, an historical work punctuated with ancient tales, spiritual interpretations, and the auguring of things to come. It had been written centuries ago by Vedek Synta Kayanil, a heroic and beloved figure from Bajor's past, and it was now considered a major canonical work of the Bajoran religion. Kira had always found it both poetic and insightful.

Entitled *When the Prophets Cried,* the narrative included, among its many stories, accounts of the discoveries of the seven Orbs known at the time of its writing. At the time Vedek Synta had penned the great book, the Orbs had been known solely as the Tears of the Prophets—they were still sometimes called that, even now—an appellation derived from the belief that the Orbs were constituent parts, small but significant, which had fallen from the Prophets to the people when direct contact between the two had somehow been lost. The Tears, it was held, were the last physical links that connected Bajor to the Celestial Temple.

The book was the lone object Kira retained from her early childhood. She had carried it with her through her many travels: through her youth during the Occupation, through her efforts in the Resistance, and now through Reconstruction and her time on *Deep Space Nine*. It was in so many regards a guidepost for her; it tethered her to Bajor's rich history, to the legacy of a family she had never really known, to her own father, and to a spiritual bedrock. So often in the course of her life, Kira had retreated to *When the Prophets Cried* in search of solace, or inspiration, or enlightenment. Most often, she had sought guidance among the words and ideas contained in the old pages. Remarkably, after all this time and after so many readings, Kira still managed to gain fresh insight from the venerable work.

It was guidance that Kira sought right now.

It had been three days since the leader of the Ferengi had announced that the Bajorans would no longer be permitted to bid for the Orb of the Prophets he possessed. Kira had grown furious with Grand Nagus Zek for his actions, and with that rodent Quark for his insensitivity and his unwillingness even to try to help Bajor. The Ferengi were little more than vermin to her, admittedly greedy, no better than thieves most of the time, and for them to stand in the way of the proper return of the Ninth Orb to Bajor was profane.

Kira also found herself angered by her own people. So many who now led Bajor, though they had fought courageously during the Occupation to expel the militarily superior Cardassians from their world, continually battled each other in their quest to bring about their society's rebirth. Such infighting, Kira felt, was not only internally detrimental, but also rendered the Bajoran leaders ineffectual in matters beyond their world; their inability to bring the Ninth Orb to Bajor demonstrated that clearly. Oh, there had been official condemnations of the nagus's actions, by both civilian and religious leaders, and there had been public outrage, but nothing had really been accomplished.

As these thoughts filled Kira's mind, her eyes lifted from the book and stared unseeing into the shadows of her quarters. When she looked back down, she found that her hands had tightened into fists. With an effort, she relaxed them, her fingers opening like the petals of a flower. Crescent-shaped indentations lined the bottoms of her palms where her nails had bitten into her skin.

Potent emotions such as anger and frustration and rage were not new to Kira; she had lived with them virtually all of her life. She had always decidedly been a woman of action, and she had often used such feelings as motivating forces. But Kira was also deeply religious, and as she had matured, she had come to understand that a life filled exclusively with violent passions held little room for genuine spirituality. Her adult life had been blessed by the presence in it of two exceptional people—Kai Opaka and Vedek Bareil—who had helped her see the need to cultivate peace within herself; they had also aided her in discovering how to make that inner journey. Both Opaka and Bareil were gone now, but Kira felt that their influences would never leave her. She reached out to those influences now as she struggled to tame her rage.

Kira paged through the antique volume until she came to the chapter called "The Third Tear." She had read this particular section of the book enough times that she could very nearly recite it verbatim. But this recounting of the finding of the Orb of Prophecy and Change, of the Orb's subsequent loss for scores of years and its eventual rediscovery, was what she needed at the moment; she needed to understand that it was all right for the Bajorans not to take custody of the Ninth Orb right now, that if it was the will of the Prophets, the Orb would one day be brought back to Bajor.

Kira had read five pages of the story and was already feeling more at ease—it helped that she knew just how the tale would progress to its conclusion—when the door chime sounded.

"Come in." Her words were expressed more as a question than as a statement; she had not been expecting any visitors, especially this early in the morning.

The door to Kira's quarters slid into the wall to reveal the Emissary standing beyond it. He leaned in from the corridor, holding on to either side of the doorway to maintain his balance. He peered left and right into the room, obviously not seeing Kira in her spot on the floor.

"Major?"

"Captain," Kira answered, closing the book and rising to her feet. Though she believed that she sounded natural, it required a deliberate effort for her to invoke the title of *captain*—or any Starfleet title—with regard to Sisko. She had served on *Deep Space Nine* as Benjamin Sisko's first officer for almost four years now, and in all that time, the basic process of addressing him had never become instinctive. Yes, he was her commander, but it was in the position he occupied in the Bajoran religion—as the Emissary—in which Kira foremost thought of him.

"Come in, Captain. Please." As Kira walked toward the door, she saw the beginnings of a grin play along one side of Sisko's mouth. She felt her face flush; she was embarrassed to have been found sitting on the floor. Thank the Prophets that she had already changed from her nightclothes into her uniform.

"Thank you." Sisko stepped over the raised threshold of the doorway—Kira had never understood the Cardassian notions of convenience and amenity—and into her quarters. "I didn't realize the station was all that comfortable," he said, pointing to the spot along the bulkhead where Kira had been sitting and reading.

"Oh, well, it isn't, really," Kira stammered. "I just . . . I don't know. . . ." Her voice trailed off. She felt silly.

Sisko laughed loudly, his lips parting and forming into a wide smile. The whiteness of his teeth was striking against the rich, dark color of his skin. Sisko had recently chosen to shave his head, and to allow the facial hair around his mouth to grow; now more than ever, he was an imposing figure.

"It's all right, Major," he told her when he stopped laughing. "Me, I sometimes stretch out on the grass when I'm watching a baseball game in a holosuite."

Kira smiled, appreciating Sisko's attempt to put her at ease, and then she began to chuckle at the image in her mind of the captain lying on his side out in a field, his head propped up on his hand so that he could observe the holographic program he was running. Sisko was in many ways an odd man, Kira thought. His love of a centuries-old Earth game seldom played anymore, his bursts of humor at unexpected times, the staccato rhythms of his speech, his command style that varied from informal and almost playful to serious and rigid . . . so many things about him were unusual. But then, he was the Emissary; how could he be anything but singular?

"Are you laughing at me?" Sisko asked, suddenly very stern.

"No, no, not *at* you," Kira said, immediately fearful that she had hurt his feelings, but then she realized that his sudden sternness had been feigned; he was joking with her. "Well, you have to admit that lying around out in a field is not exactly captain-like behavior," she teased back.

"No, I guess not," Sisko agreed, and he smiled once more. "But then again, I'm not always a captain, now am I?"

"I thought Starfleet liked its officers to be Starfleet at all times."

"You'd be surprised," Sisko countered. Then he glanced around without moving his head, his eyes darting from side to side, and leaned in close to Kira as if about to confide a secret to her. "What would you say," he whispered, apparently very serious, "if I told you that I once saw Admiral Nechayev dancing in a nightclub on Mars?"

"Nechayev?" Kira asked, mimicking Sisko's solemn delivery. She had difficulty visualizing the staid Nechayev even being out of uniform. "You're kidding. I thought she was born an admiral."

"Evidently not. I think she was even enjoying herself." Kira and Sisko regarded each other in their mock-serious manners for a moment more before both began to laugh.

When she had first come to *DS9*, Kira remembered, such an exchange with Sisko would not have been possible. It might not have been possible even a year ago. One of the reasons for that, she knew, was that she had been a very different person at the end of the Occupation than she was now. But another reason was that Sisko was a person who was not easy to get to know well. Part of that undoubtedly had to do with the loss of his wife almost seven years ago, she was sure, but there was also a strange depth to the man, and a means of thinking which did not run straight and true. She had witnessed Sisko act on intuitions and insights which would never even have occurred to another person.

And he was a man of convictions, strong, honest, and forthright. He was a good man, and Kira was pleased that she could now think of him not only as the Emissary and not only as her commanding officer, but also as a friend.

"Would you like to sit down?" Kira motioned to the sofa.

"Thank you," Sisko said, and took a seat. Kira set her book down on the small table in front of the sofa and sat down in a chair across from him. She saw him glance at the gold-flecked cover of the book, the insubstantial traces of color the only remnants of what had once been letters spelling out the title. *"When the Prophets Cried?"* he asked.

"Yes," Kira said, surprised. "Do you know it?"

"I've had occasion to read some of it, yes."

Kira suppressed a smile, but it pleased her to hear that Sisko was familiar with the ancient writings. It was just one more indication—and she had seen more and more of them of late—that the Emissary was interested in the Bajoran culture, and that he might someday come to embrace his role in it.

"I was looking for some direction," Kira told him.

"The Ninth Orb?" he asked. She nodded. "I can understand that. The nagus getting hold of it was unexpected."

"Yes." Kira sighed in frustration and stood from her chair. She paced over to the oval window and looked out into space. She tried to pick the pinpoint of light that was Bajor out of the background of stars, but she could not find it; it was probably on the other side of its orbit.

"Why him?" she asked softly, still gazing out the window.

"What?"

She turned to face Sisko, her hands coming up to her hips.

"Why him? Why the grand nagus of the Ferengi? Of all the people the Orb could have found its way to?" She paused, suddenly realizing the tension in her muscles. She dropped her arms to her sides, then moved to sit opposite Sisko once more. "Why not the Klingon emperor, or the Romulan praetor, or even the Orion chancellor? We could have dealt with one of them."

"One can typically deal with the Ferengi," Sisko noted. "It's what they do."

"But not in this case. Bajor would have paid handsomely."

"'The will of the Prophets is sometimes elusive,'" Sisko quoted. He held his hands apart, palms up, indicating that he had no other answers for her.

"How can this be the will of the Prophets?" Kira wanted to know.

"I don't know," the captain admitted. "Frankly, I'm more concerned about Bajor."

"This is hard for the people to accept," she said, "especially after the Detapa Council agreed to discuss returning all of the Orbs to us."

"It is that lack of acceptance which concerns me," Sisko said gravely. He leaned forward and picked up *When the Prophets Cried* from the table; he held the book between both hands. "Major, I'm sure you're acquainted with the account of the Third Orb."

"Of course. As a matter of fact, I was just reading it."

"Good. Then you know that it was lost to the Bajoran people for nearly a century. And in that time, the world did not fall to pieces, people's faith did not vanish."

"No," Kira agreed, although she was not sure of the point Sisko was trying to make. "But those were difficult times on Bajor. Perhaps if the Orb had not been lost, things would have been better."

"Perhaps." The captain seemed to weigh this thought before continuing. "But even given that possibility, would the mere chance of possessing the Orb have been worth fighting for?"

Kira did not answer, but only looked at Sisko. She had the feeling that he was saying more than she was hearing.

"Would it have been worth dying for?" he went on.

"What is it you're trying to tell me, Captain?"

Sisko placed the book back on the table. He let out a breath, then wiped a hand first across his face, and then across the top of his bald head.

"The official Bajoran response to Grand Nagus Zek's actions has just been issued," he revealed.

"And you're telling me that it's not just a simple protest?" Kira asked.

"That's right, Major," Sisko intoned. "It's quite a bit more than that."

* * *

Kira touched two fingertips to the signal panel set into the wall. Beyond the door, the chime sounded. She waited a couple of moments, then touched the panel once more. There was still no response.

Kira looked both ways down the corridor, almost expecting Quark to round a corner and come walking toward his quarters. But the corridor was silent and empty. Few of *Deep Space Nine*'s personnel were housed on this deck, in this particular section of the Habitat Ring, Kira knew, and so the lack of activity at this time of morning was to be expected. On the other hand, because of the early hour, she had presumed that Quark would be in his quarters.

Where would he be at this time of morning? she wondered. She knew that he did not usually open the bar until later in the day. Still, perhaps he was there checking his inventory or counting his receipts. She decided that it would not surprise her to learn that Quark actually slept with his profits.

Kira made her way to one of the central turbolifts and ordered it to take her to the Promenade. She paced in the lift—two steps in one direction, two steps in the other, her boot heels ringing on the metal floor—unable to remain motionless even in the enclosed space; she was energized by the news Sisko had given her. She did not know whether her world's official response to the nagus's actions would result in the Ninth Orb being brought to its proper home on Bajor, but she was proud of the stand her people had chosen to take. And if the deliverance of the Orb was not achieved, she mused, then at least another, lesser problem would be solved: she never did care much for the Ferengi.

The Promenade was just coming to life when she arrived there. The lighting was growing in intensity as the new day progressed, approximating the rising of the Bajoran sun. Some of the shops were just opening, while one or two were already doing business. Many of the restaurants were busy serving breakfast; the change of shifts was close at hand, and Kira spied quite a few station personnel having their morning meal before reporting to duty.

The doors to Quark's bar were closed. As she had at his quarters, Kira touched the signal panel a couple of times. There was no answer. As she considered where next to look for Quark—maybe he was in one of the docking bays, receiving a shipment—she suddenly heard him. It had only been for a second, and she had not made out the words, but she was certain it had been his voice. She waited for a moment, and then she heard it again.

"Never mind how I came by it," Quark was saying loudly. "But you want one, and I happen to have one." The words were coming from the Replimat.

Kira walked over to the self-service eatery and peered inside. The small place was nearly filled with diners, most of them wearing either Bajoran or Starfleet uniforms. Kira's gaze moved from table to table until she spotted Quark. He was near the back wall, having breakfast with somebody she did not recognize, somebody clad in civilian clothes. The stranger's light-blue skin and the bifurcated ridge running down the center of his face identified him as a Bolian, no doubt a trader on his way to or from the Gamma Quadrant.

Kira slipped into the Replimat and weaved through the morning diners. On her way past one table, she felt a tug at her arm. She was moving with such purpose that she had already taken another step before she was able to stop and see that it had been Dax trying to get her attention.

"Nerys," Dax said with a smile. "Join us for breakfast." She was sitting with Worf.

"I can't right now," Kira said hurriedly. "I have something to do." She started once more on her way toward the back of the Replimat.

"Listen," Quark was telling the Bolian as Kira approached the two, "Betazoid gift boxes aren't exported, so their availability outside of Betazed is generally very low. You couldn't find—"

"Quark," Kira interrupted. He looked up at her, his wide merchant's smile never faltering. "I want to talk to you," she told him.

"Major," Quark acknowledged. "You seem to want to talk to me a lot lately. Unfortunately, as you can see—" He nodded his head in the direction of the Bolian. "—I'm in a business meeting at the moment. If you would just—"

"This won't take long," she cut him off. "I have some news I'm sure you'll want to hear."

"I'm sure I will," Quark said in a manner that revealed he

was sure of no such thing. "But I don't have the time right now."

"That's all right," the Bolian interjected. "I think we're done anyway." He pushed his chair back from the table and stood up. Kira noticed that the Bolian had not been having a meal; there were dishes only in front of Quark.

"Wait," Quark said excitedly, jumping up from his own chair. "I haven't even described the distinctive luxury features of this particular gift box."

"I've heard all I need to hear," responded the Bolian. "Major," he said, politely bowing his head to Kira. He started to leave.

"Come by the bar later and I'll show you the box," Quark called after the Bolian, leaning to one side so that he could see past Kira. "It's quite a piece of merchandise."

Kira turned and watched the Bolian exit the Replimat; he did not look back.

"Thank you, Major," Quark said sarcastically to Kira's back. She turned to face him. "You may have just cost me a sale."

"Don't worry about it. I don't think he wanted to buy from you anyway." Quark sat back down at the table and picked up a half-empty glass of some clear liquid.

"Even if that was true," Quark said after he had drunk a couple of swallows, "I would have changed his mind." He set the glass down.

"It's *your* mind you need to worry about changing— yours and the nagus's."

"I already told you, there's nothing I can do."

Kira smiled; it was an expression, she knew, that was not filled with warmth. She sat down at the table opposite Quark.

"You'd better hope you're wrong about that," she offered conversationally. "Because if you're not, then you'll no longer have a home."

"Really? Well, then I guess I'll just have to go find myself a nice peaceful moon somewhere." It was clear that Quark did not take her suggestion seriously. He began to reach into the bowl of noodles sitting before him.

"Listen to me, Quark. Bajor officially responded this morning to being removed from the bidding for the Orb."

"And they decided that, because of what the nagus did and the fact that I can't help you, I won't be allowed to live on the station anymore?" Quark was rejecting, at least outwardly, the notion that the Bajorans would take action against him for what Grand Nagus Zek had done. But when he pulled his hand from the bowl, Kira saw that he had not grabbed any food.

"What they decided was to demand that the nagus reinstate Bajor in the final round of the auction within exactly three days."

"They demanded?" Quark seemed to consider this. "Well, Major, I suppose I understand why your people would do that, but I really don't see how that will change the nagus's mind."

"It might not," Kira granted. "But if the nagus doesn't announce within three days that Bajor will be given another opportunity to purchase our Orb—"

"'*Our* Orb'?" Quark blurted. "I think you have your facts wrong, Major."

"If we're not given another chance to purchase *our* Orb," Kira continued, emphasizing that she had not misspoken, "then *all* Ferengi will be evicted from Bajoran space."

"Evicted? I can't be evicted; I have a business here."

"Right now, you do," Kira said. "But three days from now, that will all depend on Grand Nagus Zek."

"Wonderful," Quark said. He seemed to deflate in his chair. "Who am I supposed to trust to run the bar until this pain in the lobes goes away? And what about my access to the Gamma Quadrant? It will be extremely inconvenient if I can't live on the station."

"It won't matter where you live, Quark," Kira explained. "No Ferengi will be permitted anywhere within the Bajoran system, at any time. Nor will any Ferengi shipments. That means you won't be able to travel through the wormhole, or send or receive goods through it." Quark gaped at her; he was obviously beginning to understand the practical and very serious consequences for him in this situation.

"But my business . . . so much of it depends on the Gamma Quadrant. . . ."

"Then I guess you'll just have to get there the hard way. Let's see . . . if you take a ship at warp five, it should take you—" She did a quick, rough calculation in her head. "—oh, about three thousand years."

"Thank you for your compassion."

A surge of anger rose within Kira, and she felt her face change: her eyes drew almost into a squint, her jaw set, any trace of a smile disappeared.

"Is it any less than the compassion you showed for Bajor when we were told we would not be able to bring the Ninth Orb home?"

"I did have compassion for you," Quark argued loudly. "But there was nothing I could do."

"Well, I guess you'd better find something to do now." She stood from the table. "And you won't have to find somebody to manage the bar while you're gone. If the deadline passes, your business will be nationalized and made an asset of the Bajoran people—not that it's much of an asset."

"That's robbery," Quark yelled. He stared at Kira, his eyes filled with venom.

Kira met Quark's glare with her own. A slight movement caught her attention then, and she looked at its source: the bowl sitting on the table in front of Quark. She had thought the bowl held short, stuffed noodles of some kind, but now she recognized the meal for what it was: a serving of live grubs. One had been bitten in half, she saw, and was oozing a greenish ichor. Her stomach tightened at the sight.

"You know, Major, this isn't fair." She raised her eyes to look at Quark. "I didn't do anything."

She was astonished that he could even begin to defend himself.

"No, you didn't do anything," she said. "But you *should* have." She left without waiting for him to respond.

CHAPTER 5

QUARK'S FINGERS dashed across the controls of the comm panel in his quarters like the legs of a trained and hyperactive spider. The display reacted to his movements, spinning out webs of text in all directions. His hands paused briefly, hovering, as his eyes sought to inspect the results of his queries. Then, not satisfied, he dexterously operated the panel once more.

The chaotic readout buzzed electronically, blinked, and changed. Quark leaned forward in his chair to examine the new data, but his brother, standing beside the comm panel, bent in past him and obstructed his view. Quark tried to see around him, but Rom's nose was nearly pressed against the display.

"Do you mind?" Quark scolded. Rom turned to look at Quark without managing to get out of the way.

"What?" Rom asked. A look of confusion decorated his features: his eyelids were half-closed, his mouth was half-open, his brow was furrowed.

"As empty as your head is most of the time," Quark upbraided his brother, "it's not transparent, and I'd like to be able to see what I'm doing."

"Oh," Rom offered feebly. "Sorry." He straightened and moved behind Quark's seat.

Quark returned his attention to the comm panel. The contents of the file he had just located and dumped filled the screen. He began to peruse the data, but after a few seconds, he was distracted by something he detected in his peripheral vision. He turned his head to find Rom leaning over his shoulder, peering intently at the display. The light glow of the readout shined on Rom's face.

Quark watched his brother for a few moments, expecting him to register his further irritation and back away. When that showed no signs of happening, though, Quark decided to surrender the battle and resume his work.

He scanned the comm panel. To him, the readout resembled a visual puzzle: the irregular polygonal shapes and circular sections of the station's so-called shatterframe displays always looked like related pieces that failed to fit together properly. Having spent nearly a decade on *Deep Space Nine*—all the way back to when the Cardassians had manned the station as Terok Nor—Quark had certainly gained a facility in understanding and using the graphical interface of the Cardassian-built computer, but he had never grown to like it.

Some of the splendid symbols and patterns of the Ferengi language spread across the comm panel now as Quark searched through the file he had just downloaded from a database on his native world. The Ferengi text looked like artwork, Quark thought, particularly when juxtaposed with the relatively dull characters of Federation Standard also on the screen. Unfortunately, even though the text was aesthetically pleasing, Quark found as he scrolled through the data that it did not contain the information he wanted. He sighed in frustration and weariness.

"What's the matter, brother?" Rom asked. "Can't you find him?"

Quark switched off the comm panel. The screen went dark. In the glossy, black surface of the now-empty display, he saw both his own reflection and that of his brother, and it occurred to him that Rom almost never called him by his name.

"No," Quark answered, swiveling in his seat to face Rom, who backed up a step. "I don't think he's there."

"Not where?"

"On Ferenginar."

"Oh." Rom seemed to consider this. "But where else would he be?"

"He could be anywhere, you idiot." Quark stood up, brushed by Rom, and paraded over to the sofa.

"Maybe you should leave him a message like you did for the others."

"I *would* leave him a message if I knew *where* to leave one," Quark explained, aggravated with his brother's enduring inability to understand the simplest concepts. Rom was family, and valuable in his own way—when he had worked in the bar, he had single-handedly kept its electronics up and running—but he was often an annoyance, and sometimes even a burden.

Quark let himself drop onto the soft cushions of the sofa. It was late and he wanted to sleep, but even though he was tired, he knew his mind would not rest until his fears had been allayed. He felt optimistic that the nagus and the Bajorans would arrive at a compact regarding the Orb, and that his bar would therefore remain his, and yet without actual confirmation of an impending agreement, he found that his optimism fell short of certainty.

"Maybe one of the others you left messages for will contact you soon," Rom suggested hopefully.

"Maybe," Quark agreed, though without conviction.

Rom apparently had no response to that. He started to wander aimlessly about the room, first over to the outer bulkhead and the window there, then back over to the comm panel. Quark watched as his brother made several trips back and forth, eventually stopping by the comm panel and pushing in the chair. Rom stared at the blank display for a short time, then came over and joined Quark on the sofa.

The two sat together awhile without talking. The room was dimly lighted right now, and relatively quiet; the deep thrum of the station's power core was the only sound, and it was barely distinguishable. Quark found himself staring at the wall, his mind drifting. Again, he thought about sleep, and again, he dismissed the possibility.

"Brother?" Rom finally said.

"What is it?" Quark asked, still looking straight ahead. He knew what Rom was going to say.

"I don't want to have to leave *Deep Space Nine.*"

Bull's-eye, as O'Brien or Bashir might have said.

"Don't worry, Rom."

"But I like it here."

"Don't worry," Quark repeated.

"I mean, I have friends here, and I'm on Chief O'Brien's engineering team," Rom continued plaintively. "This place is my home."

"Stop whining," Quark snapped loudly, turning quickly on the sofa to face his brother. Rom flinched away, as though Quark had moved to strike him. "Listen," Quark went on, softening his tone, "I told you not to worry about this; we're not going to have to leave."

"If you really believe that," Rom wanted to know, "then why are you trying to contact all those people on Ferenginar?"

"It's not 'all those people'; I've tried to contact four people there, and one of them doesn't even appear to be on the planet anymore."

"But why are you trying to contact anybody on Ferenginar at all?"

"I just want to make sure that Grand Nagus Zek is going to allow the Bajorans back in the auction for the Orb, that's all. Once I've confirmed that, won't you feel better?"

"Yes," Rom admitted, "but how can you be so sure that's what he's going to do?"

"Because that's what makes the best business sense."

"You may think letting the Bajorans bid for the Orb is good business," Rom said with obvious alarm, "but what if the nagus doesn't think so?"

Quark rolled his eyes and dropped his head into his hands. This had certainly been a day of surprises; it had begun with Kira telling him he might have only three days to vacate the station, and it was now approaching its end with Rom—*Rom!*—challenging his financial acuity.

That's like having a Klingon question your sensitivity, Quark joked to himself. Unless you happened to be an active volcano, the Klingon would have no basis to do so.

"Rom," Quark began, lifting his head back up. "I know you don't have the lobes for business, but even you can understand this." Quark did not really feel like explaining the situation, but neither did he feel like listening to Rom fret about it. He stood up and paced over to the window. Off to the left, he spied a lighted speck moving swiftly against the static background of the stars. Quark watched it approach *DS9* until it was near enough to recognize as one of the station's runabouts, and then he turned to face Rom across the room. "The holder of a simple auction," he said, leaning back against the bulkhead and folding his arms across his chest, "makes the most profit by selling his goods to the highest bidder."

"I know that, brother."

"Good," Quark said, genuinely pleased that Rom possessed even that much business knowledge. "But the auction for the Orb is no longer simple, since the Bajorans have placed conditions on its outcome. If the nagus sells to the highest bidder now, he'll make an immediate profit, but he'll also lose far more in future profits because he won't be able to continue his numerous business ventures in the Gamma Quadrant."

"That's right," Rom said excitedly, getting to his feet. He sounded as though he had just experienced a revelation. "The nagus does do a lot of business in the Gamma Quadrant."

"Yes, he does."

"But . . . ?"

"But what?" Quark asked, somewhat harshly. It was frustrating to think that he had calmed his brother's fears, only to discover in the next instant that he had not. But quelling Rom's anxieties and keeping him secure, Quark had long ago realized, were among the most difficult tasks in the galaxy.

"The nagus could just get other people to ship products into and out of the Gamma Quadrant for him," Rom reasoned.

"Yes, but employing intermediaries to act clandestinely on the nagus's behalf would be very costly; it would radically diminish, if not totally destroy, his profit margin."

"Oh," Rom said noncommittally. Then, after mulling it over for a moment, he added, "You're right." He actually sounded sure.

"Of course I'm right." Quark turned in place and propped his hands atop the curved sill of the window. The metal composing the bulkhead was cool against his palms. He peered out at the approximate place where the wormhole was visible when it was open. "Believe me, brother," he told Rom, "Zek needs the wormhole a lot more than he needs the few extra bars of latinum he might be able to get from selling the Orb to somebody other than the Bajorans."

Quark heard Rom's footsteps as he walked over from the sofa. He stood beside Quark and gazed out the window with him.

"Thanks. I feel much better now."

"Are you sure?"

"Yes, I'm sure."

"Good." Quark regarded his brother and saw what appeared to be an expression of genuine relief on his face. Abruptly, he was reminded of another time, back in their youth on Ferenginar, when Rom had worn a similar visage.

The incident that had led to that time had started for Quark when Rom ducked through the short, circular doorway into the front room of their family's home. Rom did not even bother to shake the rain from his clothes before coming inside. Instead, he scurried through the front room, droplets of water falling from him and spattering the floor in his wake. He ignored Quark and their parents, rushing through the house to the bedroom he and Quark shared. That was the first indication that something was not right: the usually loquacious Rom never came home without wanting to share the events of his day with the entire family.

Father immediately followed Rom to his and Quark's room; Quark and Mother trailed along behind. They found Rom manic and distraught: he bounded frenetically about the room like the ball in a dabo wheel. It took some time before Father was able to coax him into sitting down on his bed and keeping still, and even longer to persuade him to confide his troubles. When Rom finally recounted the cause of his agitation, his story came in fits and spasms, and it was mixed with tears.

Rom admitted that he had been transacting business with other boys outside of school over the course of the past several seasons. Such behavior was not atypical for a boy of Rom's age and inexperience; learning the process of deal-making was considered an important and necessary step on the journey to manhood, and figuring it out on the street was often more valuable than studying it in school.

Quark thought he saw pride in their father's countenance at Rom's disclosure, although Father hid it from Rom, whose bearing remained grave. Their mother, smiling behind a hand she raised to her mouth, also seemed pleased, and understandably so; after all, she had been the one to teach the Rules of Acquisition to both of her boys. And Quark himself was gratified that his brother was at last demonstrating the willingness and the ability to succeed at the Ferengi way of life.

But then Rom confessed that he had not succeeded.

Some of the boys with whom he had done business were older and more adept than he was, and one of them—*Breek or Breel,* Quark thought now, unable to recall the boy's name with surety—had maneuvered Rom into a desperate position. A debt had arisen from the many deals Rom had made, insignificant in its magnitude, but inescapable in its terms. Breek-or-Breel had obtained this marker on the sly and presented it during a brief period of time in which Rom found himself completely without resources. Rom had been left with no alternative but to offer remuneration in whatever manner his unexpected creditor would allow. Amid a large group of boys from school, Breek-or-Breel insisted that, as payment, he be given ownership of Rom's right hand.

Quark remembered how small and humiliated his brother had looked as he had related his woeful tale. Rom had resisted the outrageous demand, even though he had been confident that Breek-or-Breel would never require him to amputate his hand or do something with it he did not wish to do. He understood that, for the older boy, the lawful change of ownership of a part of another person's anatomy was trophy enough, proof to himself and to his cohorts that he had mastered the art of business manipulation. But for Rom, the consequences would still be cruel. In the end, though, there had been nothing else he could do but acquiesce.

As Rom finished telling his family what had befallen him, his crying became uncontrollable, his whole body shaking furiously as he sobbed. Father held him and rocked him back and forth. Mother went to him too, trying to help calm him.

Quark observed all of this in silence from the doorway, until he could watch the pathetic tableau no longer. He fled to the main room of the house in order to escape his family, but he could not escape his own thoughts. He regretted what had happened to his brother, but at the same time, he recognized that business deals created profit *and* loss; this time, Rom had lost. Quark believed that Father should not have been attempting to soothe Rom, but to educate him to be a better businessman; Rom's need to learn the craft of commerce was far greater than his need to have his tears dried.

That night, Rom dropped quickly off to asleep, evidently exhausted from his emotional day, but Quark's own emotions would allow him no rest. It was late when he heard somebody leaving the house. He jumped up out of bed and cracked the bedroom window in time to see Father making his way purposefully into the street. Quark knew right away that he was headed to confront or Breek-or-Breel's own father. That, far more than Rom's business failure, disgusted Quark: Rom had made a deal, and it was both inappropriate and weak for their father to seek redress for the lawful results of that deal. Breek-or-Breel's father evidently concurred with that opinion, for Quark learned the next day that he had refused to take any action to alter the outcome of the business that had transpired between his son and Rom.

Appalled by his father's impotence, embarrassed by his brother's incompetence, and giving no thought at all to his mother—she was only a female, and therefore without legal or financial power in Ferengi society—Quark felt the weight of the responsibility to protect his family fall upon himself. Under the pretense of tutoring Rom in business, he extracted from his brother a precise accounting of all the business he had conducted during the past year. He also began to covertly research the financial status of Breek-or-Breel and his family. Eventually, Quark constructed and implemented some deals of his own.

It took nearly a year, but ultimately, Breek-or-Breel suffered much the same fate as he had brought to Rom. Quark managed to obtain a sizable number of specific types of debts that Breek-or-Breel owed. These debts all had variable terms, with the highest margins for the creditors coming with the passage of time. But Quark did not wait to collect; instead, he called in each of the debts at the same time. Breek-or-Breel, unable to immediately discharge all of the obligations at once, was constrained to negotiate with Quark. In short order, ownership of Rom's right hand passed to Quark, and then on to Rom.

The expression of relief that had appeared on Rom's face all those years ago when Quark had presented him with the title to the legally missing piece of his own body, Quark saw, greatly resembled Rom's expression of relief now at realizing that they would not have to leave *Deep Space Nine.*

He should *have been relieved back then,* Quark thought. *I charged him next to nothing when I sold him back his hand.*

"Brother," Rom asked, intruding into Quark's reminiscence. Quark took his hands from the windowsill and straightened up. "What would have happened if we *had* been forced to leave the station? Where would we have gone?"

"It doesn't matter," Quark told him, annoyed. He could not tell whether Rom was merely speculating, or whether he now doubted what Quark had told him and was once again concerned about their immediate future. "It's pointless to even think about it."

"I guess we would have gone to stay with Moogie, huh?"

"Absolutely not." Quark despised their childhood nickname for their mother, but his brother had never outgrown using it.

Quark looked over at the doorway to his bedroom. Perhaps he should reconsider trying to get some sleep; Rom was tiring him out. But no; fatigued as he was, he knew he would only lie awake in bed. Ever since he had been a boy, incomplete or uncertain business matters had afflicted him with insomnia. Instead of heading for bed, he padded back over to the sofa and flopped back down on it.

"Brother?"

"Will you trust me, Rom?" Quark said. "We're not going to have to leave. I'm going to stay right here on the station and use my connections in the Gamma Quadrant until I earn enough profits so that I can—"

"—So that you can buy your own moon," Rom finished for him excitedly.

"Yes."

"I can't wait until you have your own moon, brother." Quark glanced over and saw Rom smiling widely, his hands joyfully clasped together in front of him; he looked like a child. Then, as Quark watched, the smile transformed into a frown. "But what if—"

"Stop it," Quark yelled, grabbing a pillow from the sofa and throwing it across the room at his brother; it flew past Rom, hit the window with a muted thump, and fell to the floor. "It's not going to happen. Listen, ever since Sisko blackmailed me into staying here and keeping the bar open, everybody else has been trying to push me off the station." Quark stopped, suddenly inundated by the memories of all the difficulties he had abided since Starfleet had taken over *DS9*. "Odo would love to throw me in the brig for all eternity, Worf'd be happy to have me as an appetizer with dinner some night, and Kira . . ." Quark trailed off without finishing, suddenly not comfortable recognizing aloud all of the animosity so often shown to him.

"She doesn't like you," Rom noted.

"Thank you, I know that." Quark stood up and walked over to the window, bent down, and picked up the pillow. "She continued to make that abundantly clear this morning when she so gleefully told me that we might have to leave. You know, I think she just hates Ferengi."

"She wasn't mean to me when she told me. She even seemed sorry about it."

"She talked to you too?" Quark asked. He tossed the pillow back onto the sofa.

"Yeah. I think she told all the Ferengi on the station about the situation. She *is* the Bajoran liaison."

"Well, she probably was mean, and you just didn't understand it."

Before Rom could respond, a signal from the comm panel sounded. Quark and Rom glanced at each other as the computer announced: "Incoming transmission."

Rom arrived in front of the comm panel first, but Quark, following, pushed him off to the side; he did not want his brother visible to whoever was contacting him. He touched a control to activate the comm panel, then another to receive the transmission. The display came to life, revealing the image of a formally dressed Ferengi. The man's jacket was accoutred with the emblem of the nagus's palace, and an impressive, bejeweled chain hung about his neck.

"Quark, you one-lobed wonder," the man squawked. He wore a broad smile on his face, his ragged dental work erupting from his mouth at all angles.

"Listen to who's talking, Zhrel," Quark retorted, also smiling. "At least I don't have to wait for the nagus's hand-me-down business tips to earn a living." Zhrel was one of Zek's financial functionaries, holding a minor place in the grand nagus's extensive commercial operations.

"That's right: you can make bad deals on your own, without any help at all."

"If you only knew what I've been up to." On the surface, Quark was playing with Zhrel, as he normally would, but he also could not stop himself from thinking about his marvelous deal of a few weeks ago.

"How can you be sure I don't know what you've been up to?" Zhrel asked.

"You don't know," Quark asserted. "But believe me, you'd like to."

"What I'd like," Zhrel declared, "are the ten strips of gold-pressed latinum you promised on your message if I returned your transmission."

"I said I'd give you *five* strips of latinum *if* you answered a question for me."

"You want information?" Zhrel asked with obviously feigned incredulity. "I think that should cost more than five strips."

"Perhaps it should," Quark agreed. "By the way, how is that crazy woman of yours? Parilka, is it?"

"Yes, Parilka. She's fine, why do you ask?" Zhrel sounded suspicious.

"Oh, I was just curious if that holorecording of her attired in that freighter officer's uniform was ever made public."

"How do you know about that?" Zhrel demanded.

"Like I said," Quark offered smugly, "there's a great deal about me you'd like to know." Quark had heard this rumor about Parilka the last time he had been on Ferenginar, but he was not actually in possession of any holorecording. He required so little from Zhrel, though, that he believed he could easily bluff his way through this conversation.

"Will I still get the latinum?" Zhrel asked.

"Just a minute," Quark said. Impatient, he expertly worked the console until he had initiated a transfer of twenty strips of gold-pressed latinum—a full bar—from one of his accounts on Bajor directly into Zhrel's holdings on Ferenginar; it was usually good practice to keep some of Zek's men on your side by bribing them with more than they deserved. "There. Do you see the transfer?"

"Yes," Zhrel said, working the controls of his own comm panel. "It's confirmed. Now, what is it you want?" He did not even acknowledge the inflated payment.

"Just one basic piece of information: Is the nagus going to reinstate the Bajorans in the auction for the Orb?"

"That's it? That's easy. The nagus was going to issue a statement tomorrow, but I can tell you now what he's going to say. There is nothing the Bajorans can do that will compel him to reverse his earlier decision."

Quark felt his lobes go cold. Off to the side of the comm panel, a shocked yelp escaped Rom's lips.

"What?" Quark asked. "Are you sure?"

"You sound surprised, Quark. Did you really think that the nagus would succumb to financial terrorism?"

"But not allowing the Bajorans . . . that doesn't make any sense . . . the Second Rule of Acquisition . . ." Quark could not seem to unite all of his thoughts into a coherent sentence. His words were being jumbled in his head by the certainty of his now-impending expulsion from *Deep Space Nine*.

"About that holorecording . . ." Zhrel said.

"Don't worry," Quark said without inflection; he was numb. "I don't have it."

"Somehow, I didn't think you did," Zhrel said evenly. "As always, Quark, it's been a pleasure doing business with you."

"And with you."

Zhrel broke the subspace connection, and the words END TRANSMISSION appeared on the display, superimposed atop the symbol of the Ferengi Alliance. Rom stepped over to the comm panel and leaned heavily against it.

"What are we going to do, brother?"

Quark gazed at Rom and answered him with the only reasonable solution that occurred to him.

"We're going to do the one thing we can do: we're going to beg."

CHAPTER
6

THE BUILDING that housed the office of First Minister Shakaar sat not in the center of Bajor's capital city, but on its outskirts. On the balcony just outside the office, Shakaar stood with his face angled up toward the clear azure sky, basking in the enchanting blanket of warmth provided by the springtime sun. The rich green landscape, dotted here and there with nascent bursts of wildflower color, was a glory to the eye, and the sweet scents of growth and renewal were an ambrosia in this season of sowing.

After fighting for more than a quarter of a century to free his world and its people from the Cardassian Occupation, Shakaar found that there were few things that pleased him more than simply gazing out at the majestic Bajoran wilderness slipping away to the horizon. In those quiet moments, he approached as close to a state of inner peace as he was ever likely to get. Years spent on the run, leading friends and strangers into guerrilla raids that often left them maimed or dead, with home not even a memory, but merely a dream of a future that would probably never come . . . all had left Shakaar scarred. Although some of those scars might pale, he accepted that none of them would ever completely vanish. In this life, he knew, serenity would never truly be his, but he contented himself with an occasional glimpse at its elusive promise.

Those glimpses were the reasons that, when he had been elected to the highest political station on Bajor, Shakaar had chosen to relocate the first minister's office here, to the periphery of the city. But while the city was not a refuge for tranquillity, Shakaar certainly acknowledged that it was beautiful in ways that the undeveloped land of Bajor was not. The loveliness of the city was different than the loveliness of nature, an art practiced not by the Prophets, but by the people themselves. Pedestrian thoroughfares and public squares accented the people's joyous sense of community, the melting together of voices in these gathering places an ever-changing song. Buildings flowed together with a remarkable fluidity and grace, a man-made sea of rounded forms and vibrant colors. The architecture was more than art: it was culture and history and hope.

Like all of Bajor, the city had been ransacked during the Occupation, its treasures plundered, its monuments abandoned to the ruinous effects of the elements. Bajor had never been a home to the Cardassians, only a conquered land to be stripped of everything of value and left to die. They had made no efforts to maintain the cities or the lands during the Occupation, and when they had finally withdrawn, it had been with a malicious contempt: buildings had been burned and soil poisoned all over the planet.

And yet, even after these obscenities had been visited upon them, the people of Bajor had remained proud of who they were and of what their world represented to them. In just three and a half years, they had made great progress in their quest to restore the physical beauty of their planet, and nowhere was that progress more visible than in the capital, a vigorous and undeniable symbol of the people's collective will to endure.

Shakaar walked to the end of the balcony, leaned out over the railing, and peeked around the corner of the building. He eyed dusty patches of brown twining through the nearby trees, unpaved roads that marked the outer reaches of the capital. Beyond, he could see the city grow until it reached its heart. At the very center of the city, the renovated structure of the Great Assembly claimed the highest point around, its wide, shallow dome sitting atop a circle of regal columns.

For Shakaar, the capital was both a link to the past and a reminder of the future. For even though the Cardassians were gone, some of their footprints remained, and that meant there was work yet to be accomplished. He did not view this as a burden; it was an inevitability. Rebuilding Bajor and its culture had become his life, and it would no doubt become his legacy. He felt no bitterness that there was no genuine peace in his love for his people and their world. How could there be peace, he often wondered, when he now knew that his duty to them would not end in this portion of his existence? When eventually he came to walk with the Prophets in the Celestial Temple, he had faith that he would at last be able to rest. Sometimes when he thought about his desire for repose, it was a struggle to avoid growing resentful, for why should a man be made to have such an acute need for something so basic?

One does with a life what one must, Shakaar told himself. He moved back to the middle of the balcony, planning to look out once more across the natural splendor of his world, but what he saw instead were the events that had defined his life. *Yes, one does what one has to do,* he thought again. Circumstances were what they were, and he would do whatever he could for his people, and love doing so, until the day his life ended.

For all of Shakaar's adult life—and even before that, in his youth—what he had been able to do for his people had been to battle ceaselessly against tyrannical invaders. The struggles of the group of Resistance fighters he had come to lead during the Occupation had evolved into something of a modern legend; the Resistance cell had even come to be known by his name. Reports and rumors of their engagements had abounded during the fighting, he knew, and both—reports *and* rumors—had now passed into the realm of history. In truth, many of the tales now told about his cell—and many other stories concerning the rebellion, he was sure—were exaggerated, or even apocryphal. There had been successes against the Cardassians—Shakaar was especially proud of his role in liberating the forced-labor camp at Gallitep, at which unspeakable atrocities had routinely been committed under the command of Gul Darhe'el—but those successes could be measured only by individuals: the man who had not been killed, the mother who had not been mutilated, the daughter who had not been raped. Those had all been laudable and important triumphs, of course, but they had fallen far short of the ultimate objective of the Resistance, which had been to repel the Cardassians. In that regard, Shakaar and his compatriots had failed: the Cardassians had left Bajor when they had wanted to leave, and that had only been once they had torn all of the readily harvested resources from it. That the various Resistance cells had been at all effective in repelling the Occupation had been an illusion, a desperate wish to cleave to on the cold nights when people had felt lost and beaten and so far from home that it had seemed they might never see it again.

What Shakaar believed he had really done for Bajor was to keep the dreams and aspirations of its people alive. And even that had been less his doing and more the deep, abiding spirituality of the people themselves. The rich heritage and religion of Bajor had truly provided the hopes to which all had clung.

And yet Shakaar continued a hero. Because of that, when the opportunity to seek the position of first minister had arisen, he had easily won the election. Shakaar had not relished the prospect of assuming the mantle of the highest office in the land, nor had he even anticipated the possibility. After the Occupation had ended, he had effectively attempted to "retire," traveling back to Dahkur, the province in which he had been born. There, with friends from the Resistance, he had sought to eke out an existence as a simple farmer.

But then First Minister Kalem Apren had died—of natural causes, in his sleep—and the provisional government had appointed Kai Winn to replace him on a temporary basis, until a special election could be organized. When it had become clear that Winn would run in the election, Shakaar, like many others, had understood the necessity that she be opposed. Because he had also felt it crucial that she be defeated, he had allowed himself to be drafted to run against her; his popularity as a hero of the Resistance, he had known, would bring him victory.

It had not been because Shakaar thought that Winn would have done a poor job that he had wanted to prevent her from being elected to a six-year term as first minister. Whether or not her means of governing would have been right for Bajor, he genuinely did not know. As kai, she had served—and would no doubt continue to serve—admirably well as the spiritual leader of the people. There was no doubt of her faith, and her actions—whether one agreed with them or not—had always seemed buttressed with the intention of helping Bajor; this had been true even during her brief tenure as first minister. She was a courageous figure as well, having lived through five years in one of the Cardassian camps; after witnessing the survivors of Gallitep, Shakaar could honestly say that he would not have wished such an experience on anyone, not even on a Cardassian.

But for all of that, Shakaar also thought that Winn was potentially dangerous. Her religious beliefs sometimes verged on fanaticism, and as a result, she had sometimes brought Bajor to the edge of precipitous issues. And although she had demonstrated on many occasions her abilities to be good and kind, she had also displayed tendencies to be unforgiving and self-righteous—and even, when it had furthered her ends, a liar.

Still, Winn was so enigmatic that it was possible that in any capacity of leadership, civil or ecclesiastic, she might yet be a savior for the Bajoran people. But because she believed that herself, Shakaar thought that she also posed a great threat to those she would be striving to help. As a self-styled messiah, Winn granted herself a moral imperative she did not truly possess, even as kai.

"Minister?"

Shakaar jumped, startled from his thoughts. He turned away from the lush vista spread out before him and around toward the doorway separating his office from the balcony. Just beyond the threshold stood Kai Winn.

"I'm sorry, Eminence," Shakaar said. "I didn't hear you come back in." At his prompting, he and the kai had taken a few moments' pause during their morning meeting; he had felt the need for a respite before moving on to discuss the issues of the Ninth Orb and the Ferengi. The kai had indulged him, but now it was clear that she wanted to continue their meeting.

"Not at all," Winn replied. Although her words and demeanor appeared neutral, Shakaar detected something in her manner—perhaps it was the forced, unnatural evenness of her voice—that suggested rancor. And he had seen the muscles of her jaw tighten when he had addressed her as "Eminence," from which he inferred that she suspected he was being less than sincere. Even though that was untrue, he understood the source of her feelings: the two had certainly had vociferous disagreements with each other in the recent past, both privately and publicly. There was also the issue of his having opposed her for the position of first minister. Winn had quickly withdrawn from the race after Shakaar's entry into it, and she had even been an advocate for his campaign, but Shakaar was unsure whether her support had been a matter of her confidence in his abilities, or of her plain, pragmatic view that she would best be served by endorsing the eventual winner of the election. He thought that it had probably been the latter case; he sensed from her a consciously buried bitterness born of a poorly hidden belief that she would have been a better selection for the high office.

"It's just that I look out at our land sometimes, and I lose myself in its beauty," Shakaar said, explaining his day-dreaming. "The Prophets have been generous with us."

Although he was not often vocal about it, Shakaar was a devout man. As a leader, though, he had always felt it necessary to hold his religious beliefs close to himself, to avoid spiritual conflicts with those who followed him. That was particularly important now, he felt, because of his position as first minister. For while most Bajorans embraced the same basic doctrine—beliefs in the divinity of the Prophets, in the existence of the Celestial Temple, in the sanctity of the Orbs—there were also differences among those who maintained that doctrine; and there were of course those who possessed a thoroughly distinct set of tenets, as well as those who held to no religion at all.

Shakaar had been chosen to lead all of his people, regardless of their personal beliefs, and so he felt it appropriate, and ultimately best, to insure that his own faith did not interfere with the business of his governing.

"We are truly blessed," Kai Winn told him, agreeing with his assessment of the bounty that was their world. "Unfortunately, there is little time right now to spend appreciating the land; we have much work to do."

She is so hardened, Shakaar thought, without antipathy. *Her time in the camps must have been so difficult.*

Shakaar held the post of kai in high esteem, and despite his numerous disagreements with her, he regarded the woman occupying that post with similar respect. Winn was not somebody whose opinions could easily be dismissed; she was insightful, and her perspective was never without reason or thoughtful consideration. Much of the time, Shakaar concurred with her viewpoints, and when he did not, she was sometimes able to demonstrate to him how his own conclusions had been reached in error. And no matter their differences, they shared a common vision: Bajor, safe and free, independent and strong, resurgent.

"Yes," Shakaar agreed. "I guess we do have work to do." He started forward, taking in a healthy breath and the wafting scents of spring—was that the savory smell of a *nerak* blossom he detected?—before stepping through the doorway and back into his office.

Inside, the kai crossed to an overstuffed chair and sat down. Shakaar followed, taking a seat on a sofa next to her. There was no conference table or desk in the office; Shakaar found it difficult to sit in one place for very long, the by-product, he supposed, of his many years on the run. During the Occupation, whenever he had needed to do something, he had managed to do it wherever he happened to be at that moment. Although he was now constrained to labor in this office much of the time, he still completed most of his work in that fashion: standing, leaning, sitting on the floor, wherever he happened to be in the room.

"We have made it clear to the Ferengi," Winn reviewed, "that all of Bajor is united in our quest for the return of the Ninth Orb."

"Yes."

"Our peremptory position is strong and unambiguous," she continued.

"I believe it is, but there's been no official response yet from the Ferengi nagus. There are reports here on Bajor of his impending compliance, but I believe those are only rumors created by the people's considerable desire to secure custody of the Orb. We have nothing conclusive, and there's been no word at all from either Major Kira or the Emissary on *Deep Space Nine.*"

"We must be prepared, then, to act on the admonition we delivered to the Ferengi," Winn asserted. Her strength and certitude were a marvel to Shakaar; he wished that he shared her confidence in the course they had chosen in this matter.

"I understand," he said, "but we should speak plainly about this, at least with each other: we did not present an 'admonition' to the Ferengi; we threatened them."

"You are entitled to that interpretation, of course," Winn said, diplomatically disregarding his point. "However, it remains that Bajor must be ready to carry forth with the actions we promised should our request not be honored. If we do not act, then we enfeeble ourselves, deprive ourselves of our own power."

"I agree, Eminence, but I have to confess that I am not entirely comfortable with our threat." Shakaar elected to ignore Winn's substitution of words like *admonition* and *request* for what their official communiqué to Ferenginar had been, just as she had elected to ignore his employment of the word *threat.*

"You do not doubt that this is for the greater good, child?"

"No," Shakaar answered. Although Winn often used the appellation *child* when speaking with individual Bajorans, chiefly with those younger than she was, Shakaar had difficulty believing that it was not intended to carry some derogatory connotation in this instance. "But it seems unfair to act against *all* Ferengi when it is only the deeds of one, the nagus, which impede us."

"It may or may not be unfair," Winn said, "but it is politically necessary. Were we to attempt to take action exclusively against Grand Nagus Zek, and not to prohibit all Ferengi from passing through our system in order to travel to the Gamma Quadrant, there is little question that there would be those Ferengi who would function as his surrogates. It might be somewhat more toilsome for him to conduct business, perhaps even somewhat less profitable, but he would not measurably be affected."

"Even if we close our borders to all Ferengi, the nagus will surely employ other agents to do business for him in the Gamma Quadrant anyway."

"Which is the reason we must also step up our customs policing, coincident with closing the borders." As was usually the case, Winn was prepared to answer all criticisms and defend all proposals.

Because she's right about this, Shakaar thought. But that did not mean they were required to ignore the unattractive aspects of what they were about to do.

"It just seems harsh to me," he admitted. Winn looked at him for a few moments before responding, taking the measure of him in some way he could not quite apprehend.

"It is harsh to me as well," Winn told him. She stood, and he moved to stand up too, out of politeness, but she stopped him with a gesture. "Minister Shakaar, I am not without a heart."

"Forgive me, Eminence; I did not mean to imply—"

"But neither am I taken with the notion of some person or faction conducting themselves heedlessly, with no consideration of—and in contrast to—what our people want and need." Winn's voice had risen slightly; she took a moment to gather herself, then paced across the office as she continued. When she spoke again, it was with her back to Shakaar. "It is critical that we do not display weakness in this matter, for Bajor is already widely perceived in that vein." She stopped near the doorway leading to the balcony and looked out.

"Frankly, I really don't care what anybody outside of Bajor thinks of us," Shakaar said, moderating his tone with deliberate effort; he did not want Winn to interpret his statement as an attack.

"I find that unfortunate," Winn said, almost as though

she were expressing an afterthought. "Four and a half decades ago, nobody cared about the Cardassians' assessment of Bajor."

Shakaar was thunderstruck. He shot to his feet.

"Are you suggesting that our people were responsible for the Occupation?" he demanded to know. He immediately regretted asking the question.

Of course that's not what she meant.

Shakaar expected the kai to whirl on him and raise her voice in anger. That would have been a normal reaction, he thought; it was the way he would have reacted. Instead, Winn slowly turned her head to face him, then returned to gazing out through the balcony doorway.

"No, child," she said. "That is not what I am suggesting at all." Winn's tone remained calm, though her words were delivered with control.

Her reserve, Shakaar thought, was remarkable; she was as unflappable as a stone. He did not know whether she lived each day with absolute peace of mind, but it was that serene state that she almost never failed to project.

"But perhaps if Bajor had not been such an obvious target for the Cardassians," she continued, "history would have been kinder to us." She slipped away from the doorway and walked back across the room to Shakaar. "To that end," she told him earnestly, "we cannot allow history to repeat."

"My pardon, Eminence. Of course that is the point you wanted to make. But this is hardly the same situation."

"If we allow ourselves to be trod upon by one group in *this* situation, it encourages the next group to try to do the same and more in the *next* situation. And they will be able to do it, because we will have lost our will, perhaps even our ability, to stop them. We will have learned to meekly accept defeat, even to justify to ourselves that this is the path the Prophets have chosen for us."

"I understand your arguments." Shakaar sighed and wiped his fingers across his forehead; they came away damp with perspiration. He had not noticed before now, but the office had grown much warmer as the day had progressed. "And I agree with your arguments. You must know I believe that, when it is warranted, a battle must be waged; I led our people—"

"I am aware of your accomplishments, Minister," Winn interrupted, "just as you are aware of mine. Now is not the time to review them."

"The only reason I—" Shakaar started, but he was interrupted by a melodic chime sounding in the room. "Excuse me," he told Winn. He walked over to a small table into which a comm panel had been set. He touched a button, opening an audio channel to his assistant's office. "Yes, Sirsy?"

"Minister, there are two gentlemen here to see you." Sirsy's voice came through the speaker with a thin, tinny quality.

"Two men?" Shakaar furrowed his brow, trying but failing to recall what other appointments he had for today beside his meeting with the kai. "Am I expecting them?"

"No, sir, but they claim that it's urgent."

"Well—"

"I'm not just *claiming* that it's urgent," came a loud male voice, obviously calling across Sirsy's outer office so that he could be heard on her comm panel. "It *is* urgent." There was a roughness to the voice, and an odd accent, as though it was not easy for the speaker to move his lips around his teeth.

"What is it they want, Sirsy?"

"We want," said the voice, clearly much closer to the companel now, "to speak with you about your intention of closing your system to all Ferengi."

Shakaar reflexively looked over at Winn, who raised an eyebrow in curiosity. The comm panel connection was severed. Shakaar waited, and after a few seconds of silence, he grew concerned. He was about to leave his office to find out what was happening when the connection was reopened and Sirsy spoke again.

"I'm sorry, Minister. These two Ferengi gentlemen reside on *Deep Space Nine,* and they say they would like to discuss amnesty for themselves should the nagus not allow Bajor to bid for the Orb."

"*Foolishly* not allow," called the owner of the voice that had already been heard. Apparently the second individual did not have anything to say, at least not in this awkward forum.

"I see." Shakaar glanced over at the kai once more. He considered what to do, then operated the controls of the comm panel and reviewed his schedule for the remainder of the day. "I am occupied at the moment," he told Sirsy, "but if the two gentlemen would like to wait—"

"Minister," Winn interrupted quietly. She came over to stand beside Shakaar, and in a whisper low enough that the comm panel would not pick up her words, she said, "A moment, please."

"Excuse me, Sirsy." He toggled a switch, closing the audio channel. "What is it?"

"Forgive me," Winn said in a tone that did not sound as though she was really interested in forgiveness, "but it sounded as though you were going to grant an audience to those two Ferengi."

"I didn't think I was going to 'grant an audience' to them," Shakaar said, "but yes, I was intending to speak with them, give their grievances a hearing."

"Are you certain that is a good idea?" Clearly, Winn did not feel the idea had much merit.

"I can't see any harm in meeting with them. Can you?"

"I'm afraid I can. Grand Nagus Zek refused any conversation with Bajor after removing us from the auction for the Ninth Orb. For us not to reciprocate in kind would be a demonstration of precisely the kind of Bajoran weakness we've been discussing."

"I understand your perspective, Kai Winn, but it could also be considered a sign of strength to be willing to listen to our adversaries, even when they will not listen to us."

"Our official imperative to Grand Nagus Zek and the Ferengi Alliance specifically stated that, in view of their unwillingness to speak with Bajor, there would be no room for negotiation with respect to our request to be reentered in the auction."

"Mustn't there always be room for negotiation?"

"No. Not always. What we want is simple and understandable. It is also eminently within the authority of the grand nagus to provide us with it. If we renege so quickly and easily on the conditions we ourselves have set, it undermines the strength of our position. Further, it exhibits our inability to effectively protect our interests."

"Yes," Shakaar said, weighing the arguments Winn had presented. Distasteful though it was to him—he had despised the Cardassians for never listening to the pained Bajoran voices crying out to them—he knew that the kai was correct in her assessment. "I see what you mean," he told her.

Winn moved back to the chair she had earlier taken. Shakaar turned back to the comm panel. He reactivated the audio channel connecting his office with that of his assistant.

"Sirsy?" he said.

"Yes, sir?"

"Please tell the two gentlemen that I will be unable to meet with them until after the—" Shakaar searched for an appropriate word, failed to find one, and settled for another. "—situation between Bajor and Ferenginar has been settled."

As Sirsy acknowledged Shakaar's orders, he heard in the background the voice of the Ferengi who had spoken up earlier.

"He won't see us? Wait. Minister . . . ?"

"If the two gentlemen refuse to leave, please have security escort them out." The mention of security appeared to inhibit the owner of the voice.

"Yes, Minister," responded Sirsy.

"Thank you."

Shakaar thumbed off the comm panel, then walked over to the sofa and sat down near Winn. They were quiet for a few moments.

"Do you think this will work?" Shakaar finally asked.

"Truly, I do not know, child," Winn answered. "I think there is an opportunity for it to work now. The Ferengi are a society for which business is, by their own word, of paramount importance. That's why we made the decision to act as we did; even if the Ferengi do not recognize that what they have done is wrong, there is every chance that this action will drive them to do as we have asked." Shakaar continued to find Winn's use of words like *ask* curious; to him, it seemed a denial of the truth. "I know this, though: I *am* confident that the Prophets will see the Orb returned to Bajor."

"I am too, Eminence. I'm just not certain when it will happen. You recall the story of the Third Orb."

"Of course," Winn told him. "But those days are long passed; Bajor is stronger now, and we are resolved."

"Yes," Shakaar said. "I suppose. . . ."

"Good. Now then," Winn said, changing the subject with apparent ease, "we have other business with which to deal. First, there is the problem of—"

But Shakaar was still thinking about the problem that they had not actually solved yet.

CHAPTER
7

As THE LIFT ASCENDED, Quark considered once more the possibility of bribery. Now more than ever before, he was in a position to practice such a tactic. Not that he had not attempted it many times in the past—he had, and often with some degree of success—but with the recent increase in his net worth, he would now be able to meet the threshold prices of more people in more situations.

But Sisko has no price, Quark thought. That was not entirely true, of course; as he had learned as a boy on Ferenginar, and as his life experience had reinforced, absolutely everybody had a price—it was a Rule of Acquisition. Very often, people even had more than one price. Unfortunately, the costs to buy some people could not always be measured monetarily. *Val-effs,* those people were called: value frauds, individuals who refused financial payoffs on the basis of their "values," but who could not even begin to tell you the worth of a bar of gold-pressed latinum. And Sisko was one of them.

Damn Starfleet, Quark railed to himself. *And damn Bajor too.* Even though he and his brother had not been permitted to speak with First Minister Shakaar, Quark realized that such a discussion would likely not have been fruitful anyway; even Shakaar's assistant had been unwilling to accept a bribe. Kai Winn's security team had also turned down his offers when he and Rom had sought to meet with her, although Quark was certain that, if they had not been escorted from the grounds of her residence, his douceur would have ended up being rejected by the kai herself.

This was why I'd wanted to leave Terok Nor, Quark thought in frustration, remembering back to when the Cardassians had abandoned the space station and the Federation had taken over. Back then, Quark had suspected that it would be impossible to do business with either Starfleet or Bajor, and he had been right; they were so uncivilized. At least some members of the Cardassian military, Quark recalled wistfully, had recognized the principles and the usefulness of graft.

The turbolift reached the apex of its journey, and Ops spread out before Quark. He stepped out of the lift onto the outer, upper level of the complex. Most of the control panels were in use at the moment, he saw, operated primarily by Starfleet personnel, but also by several officers of the Bajoran Militia. For the number of people present, he thought, the overall noise level was rather low; the bar was much louder than this on a regular basis. Of course, there was no dabo table in Ops.

"The *Calliope*'s drive reads clean," Quark heard Dax announce. He looked over and saw her seated at her sciences console on the upper level. She consulted her readouts, looked briefly over at the main viewscreen—Quark looked too and saw the image of a docked Terran freighter displayed there—and then peered down to where Kira worked at her own position on the lower level. "Their repairs must have been successful."

"Right," acknowledged Kira. "Then let's get them on their way. Releasing the docking clamps on Lower Pylon Three." As Kira operated her controls, Quark started around the perimeter of Ops toward Sisko's office. With everybody busy, he was hopeful that he could sneak past unnoticed; he had no interest in having another confrontation with Kira.

"*Calliope* acknowledges," Dax said. "They're engaging thrusters. . . ." As he passed the viewscreen, Quark saw the freighter slipping away from its mooring.

"They're clear of the dock," said Kira. "Moving away from the station. . . ."

"They signal clear," Dax reported. "They're on their way."

"Good job," Kira said. "Now, we've got to keep that dock free for the *Maurit'li'och;* it's coming in this afternoon, and it's a pretty big vess—"

When Kira cut herself off not only in midsentence, but in midword, Quark had the uneasy feeling that it was because she had seen him. His suspicion was confirmed almost immediately as she called out loudly to him.

"Is there something I can do for you, Quark?"

Quark chose not to answer, instead ignoring Kira and continuing on his way. He recognized the sound of her hurried footsteps as she left her station and mounted the steps to the upper level. She intercepted him just as he was about to reach the captain's office, moving in front of him and blocking his path.

"I asked you a question, Quark," she said. She stood with her hands on her hips and her elbows out, her pose accusatory.

"Major Kira," Quark responded, filling his voice with mock surprise. "A question? I'm sorry, I must not have heard you." He saw Kira's eyes dart left and right as she glanced at his ears, and he almost could not contain a sudden urge to laugh. She was right, of course: with lobes like his, he rarely had the opportunity to make such a claim.

"Where are you going?" Kira asked harshly. Her attitude toward Quark appeared to have degenerated even further since yesterday, when she had taken such visible delight in delivering the news of the Bajoran edict to him. With the pressure to solve his own problems escalating because of the Bajoran deadline—he had just two days to construct a means by which he could stay on *DS9*—Quark rapidly lost his ability to tolerate Kira's combative disposition.

"Where does it look like I'm going? I'm headed to the planet Risa for a much-needed vacation," Quark said sarcastically. He attempted to step around Kira, but she moved sidelong and obstructed his way once more. He looked up at her, and when it became evident that she was neither going to say anything more nor let him pass, he told her, "I'm here to see Captain Sisko."

"For what reason?" Kira demanded.

"For *my* reason," Quark fired back. "And it's none of your business."

"You mean like the way it's not Grand Nagus Zek's business to keep the Ninth Orb from the Bajoran people?" She delivered her words like photon torpedoes, discrete packets of energy targeted at her quarry.

"Listen, Major," Quark said, almost pleading for her to believe him, "I told you that there was nothing I could do."

"Yes, you did," Kira agreed. "And there's nothing I can do for you either. Captain Sisko is a very busy man; he can't just stop what he's doing to meet with whoever decides to come up to Ops."

"Which is why I have an appointment to see him—" Quark peeked at a nearby console to check the current time. "—three minutes ago." He was determined not to allow Kira to succeed in her obvious desire to thwart him however she was able.

"You have an appointment?" Kira asked him, a joyless smile on her face. "I don't believe you."

"I know you don't," Quark said, returning her empty smile. "But like everything else I've been telling you, it happens to be true." He raised his arm and pointed across toward the sciences console. "Ask Dax," he said. "She set it up for me."

They both looked over to the other side of Ops. Dax was peering back at them from her station, where she had apparently been listening to their conversation. A grin played across her features and she shrugged at Kira, mute confirmation that she had indeed scheduled Quark's meeting with the captain.

"Fine," Kira offered grudgingly, glancing back down at Quark. Her irritation was conspicuous. She was clearly unhappy to discover that Quark had done nothing wrong, that he had sought a dialogue with Captain Sisko in an appropriate manner, through an appropriate channel. Still, she did not move from in front of him. He waited for a few seconds before realizing that she had no intention of getting out of his way.

"That's all right, Major; stand right there," Quark said to her, holding his face expressionless. "I'll be happy to just go around you." He sidled past her and climbed the few steps leading up to the captain's office. He tapped the signal panel beside the doors, willfully not looking back at Kira.

"Come in," Sisko called from inside the office. Quark started forward and the doors opened, sliding horizontally apart. He entered the office and stopped just inside.

Captain Sisko was seated in the chair behind his desk, leaning back, his feet up. Behind him, the vividly drawn contrast of the starscape—the deep black of the void, punctuated by colorless pinpoints of illumination—was visible through a large, eye-shaped window. The captain was reviewing the contents of a padd he held in one hand; in his other hand, he clutched a baseball. As the doors closed behind Quark, Sisko glanced up from what he was doing.

"You're late," he said. His tone was level, his face impassive. Because his sense of humor often tended to be dry, it was difficult for Quark to know right now whether or not he was joking.

"Yes, well, you can blame Major Kira for that," Quark replied. "She didn't want to let me in here."

"I see. Is that why you wanted to see me then, so you could register a complaint about my first officer? Because if it is, I'm really not in the mood for it."

Again, it was unclear to Quark whether Sisko was being playful or serious. For now, he chose to assume the best.

"I'd love to complain, Captain," Quark jested, "but for every problem I have with Kira, I'm sure she's got ten times as many with me, and I know you don't have time for all that."

"You're probably right," Sisko responded. He slipped the padd onto the desk and swung his feet down to the floor. "So," he said, bringing his hands together around the baseball and leaning forward on his elbows, "what is it you did want to see me about?"

"It's really very simple," Quark began, endeavoring to infuse his voice with a casual quality he did not actually feel. He moved forward a couple of steps until he stood immediately across the desk from Sisko. The captain motioned to a chair there, and Quark sat down. "My brother and I don't want to leave *Deep Space Nine.*"

Sisko regarded Quark intently, as though expecting more to be said. In his hands, he spun the baseball around, the red stitching which held the pale, old-fashioned sphere together occasionally peeking out between the captain's fingers. Finally, Sisko took his elbows from the desk and leaned back.

"Is that all?" he asked with what seemed to be intentional informality. The message Quark took out of the words was that Sisko was either unable or unwilling to help.

"Surely you don't support the Bajoran edict?" Quark stated more than asked.

"I don't?" Sisko asked rhetorically, giving no indication of whether or not he agreed with the ultimatum issued to the nagus by the first minister and the kai. The captain rose from his chair and came out from behind his desk. He moved to the far end of the room, where a replicator was set into the wall.

"Captain," Quark said, "I know you consider yourself a fair man—"

"Yes, I do," Sisko interrupted before Quark could finish. Then to the replicator, he said, *"Pooncheenee."* It was a Bajoran beverage, Quark knew, typically served at breakfast. Made from the fruit of the *pooncheen* tree, which grew in the equatorial regions, the drink was very sweet. Quark used it as a mixer in the bar, but he had no taste for it at all himself.

The replicator hummed, and a tall glass filled with the orange-red liquid materialized. Sisko picked up the glass and sipped from it. He still carried the baseball in his other hand, Quark noticed.

"Something for you?" Sisko asked.

"Thank you, Captain, no," Quark answered. "But as I was starting to say—"

"—You're here to ask for my assistance," Sisko interrupted once more. "Is that it?" He returned to his desk, setting the glass of *pooncheenee* down on it.

"That's not what I was going to say, but yes," Quark admitted. "On behalf of myself and my brother."

"I'm afraid I can't help either one of you in this instance."

"What?" Quark asked. "Why not?" He was startled at the bluntness and the finality of the captain's statement. He had known that it might not be easy to enlist Sisko's aid, but he had fully expected that the captain would be able to see the injustice inherent in the actions taken by the Bajorans, and therefore at least be open to the possibility of helping. There was no indication of any of that in the captain's words or in his manner.

"I'm sure you already know the answer to that," Sisko said. "I know you have the resources and the business sense to keep up on local politics, so you must have learned about the resolution the Federation Council passed. They have chosen to view this as solely a Bajoran matter."

Quark involuntarily rolled his eyes at the mention of the Federation Council. While he had felt the chance to persuade Sisko to his cause, he had no such illusions regarding the Federation's governing body. While Sisko might have dealt with him as an individual, as a man, the Council—if they even ever would have agreed to hear Quark's case—would have dealt with him as a Ferengi. And though the Federation and the Ferengi Alliance were at peace, and even had several trade agreements, Quark knew that the people of the Federation looked down on the Ferengi. Oh, they espoused tolerance and acceptance, but they were hypocrites.

"'A Bajoran matter,'" Quark echoed, returning his gaze to the captain. "Well, that's why I tried to speak with First Minister Shakaar yesterday."

"I know," Sisko said. "At least, I suspected it was you and Rom when the minister informed me that two Ferengi, one of them very loud—"

"I'm not loud," Quark barked.

"—had come to see him about continuing to live on *Deep Space Nine*, no matter what the final disposition of the Ninth Orb turns out to be."

"That was us," Quark said. "He wouldn't even let us talk with him."

Sisko reached forward and plucked the glass of *poon-cheenee* from his desk. He took a long drink, then put the glass back down. Softly, he began to toss the baseball up a few centimeters into the air, catching it with the same hand.

"For whatever it's worth," Sisko said, "I think the minister should have spoken with you and your brother."

"Did you tell Shakaar that?" Quark wanted to know. Perhaps he would be able to resolve this situation with the first minister after all, he thought. But Sisko shook his head slowly from side to side.

"I was not asked for my opinion," he said, "and it was not my place to give it."

"Not your place?" Quark questioned. "You're the almighty Emissary; he would've listened to you." The ball continued to move up and down, out of Sisko's hand and back into it. Quark could not decide whether he found the motion hypnotic or annoying.

"Perhaps. It's difficult to know; my relationship with Shakaar is still . . . young," Sisko said. "But the possibility that he might heed my suggestion emphasizes the importance of my remaining silent. The resolution makes it clear that I cannot offer my assistance when it has not been solicited."

"*I'm* soliciting your assistance," Quark contended.

"But you are not the leader of the Ferengi Alliance. You have nothing to say about this issue."

"That's exactly my point," Quark asserted. He leaned forward and gripped the edge of the desk as he spoke. "I'm not the nagus, so why should I be punished for something he's doing?"

That stopped Sisko. The baseball came down into his hand and did not go back up. For a moment, he was silent, and Quark thought that he might have won the captain over to his side.

"You know," Sisko said at last, "I have to tell you that it surprises me that you and your brother even want to stay on *DS9*." He examined the baseball and rubbed away what looked to Quark like an imaginary blemish. "Well, maybe not Rom," Sisko amended, "but certainly you."

"Why is that?" Quark let go of the desk and sat back in his chair.

"I just didn't think that you were very happy here," Sisko explained. "And frankly, you've never really been what I would call an 'upstanding citizen' in our little community."

It took a few seconds for the impact of what Sisko had said to strike Quark, but when it did, resentment and anger swelled within him. He had learned to live with the vocal disapproval of so many of the Starfleet officers—Kira, O'Brien, Worf—but he had not known that Captain Sisko was so unappreciative of all Quark had done for him.

Very softly, he said, "Captain, I *am* your community."

"What?" Sisko asked, clearly not understanding the comment. "What does that mean?"

"It means," Quark said, unable to keep his voice from rising, "that three and a half years ago, you forced me to stay on this heap when I wanted to leave—"

"I don't know if I'd say I really 'forced' you to stay . . . I offered you a choice—"

Quark jumped up from his chair and leaned forward across the desk. His splayed fingers rested on the desktop, not far from the glass of *pooncheenee*. He glared at Sisko.

"You know you offered no real choice." Rom's son, Nog, had been caught pilfering from the assay office during Sisko's first days on the station. Sisko had given Quark the nominal choice of remaining on *DS9* and keeping the bar open, in which case his nephew would have been freed, or vacating the station, in which case the boy would have been left to the full extent of Constable Odo's brutal sense of justice. "Don't equivocate, Captain. You *blackmailed* me."

"'Blackmailed,'" Sisko repeated melodramatically. "My, that sounds wrong." This time, it was plain that the captain was joking, and thereby conceding the point. But there were still other points Quark wanted to discuss.

"You demanded that I keep the bar open for the sake of your crew's morale, not too many of whom were very happy to be here, if you recall." Quark straightened from the desk and began pacing slowly about the room. "And you wanted me to be an example to attract other businesses to the Promenade. You wanted the station to thrive, you wanted it to be—"

"—A community," Sisko finished.

"Yes. A community. I stayed here so that could happen. And it *did* happen."

"Oh, I think the wormhole may have had a little something to do with the way the Promenade—and *DS9* overall—has grown and flourished," Sisko said, standing from his chair. "*You* stayed here for the same reason you do everything," he told Quark, who had stopped moving around and now stood in a corner across the room. "To make a profit."

"Until recently, I barely made enough profit to be able to take care of my little old mother on Ferenginar," Quark said excitedly. "And now that I finally have had some success, you're not willing to help me fight to keep it." His words were coming faster and faster now, reflecting the increasing sense of anxiety he felt. He had not come here to have such a heated exchange with Sisko, but because that was the way events had unfolded, he knew that his chances of enjoining the captain to assist him were diminishing rapidly.

"I'm not sure I believe that you take care of your mother, Quark. In fact, I'm not even sure I believe that you *have* a mother." Sisko walked around the desk and toward Quark, flipping the baseball from one hand to the other and back again. "That's part of the problem: I'm not sure I believe anything you say. You live by your own rules." He stopped just a few steps from Quark.

"I live by the Rules of Acquisition, but I also live by your rules. How many crimes have I been convicted of on *Deep Space Nine?*"

"Not being convicted doesn't mean that you haven't committed any crimes," Sisko noted.

"And it doesn't mean that I have. I thought Federation law presumed innocence."

"It does," Sisko agreed quietly. For the second time, he appeared to seriously consider something, although this time, Quark could not tell whether it was something that he had said to the captain, or something that the captain had thought of himself.

"You may not realize it," Quark said, trying to focus his point, "and you certainly may not appreciate it, but I am an important part of your 'little community.' " Quark paused, satisfied with the argument he had made. Then, more to ease the tension in the room than to enhance his position, he added, "Not to mention that I cater the best parties in the sector."

Sisko laughed, and then, without warning, he tossed the baseball to Quark—it seemed to just pop up out of Sisko's hand in a lazy arc. Quark fumbled the ball several times—it rolled down and up one arm and across his chest—before getting hold of it. Sisko walked back across the office and once more sat behind his desk. As he did so, Quark held the baseball up before his eyes to examine it. OFFICIAL BALL, it said, and 1989 WORLD SERIES. Beneath it was what looked like a signature.

"A. Bart—" he read haltingly.

"—A. Bartlett Giamatti," Sisko said. "I just had that ball replicated. Giamatti was one of the true gentlemen and heroes of the game. President of the National League, nineteen eighty-six to eighty-eight; commissioner in nineteen eighty-nine, until he suffered a fatal heart attack."

"Really?" Quark said, not at all interested in what the captain was saying. He had tried to watch a baseball game once, in one of the holosuite programs he had procured for Sisko, but none of it had made any sense to him.

"Many people believe," Sisko continued, "that the loss of Giamatti—who possessed a genuine love and understanding of the game, and who had a wonderful vision for its future—ultimately ushered in the end of professional baseball on Earth."

"Uh-huh," Quark responded noncommittally.

"Oh," Sisko said, apparently realizing that he had the wrong audience for him to talk about baseball. "Sorry."

"It's all right," Quark said, coming over and sitting down across from Sisko again. "I'm used to Rom prattling on about his engineering work all the time, and that doesn't make any sense to me either." Sisko smiled, then shifted the conversation back to its original heading. With the brief diversion, though, Quark felt that the friction between the two men had lessened.

"Okay," Sisko said. "So what you're suggesting is that, because I . . . 'encouraged' . . . you to stay on *Deep Space Nine* in the first place, and since you believe you've been such an integral part of the station, I should now help you try to stay." Sisko paused and seemed to mull this over for a moment. "It occurs to me that this may all be unnecessary: it is possible that the nagus will permit the Bajorans back in the auction, and therefore Bajoran space will not be closed to the Ferengi, in which case you wouldn't have to leave."

"Zek isn't going to let them back in the auction," Quark revealed. Sisko raised an eyebrow.

"You're sure of that?"

"Yes," Quark said. "As you said, I have resources." Sisko took in a deep breath, held it for a few seconds, and let it out.

"Even if I do agree with some or all of the things you've said—and I'm not saying that I do—I just cannot get involved in this. As I told you, the Council is considering this to be strictly a Bajoran issue."

"But is it strictly that?" Quark asked. "We're talking about Ferengi being evicted from a Federation space station."

"This is a *Bajoran* space station," Sisko corrected. "In Bajoran space."

"The designation *'Deep Space Nine'* is Bajoran?"

"Starfleet is a guest here," Sisko said. "We were invited to maintain the station for the Bajorans because, after the Occupation, they did not have the tools to do so themselves. You know that."

"I know that's Starfleet's story," Quark said. "But do you think the Federation has no vested interest in being here?"

"I didn't say that."

"Good," Quark said, "I'm glad you at least see that, because this hegemony of the Federation over Bajor isn't just about responding to a cry for help; having a Starfleet presence here is a tactical advantage, and it was even before the wormhole was discovered. Face it, Captain: you denigrate the Ferengi for our pursuit of profit, but you are imperialists."

"If you're trying to get on my good side," Sisko said, "it's not working."

"Do you want to talk about good?" Quark asked. "Forget about my business, forget about the Federation needing to support the Bajorans. Do you know why you should help me?"

"Apparently I'm going to find out," Sisko answered.

"You should help me because it's the right thing to do."

"Is that a moral argument?" Sisko asked. "You surprise me, Quark."

"Is it working?"

"Let me ask you this: Don't you think the right thing would be for the Bajorans to be given possession of their sacred religious artifact?"

"If they pay enough for it," Quark said. "Sure, fine, let them have their artifact. What do I care?"

"But wouldn't it be the *right* thing to do to give them the Orb?"

"'*Give* them the Orb'? No. The nagus owns the Orb. He didn't steal it; he purchased it."

"The Orb was stolen from Bajor by the Cardassians," Sisko argued.

"The spoils of war, I suppose," Quark said. "The fact is that the nagus didn't steal the Orb, but made a legitimate purchase. So why should the Bajorans be allowed to lay claim to something which they no longer own?"

"Understand," Sisko urged him. "They are a very religious people. The Orb is sacred to them."

"It's sacred because they say it is. What if the Bajorans were to say that the planet Earth is sacred to them? Would humans—" *Hyoo-mons.* "—give up their world?"

"Look, we're not accomplishing anything here," Sisko said tiredly. "Now, it seems to me this is not a debate you and I need to have. Even if we were to come to some understanding between ourselves, it would mean nothing to the actual participants."

"I agree with you. So help me debate the issue with Shakaar."

"No. The first minister made it clear when he and I spoke that because of the edict, both he and the kai believe it would be inappropriate for either of them to meet for any reason with any Ferengi."

"Then *you* talk to him," Quark insisted. "Tell him you think he should let Rom and me stay on the station."

"I didn't say that's what I believed," Sisko corrected Quark. "I only said I thought that the first minister should allow you to speak with him. It would still be his prerogative to stand by the Bajoran edict."

"But how can Starfleet—how can *you*—possibly support such an unjust policy?" Quark wanted to know.

"Racist? I don't see the policy as unjust. The Bajoran government is reacting to a specific action taken by the Ferengi."

"By an *individual* Ferengi."

"Yes, but that individual Ferengi is the leader of your entire alliance."

"But because of that one Ferengi's actions," Quark contended, "regardless of whether I agree with those actions, I am being required to abandon my home and my business."

"I understand how you feel," Sisko said, not unsympathetically. "As it happens, I agree with much of what you've said. The Bajorans should not punish innocent Ferengi—if there is such a thing—for the actions of the nagus. But that's only what I believe; the Bajorans believe differently, and so my hands are tied."

Quark was running out of options. He looked at Sisko, desperately trying to think of another argument to make.

"Would you talk to Shakaar," he finally asked, "as a personal favor to me?"

"A favor?" Sisko asked, seemingly incredulous.

"Yes," Quark said. "Out of friendship." Sisko laughed aloud.

"Don't try to sell me that line. We are not friends." Sisko raised a hand and aimed a finger at Quark. Smiling broadly, he said, "I wouldn't be your friend if you paid me."

"You're right, we're not friends," Quark admitted. "But I would be your friend if you paid me to be." Quark stood up and walked to the doors, which opened at his approach. He saw several faces in Ops—Kira's included—look up in his direction before he turned back to Sisko. "I might even be your friend," he said, "if you applied your vaunted Federation morality to the Ferengi." Sisko's smile evaporated.

"You're calling me a hypocrite," he said angrily.

"If it was somebody else who had the Bajorans' Orb, Starfleet would be offering to negotiate between the two governments. *You* would be offering. But in this case, you're happy no matter the outcome: either the Bajorans get the damned Orb, or you don't have to put up with Ferengi in the Bajoran system and the Gamma Quadrant."

Quark suddenly realized that he was still carrying the baseball. He let it drop from his hand. It struck the floor with a thick, dull sound and rolled a short distance toward the desk. He pivoted on his heel and exited the office, unsure where he was going or what he would do next.

8

CHAPTER

8

JACKIE ROBINSON swung at the first pitch. He made solid contact, but high: the baseball shot downward into the summer-baked hardpan in front of home plate. The ball bounded up and over the pitcher, whose leap atop the mound brought his glove just under the chopper as it shot past him, headed toward second. The shortstop and second baseman both sped toward the middle of the diamond, instinctively measuring the trajectory of the ball. The two fielders covered a lot of ground, but the ball landed on the infield dirt and rolled into the outfield ahead of them.

A tweener, thought Sisko from his place in the stands. *That ball had eyes.*

Robinson reached first base and took a wide turn. In center, the outfielder ran in and bent low to gather in the ball, but he was momentarily distracted—*did he glance toward first, concerned about how far past the base the batter had run?*—and it kicked off the heel of his glove. Robinson did not hesitate; he immediately raced toward second. The center fielder quickly retrieved the ball and threw it in to the shortstop, who had circled back to cover the base, but too late: a cloud of dust marked where Robinson had already slid in safely.

"Beautiful," Sisko said aloud. He was sitting on the edge of his seat, his hands resting on the back of the Brooklyn Dodger dugout. All around him, the hometown crowd at Ebbets Field roared their approval of Robinson's base-running theatrics.

"Dad?"

Sisko turned in his seat and looked up into the stands, hunting for the source of the voice. At the top of the cement stairs leading down to the section in which he was sitting, the holosuite doors stood open. On the other side of the threshold, Sisko knew, a simulated night had fallen on a space station hundreds of light-years from the world of his birth; on this side, it was a crisp summer afternoon on Earth. Beyond the doors, gazing out over the stadium from a hallway on the second level of Quark's, was his son. Sisko waved up to him.

"Jake, down here," he called loudly. "Here."

Jake looked down toward the dugout, scanning the rows of spectators there. He spied his father and waved, then started down the steps. Behind Jake, the holosuite doors closed with a hard, metallic sound and vanished.

"Jake-o," Sisko said as his son reached him. "What are you doing here?"

"Hi, Dad."

"Here, sit down," Sisko said, offering up his own seat. He began to move over to the next seat, but it was already occupied by a rather burly man. The man was paying no attention at all either to the people around him or to the game being played in front of him, instead focusing his energies on devouring a hot dog piled high with ketchup and relish; a fresh red stain stretched down the center of his white shirt. "Computer," Sisko ordered, "delete the fan in the seat next to mine." The image of the burly man blurred slightly as it faded out of existence. Sisko moved into the vacated seat, and Jake sat down next to him.

"What game is this?" Jake asked, peering out at the two teams on the field.

"Oh, just a regular-season game from the nineteen-forty-nine Major Leagues," Sisko said. "The Brooklyn Dodgers hosting the Boston Braves. Nothing special."

"I thought they were *all* special," Jake said in a playfully mocking manner, a boyish grin on his face.

Sisko smiled and clapped his hand on his son's back. While Jake shared his interest in and enjoyment of baseball, Sisko knew that he did not possess his overriding passion for the game. Few people did—few enough were even aware of the existence of the game itself—which was hardly surprising, considering that the sport had last been played professionally more than three centuries ago. Still, Sisko was delighted that Jake had grown up knowing and liking baseball, and that their mutual appreciation of the game had helped to enhance and even strengthen their relationship through the years.

"I guess you're right," Sisko said. "To me, they are all special."

The sharp report of a swinging bat striking a pitched ball rang out, and the crowd around Sisko and Jake rose to its collective feet as one. They automatically did the same. Sisko's first reaction was to look toward the outfield, thinking that the batter had hit the ball deep, but there had been no roar from the crowd, and the people around them were looking straight up into the air. Sisko and Jake quickly tilted their heads back as well, their eyes searching the sky. They both spotted the foul ball at about the same time; it landed twenty or so rows in back of them. Nobody caught the ball; it landed in the stands and ricocheted about the slatted, wooden seats. Several people scrambled to retrieve it, and a young man finally recovered the ball and held it aloft, displaying his trophy from a day at the ballpark. There were scattered cheers and applause for the boy as people sat back down.

"So, Jake," Sisko asked a second time, "what are you doing here?"

"Well, I got back to our quarters and I saw your bedroom door was open," Jake explained. "I looked in to see if you were there, but all I saw was your uniform lying on the bed, so I figured you might be here." Sisko almost always wore his Starfleet uniform when he was on the station and not in his quarters; as the commander of *Deep Space Nine,* he had a responsibility to maintain a public air of authority. One exception to this was when Sisko spent time in a holosuite; he liked to dress in an appropriate style whenever he visited one of Earth's old baseball stadia: right now, he was wearing black slacks, a white, button-down shirt, and a herringbone sport coat. "I knew you had an early meeting tomorrow," Jake continued, "so I got a little worried when you weren't home."

"You're right," Sisko said. "I have to be in a briefing at oh-seven-hundred. But it's not that late, is it?"

"Almost oh-one-thirty," Jake answered.

Sisko groaned; he had not realized the lateness of the hour. For him, baseball was a time machine, able to transport him through hours in the blink of an eye.

"I know, I know: time flies when you're watching a good game," Jake teased, as though he had read Sisko's thoughts. "What's the score, anyway?" he asked, at the same time looking out toward right field, where the scoreboard was set into the outfield wall.

"It *is* a good game," Sisko told him. "One to one in the bottom of the seventh, but the Dodgers have a man on second with nobody out." Jake gazed out at the middle of the infield, to where the runner danced off second base.

"Jackie Robinson?" Jake asked, pointing out at the runner.

"Number forty-two himself," Sisko confirmed.

He and Jake watched as the pitcher delivered the ball to the plate. The batter swung and hit a grounder toward right field. The second baseman moved to his left and gloved the ball deep in the hole, then pivoted and threw to first base ahead of the batter. The cheers of the crowd rose and fell as what had appeared to be a run-scoring single became the first out of the inning.

"Good play," Jake commented.

"Eddie Stanky," Sisko said, identifying the player. "Used to be on the Dodgers." On the play, Robinson advanced to third base, where it would take only an outfield fly to score him at this point.

The action on the field captivated Sisko now, and evidently Jake as well: the game could turn on this at-bat. They looked on as the next hitter marched to the plate. He swung and missed the first pitch, then took two balls. Through each of the pitches, Jackie Robinson was constantly astir, darting quite a few steps down the third-base line toward home, then darting back when the ball reached the catcher. He was always in motion, both to distract the pitcher and to achieve as long a lead as he could, Sisko guessed. The infielders had crept up onto the grass, Sisko noticed; they would try to throw Robinson out at home if the ball was grounded to them.

Something else suddenly occurred to Sisko, pulling his focus away from the game.

"Jake, if it's almost oh-one-thirty, then why is it that you just got home?" he asked. "Where were you so late? Just because you're closing in on eighteen doesn't mean—"

"I was over at the O'Briens'," Jake rushed to say, no doubt to preempt the lecture he thought was about to begin. "The chief was telling me some of his family's ancestral stories about old Ireland." Jake had recently decided that he wanted to be a writer, and in pursuit of that goal—or in the creation of it—he had developed a love of storytelling. Sisko was impressed at the breadth of his son's appreciation for almost any sort of tale: contemporary or classic, human or alien, short stories or novels, written or spoken. To Jake, each combination of style and form was apparently one facet of the overall art. "What I want to know," Jake said, "is why are *you* here so late?"

"Oh, I don't know," Sisko hedged, unsure whether he really wanted to discuss what it was that was bothering him. "I think I just needed to get away for a little while."

"Did something happen?" Jake wanted to know.

Sisko hesitated before answering, and then said, "He popped it up," referring to what was happening on the field and at the same time evading his son's question. Jake looked out at the diamond to watch the play—the batter had hit a ball high into the air, and the third baseman drifted back and caught it on the edge of the outfield grass—then returned his attention to his father. "Two outs," Sisko said, feeling Jake's gaze upon him. "Now they'll need a hit to score the go-ahead run." He continued to look straight ahead, out at the field.

"Dad, you don't have to tell me what happened," Jake

said softly. "Just tell me if you're okay." Sisko turned to Jake, proud and pleased that his only child had grown up not only to be a good son and a fine young man, but also to be his friend.

"It's a complicated story." *And maybe one it would be good for me to talk about,* Sisko thought.

"I love stories."

"I know you do." Sisko did not think Jake was pressuring him to discuss what had happened, but merely letting him know that there was somebody who would listen if he wanted to talk. "It was nothing terribly significant, just a meeting I had earlier today with Quark."

"Quark?" Jake sounded surprised.

"He asked me to help him and his brother," Sisko said. "The nagus has announced that he isn't going to let the Bajorans back in the auction—" *Just as Quark predicted,* Sisko thought. "—and so the Bajorans may now carry through on their threat to close their system to all Ferengi. But Quark wants to stay on the station."

"Is that because he can't find a buyer for the bar?" Jake asked.

"What?"

"I talked to Rom on my way up here. Quark is so desperate to sell the bar that he's got Rom and Broc running it while he tries to locate a buyer."

"I saw Broc when I came in," Sisko said. "He was the one who let me into the holosuite, but I thought I saw Quark working."

"If he's there," Jake told him, "I'm sure he's not taking orders and serving drinks. Rom told me Quark's doing everything he can to sell the bar."

Sisko thought about this for a moment. He considered the possibility that Quark's inability to liquidate the assets he held in Bajoran space might have been what had motivated him to want to remain on the station. In light of their earlier conversation, though, Sisko was fairly certain that the circumstances had been reversed Quark now wanted to sell the bar only because he feared that, if he did not sell it by the time the deadline passed, the Bajorans would take it from him.

Around Sisko and Jake, the noise generated by the crowd

suddenly increased. Many people rose to their feet. Sisko looked out at the field and saw an instant of motion followed by a billow of dust rising up around home plate. The umpire's arms went wide, almost as though he were a huge bird attempting to take flight.

"Safe," the umpire bellowed, loud enough for Sisko to hear it in the stands. The crowd grew even louder, yelling their admiration for the man who had just scored the run that put the Dodgers ahead in the game.

"Jackie Robinson stole home?" Jake asked.

"I guess so." Robinson picked himself up and jogged toward his team's dugout, at the same time trying to brush away the infield dirt he had collected on his uniform during his trip around the bases. "He was quite a ballplayer," Sisko said, but in an offhand way; his mind was still busy toiling over his meeting with Quark.

"Dad, do you want to stop the game so we can talk?" Jake was still so much a boy—he could get so exuberant about little things, he was often shy around girls, he had difficulty keeping his room clean—but there were glimpses more and more often now of the man he would soon become.

This is one of those glimpses, Sisko thought.

"Sure," he told Jake. "I'd like that." Then, in a slightly louder voice, he said, "Computer, pause program and save." All about Sisko and Jake, movement stopped: baseball fans froze in position as they stood up or sat down or cheered, the Dodgers and Braves themselves became motionless on the field, the wispy clouds overhead ceased scudding across the sky.

"Program saved," replied the computer.

"Come on," Sisko said, "what do you say we take a walk." Sisko climbed up onto the roof of the Dodger dugout, and Jake followed. They made their way to the end of the roof and jumped down onto the playing field. As they strolled over to the first-base line, Sisko marveled, as he always did, at the cushiony spring of the grass, which was as thick and as full as a carpet. When they reached the line, they headed toward right field.

"I don't think Quark asked me to help him because he couldn't sell the bar," Sisko began to tell Jake, endeavoring to articulate what it was that was troubling him—not only to his son, but also to himself. "I think he's trying to sell the bar because I wouldn't help him."

"Is that what's bothering you?" Jake asked. "That you refused to help Quark?"

"Not exactly," Sisko said. "The Federation Council's resolution is pretty clear on this: we cannot interfere in this situation between the Bajorans and the Ferengi."

"How come?"

"Well, I told Quark that the Federation was considering this a Bajoran matter, but the truth is that siding with either faction would place the Federation in a precarious position," Sisko explained. "We can't side with the Ferengi because of our relationship with the Bajorans, but if we side with the Bajorans . . . well, their current stance is considered extreme. The Council believes the proper thing for the Federation to do is to remain neutral in the face of opposing viewpoints, neither of which we feel is right."

"Why not try to help both sides?" Jack asked. It was something Sisko had been asking himself all day.

"We could try to elevate both sides," Sisko said, "but the Council is handling this in much the same way that Starfleet handles Prime Directive situations." As he walked, his foot brushed against the baseline, sending up a puff of white chalk into the still air. "Our belief that both the Bajorans and the Ferengi are wrong does not give us a moral basis to impose that belief, either explicitly or implicitly, on their cultures. In fact, we have an obligation to *avoid* doing so."

"Okay," Jake said. "So what's the problem?"

Sisko opened his mouth to answer, but stopped: this was hard. After Quark had been in his office this morning, Sisko had begun to feel vaguely uneasy. There had been much to occupy him throughout the day, diverting him from that uneasiness, but he had discovered when he had gotten off duty this evening that the feeling had not abated. He had tried to define the emotion, had tried to understand and deal with it, but even now, its precise cause remained elusive.

The two walked all the way into right field without saying anything further, Sisko grateful that Jake respected his silence. At the outfield fence, the grandstands angled in close to fair territory. Sisko looked up and read some of the advertising that covered the wall: ESQUIRE BOOT POLISH, GEM RAZORS AND BLADES, and the famous ABE STARK sign, on which the tailor proclaimed to batters HIT BALL, WIN SUIT.

Underfoot, the manicured emerald grass gave way to dirt. It was the warning track, a band three meters or so wide at the edge of the playing surface, intended to alert fielders of their proximity to the fence. Sisko and Jake turned to follow the track across the outfield. To their left, not too far away, stood the immobile figure of the right fielder.

"The problem," Sisko said, speaking slowly as he resumed the conversation, carefully measuring both his words and his thoughts, "is that the Federation has sent Starfleet to mediate disputes between other cultures before, cultures with motives that were far more suspect. *I've* mediated such disputes. Would it really be wrong to do that in this case?"

"I assume Starfleet hasn't been asked to mediate," Jake commented.

"No, it hasn't," Sisko granted. "And the Council has ruled that even offering assistance would be a bad idea. But the Bajorans and the Ferengi are both mature cultures; merely suggesting that they might benefit from a third-party moderator is not going to unduly influence their civilizations."

"I don't know," Jake said. "Maybe because you're the Emissary . . ."

"Maybe," Sisko agreed. "But I don't have to be the one to actually help, or even to offer help."

As they walked, the scoreboard loomed up to their right, built into the outfield wall. It rose to a height of about ten meters and stretched away into right-center. Its configuration was peculiar, Sisko knew, even for the time in which it had been constructed: its upper half was vertical, but its lower half was concave and sloped away from the playing field. During the 1916 season, Sisko remembered from his baseball references, a player on the Robins—as the Brooklyn team had then been known—had hit a ground ball that had struck the oddly angled scoreboard and vaulted up the fence and out of the ballpark for a home run.

"Dad," Jake said, "what does this have to do with your meeting with Quark?"

"Quark proposed that the reason the Federation isn't interested in lending a hand to resolve this situation is because the people being wronged are the Ferengi." Even repeating Quark's belief, Sisko found, was not easy; the values embodied by the Federation were very serious to him, and very personal. To even consider that those values were not practiced—or worse, that they had somehow become corrupted—seemed unthinkable.

"Well," Jake said, "is Quark right?"

Now, that's the important question, isn't it? Sisko thought.

"My immediate reaction is: no," he said. "Certainly, it's my belief that the history and the actions of the Federation reflect that it treats all peoples equally."

"But?" Jake asked, either hearing doubt in Sisko's tone, or anticipating that an "immediate reaction" implied an additional response.

"But I can't honestly speak for the members of the Federation Council. I can only speak for myself."

"That's all any of us can do, right?" Jake noted.

"Right," Sisko said.

"So why are you letting something Quark said get to you?"

"There was a time when I never would have allowed that to happen," Sisko said, recalling another conversation he had had with Quark, some time ago. "Remember back a couple of years when you and Nog and I went on that camping expedition to the Gamma Quadrant, and Quark insisted on coming along?"

"Sure," Jake answered. "That's when you and Quark were captured by the Jem'Hadar."

"Quark and I were together for a long time when we were being held, and we talked a lot." Sisko thought back to the incident, and to all of the observations Quark had offered up about humans. "Well, Quark talked a lot, anyway," Sisko amended. "And one of the things he claimed was that humans generally disregarded out of hand anything any Ferengi had to say because of the nature of the Alliance's capitalist culture. He specifically said this was true of me, that I never paid any attention to him or took him seriously, strictly because he was a Ferengi."

"I remember that," Jake said. "Quark repeated some of it to Nog, and Nog told me about it."

"Yes, well, I told Quark that he was wrong, but when we returned to *Deep Space Nine,* I began to notice that there was a certain . . . insensibility . . . even sometimes a callousness . . . with which Quark was treated by many people on the station. I therefore took pains to be sure that was not true of me."

"How'd you do that?" Jake asked, sounding genuinely curious.

"For one thing, I tried to be more receptive to Quark," Sisko said. "I also tried to keep an open mind about the views he expressed. As it turned out, I think he may have been right about me not paying him much attention, because I found that I quickly learned something about him."

"What was that?"

"I came to realize that Quark lives his life under a fairly strict set of rules—"

"The Rules of Acquisition," Jake supposed.

"The Rules of Acquisition, yes," Sisko concurred, "but as interpreted through Quark's own unique perspective. And as he pointed out to me this morning, he also lives by our rules."

"Yeah, I guess he's never been in one of Constable Odo's holding cells for too long," Jake joked.

"That's exactly what I mean, though," Sisko said. "He's never been convicted by Bajor or the Federation of any crimes. And yet I'd always perceived him as a lawbreaker."

"I don't think I'd actually describe Quark as honest, Dad," Jake said.

"I'm not talking about honesty. I'm not even really talking about Quark as much as I'm talking about myself. I'd always thought of Quark as having a complete lack of respect for the laws and rules of the Federation and Starfleet. Of Bajor too. But he's actually lived for a long time within those parameters."

"So what does that mean?"

"It means that, at least in some ways, I was wrong about

Quark," Sisko admitted. He saw that they had come to the point where the right-field fence met the center-field fence in an oblique angle. It was the deepest part of the ballpark. Sisko looked back toward the infield and saw that they were indeed a long way from home plate.

"Okay," Jake said as they passed the place where the fences joined together. "But that's not a crime. People do make mistakes."

"It's not criminal if I made those false estimations of Quark based upon who he was and how he acted, rather than upon the fact that he was a Ferengi."

"That's what's really bothering you, isn't it?" Jake asked in a grave tone. "You're worried that you're a racist."

Sisko took a deep breath and let it out very slowly. The words, spoken aloud and without pretense, were very heady.

"No, I don't think that's the case, but I am concerned that some—or *any*—of my actions have been motivated or tainted by racial biases."

"I think it's probably impossible to prevent yourself from behaving that way some of the time," Jake said. "Don't we all? I mean, everybody has biases."

"I didn't think I did. Not those types of biases, anyway."

"You do, Dad. Everybody does." Jake spoke with apparent certainty.

"You're talking about something specific, aren't you?" Sisko asked.

"No," Jake said. "Well, not on purpose. I was thinking about the way you treat Nog."

"Nog? I helped him get into Starfleet Academy. I *sponsored* his application."

"Yes, you did," Jake said hesitantly, "and he's grateful to you for that. And I am too. But it took a lot of convincing before you were willing to recommend his admittance."

"Well, no Ferengi had ever—" Sisko stopped, shocked at what he was hearing himself say.

"Right: no Ferengi had ever entered the Academy. But that says virtually nothing about Nog as an individual."

"I see your point."

"And you were never very nice to Nog," Jake continued. "I'm sorry, Jake, but the truth is, I didn't always like

Nog." Sisko spoke more harshly than he had intended; he was suddenly feeling very defensive.

"Why not?"

"For one thing," Sisko said, deliberately moderating the timbre of his voice, "when you and I first got to the station, Nog was arrested by Constable Odo for stealing. Not exactly the type of influence I wanted to have around my teenage son."

"So that was a reasoned criticism?"

"Yes."

"And therefore not based on the fact that he was a Ferengi."

"Okay, Jake, so you've made both points: that I am biased against Ferengi, and that I'm not."

"What I'm saying is that everybody has biases, Dad; they can't help it. It's only natural to draw inferences from the compilation of your life experiences. It's only when somebody does that without thinking, or to adversely affect another person, that it's a bad thing. In your case, your biases showed with Nog—and maybe with Quark—but you recognized that fact and overcame them. The fact that you're now questioning yourself about the Federation's role—and your own role—in this affair between the Bajorans and the Ferengi is an indication of that."

"I guess the problem I have is that I usually fight to defend the things I believe in, and in this case, I think the Bajorans are wrong to threaten to close their borders to *all* Ferengi if the nagus won't reinstate them in the auction. And yet I'm not fighting to reverse that course."

"Do you really think the Bajorans will do that? Do you really think they'll expel Quark and Rom and the other Ferengi from their system?" Jake asked. These were issues Sisko had been wrestling with since he had learned of the edict.

"Honestly, no, I don't think so," he said. "It seems so cold and . . . so unjust . . . an action. Quark was right about that, at least. But even though I don't think innocent Ferengi should suffer the consequences of the nagus's actions, that doesn't mean I think what the nagus is doing is right. The Orb was stolen from the Bajorans in the first place."

"And that's not right," Jake commented, "but they've done fine without any of the Orbs the Cardassians took."

"Yes, but it appears as though the Bajorans may be taking all of the others back fairly soon. In fact, they're in negotiations right now with the Detapa Council to do just that."

"So why not talk to the Bajorans about the edict?" Jake asked, and then immediately answered his own question. "Oh: the Council's resolution?"

"Yes."

It's a circle, Sisko thought. And there did not seem to be an answer anywhere on its circumference.

He and Jake walked again without speaking for a while. They were nearing the left-field line, having traversed most of the outfield, when Jake broke the silence.

"You know, Dad," he said, "it seems to me that somebody biased against the Ferengi wouldn't be thinking about these issues; he wouldn't be asking these questions of himself."

"I guess I don't really believe that I treat Quark and his people unfairly," Sisko said, "but I find this problem between the Bajorans and the Ferengi very troubling."

"I know," Jake said. "Well, as far as the Ferengi are concerned, I think it's important for you to realize that it's because you believe so deeply in your own philosophy—including the Federation Constitution, Starfleet regulations, and the Prime Directive—that it's difficult for you to credit not only a foreign notion of right and wrong, but something that was previously considered wrong in Earth's past. Capitalism and greed almost destroyed our world."

"And yet, somehow it seems to work for the Ferengi," Sisko said, shaking his head at the strangeness of the idea. Jake shrugged his shoulders comically, and Sisko chuckled. "Come on," he said to his son, "we better get out of here. I have that briefing in the morning." The two stopped walking as Sisko called, "Computer, exit."

The hydraulic sound of the holosuite doors opening drifted to them from behind and to their left. Sisko and Jake turned to see the doors in the middle of left field, an incongruous sight amid the spectacle of the ancient baseball cathedral. The rich texture of the grass and the bright sunshine seemed far more inviting than the cold deck plating and dim night lighting waiting on the other side of the doorway.

"End program," ordered Sisko, and Ebbets Field and its thousands of occupants disappeared, revealing a room far too small to accommodate anything of so grand a scale. Sisko walked with his son across the empty holosuite floor. The holographic imaging system embedded in the walls and ceiling and floor was an impossible and unrecognizable echo of the sights and sounds it had created.

With Jake at his side, Sisko exited the holosuite, leaving behind reproduced images and approximated moments out of history, but taking with him his son's insight, his own introspective questions for which he still needed answers, and—far back in his mind, but still there—the memory of a man named Jackie Robinson.

116

CHAPTER
9

TWO HOURS before the Bajoran deadline, Quark did not have a buyer for the bar.

"I'm ruined," he told his brother. Rom, though, seemed unconcerned. He had apparently made peace with their impending expulsion from *Deep Space Nine*, no doubt confident that his older brother would take care of him. Where he thought they would go, Quark did not know, nor did he even really want to know.

He probably thinks we're going back to Ferenginar to live with Mother, Quark realized with a shudder.

"Don't worry," Rom said in response to Quark's talk of ruination. "You made that great deal a few weeks ago; I'm sure you'll be able to make others."

"Don't you understand, you idiot?" Quark growled. "The reason I was able to make that deal was because of my contacts in this area of space and my proximity to the Gamma Quadrant and the wormhole. When I start doing business in another location, it'll take me years to reestablish all the advantages I had from being here—if I'm able to do it at all. If I could afford my own moon right now, that would be a different matter, but I can't."

"Well," Rom offered, "at least we have each other."

"Wonderful," Quark muttered. "That and two slips of latinum'll get me a cup of *raktajino*." He could not even force a sardonic smile. It was early morning and they were in the bar—it was closed, with only a few lighting panels switched on—and Quark was attempting to contact what he knew would be his last hope of making any kind of a profit before the Bajorans made it illegal for him to be here and they took possession of his business.

In the two days since he had met with Sisko, Quark had relentlessly sought a purchaser for the bar. Few parties had shown any desire to buy Quark's, and those who had shown interest had also believed that they would be able to make a better deal in just a few days; after all, the Bajoran government was not likely to want to maintain ownership of a drinking and gaming establishment. Quark had exhausted virtually every avenue available to him. He had slept poorly during the intervening nights, and now he was drained, physically, mentally, and emotionally. His ears felt as though they might shut down at any moment and not hear another sound for a week.

"Are you trying to contact cousin Gaila again?" Rom asked. He was seated at the bar, across from where Quark stood at the comm panel. Rom was picking at a plate of food, a human breakfast that included scrambled eggs. It nauseated Quark even to look at the amorphous yellow mass. It was amazing to him what some people could eat.

"Yes. Trog told me where I could supposedly find him." Trog was one of Gaila's business associates. Quark had tried numerous times over the past couple of days to reach his cousin, but he had so far been unsuccessful. His search had ranged far: he had hunted—via subspace transmissions—in scores of different locations, scattered across Gaila's moon, a dozen different planets, and twice as many spacecraft. He had left messages everywhere, but there had been no response to any of them. Finally, just moments ago, he had managed to find Trog. After accepting an appropriate fee, the opportunistic Trog had purported to reveal where Gaila could be reached, although Quark was dubious about the authenticity of that information; Trog was not a man known for his probity.

Quark operated the comm panel, and the words ESTABLISHING LINK . . . appeared on the screen. He waited tensely as time dragged on, each second bringing him closer to the certainty that he would be unable to contact Gaila before the deadline.

Suddenly, an image replaced the words on the screen: a striking young woman with piercing eyes and a smooth, bald head, she was obviously a Deltan. It was equally obvious from the expression on her face that she was not pleased to be responding to this communication. She said nothing.

"Uh, my name is Quark."

She still said nothing.

"I was looking for Gaila," Quark said uncertainly.

"I cannot help you," the woman replied. Her distinctive accent clearly distinguished her as a native of Delta IV.

"What? Why not?"

"Gaila—" the woman said, and stopped. She looked off to the side for an instant, and then back at Quark. "Gaila is not available," she finished.

Not available! Then at least this woman knows Gaila, and perhaps knows where he is.

"Who are you?" Quark wanted to know. "If you don't mind my asking."

"I do mind."

"All right." Quark automatically suppressed the anger he felt, knowing intuitively that he would learn nothing from this woman if he displayed a temper. "I realize this is a terrible inconvenience," Quark said, using one of his many salesman's voices, "but I really must speak with Gaila as soon as possible."

"Does he know you?"

"Yes, yes, absolutely," Quark answered. "I'm his cousin."

"You're Gaila's cousin?" The woman sounded skeptical.

"Yes," Quark said. "I'm his cousin and—" He quickly reviewed the woman's reactions and demeanor in his mind, trying to decide the proper tack he should use with her. "—I'm his cousin and I need his help," he ventured.

Once more, the woman was silent.

"He owes me," Quark said at last, desperate for a response. He got one.

"I wouldn't exactly say I owe you," came a voice from offscreen.

"Gaila? Please tell me that's you."

A Ferengi male appeared on the comm panel beside the young Deltan woman, pushing her partially out of the picture. The man was a contemporary of Quark's, though somewhat older, and there was at least some small resemblance in the lobes.

And not just physically either, but businesswise. Quark had often told himself that, anyway, particularly after his cousin's many successes.

"Gaila," Quark said, delighted.

"Quark," Gaila acknowledged. "How did you find me here?" It did not sound as though Gaila was happy to have been found.

"I think that, when you return, you'll discover that Trog is a few bars of latinum richer than when you left," Quark explained.

"Ah, Trog," Gaila said, smiling, his displeasure at having been located evidently mitigated because it had merely been as a result of his cousin bribing one of his business partners. "He's like family."

"Obviously," Quark said. "He took my money."

"What is it you want, Quark?" Gaila asked.

"Do you know about the situation going on with Bajor and the nagus?"

"I heard the Bajorans were angry about making a poor bid in the auction for that relic of theirs."

"There's more," Quark said. He explained what had happened—and what was likely to happen—in detail.

"And what is it you want me to do?" Gaila asked when Quark had finished. "Even if I was inclined to buy the bar from you, what would be the point? The Bajorans would take it from me for the same reason they're going to take it from you."

"I realize that," Quark said. "But I thought you might know somebody who—"

"Quark, what are you doing on a Federation space station anyway?" Gaila interrupted. "Listen, this could be the best thing for you. Why not join my business?"

"I don't want to join your business. I want to keep *my* business."

"But you can't keep your business; that's why you've contacted me." Beside Gaila, the Deltan woman rolled her eyes and moved completely out of view.

"I know," Quark said, "and if you could just—"

"This is not an offer I make every day, or to many people," Gaila cut Quark off again. "Actually, I don't ever make this offer to anybody. But you helped me out when I needed it." Years ago, Quark had helped Gaila out of some trouble, eventually loaning him the funds to establish his arms-dealing business, which had subsequently prospered.

"So you *do* owe me," Quark argued.

"I gave you that small ship," Gaila said.

"A defective ship that crashed," Quark countered.

"Cousin, I'm trying to help you," Gaila replied. "I've presented you with this proposition before, and you've never taken it. Why not? I'm doing well . . ." He made a motion off to the side which Quark could not see, but the beautiful Deltan woman reappeared on the comm panel as she returned to Gaila, who slipped an arm around her. ". . . *extremely* well . . . as you can see."

"Yes, I see, but I just can't join your business."

"What's the matter with you?" Gaila asked, clearly confounded by Quark's rejection of his offer. "I think you must have gotten soft living among humans and Bajorans; your values have become tainted by the Federation and Starfleet. Where is your sense of profit, your instinctive need for gain?"

"My need for gain is fine," Quark snapped back. "But I can't make any profit if I'm dead. Your business is dangerous, and I'm not a brave man. I don't want to get involved with the people you deal with."

"Well, then," Gaila said, surrendering, "there's nothing more I can do for you."

"'Nothing *more*'?" Quark said. "You haven't done *anything*."

"He gave you an opportunity to join his business," the Deltan woman bristled.

"And the opportunity will remain open to you, Quark, at least for now," Gaila said.

"Are you sure——" Quark began, but the comm-panel screen went dark, the image of Gaila and his consort replaced by the words END TRANSMISSION.

"That didn't go so well," Rom observed over his breakfast.

"No," Quark agreed. He was stunned. He had finally been able to locate Gaila, his final hope, and now that hope was gone.

"Now what, brother?" Rom asked.

"Now," Quark answered, "I'm ruined." He came out from behind the bar, barely aware of the movement of his limbs; he felt as though he were in a trance. "The best deal of my life . . . all that profit I made . . . it'll have to sustain us for a long time, until I can establish a whole new business somewhere else." He walked over to the front doors and operated the lock.

"What are you doing?" Rom asked.

"I'm opening the bar." It was hours away from the time Quark typically opened for business, but what else was there to do? "I might as well make the last few strips of latinum I can before the Bajorans come up here and steal my bar from me." The lock mechanism disengaged with several electronic beeps and an audible *snik.* Quark touched a button on a nearby control panel and the doors parted and slid open. He touched another button and activated all the lights in the bar, throwing the place into bright illumination.

"But who'd want to come to the bar so early in the morning?" Rom wanted to know.

"People coming off the night shift, maybe," Quark guessed, joining Rom back behind the bar. "I don't know; that's why we're never open at this hour."

"I thought it was because you liked to sleep late," Rom said.

Quark started to reply, but he was distracted by the sudden, slightly metallic sound of something being moved across the floor. He and Rom looked over and saw the source of the sound: at the end of the bar, near the doors, Morn had taken a seat.

* * *

Thirty minutes later, there were two dozen customers in the bar. Most were on their way to their day shifts and were having breakfast, but there were a few who were winding down after a long night's work.

"I guess we should have been opening the bar earlier all along," Quark said from where he stood next to the replicator. "People apparently want another option for breakfast."

"It can get pretty boring always eating in the Replimat," Rom said. He was still seated at the bar, although he had by now finished his morning meal.

"Of course, I find this out," Quark said, not without some bitterness, "just as I'm about to be banished from the station."

"Are you sure that's going to happen?" somebody asked. Quark turned to find that Dax had entered the bar. She sat down on a chair next to Rom.

"These days, Commander," Quark said, "it's about the only thing that I am sure of."

"Sounds like you're feeling sorry for yourself," Dax noticed.

"Sure, and why not? I'm about to be punished for something I didn't do—more than that, for something I had absolutely nothing to do with at all." To his brother, he added, "At least Odo only ever tried to catch me breaking the law; he never wanted to charge me with a crime I didn't commit."

"Such praise," Dax said. "I'll have to make it a point to let the constable know how highly you regard him." She smiled in her playful way. Quark ignored the comment.

"What can I get you, Commander?" he asked.

"I don't know," she said. "I could use something."

"Tough shift?" Rom inquired.

"Uh-huh. I worked a double. I'm tired, but I felt like relaxing a little bit before I headed for my quarters. I was just going to get something to eat at the Replimat when I saw that the bar was open."

"For a limited time only," Quark said loudly. "So, what'll it be?"

"I think I'd like something different."

"Well, I'm clearing the decks," Quark said, spreading his

arms wide as he peered beneath the bar at the stock there. Across the room, a customer waved. "You're needed over there," Quark told his brother, pointing. Rom looked around at the customer with her hand raised; it was Ensign Holdbrook. Rom stood up and headed for her table.

"I thought Rom wasn't working here anymore after his appointment to Chief O'Brien's engineering team," Dax said.

"He wasn't, but now he's about the only one who is," Quark replied, pulling out a bottle from beneath the bar. "Except for Broc, the rest of my waiters have already packed up and left the station." All of the waiters previously employed at Quark's had been Ferengi and, in view of the Bajoran edict, they had each been anxious to depart DS9. The consensus was that any Ferengi remaining on the station after the deadline had passed would be arrested and jailed. Quark had been able to convince only Broc to stay this long, although Quark had also demanded that Rom forgo his engineering duties in order to help out at the bar.

"What's this?" Dax asked, referring to the bottle Quark was holding in his hand.

"Just a little something from Earth I think you might find . . . intoxicating," Quark said, removing the stopper. The bottle was rectangular in shape, clear, and almost completely full of a pale, amber liquid.

"What is it?"

"It's called tequila," he said. "It's got quite a kick, from what I understand. Naturally, I thought of you when I heard that." Dax frequently claimed to be seeking out new experiences and new ways of enjoying her life.

Quark set the open bottle down on the bar, and Dax bent in close to the neck. She sniffed the liquor, then examined it visually. After a moment, she wrinkled her nose in apparent confusion.

"What is that?" she asked, her fingertip pressing against the side of the bottle.

"What?" Quark leaned in toward the bottle to see where she was pointing. "Oh, that. That's just a worm of some sort. It's an old custom, I'm told."

"Uh-huh."

"Can I pour you a round?" Quark asked.

"You know, I think I'll just pass."

"Whatever you say." Quark replaced the stopper and returned the bottle to its location beneath the bar. "How about a *kiriliona?*"

"No, I think I'll try a—"

"What are you doing open?" a loud voice interrupted.

Quark and Dax spun around to the source of the voice: it was Kira, standing just inside the doorway, her hands perched on her hips. Having gotten Quark's notice, she marched over to the bar, where she stood beside Dax. At the same time, Rom returned.

"What did the ensign order?" Quark asked his brother, referring to the customer who had summoned Rom. He did not respond to Kira.

"Nothing," Rom said. "She just wanted to pay." He handed over several slips of gold-pressed latinum.

"Latinum instead of a charge," Quark said. "How thoughtful."

"Did you hear me, Quark?" Kira asked. "The deadline is up in ninety minutes. Shouldn't you be packing?"

"Don't worry, Major," Quark told her. "I'll be gone soon enough."

"Not soon enough to suit me," she retorted. "But I'm not *worried* at all. What I am is delighted that *Deep Space Nine* will finally be rid of its infestation."

"Kira—" Dax started, but Quark talked over her.

"You and your people have certainly left me no choice in the matter but to leave," he said, then raised his voice nearly to a shout as he finished, *"even though I didn't do anything."*

"I don't care what you did or didn't do," Kira told him. "This couldn't happen to a more deserving person."

"You know, Major Kira," Rom interjected, "my brother's right: we really didn't do anything wrong." Kira looked at Rom as though she had not seen him until just now.

"Oh, you consider me a person now, not an infestation," Quark said. "I suppose I should be flattered."

"You should be flattered," Kira said, returning her attention to Quark, "that I haven't chased you away long before this."

There was a pause as Quark developed—and Kira waited

for, he was sure—a harsh response. Instead, though, Quark chose to lower his voice and calm his manner.

"You're right, Major," he said, which seemed to startle Kira. "Then again, I was ready to leave here when Starfleet took over, but the Emissary invited me to stay. In fact, he *insisted* that I stay."

"You're lying," Kira said.

"Ask him yourself. It doesn't matter, though. I'll be leaving now—" He glanced over at Rom. "My brother and I will be leaving now so that the great Bajoran religion can exact its revenge on innocent people."

"You call yourself innocent?" Kira exclaimed. "Ha."

"Kira, I think—" Dax said, standing from her chair, but Kira continued.

"I can't wait until you're gone. You never deserved to pass through the Bajoran system, much less live here. You're a—"

"Major Kira," Dax said forcefully. "I need to speak with you." Kira looked at her and, after a moment, smiled bemusedly.

"Can't it wait?" she asked.

"I need to speak with you now." Dax had lowered the volume of her voice to just above the level of a whisper. It apparently convinced Kira of the serious and imperative nature of her appeal.

"All right."

Dax touched Kira lightly on the arm and led her a dozen or so steps away from the bar.

Quark watched Dax lead Kira over toward the dabo table, which was currently empty. There, the two officers faced each other. Kira still seemed perplexed, but Dax looked as though she had reverted to her usual cool and composed self.

From his place at the bar, it was an easy matter for Quark to overhear what they were saying, despite his fatigue. The women were only halfway across the room, after all, and the bar was not exactly filled to capacity.

"What is it, Jadzia?" Kira began.

"I just wanted to stop you before you embarrassed yourself any further."

"Excuse me?" Kira asked in an incredulous voice. Quark, too, was surprised at Dax's words.

"Whether you believe it or not," Dax stated, "Quark *is* innocent in this matter. But even if he weren't, your behavior is still inexcusable. If Quark had suggested to the nagus himself that the Bajorans should never be given an opportunity to purchase the Orb of Wisdom, then he would now be suffering the consequences of his actions with the loss of his bar and his forced departure from Bajoran space, and your behavior here would still be poor."

"You don't understand," Kira said. "I was just—"

"Just what?" Dax demanded. "By coming in here now, you've gone out of your way to berate Quark. Did you think he didn't know how you felt? Of course he knows. And you came in here anyway to tell him again, maybe even to hurt him. Hardly the kindness and caring that the Bajoran religion advocates."

Quark almost could not believe the vehemence with which Dax delivered her words. He understood that her remonstration was less a defense of him and more a rebuke of Kira's conduct, but he found that it nevertheless pleased him.

"But the fate of the Ninth Orb is at stake," Kira protested. "We're not just talking about some valuable piece of property, some object the Bajoran people want to own for no good reason. We're talking about a sacred artifact created by the Prophets themselves."

If the Prophets wanted you to have the Orb, Quark thought cynically from across the room, *then why did They ever let it be removed from Bajor?*

"I realize that, Nerys," Dax said, her tone softening as she used Kira's given name. "But is that really a reason to treat Quark—or anybody—so badly?"

There was a brief silence during which Quark thought Kira was going to answer Dax's question, but it was Dax who spoke next.

"Has Quark ever told you that he's happy that the Ninth Orb isn't on Bajor," she asked, "or that he's pleased that your people were expelled from the auction?"

"No," Kira admitted, "but he refused to try to persuade the nagus to reinstate Bajor in the bidding."

"I know that," Dax said, "but I also know that Quark opposing the nagus would be like you opposing the kai."

"Well, when I've believed she was wrong, I have" Kira argued. "I've certainly had my disagreements with Kai Winn."

"But what about with Kai Opaka?" Dax asked, bringing up Kira's old friend and mentor.

"That was different," Kira claimed. "I liked Opaka. I respected her as a person and as a leader, not just as a religious figure."

"Aren't those the same types of feelings that Quark has for Grand Nagus Zek?"

"You sound like you're on Quark's side," Kira said indignantly.

"I'm not on anybody's side. But I honestly think the way you've behaved here is wrong. I'm saying this to you as your friend: Kira, you can be better than this."

"Why don't you tell Quark that he can be better than he's being, that he could at least try to help bring the Orb back to Bajor." It was not a question, Quark thought, but an accusation.

"How do you know I haven't?" Dax asked. Kira's jaw dropped in surprise.

"Have you?"

"No." Kira's expression hardened immediately. "I haven't told Quark he can be better in this situation because I don't necessarily think that he's done anything wrong."

Kira was quiet again for a moment. She looked down, shaking her head slowly left and right a couple of times. Her hands tensed into fists very briefly, Quark saw, then opened again as she brought her emotions under control. Finally, she looked back up at Dax.

"Then Quark's not the only one who's wrong," she said. She spun on her heel and paced quickly out of the bar, not even glancing at Quark on her way out the door.

"She sure looked angry," Quark said as Dax returned to the bar. He nodded his head in the direction Kira had taken.

"Mad enough to chew neutronium," commented Rom.

"Don't pretend that you didn't hear every word we said," Dax told Quark.

"With such good hearing, Commander, I really couldn't help myself." Quark glanced over at the chronometer on the comm panel. The Bajoran deadline was not much more than an hour away. "But there's very little point in chastising me for eavesdropping; Rom and I have to be on our way."

Despite Kira's remarks suggesting the contrary, Quark and Rom had already packed up their personal belongings, along with a few particularly useful and valuable items from the bar. Quark had discovered that shipping the entire contents of his business out of Bajoran space would have been cost prohibitive; consequently, he was going to abandon everything in the bar. If there had been more time, he would have held a sale, but the three days leading up to the deadline and his frantic efforts, first to find a way to remain on the station, and then to sell the bar, had left him no opportunity to do so.

"In fact, you should go make sure everything's ready for our trip," Quark told Rom. "And make sure Broc's ready to go too."

"Okay," Rom said. He headed for their quarters.

"I never did get that drink," Dax said, sitting down.

"What was it you wanted?" Quark asked.

"How about a Finagle's Folly."

"Coming right up." Quark pulled a glass and the necessary ingredients from beneath the bar and began mixing the drink.

"Where will you be going?" Dax asked.

"Alastron Four, for now."

"There's not much there, is there?" Dax said. "Why did you choose that place?"

"The only ship departing the station this morning before the deadline is an Alastron shuttle headed back to their world."

"Where will you go after that?"

"Who knows? I haven't really had much time to make any concrete plans." Quark finished preparing the Finagle's Folly and pushed it across the bar.

"I see," Dax said, lifting the drink to her lips and taking a sip. "So tell me again, why is it that you're leaving?"

"Pardon me?" Quark said. "I may have excellent hearing, but sometimes I can't believe the words that come out of people's mouths."

"I wanted to know why you're leaving," Dax repeated. "I know about the Bajoran edict, but what is it you expect to happen if you don't go?"

"If I stay on *Deep Space Nine*," he said, "then they'll probably arrest me and throw me in jail." Remaining on the station in violation of the edict had never seemed like a reasonable alternative.

"Who would?" Dax asked. "Odo? Do you really think he'd arrest you for no good reason?"

"He's been trying to arrest me for any reason at all for years."

"But think about that for a minute," Dax said. "The constable could have arrested you whenever he'd wanted to during that time. Why didn't he?"

"Because he never caught me committing a crime."

"Exactly. You know what Odo says: 'Laws change, but justice is justice.' And if it's justice he's interested in, do you think he's going to arrest you when you really haven't done anything wrong?"

"I don't know." This had never really occurred to Quark.

"Besides, this isn't a matter of station security, and so it doesn't fall within his responsibilities. And you know that no Starfleet officer is going to arrest you; we're keeping out of this."

"Well, then I suppose they'll send somebody here from the planet."

"Maybe," Dax allowed. She took another sip of her drink. "But I'm not so sure how well Starfleet would like that happening on their space station."

"As Captain Sisko likes to point out," Quark said, "this is a Bajoran space station."

"And how do you think it would reflect on Bajor, in light of their petition to join the Federation, for you to be arrested?"

"What are you saying, Commander?" Quark asked. "Do

you know for a fact that nothing's going to happen to me if I decide to stay here?"

"I can't say that, no," she said. "But do you really want to leave this place? It's become your home."

"I'm not sure how much of a home it is," Quark said, "but it is where my business is." And that was everything to him.

"That's what I'm saying," Dax said. "Are you going to let somebody destroy your business for something you didn't do?"

"I don't appear to have much choice," Quark said.

"I think you do."

"Well, I don't think we're going to have a chance to find that out," Quark said as he checked the chronometer once more. It was getting late; he and Rom and Broc were scheduled to be on a shuttle departing the station thirty minutes prior to the deadline—just long enough for them to get clear of Bajoran space—and that time was approaching.

"I really have to be going, Jadzia." He took a step away from the bar and addressed the customers remaining. "Last call," he told everyone. "And I do mean 'last.'"

From the end of the bar, Quark saw Morn was gazing at him with an expression that seemed equal parts sadness and terror.

The cogwheel-like inner hatch rolled to one side along its track, revealing the short corridor that was Docking Bay One. Attached to the outside of the bay was the Alastron shuttle *Aran'tsah*. Quark, Rom, and Broc stood on the station side of the hatch with the bags they would be carrying with them on the shuttle; Rom and Broc had seen to it that the remainder of their personal belongings had already been loaded aboard *Aran'tsah*.

After the hatch had opened fully, Rom and Broc hefted their duffels and passed through it, on their way to the shuttle. Quark lifted his bag as well, but he did not move from where he stood. At the inner hatchway, obviously realizing that Quark was not with them, Rom and Broc turned around.

"Are you coming, brother?" Rom asked.

Now, that really was a legitimate question, wasn't it? Because when it came down to it, Quark found that he did not really want to leave *Deep Space Nine*. Dax had talked about this place being his home, and even though Quark felt that was a subject for debate, it certainly was the case that *DS9* was the place where he practiced his livelihood. And since Quark's business was his life, well, then that meant that this was where his life was.

But what price was he willing to pay to keep it? He had told Gaila that he was not brave, and that was positively true; Quark ran from fights not just as a rule, but as a way of life. It had not been a lie when he had told Gaila that he had not wanted to get involved in dealing arms because the people involved in that business—and the very nature of the business itself—scared him.

What about that lucrative deal you just made, then? he asked himself.

Well, that had not been an exercise in dealing weapons per se. And Quark had taken the time and had made the effort before embarking on that deal to assess its risk factors with respect to its participants. Had they even been moderately high, he would not have engaged in any of the transactions. At any rate, he had only been an intermediary—not even an intermediary, really, but more of a facilitator. And the people he had been dealing with had been, well, reputable.

So he was not a brave man, but just how much bravery would would be required of him if he stayed here, if he made the stand that Dax thought he should? Would he be arrested? Would he be jailed? There seemed to be some truth in Dax's argument suggesting that those things would not happen, but could he be sure of that? After all, she had only been speculating.

What courage will you need for what lies on the other side of that docking bay? Quark asked himself then. A complete loss of his business, an uncertain future. Could he really face starting all over again on his climb up the Ferengi ladder of success?

I don't know, he answered himself. *I don't know.*

"Brother?" Rom called again from the inner hatch.

Quark looked up at his brother, whose two hands were clasped together on his shoulder, grasping the drawstring of the duffel bag he carried. Broc stood beside him in a similar pose.

Quark regarded the two men. After a moment, he set his own bag back down on the deck.

CHAPTER
10

ODO ADJUSTED HIS MOVEMENTS as he exited the turbolift onto the Promenade. He tensed as best he could the internal structure of his body, trying to reduce as much as he could any interior flow of his changeling anatomy. The thorough bracing of his form in this fashion was not intuitive to him, and it therefore required a concentrated effort to accomplish it.

He strode carefully down the Promenade, cushioning his feet as they came in contact with the deck. He walked past the Replimat and other shops on his way to Quark's. From a distance, he could see that the bar was open for business, as it had been yesterday and the day before, despite that the deadline specified by the Bajorans had passed and the nagus had not reinstated them in the auction for the Ninth Orb. According to the edict, any Ferengi within Bajoran space were now there illegally, but if there had been any effort to expel or arrest—or even identify—such Ferengi, Odo was not aware of it. Of course, as best he could tell, most of the Ferengi on *Deep Space Nine* had left the station prior to the deadline; he assumed the same was true of those who had been on Bajor itself, or elsewhere in the system. As far as he knew, the only Ferengi violating the edict were Quark and Rom.

As Odo neared the bar, he spied Quark inside the doors, his back to the Promenade walkway. That was good: it would allow Odo to easily test his ability to restrict the internal motion of his body when in humanoid form.

Odo entered the bar and approached Quark from behind. He stopped just in back of the Ferengi and waited. Quark was surveying the room—the bar was busy, as it often was in the evening—and he had given no indication that he had heard the constable arrive.

Odo also looked around. With the exception of Rom, all of the waiters were new to the bar, he noticed, and none of them were Ferengi. Broc, who had remained on the station right up until the deadline, had chosen not to stay beyond it. All of the women working at the dabo table had also been newly hired, and unlike their predecessors, they were not Bajoran. Of course: either the locals had elected not to work for a Ferengi after the deadline had passed, or Quark had opted not to explore their loyalties.

"Quark," Odo said at last. He was pleased to see Quark start at the sound of his voice. The Ferengi turned and gazed up at him.

"Where did you come from?" Quark asked, seemingly flustered. "How long have you been standing there?" Odo did not believe that he was acting, but it was difficult to know with certainty; Quark was nothing if not devious.

"I didn't come from anywhere," Odo replied. "I'm always by your side, Quark. How else would I be able to catch you in the act of committing a crime?"

"You haven't caught me yet," Quark remarked. "Then again, it's always been my policy not to break the law."

Odo tried to laugh. It came out as a quick exhalation of breath, a fleeting burst of noise. He had learned much about humor in his life, but it still often required an effort for him to participate and react the way other people did. It was less the result of his changeling nature, he thought, than the philosophical rigidity born of his dedication to justice.

"You're breaking the law right now," Odo reminded Quark, "just by being in Bajoran space."

135

"And yet you don't seem to be arresting me," Quark noted.

"Don't think I haven't thought about it," Odo told him truthfully. "But the edict that the Bajorans issued is not a matter of station security; it is therefore not within my jurisdictional purview." Which was also true, although Odo also realized that he might have found it difficult to arrest Quark and Rom even if he had been ordered to do so. For all of the time and effort the constable had expended through the years attempting to find a legitimate reason to apprehend Quark, he had no desire to take him into custody when, at least in his own view, no real crime had been committed.

"Well, you shouldn't sneak up on people," Quark said. "It's not right."

"It wouldn't matter whether or not I sneaked up on you if you had nothing to hide, now would it?" Odo responded.

"My life and my business are open books," Quark claimed.

"If you ever opened your books, I'm sure they'd read like a fairy tale."

"They do have a happy ending, though."

"For you, yes, I'm sure they do." Odo turned to go.

"Next time," Quark called after him, "make some noise when you come into the bar."

Odo did not bother to respond.

The Daily Criminal Activity Report was going to be propitiously short. In his office, in preparation for his morning meeting with Major Kira tomorrow, Odo recorded and described the one minor incident that had occurred that day. Odo glanced up at the security monitors and saw that the two detainees in the brig were quiet at the moment; one was a local Bajoran shopkeeper, the other a Bolian freighter who had apparently felt cheated in some transaction. Their altercation had landed them here, where they were currently cooling off in separate cells.

Odo paused as he ended the report, debating as he had the previous two nights whether or not to append it with an informational notation. It should have been easier to make the decision tonight, he thought, considering that he had made it twice already. And yet the same arguments for and against the addendum raged with each other in his mind. Ultimately, he came to the same conclusion he had reached in preparing his two previous reports. Under the heading ADDITIONAL NOTES, he recorded:

> In defiance of the Bajoran decree that all Ferengi depart the system, two individuals remain on *Deep Space Nine*. As such matter does not come under the heading of station security, no action has been taken.

In some sense, Odo felt that, in not acting on Quark's and Rom's refusal to leave the station, he was disregarding the order that had been issued with the force of law by the Bajoran government. At the same time, he assuaged to some degree these concerns by including in his reports his lack of action with respect to this matter. When he had first done this, Kira had questioned his decision not to arrest Quark and Rom, but she had then accepted his explanation of his insufficient authority to apply this particular law on the station. Further, no word had yet been issued on Bajor regarding any penalties or law-enforcement procedures for individuals who were in violation of the edict.

Odo finished the report and was about to move on to his next order of business when the doors to the security office slid open. Odo looked up from his console to see Captain Sisko enter, accompanied by two individuals with whom the constable was not familiar. The two, a man and a woman, each wore the apricot-colored uniform of the Bajoran Militia. The woman carried a Bajoran padd, while a small instrument pouch was slung on a strap across the man's shoulder.

"Captain," Odo said, rising from his seat.

"Constable Odo," Sisko returned. The captain's face was barren of expression. "This is Lieutenant Carlien and Sergeant Onial," he said, introducing first the woman and then the man. Carlien was a head shorter than Odo, fit but not skinny, with wavy red hair falling to her shoulders; her most striking feature was the greenish tint of her eyes. Onial was slightly taller, and slim; his straight brown hair, combed back away from his face, was nearly as long as that of the lieutenant.

"How do you do," Odo said with appropriate formality. He knew why the two Bajorans were here even before Sisko told him.

"The lieutenant and the sergeant have come from Bajor to enforce the edict regarding the banishment of all Ferengi from Bajoran space," Sisko said. "Apparently there have been reports from Bajorans living on the station indicating that there are still several Ferengi aboard *Deep Space Nine.*"

"Not several, Captain," Lieutenant Carlien corrected. At least on the surface, Odo noted, she did not seem to be in the presence of the Emissary, as so many Bajorans often were. "Two individuals named—" She consulted her padd. "—Rom and Quark. Do you know of them, Constable?"

Odo glanced at Sisko. The captain inclined his head slightly to the side, shrugging his shoulders almost imperceptibly. The two men had discussed the situation regarding Quark and Rom. While they both disagreed with the Bajoran position, neither of them were prepared to lie about anything.

"Yes, I believe they are still on the station," Odo informed Carlien and Onial.

"May we ask why they have not yet been taken into custody?" Onial asked.

As explanation, Odo related the range of his authority as he interpreted it. Carlien and Onial seemed to accept the rationale at face value.

"I understand the limitations incumbent upon your position," Carlien said to Odo. Then, to Sisko, she continued, "As militia officers representing the government in the role of system-wide law enforcement, however, we *do* possess the authority to act in this matter."

"Of course," Sisko acknowledged. He held out his hand to Carlien and said, "May I?" She handed him her padd, and he passed it on to Odo. "First Minister Shakaar himself has signed arrest warrants for all Ferengi in the system."

Odo perused the document on the readout. When he finished his examination, he came around his security console and delivered it back to Carlien.

"All seems to be in order," Odo confirmed.

"So," Carlien said, "will you please take us to these two men, Constable?"

Again, Odo looked to Sisko for assistance.

"Yes, of course," the captain answered, motioning toward the door. "Constable?"

Odo sighed—a habit he had learned to unconsciously mimic by observing humanoids in moments of frustration—and turned to pick up a tricorder from atop his console. Reluctantly, he then led Sisko and the two Bajorans out of his office.

"This way," he told them.

CHAPTER
11

"RIGHT THIS WAY, Lieutenant, Sergeant."

Odo's voice was not extremely loud, but it did not need to be in order for Quark to hear it. Even the constable's footsteps were conspicuously audible as he marched through the Promenade toward the bar. All of which was strange, Quark knew, since Odo's appearances were so often unheralded.

"The bar is just down here, on the left," Quark heard Odo say.

Lieutenant, thought Quark. *Sergeant.* Sergeant was not a Starfleet rank; it was a Bajoran one. It could be one of the Bajoran officers assigned to *DS9,* but—

—No. They were coming for him, he realized.

"Rom," Quark called across the room. Rom looked up from where he was taking a customer's order at a table. Quark beckoned him with a gesture, then raced over to the end of the bar, to where Morn was sitting in front of a mug of lager. Quark grabbed his elbow and leaned in close to him. Morn's breath smelled liked his drink.

"It's time," Quark told him. "You're in charge."

Morn spun around on his stool to face Quark, the smile

on his otherwise-droopy countenance by far the biggest Quark had ever seen there. It was unnerving.

"Don't drink all the profits," Quark enjoined him. Morn said nothing, but he continued to smile as he got up and moved behind the bar.

"Is it time, brother?" Rom asked, arriving beside Quark. "Are they coming for us?"

"They're coming," Quark said, ducking behind the bar for a moment to retrieve a satchel. "Let's go." He shoved the satchel into Rom's arms and pushed him toward the nearer of the two winding staircases that led up to the second level. They had just started up when Odo spoke again.

"Right over here," Quark heard him say. From the volume and direction of his voice, Quark judged the constable to be just outside the entrance to the bar. Rom must have heard him too, because he stopped halfway to the second level and peered over the staircase railing at the main doors. Quark pushed him again to get him moving.

By the time they had dashed the rest of the way up the stairs, Quark could make out the sound of a portable sensing device down below them.

Odo watched as Sergeant Onial swept the handheld Bajoran scanner back and forth in front of himself, attempting to detect any Ferengi life signs. The two Bajoran officers stood ahead of Odo and Captain Sisko, just inside the doors to the bar.

"Anything?" Lieutenant Carlien asked her subordinate over the electronic whine of the scanner.

Odo gazed about the room. Neither Quark nor Rom were there, he saw, but Morn was working behind the bar, a clear indication that Quark believed the situation to be desperate. Morn was smiling broadly as he poured a tall glass of some brightly colored liquid. Odo wondered idly whether the drink was intended for a customer, or if the new bartender was indulging in what he considered to be a perquisite of the job he had been asked to do.

"Yes," Sergeant Onial answered the lieutenant. He held the scanner pointed in the direction of the stairway near the end of the bar. His hand then rose until the device was aimed upward, toward the second level. "They're on the deck above us."

"Both of them?" Carlien asked.

"Yes."

The lieutenant headed immediately for the stairs. The sergeant followed in her wake, and Sisko and Odo trailed along after them. Odo noticed several of the bar's customers look up from their drinks and their conversations as the quartet passed.

Once they had reached the second level, Onial paused to confirm his sensor readings. He started toward the walkway of the Upper Promenade, on a zigzag course amid the people seated at the tables there.

"This way," he said, but then he halted abruptly in his path.

"What is it?" Carlien asked.

"The readings are fluctuating," he said. "It's almost as if they're intermittently being masked."

"Constable?" Sisko said, but Odo was already activating his own tricorder. His actions were born more out of habit than out of duty, Odo recognized, as were those of the captain, he was sure.

"They are trying to mask their life signs," Odo verified. "If they're successful, we won't be able to read them at all."

"Can you pinpoint their location, Sergeant?" Carlien wanted to know.

Onial studied his scanner. Holding the device steady, he pivoted on his heel; Odo found the movement reminiscent of a compass needle finding a magnetic pole.

"They're through there," Onial said, indicating a doorway.

"Confirmed," Odo said, looking at his own sensor readings.

"What is through there, Captain?" Carlien asked.

"Holosuites."

"That may be how they're trying to block our scans," Onial theorized.

"The readings we're getting aren't just holosuite projections, are they, Constable?" Sisko asked.

"Negative," Odo said, checking his tricorder. "I'm reading two actual life-forms, both of them Ferengi."

"Then let's go," Carlien said.

Onial led the way this time. Through the doorway, a short hall led to Quark's holosuites. Onial stopped at the first one and examined his scanner.

"They're in here," the sergeant announced. Carlien stepped up to the doors, but they did not open. Odo slipped past her to the other side of the doorway, where the control panel for the holosuite was set into the wall. Odo operated the panel.

"The doors have been locked," he told everybody. "There's a program running in there."

"Shut it down," Sisko ordered.

Odo worked the controls.

"I'm not getting any response," he said. "I'll initiate the override protocols." Sisko walked over and stood beside Odo, observing him as he worked. After a few seconds, Odo glanced back over his shoulder and said, "There's no response from the overrides either."

"Cut the power."

Odo acknowledged the captain with a nod and set to bypassing the primary holosuite functions. He accessed the emergency power shutdown procedure and triggered it. There was no effect.

"Nothing's happening," Odo said. "I think the panel's been reconfigured. In fact, I'd guess that the whole system has been thoroughly modified."

"Can you shut it down manually?" Sisko asked.

"I can try." Sisko backed away as the constable dropped to one knee. Odo set his tricorder on the floor and removed the access plate situated on the wall beneath the main holosuite controls. He peered inside at the circuitry junction there, located the manual cutoff switch, and reached for it. There was a *snap* as he threw the switch. He retrieved his tricorder, stood up, and checked the control panel. Sisko moved back in next to him and looked at the panel as well.

"Nothing," Sisko said.

"They must have shunted the power through another system," Odo concluded. "It'll take some time to isolate the circuit."

"Is there any way to unlock the doors?" Carlien asked.

Odo used his tricorder to learn the answer.

"This looks like one of Rom's specialty jobs," he said. "Getting past the security locks he's put in place will also take some time."

"Can we beam in?" Carlien persisted.

"No," Odo replied. "Part of Rom's locking strategy is to set up repeating, low-level antiresonance bursts. It makes it impossible to focus a transporter beam."

"A transporter beam originating outside the antiresonance field," Sisko said. "But the holosuite is active. What if we tapped in to its internal transporter system?"

"Hmmm," Odo said, considering the suggestion. "We could use the station's transporters, but direct the rematerialization subroutine to use the holosuite's emitters."

Sisko tapped his combadge. "Sisko to Chief O'Brien."

"O'Brien here," the chief responded. Sisko quickly described what they wanted to do. It took only a few moments for O'Brien to make the necessary adjustments to the station's transporter software.

"We're ready whenever you are, Captain," O'Brien reported. "But once we put you down inside the antiresonance field, we won't be able to fix a transporter lock on you to beam you out of the holosuite."

"That's all right, Chief," Sisko said. "Once we're inside, Rom should be able to get us out. If you haven't heard from us in thirty minutes, then cut your way through the doors."

"Aye, sir."

"Energize."

There was a pause, and then Odo heard the faint, high-pitched hum of the transporter effect arise in the corridor. Pearls of soft red light closed around him, flooding his vision, then released him after a subjectively immeasurable span of time. When his sight cleared, he saw right away that there was indeed a program running in the holosuite.

The four officers were standing on a large veranda overlooking a tropical landscape. A breeze blew, taking the edge off the high temperature. Above the group, gently undulating in the moving air and providing sanctuary from the sun, a light fabric covered the veranda in tentlike fashion. A few small tables were scattered about, as were several sunken tubs. People congregated in twos and threes, here and there in larger groups, everybody clad—or unclad—in an appropriate manner for the climate. Servers wandered unobtrusively through the scene, delivering food and beverages and taking people's orders. Everybody appeared happy and serene.

Beyond the veranda, off to the right, a lush forest swept up a mountainside. Extending away from the base of the mountain was a beach of pale sand, connecting the verdancy with the crystalline waters of a vibrant, blue-tinted sea. Here too there were people, swimming in the surf, playing in the sand, relaxing.

"Risa," Sisko informed everybody.

Risa, Odo thought. He had heard of the world, of course—it was famed for its weather-controlled beauty and its magnificent resort facilities—but he had never traveled there. Until now, he had never even seen a holographic representation of the place; Odo was not enamored of fantasies.

"Wow," Onial said quietly. "I've never been to Risa."

"And you still haven't," Lieutenant Carlien told him brusquely. "Where are they?"

Onial flushed as he raised his scanner, obviously embarrassed at his reaction to the holoprogram. He operated the device, again swinging it around in an attempt to pick up Ferengi life signs. Odo consulted his own tricorder.

"They're down on the beach," Onial said finally, just as Odo reached the same determination. Carlien started for the stairs that led down to the sand. Onial, Sisko, and Odo followed.

Walking on the beach, Odo discovered, was not an easy matter, at least not for him. He felt awkward and uncomfortable, unsure of his movements; the rises of the fine grains of sand did not provide adequate support for the weight of his faux Bajoran body, perched as it was on his faux Bajoran feet. He therefore willed his feet to flatten and widen as he tramped along, which shored up his footing considerably.

Onial led the way with his scanner, with Carlien at his side and Sisko and Odo behind them. They passed imaginary patrons of this imaginary Risa, none of whom paid them any attention. Above, the projected cerulean sky was cloudless.

They stopped about two-thirds of the way to the water, when they reached two lounge chairs. Onial motioned with his scanner, indicating that the two Ferengi were in the chairs, which faced away from the officers. Carlien circled around to see for herself. The others followed.

Odo was surprised by what they found. Because Rom was a capable and creative engineer, and because the trail had taken them to a holosuite, Odo realized now that he had suspected they were chasing a ruse, the Ferengi life signs they had been reading an artifice somehow devised and executed by Rom. Consequently, he had not expected to find what they did: lying in one lounge chair was Quark, in the other, Rom.

"Is one of you Quark?" Carlien demanded.

"Do I have to answer that question, Captain?" Quark asked. In his hand, he held what looked to be some sort of a tropical drink, a straw emerging from it, the container brightly decorated.

"I don't think not answering will make any difference," Sisko replied.

But Quark did not answer. Neither did Rom.

"Captain?" Carlien asked.

"This is Quark," Sisko said, pointing. "And this is Rom."

"I am Lieutenant Carlien of the Bajoran Militia," she told the two Ferengi. "I am informing each of you that you are under arrest, charged with violating the statute established by the Chamber of Ministers, which prohibits Ferengi from being within Bajoran sovereignty. In accordance with that law, you will now be taken into custody."

"Captain Sisko," Quark said, not moving from the lounge chair. "I implore you: This isn't right. I've committed no real crime."

"According to them, you have," Sisko said.

"Stand up," Carlien ordered. Next to the lieutenant, Onial opened the pouch he was carrying, placed his scanner inside it, then removed two sets of hand restraints. Odo wondered if such measures were truly necessary, but he did not say anything.

"Captain, please," Quark tried again.

"If you do not stand up," Carlien said, "Sergeant Onial and I will force you to your feet."

"I suggest the two of you comply," Odo said. "The warrants for your arrest authorize the use of whatever force is necessary in order to apprehend you."

Quark looked over at his brother, and then the two of them rose to their feet. Quark set his drink down on the sand. Neither he nor Rom seemed as upset as Odo would have expected.

"Turn around," Carlien said.

Quark and Rom did as they were told. Onial handed the lieutenant one set of restraints, and she affixed it about Quark's wrists, his arms behind his back. Onial secured the other set of restraints on Rom in the same manner.

"Will we have to wait for your officer to break us out of here, Captain?" Carlien inquired.

"I don't know," Sisko said. "Let's find out: computer, exit."

Several paces down the beach, the holosuite doors appeared. They parted and slid open, revealing the corridor on the second level of the bar from which the four officers had transported to this simulated Risa. Carlien reached out and took hold of Quark's forearms. Onial did the same with Rom. The two Bajoran officers propelled their prisoners ahead of them. Once more, Sisko and Odo followed.

The group crossed the sand to the doors. At the threshold, Quark and Rom suddenly stopped and turned, each attempting to wriggle free of their captor's grasp.

"Captain Sisko," Quark said, "I really must protest this treatment."

Before Sisko could respond, Carlien forced Quark back around and planted her hand between his shoulder blades. When he did not begin walking, she pushed him. He moved forward through the doorway . . . and vanished. The hand restraints clattered to the deck. Everybody seemed startled.

Everybody but Rom.

Carlien reached for Rom. She grabbed him by the upper arm, pulled him from Onial's grasp, and strode with him through the doorway. Rom disappeared too, the second set of restraints landing on the floor beside the first.

Lieutenant Carlien looked back through the doorway into the holosuite, first at Onial, and then at Sisko and Odo.

"Where are they?" she asked.

Quark stood by the sealed inner hatch with his mouth hanging open. He was dumbfounded.

"Where's the transport?" he wanted to know. Staring through the portholes in the inner and outer hatches, Quark could only see the dark of space where he had expected a ship to be.

"It was supposed to be here," Rom said. He pulled a padd out of his satchel and switched it on. Quark wrenched it from his hands.

"Give me that," he said. He accessed the readout of ships scheduled to depart the station that day. He slid his finger down the list of times until he came to 1955. The corresponding entry under the heading SHIPS read PERIN CHENASE (REGISTRY: RIGEL V); the entry under BAY read 6. The list confirmed what Rom was claiming the transport was supposed to be leaving from this docking bay in ten minutes.

Unless the list is wrong, Quark realized.

"When did you download this schedule from the station computer?" he asked his brother.

"When you told me to," Rom said.

"When I told you to what?"

"When you told me to record all the departure schedules," Rom answered. "So we could get out of Bajoran space if the Bajorans decided to come after us." Rom's words came very quickly, a sign Quark recognized: his brother was nervous that he had made a bad mistake. Quark was suddenly nervous too.

"I told you that two and a half days ago," he said.

"Right."

"Right?" Quark asked. "Don't you think that the schedule might've changed between then and now, you idiot?"

Rom did not answer.

It really was unbelievable, Quark thought. Rom could construct out of scrap parts a system to project false Ferengi life signs, and another to conceal their actual life signs, but he could not manage to successfully complete other, simpler chores.

interested not only in violating the Bajoran edict, but in fleeing from the authorities, Lieutenant Carlien had requested the use of *Deep Space Nine*'s sensors to aid in her search for the fugitives. Sisko and Odo had led Carlien and Onial up here to Ops, where a scan for Ferengi life-forms had turned up negative.

"How long will this take, Captain?" Sergeant Onial inquired. Sisko looked to Odo, who had been observing the operation from the outer, upper level.

"That depends on a number of factors," Odo said, padding down to where Sisko stood with Carlien and Onial. "One of which is luck. But a sensor sweep of this type, across the entire station, should take several hours, at least."

"How many ships are scheduled to leave within that time frame?" Carlien wanted to know.

"A few, I'm sure," Sisko answered. "Why?"

"Isn't it obvious?" Carlien asked, rather impertinently, Odo thought. "We want to prevent the Ferengi from escaping Bajoran space."

"I thought that was what you wanted," Odo commented. "The Ferengi out of Bajoran space."

"We do, but Rom and Quark are in violation of the law," she explained. "They must be arrested."

"Frankly," Sisko said, "their violation of the law notwithstanding, I'm not clear on why you wouldn't welcome their departure. Denying the Ferengi access to the wormhole is, after all, the real threat contained in the Bajoran injunction to the nagus. It's that which may have an influence on Ze... not jailing a couple of Ferengi citizens whose incarceration will have no effect at all on the grand nagus's business interests."

"My orders are unambiguous, Captain," Carlien stated coldly. "We are here specifically to apprehend the two Ferengi on *Deep Space Nine* who refused to comply with the edict. They must not be permitted to abscond from us."

Sisko took a deep breath, then walked away from Carlien and Onial. He mounted the steps to the upper level of Ops, paced a short distance around its periphery. Finally, he faced Carlien again, though now from a distance.

"I will not prevent you from searching for Quark and

Profit and loss, Quark told himself. *Profit and loss.*

Quark reached over and took the satchel out of Rom's hands. He opened it, pushed the padd in next to a small contrivance that was currently emitting an electric hum, and pulled out three isolinear rods, orange-hued and about ten centimeters long each. Quark was not authorized to possess any of these rods; one of them contained various station security programs, and it was this one that he selected for use right now.

Quark knelt down to the side of the inner hatch and pulled an access plate from the wall to reveal a circuitry junction. He studied the configuration for a moment, then slipped the isolinear rod into a suitable slot.

"Open the hatch," he told Rom.

Rom operated the control panel on the wall and the hatch rolled open along its toothed track. Quark removed his isolinear rod from the junction and replaced the plate. He stood and pushed his brother into the short corridor of Docking Bay Six, then followed him inside.

"Close it," Quark said, knowing that Rom would not require a security override to do so. It was important that they get out of sight as quickly as they could. It would probably not be long before Odo and the Bajorans discovered that they had been duped, and they would assuredly commence a search of the whole station.

Rom worked the controls located inside the docking bay. The inner hatch spun closed.

"Now what, brother?" Rom asked.

"Now we try to figure another way off the station and out of Bajoran space."

"Maybe we should've left before the deadline," Rom said. "When we wouldn't have had to run and hide."

Maybe we should have, Quark thought. Somehow, though, he had not believed that the Bajorans would carry out the threat they had issued in their ultimatum to the nagus. He had prepared for it—the satchel, telling Rom to track the station's departure schedule, transferring all of his financial accounts to institutions off Bajor—but he had not actually thought that such precautions would be necessary. And, when Quark had finally been willing to think about it, he had found that he had not really wanted to leave the bar.

Perhaps he had also invested too much in what Dax had said to him. He had figured that if the Bajorans came looking for him, he could just board the nearest ship and flee the system. But until that time, he had planned to continue running his business and making profit, working toward his dreams. His real mistake, he knew now, had been to trust Rom with anything.

Quark removed the access plate in the docking bay. He exchanged the isolinear rod he had just used for a second one. He installed the new rod, then worked the control panel and brought up a readout of the departure schedule for today. There was only one ship leaving the station within the hour: an Andorian freighter. Of course, true to his luck, the ship was on the opposite side of the Docking Ring.

"An Andorian freighter, headed back home," Quark said to himself. "Wonderful." It was bad enough that Andorians were a self-described violent race, but if Quark could not convince the pilot of the freighter to make an unplanned stop at some other world, he and Rom would end up on the other side of Federation space—deep in foreign territory, and a very long way from the Ferengi Alliance. Quark had worked on a freighter himself for eight years, though—a Ferengi freighter, but still a freighter—and he hoped that his experience would help him deal with the Andorian pilot.

Quark shut down the control panel, then bent to retrieve his isolinear rod. He replaced the access plate and stood to face Rom.

"All right," he said. "We've got to get all the way over to Dock Eleven."

"That's on the other side of the station," Rom protested.

"What do you want to do?" Quark asked sharply. "Wait here until salvation arrives on the other side of one of these hatches?" He thrust one thumb in the direction of the outer hatch, one thumb in the direction of the inner hatch.

"I guess not."

"You guess not. Well, good." Quark opened the satchel and dropped the isolinear rod inside, then reached in and pulled out a small, homemade device. "Will this thing continue to mask our life signs until we get across the station?" Rom took the device and examined it; it was humming faintly.

"I think the power'll last," he said. "But it may not do us

much good. If they get into the holosuite and find created false sensor readings, they'll probably start s for a sensor hole."

"How long will it take them to find us?"

"That depends. It could take a few hours."

"That's all the time we need."

"Or it could take five minutes. If they're lucky."

"Wonderful."

"Even if we get to the Andorian ship," Rom said, ' makes you think Captain Sisko will let it leave the stat

"The freighter's already been scanned and cleare departure," Quark explained, "so unless Sisko catch boarding the ship, he'll have no legal grounds to sc again. And anyway, I know the Andorians. They're going to let anybody prevent them from meeting schedule. If they had to, they'd blast their way out of h

"Are you sure?"

"Of course I'm sure," he told Rom. He was not sure he did know that even though they were members o Federation, the Andorians had a passionate distrust— be even a hatred—of Starfleet. If he needed to, Quark probably use that fact to help them get aboard the frei and Sisko would not be able to search the ship or docked indefinitely without starting a diplomatic ir Such an incident with a member world of the Fe would be something the Bajorans would want to a

"Okay," Rom said. "So we'll be okay if we can freighter, and we can probably hide our life signs there, but how are we going to prevent ourselves seen?"

In response, Quark pointed at the ceiling.

"Can you scan for sensor holes?" Lieut asked.

It was precisely the course of action O taken, he thought, if this had been his inve

"We can," Sisko answered. He was stan lien, on the lower, inner level of Ops. "D

"Yes, sir," she said from her positi console. "Beginning scan."

After it had become clear that Qu

Rom on *DS9*," he said. "I'll even help you do so—" Odo knew that Sisko had little choice but to help; despite Starfleet's presence, this was still a Bajoran space station. "—but I cannot search or detain any ships without just cause."

"Harboring outlaws who are evading arrest is just cause," Carlien maintained.

"And so if our sensor sweeps show Quark and Rom boarding a ship docked at *DS9*, then you can search that ship," Sisko granted. "Otherwise, if you wish to delay any ships, I'm afraid you'll have to find the means to do it yourself." That, Odo knew—as Carlien must have as well—would not happen both *Defiant* and the tractor beam on the station were Starfleet property, and Bajor had no spacefaring fleet beyond a small number of cargo vessels, personnel transports, and short-range impulse ships; that was one of the primary reasons the Bajorans had invited Starfleet to operate *Deep Space Nine* in the first place.

"I understand," Carlien said, acknowledging the limitations Sisko was imposing upon her. "Will you show me the schedule of upcoming departures?"

"Major Kira should be able to provide you with that information."

"I can bring up the data here at my station," Kira said.

Odo realized that the major had been unusually quiet since he and Sisko had escorted the Bajoran officers up to Ops. Odo was aware of Kira's antipathy toward Quark, and of the resentment she felt because of the situation involving the Ninth Orb, but he was not sure whether he understood her silence now. Did she not trust herself to speak because of her feelings of acrimony? Or had she perhaps been the person who had reported to the Bajoran government that Quark and Rom were still on the station, causing her now to experience recriminations for that action? Neither reason satisfied Odo—they did not seem consistent with Kira's character—but he could not at the moment conceive of any others.

Carlien and Onial went over to Kira's console as she retrieved the information they desired.

"Here," Kira said after she stopped working her controls. She pointed to an entry on her screen. "Two vessels will be leaving within the next ninety minutes, both freighters. One is Andorian, the other, Bolian."

"After that, when does the next ship leave?" Onial asked.

"Not for four hours," Kira said.

"Which of the two freighters departs first?" Carlien asked. "And where are they headed?"

"The Andorian ship leaves first," Kira said. "But it's on a direct voyage back home. The Bolian ship is going to—" Kira tapped a control on her console. "—it's going to Alastron Four."

Alastron Four, Odo thought. According to Dax, that had been Quark's intended destination before he had opted to remain on the station. *Should I say anything?* Odo asked himself. His beliefs regarding Quark's character to the contrary, he still had misgivings about this entire affair. As chief of security, though, he had an obligation to—

"Dax, didn't you say that Quark booked passage on a ship headed for Alastron Four a couple of days ago?" Kira asked.

"Yes," Dax said, with apparent reluctance. "I did say that."

Although Kira had effectively relieved the constable of the necessity of making a decision about whether to reveal personal information regarding Quark, Odo felt no relief. This matter was monstrously troublesome for him. He had devoted his life to the one thing about which he felt most strongly: the pursuit of justice. But when the law and what he believed justice to be were at odds, what was he to do? To arbitrarily disregard the law—or worse, to transgress it—was anathema to him.

"Captain, to eliminate the possibility that the Ferengi will beam over to one of the docked ships," Carlien said, "I'd like to ask that the station's transporters be shut down."

"Very well," Sisko said.

"And that all transporters on the docked ships be deactivated."

"I don't have that authority," Sisko said. "Those ships are not my personal property, Lieutenant, and the crews on them have rights."

There was a tense stillness when Carlien did not respond. After a moment, Kira looked up from her console.

"Rather than shutting down the transporters, we can

raise the deflector shields around the station," she suggested, "and send antiresonance bursts through the open hatches to inhibit transport through them. That should accomplish the lieutenant's objective."

"Thank you, Major," Sisko said. Odo did not know with certainty—the captain was frequently circumspect about revealing his feelings—but it seemed to him that Sisko was not pleased that Kira had chosen to offer such counsel at this time. "Will that satisfy you, Lieutenant?" he asked.

"Yes, it will."

"Very well," Sisko said. "Take care of it, Major."

"Yes, sir." Kira operated the controls at her station.

"I would also like to watch the Andorian and Bolian ships, maintain surveillance on all avenues of entry to both," Carlien ventured. "With your permission, Captain, I'd like Sergeant Onial to assemble two squads of off-duty Bajoran security personnel." Odo was not sure that Carlien required Sisko's permission for such an action, but she was obviously bright enough to sidestep any possible issues by explicitly requesting the use of Bajoran officers quartered on *DS9*.

"Of course," Sisko said. "Constable Odo can help coordinate. *He* is the ranking security officer of the Bajoran Militia on the station." The captain's message to Carlien was plain: Sisko would offer his assistance in her mission to arrest Quark and Rom on *Deep Space Nine*, but his officers would be in command.

"Thank you," Carlien said, obviously perceiving that she should press no further. Sisko did not respond, but turned and walked into his office.

"Constable?" Onial asked.

"I'll bring up the deck plans for the Docking Ring," Odo said, moving to an unstaffed console, still wondering how he felt about what was transpiring.

Quark stopped when the systems-access tunnel in which they were crawling intersected with a vertical tube. The joints in his arms and legs ached from the long journey across the station, but he and Rom were close to Docking Bay Eleven now. He looked back over his shoulder to check on his brother. Rom was nowhere in sight.

"Rom," he called in an urgent whisper. There were several thumps, and then Rom came scrambling around a corner, dragging the satchel behind him.

"I'm here, brother," he said. "I was just looking at a new dynamic relay conduit—"

"Does it have anything to do with us?" Quark asked in frustration.

"No," Rom answered.

"Then forget about it," he said. "Now, is that—" He pointed down the vertical tube. "—where we're headed?"

Rom pulled the satchel up beside him and rummaged through it. He found the padd and consulted it.

"That's it," he said. "The access panel at the bottom of the shaft leads directly into Docking Bay Eleven."

"All right. Let's get going then."

Quark hoisted himself out of the tunnel and onto the ladder that extended up and down the length of the tube. He climbed down to the floor at the base of the tube, then waited for Rom to join him. Once they were together, Quark moved to the access panel that led into the docking bay. Moving his ear close to the panel, he listened.

"I hear footsteps," he told his brother. "Back and forth between the inner and outer hatches."

"Could it be somebody from the freighter?"

Quark wanted to say *yes*, because that was what he wanted to be true. But he knew that it was not.

"No," he said. "Security's patrolling for us." Odo and the Bajorans had uncovered their ploy, and now they were guarding all of the docking bays on *Deep Space Nine*. Even if Rom could renew the power in the device he used to mask their life signs, they could not continue to hide out on the station; either a sweep for sensor holes or a physical search would eventually see them captured. No, they somehow had to board one of the docked ships and get away. But there was no other way onto any of the ships other than through the docking bays.

Except—

"Rom, can you patch in to the station's transporter system?" Quark asked.

"Uh, maybe," he said.

"Do a site-to-site transport to get us on to the freighter?"

"Maybe."

"Don't tell me that. Yes or no?"

"Well, yes," Rom said. "But I can't do it if we're shielding our life signs. The same interference that blocks the sensors would make it impossible to fix a transporter lock on us."

There was not much of a choice. Whether they confronted a security officer while trying to board a ship, or allowed themselves to be scanned by dropping the sensor mask, they had to come out of hiding. But the likelihood that their life signs would be scanned in the brief moment it would take them to beam across to the Andorian freighter seemed remote compared to the chance of them being seized attempting to make their way past a security guard. Of course, in either case, Quark would have to talk quickly to the pilot in order to explain their presence aboard the freighter; then again, Quark possessed an aptitude for cold selling.

"Tap into the transporter," Quark told Rom. "Get us aboard that ship."

Odo noticed it at the same time that Kira did.

"Lieutenant Carlien," the major said, "I think we may have something." Kira's fingers sped across her console, and Odo guessed that she was trying to gather all of the information available about what they had just seen.

"You found something?" Carlien asked anxiously, coming down to Kira's station from where she had been pacing the perimeter of the upper level.

"Captain Sisko to Ops," Kira called, the communications monitor automatically opening a channel and relaying her message. Then to Carlien, she announced, "Transporter contact with the deflectors."

"Transporter contact?" Carlien seemed confused. "But I thought—"

"They tapped into the system directly," Kira explained, "bypassing the transporter controls, which we'd shut down."

"What have you got, Major?" Sisko asked as he entered from his office.

"Somebody just attempted to beam off the station," she said.

"They were unsuccessful," Odo amended. He studied the data marching across Kira's console. "It looks like the transporter contact may have been on the Docking Ring."

"Where did they try to transport from?" Carlien wanted to know. She crowded about Kira's console, but she was obviously unable to understand the readouts.

"Chief?" Kira said.

"Working on it," Chief O'Brien said at his station on the upper level. His brow furrowed as he worked, his eyes darting from side to side as he scrutinized the data coming up on his console. Finally, he looked up. "Reflecting back from the point of transporter contact with the shields, it looks like the transport signal originated right outside Docking Bay Eleven."

Odo watched as Kira furiously worked her controls.

"I'm reading a sensor hole there," she reported. "In a systems-access tube leading directly to the bay."

Lieutenant Carlien activated her combadge.

"Carlien to Sergeant Onial," she said.

"Onial here," came the sergeant's disembodied voice.

"Where are you, Sergeant?"

"I'm in a corridor leading to the inner hatch of Dock Two." It was where the Bolian ship bound for Alastron IV was moored.

Carlien related the location of Quark and Rom.

"I understand," Onial replied.

"Sergeant Onial," Sisko said after activating his own combadge. "This is Captain Sisko."

"Yes, Captain?"

"I want you to wait for Constable Odo to arrive before taking any action." Sisko peered over at Odo; he was already breaking away from Kira's console and heading for the steps to the upper level.

"Captain, please," Carlien appealed to him. "The Ferengi could run off in the time it will take the constable to get down there."

"And where will they run to, Lieutenant?" Sisko asked. "Don't worry; we'll keep a close watch on them from up here." Then, looking across to the sciences console, he said, "Dax?"

"I'll put a sensor lock on the hole," she said.

"Lieutenant?" Sisko said.

"Very well." She tapped her combadge again. "Sergeant Onial, you are to wait for Constable Odo."

"Yes, Lieutenant," Onial responded.

"And Sergeant," Carlien said, "do not contact the guard inside the docking bay; the Ferengi have exceptional hearing."

"Acknowledged."

Odo had reached the upper level and was on his way to the turbolift when Sisko called after him.

"Constable."

"Sir?" Odo said, stopping and turning to face Sisko.

"You're in charge. I don't want things to get out of hand down there."

"I understand," Odo said, recalling that Carlien and Onial were authorized to use force to apprehend Quark and Rom. Since the two Ferengi had not been able to depart the station by now, it was clear that they would be taken into custody. It was apparent to Odo that the captain did not want them hurt—for their own sakes, of course, but also to avoid any escalation of the troubles between the Bajorans and the Ferengi.

Odo would make sure that the arrest went smoothly. He entered the lift and ordered it to take him to the Docking Ring, Bay Eleven.

"What happened?" Quark asked. They had begun to transport, but when the beam effect had dissipated, he found that they were still at the base of the systems-access tube.

Rom operated his padd, which was now patched by means of a fiber-optic line into one of the data-transmission cables in the access tube.

"What's taking so long?" Quark demanded when Rom did not immediately reply.

"I have to locate the transporter logs to find out why we weren't successful," Rom said.

"Well, hurry up." Time was growing short, Quark knew. As each moment passed, the possibility of being found increased, as did the level of his anxiety.

After a while, Quark heard the inner hatch of the docking

bay open, followed by the sounds of voices. Just then, Rom discovered the information for which he had been searching.

"The deflectors are up around the station," Rom told Quark.

"Wonderful," Quark said. "Now what are we going to do?"

He did not have to wait long to have his question answered. Right next to him, the access panel leading from Docking Bay Eleven opened.

On his way to the Docking Ring, Odo redeployed the security force. He stationed a pair of guards outside each of the access panels that led in to the network of systems-access tubes and tunnels surrounding Bay Eleven.

When Odo arrived at the dock, he found Onial pacing back and forth in front of the closed inner hatch. He verified with Kira that Quark and Rom were still in the same place, quickly briefed the sergeant on his intended plan of action, then operated the control panel beside the inner hatch. The door wheeled open. Inside the bay, the security officer posted there looked up, his hand phaser drawn and aimed at Odo and Onial. When the guard saw who had opened the hatch, he lowered his weapon.

"Report," Odo said as he entered the docking bay. Onial was at his side.

"All's been quiet, sir," declared the guard.

Odo motioned to Onial and then pointed to the access panel just inside the inner hatch, on the left-hand side. As Onial bent beside the panel, Odo gestured to the guard, holding two fingers to his lips, indicating that the guard should not ask about what Odo and Onial were doing.

"No sign of Quark and Rom?" Odo asked as cover.

"No, sir."

Odo squatted beside a second access panel, this one set opposite the first, in the wall to the right of the inner hatch. Odo made a rhythmic movement with his hand, then counted out with his fingers: three, two, one. On the last beat, Odo opened the right access panel; on the other side of the bay, Onial opened the left.

Odo peered through the opening and saw nothing. He

quickly turned to look in Onial's direction. Visible past the sergeant's body was Quark, and past him, Rom.

Onial grabbed for Quark, but the Ferengi kicked out, more a reflex than an attack, Odo thought. Because the access panel was set low on the wall, Onial was squatting, his body weight fully on his toes, and the force of Quark's kick sent him over backward. Rom disappeared up the ladder. Quark quickly followed.

Odo slapped at his combadge.

"Odo to security detachment. Go." The officers stationed at the access panels would now open those panels and enter the systems-access network, then wait for Quark and Rom to come to them.

Odo raced across to Onial to ascertain whether or not he had been injured. The sergeant brushed off his efforts.

"I'm fine, I'm fine," Onial squawked. "Go after them."

Odo knelt and thrust his head and shoulders through the opening. He was in time to see Quark's foot disappear down the horizontal tunnel that intersected with this tube.

"Quark," he called. There was no response. Only the sounds of the two Ferengi scrambling to escape drifted back to him.

In his mind, Odo saw currents, drifting rivers of motion sliding effortlessly through space and time. Within the currents, he conjured the images of eddies, and within the eddies, he perceived their intangible derivatives: dimensionless points in space defining instantaneous rates of change.

Odo envisaged the change he sought, although he had never experienced this change in exactly this way. It was always new, anyway, with only the vaguest reminiscences connecting him to what had transpired previously, to what he had been previously. That was the primal aspect of the joy of being a changeling, that the universe within was always archetypal.

And so: the change, proprioception delivered into the consciousness, driving up through the queue in reverse, from the fluxion of the nonexistent point, through the eddies circling in countermovement to the current, which grew encompassed by the internal tide, became directed, and so: the change.

Odo felt himself go, his mercurial corporeality softening and shifting, becoming something other than it was, becoming more than it was, becoming the embodiment of his own thought. There was quicksilver movement, and his humanoid shape was a memory only.

And he *became*—

—Became a cyclonic mass swirling inward on itself, and upward against gravity, and through the vertical systems-access tube. Sight was gone, and hearing, and even touch in the humanoid sense, but there was yet *sensation*, full sensation, and with it a knowing, a perception of the outer universe.

Up through the tube, and then over, in that direction, into the access tunnel, and down with gravity, to the floor of the tunnel, landing, and the process of becoming again, just a mass now, but a unique mass, unique because it was him, because it was Odo, but also because it was something he had never been, not precisely, that was not the nature of his existence, even when he was the humanoid, he was the humanoid anew each time. And there again, in that direction, with sense came knowledge, the understanding that Quark and Rom were fleeing in that direction, toward whichever security officer was patrolling at the next junction. There would be no escape, Odo knew.

Becoming again, a tube in a tube, flowing not directly against gravity now, but perpendicularly to it, again something different, but also with spiral motion, always circles within circles, and points without shape creating shape—

—And becoming the humanoid constable once more.

"Quark."

Quark stopped. He was on his hands and knees. He looked back past his body.

"It's over," Odo told him.

Quark peered back and saw Odo lying in the tunnel. *Good,* he thought. Now at least he could stop running—or crawling, to be more accurate. After the trip here from the other side of the station, and then this frantic attempt to flee, his knees and elbows felt raw.

"Brother?" Quark looked ahead and saw that Rom had also stopped. "What should we do?"

"Do?" Quark asked. "I think we should rest." He collapsed onto his side, still breathing heavily from the exertion. "What do you think, Odo?"

"I think you have to surrender now, Quark," he answered. "There are security officers stationed at all of the tunnel junctions around Dock Eleven. There's no way for you and Rom to escape."

"Well then," Quark told Odo, "congratulations. You finally got me."

Odo crawled backward down the tunnel, keeping Quark and Rom in view as they followed along after him. At the junction with the vertical tube leading directly to Docking Bay Eleven, Odo climbed onto the ladder and upward, allowing his two captives to mount the ladder and descend to the floor. Finally, the three of them clambered through the access panel.

When Quark and Rom had agreed to surrender, Odo had contacted Ops and informed the captain. Consequently, they found Captain Sisko and Lieutenant Carlien waiting in the docking bay, along with a number of the station's Bajoran security officers. Once Quark and Rom had risen to their feet, Carlien stepped up to Quark and gazed down at him.

"I am Lieutenant Carlien of Bajor. I am informing you—" She glanced from Quark to Rom and back again. "—both of you, that you are under arrest. You are both charged with violating the law that prohibits Ferengi from being within Bajoran sovereignty. In accordance with that law, you will now be taken into custody." She raised her hands, in which, Odo saw, she held the restraints. As Odo wondered again whether such measures were truly necessary, Captain Sisko moved next to Carlien and raised his hand between her and her prisoners.

"Are those really required, Lieutenant?" he asked.

"With all due respect, Captain," Carlien said with great sincerity, "I think they are. These two have already demonstrated that they are willing to flee from arrest."

"And yet they just surrendered peaceably, without the use of weapons," Sisko argued. "I think they're no threat to run if you simply keep an eye on them."

"Again, I must disagree. . . ." Carlien's words trailed into silence.

There was a pause. The tableau was frozen: Carlien and Sisko staring at each other, Quark and Rom waiting for something to happen, Sisko's hand motionless between captor and captives. Odo wondered what the captain's response would be and how he felt about what was happening. And Odo considered his own feelings.

How strange, he thought. All these years pursuing Quark, seeking to bring him to justice, and now that he had just assisted in apprehending Quark for violating the law—more than one law, if you included his flight from arrest—he felt no satisfaction.

At last, Sisko moved, dropping his hand and stepping back.

"As you wish," he told the lieutenant.

Carlien opened the restraints. Quark stood with his hands at his sides.

"Please turn around and present your hands," Carlien said.

Quark did not move. Rom glanced over at his brother with what Odo thought was a concerned look. As badly as Rom was so often treated by Quark, Odo had no doubt that he still loved his older brother.

"Quark," Rom said. "Don't you think—"

Carlien signaled to Sergeant Onial, who approached Quark from behind, causing Rom to swallow his words. Sisko quickly stepped forward again.

"Force will most definitely not be necessary," Sisko insisted strongly. Softening his voice, he said, "Quark, I think you need to make this easy on yourself and your brother."

Quark said nothing, but he looked up at Sisko with an expression that Odo interpreted as contempt. After a tense moment, Quark raised his hands, although he did not turn around. Carlien attached the restraints—compromising with Sisko in some way, Odo realized, because she secured Quark's hands in front of him this time—then moved sideways to stand in front of Rom. Before she had even **opene**d the second set of restraints, Rom had lifted his hands, his wrists up as though in supplication. She opened the restraints and attached them.

"You must be enjoying this," Quark suddenly said. His voice was low, clearly filled with enmity. Odo looked over to see who he was addressing and was startled to find that Quark was glaring at him.

"What?"

"You've wanted this for so long," Quark said. "You only wish it was you applying these manacles, don't you?"

Because his true feelings were not so uncomplicated, Odo was appalled by Quark's comment. But of course Quark would feel that way, Odo realized; if events had been different, if Odo had caught him violating the law—other laws, *fair* laws—then he no doubt would have felt as Quark had suggested.

"I—" Odo started, not knowing what he was going to say, or even what it was he wished to convey. "I must admit," he began again, "the sight of you in shackles does seem appropriate." But the words were hollow, barren of the righteousness they should have had. Where Odo should have felt a sense of justice, he only felt a sense of inequity. "Of course, Rom doesn't belong in restraints," Odo added weakly, attempting to temper his previous statement.

"But he does, Constable," Carlien said. "Both of these men have broken the law." To Sisko, she said, "May we go now, Captain?"

Sisko nodded but did not say anything. Carlien circled around Quark until she stood at his side. Onial shifted over to stand beside Rom.

"Please thank your crew for their efforts," Carlien told Sisko. "And we thank each of you," she said, looking at both Sisko and Odo. She took hold of Quark's arm and led him out of the docking bay. Onial followed behind her with Rom.

Once they were gone, Odo looked around until he picked out the ranking security officer present.

"Walenista," Odo addressed her.

"Sir?"

"Dismiss the security teams," he ordered.

"Yes, sir," Walenista acknowledged. She directed her

contingent out of the docking bay and away, leaving Odo alone with Sisko.

Odo looked over at the captain, and he found that he wanted to say something, to talk about what had just happened, about how he felt about it. But he was not sure how to begin, or even if he was capable of beginning. Instead, the docking bay was filled with silence and stillness.

Finally, the two men left together without saying a word.

CHAPTER
12

QUARK EYED HIS BROTHER across the breadth of the shuttle. Rom had been completely silent ever since they had boarded the shuttle at *Deep Space Nine* and started their trip to Bajor. He was seated facing forward, the restraints about his wrists secured to the back of the chair in front of him. Quark was positioned in the same attitude on the other side of the compartment. They were in the middle of the shuttle, in the third of six rows of bench seats, a center aisle running between those seats to port and those to starboard.

Lieutenant Carlien sat with her back to the bulkhead that separated the pilot—Sergeant Onial, Quark supposed, though there could have been somebody else up there—from the passengers. The lieutenant was pretending to watch both of her prisoners, but for the most part, she kept her eyes trained on Quark. She carried a weapon at her side.

"Do you really think we're that dangerous?" Quark asked, shifting his gaze from Carlien's eyes down to her sidearm. When he looked back up at her, she looked away, ignoring him. "We may have run," he told her, "but we were unarmed. As you know from searching us."

167

She still did not respond to him.

"Since you have a weapon, though," he went on, keeping his tone light, "it's possible that we might somehow get possession of it and force you to free us. We would leave the system, nobody would get hurt, and you'd never have to see either one of us ever again."

He had her attention now, he saw, although she still refused to say anything.

"Now, how could we possibly get hold of your weapon?" Quark asked rhetorically. "You're not likely to drop it, are you?"

He waited for a moment, allowing her time to answer, knowing that she would not.

"And there doesn't seem to be much chance of us overpowering you," he continued. "Hmmm. I wonder how we can get it." He tilted his head back and looked toward the ceiling, as though in vigorous thought. He contorted his face continuously, trying to comically reinforce that impression. Eventually, he returned his gaze to Carlien. He was pleased to see that her eyes were still focused on him.

"I know," Quark said, with a suddenness that suggested that what he was about to say had just now occurred to him. "We could buy your weapon from you." Quark caught a slight movement in his peripheral vision, and heard the sound of flesh brushing against fabric; he knew that Rom had turned to watch him.

Although Carlien had already been regarding Quark, it seemed that only now did she actually see him. When she did not say anything, though, Quark pushed on.

"Of course, I'm sure such a weapon must be very expensive, and considering how much—"

"Shut up, Ferengi," Carlien ordered. Her facial features appeared rigid, her jaw was clenched.

"Is that supposed to be an aspersion?" Quark asked. "Because it's not; I happen to be a Ferengi. Would you be insulted if I called you 'Bajoran'?"

"I can be proud to be a Bajoran," she said.

"I'm proud to be a Ferengi."

Carlien laughed derisively.

"Yes," she said. "Your culture is so *rich*—" Her use of the word was clearly as a double entendre. "—that you feel completely comfortable engaging in graft."

"If you're referring to my attempt to bribe you," he informed her, "you're using the wrong word. I'm in no position to practice graft right now. And anyway, graft is more of a strategy; bribery is simply a tactic."

"You actually do sound proud," Carlien said. She stood up and took a couple of paces toward Quark. "And yet you are insolent enough to ask me to betray my government, my duty, for mere profit."

"There is no such thing as 'mere' profit," Quark said. "You shouldn't be offended, Lieutenant; even you must realize that everybody has a price."

"You disgust me," she said, taking several more steps toward Quark. Then she stopped abruptly. She seemed suddenly to realize that she was getting too close to her prisoner, as though he had been trying to antagonize her so that he could draw her in and somehow physically subdue her.

Quark chuckled to himself: such an idea was preposterous; he would no sooner do battle with Carlien than he would ask someone to cut off his lobes.

"Are you sure it's me that's disgusting you," he asked her, "or have you perhaps thought of a price you would be willing to accept?"

Carlien's eyes narrowed briefly, then she turned and marched back to her seat. But instead of sitting, she removed her weapon from her side and placed it on the chair. Then she walked down the aisle of the compartment, between Quark and Rom, and sat down in the seat behind Quark. He snapped his head around, unsure—and fearful—of her intentions. Slowly, she leaned toward him, evidently to say something to him. She brought her mouth close to his ear—which was unnecessary, of course, considering the quality of his hearing.

"Actually," she told him quietly, "I do have a price." To Quark's surprise, there was no lilt in her voice, no quality which readily identified the statement as sarcasm or mockery. The lieutenant sounded serious.

Did she just think of something she wanted? Quark

speculated. *Something important to her, or something she'd ever given up hope of acquiring?* If so, it did not necessarily bode well for Quark's ability to provide her with what she wanted, but at least there was a chance.

Quark struggled to turn his head around further. Carlien leaned forward more, until they faced each other at close range, over Quark's shoulder. They locked eyes. She appeared very serious indeed. He smiled at her, not broadly, and not just a grin, but a little smile, filled—he hoped—with charm and a sense of understanding.

"Tell me," he whispered to her.

She said: "I want the Orb of Wisdom returned to Bajor."

Quark stared at her for a long moment, then turned his head to face forward again. Carlien rose and returned to her seat at the front of the compartment, retrieving her weapon as she did so. Quark looked up at her and saw that she had returned to her businesslike demeanor. But there was no business in that behavior, only a warped notion of duty. He saw no hope for himself with this woman.

"You could have had the Orb," Quark told her, "if only your people had possessed some sense of its worth." In spite of everything that had happened, Quark still did not understand why the Bajorans had not been willing to pay the nagus's price, to tender the highest bid and buy the Orb; were they that poor, or were their business faculties that bad?

"Apparently," Carlien said, "the Orb is worth more than your freedom."

Quark closed his mouth. Right now, there was nothing more to say.

The trip through the atmosphere of Bajor was bumpy but uneventful. There were no windows to look through in the passenger compartment, and Carlien had not told them where on Bajor they were going. To the capital, Quark supposed, to stand trial and be sentenced. He could not imagine that he and Rom would receive much of a prison term; they might even be escorted out of Bajoran space immediately, although he guessed that Shakaar and Winn would probably want to try to make some sort of a statement to the nagus by actually jailing a couple of

Ferengi for at least a few days, or even a few weeks—as if that would impress the nagus at all.

The shuttle slowed in its approach to its landing area, hovered momentarily as it ceased its forward momentum entirely, then began a short, vertical descent. There was another bump as it finally touched down.

Carlien stood from her chair and touched a small control panel set in to the bulkhead against which she had been sitting.

"Are we secure, Sergeant?" she asked.

"Not yet," came Onial's response through the panel. "Colonel Mitra wants to meet and inspect the prisoners personally. He should be out shortly."

"Acknowledged," Carlien said. She sat back down and waited.

Colonel? Quark thought. Why would such a senior officer of the Bajoran Militia be involved in this? For the first time, Quark began to realize that the Bajorans were considering this matter—not just with respect to the Orb, but regarding his and Rom's failure to vacate Bajoran space before the deadline—very seriously. Up until now, he had not believed anything worse than losing the bar would happen to him and his brother. Suddenly, he was not so sure.

About five minutes later, the door in the bulkhead that separated the pilot from the passengers slid open, and Onial entered.

"They're ready for us now, Lieutenant," he reported. Carlien nodded and stood. She drew her sidearm, and Onial drew his.

"Ready?" Carlien asked the sergeant.

"Ready."

She turned and operated the control panel again as Onial trained his weapon on Quark and Rom. There was a loud hum and then a click, and the magnetic locks holding Quark's and Rom's restraints to the backs of the chairs in front of them let go. Carlien turned and raised her weapon.

"Come forward," she said.

Quark and Rom did as they were told.

"There," she said, pointing with her weapon at the hatch. She worked the control panel once more, and the hatch split horizontally in two halfway up its height. The top portion lifted upward, the lower portion opened away from the shuttle and became a ramp down which they could exit. The air in the cabin cooled noticeably.

"Move," Carlien said as she and Onial fell in behind Quark and Rom.

The quartet walked down the ramp and out into an overcast Bajoran day. When they stepped off the end of the ramp onto hard, lifeless soil, Carlien ordered them to stop.

Quark looked around and found it difficult to comprehend what was happening. The sky above was uniformly gray, with not even a hint of blue. A wind gusted about them, lowering the already cold temperature even closer to the freezing point. He shivered only partially from the cold as he looked into the distance and saw nothing: no trees, no mountains or hills, nothing but desolate plains. Closer, he saw a tall wire fence, with sentry posts at regular intervals. Quark could not reconcile what he was seeing with what he had expected to see. This was not the capital. It was not even the right hemisphere, he realized: it was almost summer there, and it was definitely nowhere near summer here.

A line of five Bajoran Militia officers stood at attention by the end of the shuttle ramp. The one in the middle stepped forward, the rank insignia on the collar of his uniform indicating that he was a colonel. He was an older man, but solid, with chiseled features, and penetrating eyes, both colder and grayer, Quark thought, than the weather around them.

"Welcome," he said to Quark and Rom, his voice full of gravel and fire, "to Gallitep."

PART II

Resolution 49-353

CHAPTER
13

SISKO READ the entire report again, attempting to put all of the figures into perspective. But the second time through, the implications engendered by the report grew no brighter: something was definitely wrong.

The door chime warbled.

"Come in," Sisko called from where he sat behind his desk. The doors parted, allowing a momentary rush of noise in from Ops—voices, footsteps, the electronic clamor of consoles being operated—and then the doors closed behind Major Kira as she entered the office.

"You wanted to see me, Captain?" she said.

"Yes, Major. I've just been going over your report." He held a padd up so that she could see it, then shoved it onto his desk; it slid halfway across the smooth, glass surface, coming to rest just short of a stand holding the 1989 World Series baseball. "There are some disturbing numbers in here."

"That's why I wanted you to look at it as soon as possible." She walked further into the room.

"Frankly," Sisko said, folding his hands together atop his

desk, "I'm a little surprised you didn't come to me sooner with this."

"I really wasn't sure there was a problem before now," Kira told him. "In fact, I'm still not sure there *is* a problem. We have ships scheduled to dock at the station all the time that are days or weeks overdue, or that never even show up at all. A lot of ships—freighters especially—run late or change their itineraries. Some shipments get canceled. In most cases, we only find out about the changes when a ship doesn't show up when it's supposed to."

"But this . . ." Sisko's voice trailed off as he reached over, picked up the padd, and looked again at the report. Within the lines of text that filled the small screen, numerous italicized words—the names of ships—stood out. "Twenty-nine vessels slated to dock at *Deep Space Nine* within the past week . . . all missing."

"If we knew that these ships were missing, then I really would be worried," Kira said, taking one of the chairs in front of the desk. "But we don't know that any of them *are* missing, and we do know that at least some of them *aren't;* they just never showed up here. It's the trend that concerns me."

Sisko thumbed the controls on the padd and paged through the report. Blocks of text paraded up the screen, recounting Kira's findings. Two ships absent each of the first three days, three the next, then four, seven, and finally nine today.

"We know that some of these ships are all right?" Sisko asked.

"Yes. After the leap from four to seven no-shows yesterday, I began contacting the ports of registry of the absentee ships. A couple have sent messages indicating that the ships in question are fine."

"Any explanation for why they didn't arrive at *DS9?*"

"No," Kira said. "The ports themselves wouldn't necessarily know that, and a lot of shippers don't like to part with that kind of information over subspace."

"I'd guess that a lot of them don't like to part with any information at all," Sisko said, and he saw from the expression on Kira's face that she agreed with him.

Sisko leaned back in his chair, the padd still clasped in one of his hands. Kira was right, he thought, when she said that there was no concrete evidence that there was truly a problem here, but she was also right that the pattern of more and more ships not arriving at the station as scheduled was troubling. If there was a cause, if this was not mere coincidence, then Sisko wanted to know what was happening, and why.

"What does Commander Worf have to say about this?" Sisko asked.

"I haven't consulted with him about it," Kira replied. "None of the ships we're talking about are from Starfleet."

Sisko nodded his understanding. As the strategic operations officer for this sector, Worf's primary duty was to coordinate the activities of Starfleet vessels in the region. Still, within that context, his routine observations of the Bajoran sector might allow him to provide some insight into the situation. Sisko activated his combadge with a touch.

"Sisko to Worf," he said. He looked up toward the ceiling but did not see it, automatically visualizing the commander in his mind's eye as he spoke. There was a short pause before a response came.

"Worf here," answered the bass Klingon voice.

"Mr. Worf, I'd like to see you in my office."

"Aye, sir. I'm on my way."

The communication ended, and Sisko looked back over at Kira.

"Perhaps he can shed some light on this from an intelligence standpoint," Sisko explained. He glanced down at the padd in his hand, then back up at Kira. "Major, since all of these ships are freighters or trading vessels of one kind or another, should we be considering piracy?"

"It's possible," she allowed. "The businesses on the Promenade have certainly been affected by their failure to receive shipments this week."

"I was down there yesterday," Sisko told her. "I noticed that the crowds seemed a bit thin. I just assumed it was because Quark's was still closed down." Quark had been gone from the station for more than a month now. His business had been officially nationalized on the day after his arrest. Sisko assumed that the Bajoran government had not yet sold the bar, as it had remained closed since that time.

"Quark?" Kira laughed, although Sisko thought she did so without humor. "I don't think anybody misses him."

Sisko tilted his head slightly to one side as he regarded Kira. He knew that his first officer had never gotten along well with Quark, but her attitude now surprised him. She was bright enough and honest enough that she should have been able to know and admit the truth about Quark: he—or at least his bar—had been well liked.

"I wouldn't be too sure that nobody misses him," Sisko said. "I think the closure of Quark's has had quite a detrimental effect on the businesses on the Promenade—and on the people who live on the station. Like it or not, Major, Quark's was popular."

"A small price to pay to be rid of that Denebian slime devil," she said. "*I* don't miss him."

"I'm sure you don't. But obviously some—"

The door chime sounded. Sisko called for the visitor to enter, and the doors opened to admit Worf. Again, there came a brief surge of sound from Ops.

"Commander," Sisko greeted him. "Please have a seat."

"Yes, sir," Worf said—rather stiffly, Sisko thought. Worf had not served on *DS9* for very long, and so Sisko suspected that he had not yet fully acclimated to his new environment. Fresh from duty aboard a starship, it seemed likely that Worf still did not understand the rhythms of the station and its crew, nor the sometimes-unorthodox manner in which Sisko commanded.

As Worf took the chair next to Kira, Sisko worked the controls on the padd, paging through the report. The device blinked and chirped until he stopped at the summary of the situation that Kira had prepared. He handed it across the desk to Worf.

"I'd like you to take a look at this," Sisko said.

Worf took the padd and read through the displayed text. When he finished, he looked up.

"I take it this is unusual," he said.

"Not entirely," Sisko answered.

"We have ships arrive late, or not show up, all the time,"

Kira clarified. "But not on such a regular basis, and not with such steadily increasing numbers."

"I see."

"It may be nothing," Sisko said, "but I don't want to take any chances. Is there anything that you know of, Mr. Worf, that might help us explain this? Ships missing in a particular area, perhaps a new navigational hazard . . . anything?"

"There have been no incidents in the sector involving Starfleet vessels," Worf declared. "But there have been several rumors about small ships being attacked in nearby space. Nothing has been confirmed, but if it's true, it might account for this." Worf held up the padd, just as Sisko had earlier done.

"Have you heard anything specific?" Sisko wanted to know.

"The reports I've received have been extremely sketchy, and from sources I do not consider to be credible."

"Still, coupled with the increasing number of ships not making scheduled stops here," Sisko said, "there may be something to what you've heard."

"Even rumors are sometimes true," Kira noted.

"Any word in those reports on who the attackers might be?" Sisko asked Worf.

"No, sir."

"Could it be the Cardassians?" Kira proposed. Sisko thought he detected in her voice an undercurrent of—what? Fear? Anger? Probably a complicated mixture of those emotions and others.

"I think Central Command has its hands full right now," Sisko said, referring to the civil revolution on Cardassia Prime that had not long ago wrested control away from the military and placed it in the hands of the Detapa Council.

"The Klingons then?" Kira ventured. "The Romulans?"

"Perhaps the Dominion is attempting to disrupt life in the Alpha Quadrant," Worf suggested, "in preparation for an offensive."

"Perhaps," Sisko said, but another possibility occurred to him.

"Major," he said, "have you spoken with First Minister Shakaar recently?"

"Not within the last few days, no," she said. "Why?"

"Maybe you should," Sisko said. "See if Bajor has experienced any problems similar to the ones we're having."

"Yes, sir," Kira said. She stood from her chair, evidently prepared to leave to follow her orders, but then she gave Sisko what he thought was an inquiring look. "Do you know what's been going on, Captain?"

"I have an idea," Sisko told her. "But it's only speculation at the moment, and I want to try to remedy that." Sisko shifted his gaze from Kira to Worf. "Commander," he said, "prepare the *Defiant.*"

From the command chair in the center of *Defiant's* bridge, Captain Sisko watched his crew work. Dax was stationed at the flight-control position, O'Brien was at operations, Worf at tactical. Dr. Bashir also hovered about the bridge, his presence on the ship precautionary; should the rumors of ships in the sector being fired upon prove true, Sisko wanted to be able to provide medical aid to any casualties they might discover.

"We're approaching the Bajoran trade routes," Dax announced, as Sisko had requested her to do.

"Mr. Worf," Sisko ordered, "engage the cloaking device."

"Sir?" Worf asked with obvious surprise. In a way, it pleased Sisko: his newest crew member was perhaps not as stiff and as unacclimated as he had previously thought; Worf was at least comfortable enough—and obviously strong and independent enough—to question his commanding officer.

"You heard me," Sisko said. He saw Dax glance up from her console, first at him and then at Worf, an amused grin on her face. At his station, Worf complied with the order. The interior lighting of the bridge dimmed as the cloak began operating. About *Defiant*, Sisko knew, an energy screen was being generated, a screen that refracted light and energy waves in an unusual way, rendering the ship invisible both to the eye and to most types of sensor scans.

Sisko understood why Worf had felt the need to question his order: the Romulan Star Empire had agreed to loan the Federation the cloaking device for installation aboard *Defiant* under the condition that it never be used within the Alpha Quadrant. Sisko did not take this stipulation lightly—nor did Lieutenant Commander Worf, apparently—but this was not the first time the captain had found occasion to break it. But Sisko's justifications for transgressing the accord with the Romulans were not based in some Machiavellian ethic. Each of the few times he had used the cloaking device, he had weighed heavily the moral implications of doing so, the possible consequences, and whether he was violating the intent of the agreement that had been forged with the Romulans. The Empire had provided the cloak to enhance Starfleet's ability to protect the Alpha Quadrant—and therefore the Empire—from Dominion attack, but the Romulans did not want to have their own ordnance used against them, or used to fortify the relative power of the Federation. Sisko was always sure that he in no way acted in contravention of that covenant.

Defiant reached the location Dax had identified, and Sisko ordered a change in course. The warship came about and began tracing the trade route, traveling away from Bajor. The way ahead looked clear on the main viewer. As Sisko watched and waited for whatever it was they would find out here—if they found anything at all—he wondered whether his suspicions would be borne out. It was not long before he learned the answer.

"I'm reading a vessel," reported Worf.

On the viewscreen, Sisko saw, there were still only stars; the sensors had found the ship before it had even become visible to the crew of *Defiant*.

"Is it a freighter?" Bashir asked from where he stood at the back of the Bridge. Sisko had forgotten that he was there.

"It is impossible to tell at this distance," Worf said. "But the vessel is of an appropriate size to be a freighter."

"Slow to one-half impulse as we approach," Sisko told Dax.

"Aye," Dax acknowledged.

"Entering visual range," said Worf.

Sisko studied the main viewer. He watched as a small, unidentifiable shape materialized amid the scattered stars.

"Magnify," he said.

Worf jabbed at a control and the image on the viewer shifted. The starscape did not change, but the shape increased in size, became discernible as a slender, gray ship. It was long and roughly tubular, with a pilothouse located toward the bow, and what looked to be a large cargo bay encircling the primary hull amidship.

"That's an old Earth vessel," O'Brien commented. "Similar to the D-Y-eleven-hundred class."

"Much older," said Worf, who was an expert at spacecraft classification. "D-Y-seven-hundred, to be exact. It's navigational beacon identifies it as the *Alerica.*"

"What can you tell us about it, chief?" Sisko asked.

"Records show it was built on Earth," O'Brien reported after consulting the ship's database, "but it was later sold to a Frunalian shipping company."

As *Defiant* closed on *Alerica,* surface details of the freighter became visible. Interior lights shined through windows fore and aft, docking clamps were secured beneath the pilothouse, Frunalian markings decorated the hull.

"One of the running lights is out," Sisko noticed. As he looked closely, he saw several dark streaks along the main body of the ship near the extinguished light. "What are those black patches?"

"They appear to be some sort of heat distress," Worf said. "I'm picking up some very odd residual energy signatures from them. They almost look like the remnants of phaser fire."

"They are," O'Brien said, checking the readings on the operations console. "But from phasers fired at a power level about ten percent of normal."

"What's *Alerica's* status?" Sisko asked.

"All systems are operational," Worf said. "No major damage. It is heading under its own power away from Bajoran space."

"Can you find the attacker?" Sisko asked.

"Scanning," answered Worf.

"I don't understand," Bashir said, walking forward until he came abreast of Sisko. "Did somebody attack that ship with their phasers intentionally set at a useless level, or did they just have inferior weapons?"

"I hope it's the latter, Doctor," Sisko said, "but I doubt that's the case."

"Do you know something, Benjamin?" Dax asked, turning in her seat to face Sisko.

"I *suspect* something," he told her.

"Sensor contact with another vessel," Worf said.

"It's not a freighter, is it?" Sisko asked.

"No," Worf said. "It is much larger." He worked the controls on his console. "The configuration is—" He stopped and looked up at the captain. "It's Ferengi."

"Damn," Sisko blurted, launching himself up out of his seat and forward to where Dax sat at the conn. He searched the readouts on her console for information. "What type of ship?"

"Definitely a Marauder," O'Brien said. *"D'Kora-*class."

It was the largest, most powerful type of vessel in the Ferengi fleet. And it was what Sisko had feared.

"If the *Alerica* is a freighter," he said, "I want to know what it's carrying."

"I've got it, Captain," O'Brien said. "It's definitely a freighter: it's fully loaded with a cargo of grain."

"Wait a minute," Bashir said. "That doesn't make any sense. I thought the freighter was headed *away* from Bajor."

"It is," Sisko said, although he did not bother to check any readouts to confirm this.

"But Bajor doesn't export grain," Bashir said. "Thanks to the Cardassians, there's not even enough arable land for the Bajorans to grow sufficient crops for themselves."

"Dax," Sisko said, ignoring the doctor for the moment, "I want you to circumnavigate the Marauder on a sphere with radius equal to—" He considered what an appropriate distance would be. "—twice our maximum sensor range."

"What do you expect to find?" Dax asked as she executed the captain's command. *Defiant* responded immediately onto its new course. The image of *Alerica* was swept from the viewer, the stars now streaks of light as *Defiant* maneuvered on its axes. Sisko walked back to the command chair and sat down.

*"D'Kora-*class vessels are typically equipped with two levels of weaponry, firing electromagnetic pulses—or in this case, I guess, phasers—and powerful plasma-energy bursts," Sisko explained. "If the commander of that vessel

had wanted to destroy that freighter, he would have. But he wasn't trying to destroy it, or even damage it; he just wanted to force it to change its course."

"I have another sensor contact," Worf reported. "Another vessel." Worf worked his controls. "It is another *D'Kora* Marauder."

"Another Marauder?" Bashir asked incredulously. "The Ferengi can't possibly be preparing to attack Bajor." To Sisko, the statement sounded like a question.

"They're not going to attack," Sisko told his crew. "It's a blockade of Bajor." *Which is almost as bad as an attack,* Sisko realized; before long, the population of Bajor would be facing starvation. "At least," Sisko amended, "they're not going to attack *yet.*"

CHAPTER
14

KIRA SAT IN A CHAIR inside the office of the first minister and looked across the room at him. He was standing in the doorway that led to the balcony, peering out at the Bajoran countryside as the last vestiges of day prepared to abandon the capital to darkness. His shadow had grown long and dim on the wall behind him, outlined with the fading orange-red of sunset. The entire room had grown dim, actually; the generous amount of illumination that entered through two skylights during the day was nearly gone now.

This was only the fourth time Kira had seen Shakaar in as many weeks, and none of those visits—including this one—had been of a personal nature. As she watched him, she could see that the past month had taken its toll: he seemed thinner, but worse than that, his wilted posture betrayed his great fatigue—so much so that she was not entirely sure how he was still managing to function. Of course, Kira knew that this was not the first time in his life that Shakaar had faced difficult, sleepless nights.

I miss you, Edon, she thought. And in her mind, she answered for him, hearing his voice in the soft tones she knew he reserved only for her: *I miss you too, Nerys.*

Kira was here on the outskirts of the capital city, as she had been on the three previous occasions, in her official capacity as the Bajoran liaison to *Deep Space Nine*. In this difficult time, Shakaar was unwilling to leave his world, even to meet with the Emissary on the station. For his part, the captain was doing what he could back on *DS9* to avert the impending calamity on Bajor; this was what Kira conveyed now to the first minister and the kai.

"And how does Captain Sisko propose to help us, child?" Winn asked in response. She was sitting opposite Kira across a low, circular table, her facial features indistinct in the developing gloom. There was skepticism evident in her voice, a skepticism Kira recognized as the kai's doubt—seldom stated outright, but often intimated—about whether Benjamin Sisko was truly the Emissary. "We are only days away from a terrible crisis," she finished.

"Days?" Kira asked, stunned. She had known that the blockade had begun to have a significant impact on Bajor—even *DS9* had been affected: at least a third of the shops on the Promenade had been forced to close during the past month—but she had thought that there was still time before circumstances would become critical. "I understood that the situation wasn't that desperate yet," she said. She looked to Shakaar for verification.

"It's not," confirmed Shakaar. He came away from the balcony doorway and walked over to Kira and Winn.

Winn peered up at Shakaar, and for a moment, her face left the shadows and became visible in the dying light of the room. She was smiling, Kira saw, despite being contradicted, but Kira also saw that the smile did not touch Winn's eyes.

"With all respects," the kai said, "I have been in contact with many of the provincial ministers, and they all report that their local food supplies are extremely low."

"Yes, I know," Shakaar said. "I've spoken to them as well." Kira heard the weariness in his voice—the drawn-out syllables, the diminished volume—and she understood that he was not only physically tired, but emotionally tired as well. "I've heard those same things."

"Surely you don't disbelieve the ministers?" Winn said.

"Not the ministers, no," Shakaar said. As he spoke, he

squatted down before the table—his knees crackling like the sound of electric sparks—and reached out to open a narrow wooden box sitting atop it. From the box, he extracted a long, thin match. "I do disagree with their assessments, though. We've been rationing food for weeks now, and we'll continue to ration food; their projections don't seem to adequately take that into account."

"How long do *you* estimate before people begin going hungry?" Kira asked.

"They're already hungry," Shakaar replied, not without some bitterness. Such hardships, Kira realized, harked back to the brutal times under the Cardassians. "Three or four weeks from now, though—perhaps as few as two—things will be much worse than they are now." Shakaar swept the match across the bare stone floor of his office; the tip flared to life. He lifted the glass chimney of an oil lamp that was sitting on the table and ignited the wick.

"Weeks are better than days," Kira offered, "but that's not all that far off."

"No," Shakaar agreed. He replaced the chimney on the lamp and turned the regulator; the flame blossomed, tall and bright in its pellucid enclosure. Kira gazed across the table and saw the faces of Shakaar and Winn kindled yellow in the lambent glow.

"Regardless whether our stores of food last weeks or days," Winn said, "we have an even more immediate concern: medical care."

Captain Sisko had told Kira that he feared that would be the case. While health-related resources were obviously not being dispensed as quickly as food was, they were far harder to ration. An individual in need of medicine or a surgical procedure often could not be given a reduced dosage or have a different operation performed on them.

"This is one of the ways Captain Sisko believes he can help us," Kira apprised Shakaar and Winn. "He is seeking approval from the Federation Council to petition the nagus to allow humanitarian aid through the blockade."

"Captain Sisko wants to negotiate with the Ferengi?" Winn asked with obvious contempt. "It is the Ferengi who are keeping food and medicine from our people in the first place."

Kira felt her mouth open and close several times in surprise at the kai's reaction, like the maw of a great fish soundlessly breathing water in. She had expected her news to be met with optimism and hope. Once more, she looked to Shakaar.

"Such assistance would be helpful, of course," he said, his tone more moderate than the kai's, "but it seems unlikely that the captain will be able to provide it." Shakaar still held the burning match in his hand, and he got up now and walked to over to where another lamp sat on a shelf. "The Ferengi have made it clear that they are using their blockade—an attempt to starve our population—as leverage to force us to allow them access to the wormhole. Why would they gainsay their own strategy by allowing food and medicine to be brought to Bajor?" He lighted the lamp and moved across the room to another.

"They are barbarians," said Winn. "Materialistic in the extreme. They're not even interested in the welfare of their own people who were taken into custody by the Militia."

"What's happened to them?" Kira asked. "The Ferengi that were arrested?"

"They were being held for trial," Shakaar explained, firing the third lamp, "but because of the blockade, they are now being interned as political prisoners."

"Oh," Kira said, unsure whether she was comfortable with the notion of detaining people not because of the crimes they had committed, but because of who they were. The Bajorans had every right to close their borders to the wretched little Ferengi because of the actions of their leader, but to hold people in prison because they were Ferengi . . . to her, such an action was dangerously reminiscent of those taken by the Cardassians during the Occupation.

"I suppose one way to end the blockade would be to rescind the edict," Kira suggested. She personally thought it would be wrong to capitulate to the Ferengi, but at the same time, she understood the need to balance that view against the possibility of saving Bajoran lives.

"We will not bow to the will of the nagus," Shakaar said flatly. He blew out the match—a curl of spoke drifted up from its spent tip—and returned to the table. The room had been transformed now, the cast on the walls no longer the orange of twilight—the sun had wholly departed—but the yellow of lamplight. "What we require is another kind of assistance."

"What would that be?" Kira asked, confused; she had thought the help Bajor needed was obvious: food and medical aid.

"We need to break the blockade," Shakaar said.

"Well, yes, of course," Kira said, "but how do you propose to do that?"

"Captain Sisko could help us," Shakaar said.

"What does that mean exactly?" Kira asked. She rose from her chair and faced Shakaar, an anxious feeling beginning to take hold of her as she inferred what it was he was proposing. "Do you want Starfleet to confront the Ferengi fleet?"

"What we want," Winn said, "is to be left alone to live in peace."

"We're not asking the Federation to defend us," Shakaar clarified. "We just want the means to be able to defend ourselves."

Kira stared at him. The flame of the lamp on the table flickered, sending fleeting changes in light and hue rolling across Shakaar's features like the shadow of a cloud moving over land. Kira wanted him to articulate exactly what it was he was suggesting. Eventually, he did.

"In this case," Shakaar said, "that means ships."

"Ships?" Kira asked. She walked across the room, away from Shakaar and Winn, unable to contain the feelings of shock and disbelief that overwhelmed her. Her views were usually in harmony with Shakaar's, particularly in matters of such importance. When she reached the far side of the room, she turned back around, not even attempting to check her emotions. "You're going to plunge Bajor into a war in space?" she asked angrily.

"*We* are not trying to starve the Ferengi," Shakaar said.

Kira laughed once, a short, harsh sound that escaped her unsmiling mouth before she could stop it. The sense that this conversation was not really happening—that it could not possibly be happening—washed over her. She paced back over to Shakaar and Winn and looked this time to the kai.

"You can't possibly agree with him?" Kira asked, disturbed at having to seek the support of this woman she had so often opposed, against a man she had followed through the Occupation, into his role as first minister, and finally, into her heart.

"The minister and I are united," Winn declared. The flame of the lamp was reflected in the black of her pupils.

Kira was quiet for a moment, her mind tallying all of the reasons this was a bad idea. She decided to focus on the most practical matters.

"Who would fly these ships?" she asked.

"There are plenty of Bajorans with experience commanding and crewing freighters and impulse ships and the like," Shakaar said.

Freighters? Kira thought. Surely it was obvious that piloting a freighter, or even the impulse ships used to defend the high orbit of Bajor, hardly qualified somebody for interstellar combat. Even the so-called assault vessels of the Bajoran Militia were little more than personnel carriers.

"This would be a war we couldn't possibly win," she said.

"It was said that we would never be able to repel the Cardassians," Winn said, "and yet, here we are."

"The Cardassians occupied Bajor for *forty* years," Kira exploded. "It was a miserable existence, costing millions of lives and immeasurable suffering." She paused to calm herself before continuing; nothing incited stronger emotions in her than recalling the Occupation, the event that had most defined her world within her lifetime. But she also realized that there was nothing she could tell Shakaar and Winn about the Occupation that they did not already know. Instead, she told them, "I guess I can take solace in the fact that the Federation will never go along with this."

"Nevertheless, this is the official position of the Bajoran government," Shakaar said firmly and coolly. Kira recognized that he was speaking to her specifically on a professional level. "And we want you to make the request of Captain Sisko on our behalf."

"Perhaps the major might be uncomfortable doing so," Winn said, talking to Shakaar as though Kira were not present. "We could send another representative—"

"I am the Bajoran liaison," Kira interrupted. "I will talk to Captain Sisko."

"Major," Shakaar began, his employment of her title sounding strange to her, "if this will be too difficult for you—"

"I'll do it," she said. She headed for the door. Shakaar called after her. When she did not turn, she heard the quick pace of his footsteps as he raced across the room and intercepted her before she could leave. He put a hand on her elbow and coaxed her to stop.

"Nerys," he said, lowering his voice to just above a whisper. "Nerys, this is the right course of action to pursue. You remember what it's like to live under oppression. We can't let the Ferengi destroy our way of life, especially not after we just recovered it."

"Of course I remember what it was like," she told him. "And what I remember most is counting our numbers after a fight to see how many of us were still left alive. I remember patching wounds with improvised medical supplies . . . seeing my friends maimed . . . Furel lost an arm." Her gaze wandered from Shakaar as she thought of her old friend, so large and filled with life, now reduced by war. And she thought of others—there had been so many of them—not lucky enough to have been merely wounded.

Kira pulled herself back to the present. She peered over at Winn, who was still sitting placidly, as though nothing troubling had been discussed here at all. Kira looked up at Shakaar again and then wrenched her elbow from his hand. She thought once more, *I remember,* but she left without saying another word.

CHAPTER
15

"HE WANTS *what?*"

"I know," Kira said. "I agree that it's ridiculous."

"'Ridiculous' doesn't even begin to describe it, Major,"
Sisko fumed. They were in his quarters aboard *Defiant*. The
cabin was very small, almost confining, although it was
slightly larger than all of the others on the ship, and the only
one with just a single bunk. Even aboard the Spartan
battleship, it seemed, rank had its privileges.

Sisko had been on the bridge when Major Kira had
arrived back at *Deep Space Nine* after her meeting with First
Minister Shakaar. He had been awaiting her return, as well
as preparing for a meeting of his own out on the Bajoran
trade routes. Sisko had brought Kira here, to his quarters,
so that he could debrief her privately, and he was pleased
now that he had. Morale was low enough on the station—
with more Promenade shops closing each day, there were
continually fewer services and fewer forms of recreation
available to the crew and the local inhabitants—without
people witnessing the anger and frustration of the captain.

"I told Shakaar that the Federation Council would never
authorize Starfleet to provide Bajor with ships," Kira said.

192

She was seated at a desk built into one bulkhead, in the cabin's lone chair.

"Of course they won't," Sisko agreed. He moved anxiously about the compact room like a wild animal newly caged. "I just don't understand this," he went on. "These people refuse to negotiate with each other, and yet Zek is prepared to starve the population of Bajor, and Shakaar is prepared to wage war with Ferenginar. It would be laughable if the situation weren't so grave."

"Are you going to pass the minister's request on to the Federation Council?" Kira asked.

"As much as I'd like not to," Sisko said, "I don't really see what choice I have." He stopped near the door and rubbed his temples with the tips of his fingers. He found that he suddenly had a headache; he had been struck with quite a number of them in the past few weeks. He dropped his hands to his sides and sighed heavily. "I'm afraid this will not reflect well on Bajor."

"What?" Kira asked. "What do you mean?"

Sisko was surprised by the question. How could Kira have failed to assess the consequences of the first minister's request?

"What I mean is that this is the type of behavior that will be evaluated as Bajor is considered for admission to the Federation," he said. "And wanting to start a war is hardly an indication of a healthy and mature society."

Kira's jaw dropped; what Sisko had said had obviously had a serious impact on her. She rose to her feet, her hand gripping the back of the chair tightly. Her face appeared barren of expression, which Sisko knew from experience to mean that she was angry. He thought that she was either struggling to control her emotions or searching for a way to respond.

"Bajoran culture has existed for five hundred thousand years," she finally managed to say. "Far longer than the culture of Earth." She spoke the words in an oddly neutral tone, but Sisko suspected that if she had not believed him to be the Emissary, her defense of her people would have been far more spirited.

"You're right," Sisko said. "Your culture is much older than mine. And in the short history of my people, we've practiced slavery, internal exile, and genocide. But we evolved from that."

"Slavery and genocide? *What* are you talking about?" Her voice was no longer neutral. She paused, appearing to calm herself with an effort. "As much as I disagree with the first minister's decision to ask the Federation for military aid, all he's trying to do is afford Bajorans the opportunity to defend themselves."

"I understand that," Sisko said. "But they're trying to defend themselves against a response to their own unjust actions." Sisko felt a twinge of guilt as he echoed Quark's characterization of the Bajoran edict.

"What?"

"Major, the expulsion of all Ferengi from the Bajoran system because of the actions of one Ferengi—"

"—the *leader* of the Ferengi."

"Again, I understand your point. But punishing innocent people for the actions of another . . . I'm sorry, but that's unjust."

Kira took a small step backward. Her foot struck the leg of the chair and she nearly tripped. Instead, she fell back down onto the seat.

"I'm sorry . . . I . . . I'm not having an easy time with this," she said. Her hands twisted together nervously in her lap, and she looked away from Sisko. "The truth is, I'm not entirely comfortable with the way this situation has progressed either, but . . ."

"But?"

"It is difficult," she said, looking back up, "to hear you saying that the Ferengi are right and the Bajorans are wrong." She seemed both to be accusing him of siding with the enemy and to be pleading with him to tell her that he was really on her side.

Sisko crossed the room to Kira. He peered down at her for a moment, then gently placed a hand on her shoulder.

"I think the blockade is wrong," he told her, because he thought she needed to know that was the case. "But I do think the edict is wrong too. Those are just my opinions, though; they needn't be yours."

"I know," Kira said. "But it troubles me that this is what the—" She had been about to say "Emissary," Sisko was sure, but she stopped herself, probably because she was aware of his discomfort with his supposed place in her religion. "—that this is what you think," she finished.

"Nerys," he said, "since the day I took command of *Deep Space Nine,* the depth of my appreciation for the Bajoran people has only increased. I wasn't saying that your society is immature or unhealthy, but I do think that what they're doing in this situation is a mistake. What I fear is that, before the mistake is corrected, people will suffer."

"You want what's best for Bajor, then," Kira said.

"Yes, of course I do," he said. "Which is why the *Defiant* should get under way."

"You got permission to ask the Ferengi to let Starfleet transport humanitarian aid to Bajor?" Kira asked, hopeful.

"Yes. The Federation Council agreed to let me make the request in the name of altruism."

"Somehow," Kira said, "I don't think there's much chance of altruism persuading the nagus."

"We'll see," Sisko told her. He knew that she was right, of course: the nagus would never allow food and medical provisions through the blockade. But Sisko had something else in mind.

"You're in command of the station, Major," he said. They left his quarters together, but quickly parted, Kira headed for *DS9,* and Sisko for the bridge.

Defiant flew at full impulse speed. The bantam vessel ran uncloaked, on course for the Bajoran trade routes and the Ferengi armada.

"We're approaching the blockade," Dax announced.

"Mr. Worf?" Sisko asked from the command chair.

"Scanning for Ferengi vessels," Worf said. Then, after a few moments: "I've got one. A Marauder. Range: twenty million kilometers."

"Reduce speed to one-quarter," Sisko ordered. "Close to within one thousand kilometers."

"Reducing speed," Dax acknowledged. As she worked her console, the pervasive vibrations of *Defiant's* sublight fusion generators moderated, the only noticeable indication that the ship had slowed.

"Give us a picture when you can, Mr. Worf," Sisko said.

The bridge crew was quiet as *Defiant* maneuvered into position. Finally, the ship came within viewing range of the Marauder.

"I have the Ferengi vessel on screen," Worf said. "Maximum magnification."

The image on the main viewer blinked and the *D'Kora*-class Marauder appeared, centered on a background of distant stars. A two-pronged, angular forward section—presumably a control center—was connected by a squat neck to the main body of the ship, which fanned out and forward in a shape approximating an eighth of a sphere, and which resembled, Sisko thought, the sweeping wings of a large bird. The ship grew in size on the viewer as *Defiant* drew closer.

"One thousand kilometers," Dax called from the conn.

"Full stop," Sisko said.

The resonant hum of the impulse drive faded to silence as the velocity of the ship fell to zero.

"Engines answering full stop."

"Mr. Worf," Sisko said, peering over to the tactical station, "hail the Ferengi vessel. Identify us, and let them know that I wish to speak to a representative of Grand Nagus Zek. Tell them I have a business proposition for him."

"Yes, sir," Worf replied with obvious reluctance. It was plain to see that the Klingon believed proposing anything to the Ferengi would be unseemly.

"How can you be sure there'll be a representative of the nagus here, sir?" O'Brien asked.

"Commander Dax is our resident expert on the Ferengi," Sisko said in response. Recognizing that his science officer possessed more practical knowledge about Ferengi society than any other Starfleet officer on *Deep Space Nine,* he had consulted her before embarking on this mission.

"Zek has somebody working for him in *every* Ferengi operation," Dax answered for the captain.

"We are receiving a response," Worf reported. "Readout only." He paused, and then said disgustedly, "They want to know what the 'proposition' is."

"Tell them that when an official representative of the nagus steps forward, he'll find out."

"Yes, sir." Worf relayed the message. There was no reply. After a full minute, Sisko asked, "Anything?"

"Negative."

"Dax, bring us about," Sisko said. "Take us back the way we came."

"Coming about," Dax said. The Marauder slipped from the main viewer as directional thrusters fired and turned *Defiant*.

"Ahead at one-quarter impulse speed."

"One-quarter impulse," Dax said. She worked her controls to power up the sublight drive. The beat of the fusion generators began to pulse once more through the ship.

"Prepare to go to full impulse," Sisko said, frustrated at the failed attempt to send a personal message to the nagus. He would now have to—

"We are being hailed," Worf said. "They will talk to you, Captain."

"They just can't resist hearing an offer, can they?" Dax commented, smiling.

"Stop engines," Sisko ordered a second time. "On screen, Mr. Worf."

On the main viewer, the empty field of stars vanished, replaced by the figure of a lone Ferengi officer. He was standing in what appeared to be a crew cabin, presumably his own. The walls in the room behind him were a bright green; the predominant colors among the room's furnishings were purple and yellow. The garish combination reminded Sisko of Quark's wardrobe.

"I am Bractor," the officer introduced himself, "daiMon of the Marauder *Kreechta,* and commander of this wing of the Ferengi fleet."

"Captain Benjamin Sisko of the *Starship Defiant* and station *Deep Space Nine,"* Sisko said. "DaiMon Bractor, are you an official representative of the grand nagus?"

"I am," said Bractor.

"Forgive my brashness, DaiMon, but I have little time for diplomacy." This statement was itself diplomatic, Sisko realized, considering that the Ferengi were not known either for practicing or appreciating circumspection. "How can I be sure you're telling me the truth?"

"I guess you can't," Bractor answered. "You'll just have

to trust me, human." As with Quark—as with so many Ferengi—the word came out pronounced *hyoo-mon*.

"Funny," Sisko said, "I don't recall the word *trust* being mentioned in any of the Rules of Acquisition."

"Actually, the 47th Rule states—"

"—Nothing I'm interested in hearing right now," Sisko interrupted. "But I'm sure you'll want to hear what I have to say. May I transport aboard the *Kreechta* to meet with you?"

"Captain," Worf called before Bractor could respond. Sisko looked over to the tactical console. Worf glanced up at the main viewer, then stood up and moved away from his station and over to the center of the bridge. With his back to the screen, he addressed Sisko discreetly. "Captain, the Ferengi are not to be trusted, particularly in light of their superior numbers out here. I strongly recommend that you meet with Bractor aboard the *Defiant.*" Prior to his posting on *DS9*, Sisko knew, Worf had served for seven years aboard a Galaxy-class starship, six of those as chief of security; apparently, such training died hard.

"Mister Worf—" Sisko began, but Bractor spoke over him.

"—Perhaps your officer is right, Captain," he said. Worf spun quickly to face the viewer. He seemed startled that the daiMon had heard his whispered words. "I would be willing to beam over to your ship."

Of course you would be, Sisko thought. Worf was right: with all of the other Ferengi vessels that comprised the blockade patrolling nearby, Bractor would feel well-protected. But Sisko also suspected that the daiMon wanted to transport aboard *Defiant* in the hope that he would have an opportunity to learn something about the unique state-of-the-art vessel. It would also allow him to prevent any of his crew from overhearing any personal side deal he might be able to negotiate with Sisko.

"We would be happy to have you aboard," Sisko said.

"Your vessel is presently positioned near the Marauder *Bokira,*" Bractor said, consulting something offscreen. "My tactical officer will provide the location of the *Kreechta,* as well as transporter coordinates. We'll inform you when we're ready."

"Very good."

Bractor jabbed at a control and his image was replaced on the viewer by the emblem of the Ferengi Alliance. Worf walked over to his station and touched a control. The desolate starscape reappeared on the screen.

"You know, Worf," Dax teased, "the Ferengi aren't afraid to use those ears of theirs."

As far as Sisko could tell, Worf was not amused.

Sisko entered Transporter Room One. A square-shouldered, sandy-haired officer only recently assigned to *Deep Space Nine* stood at the console. Sisko did not recall his name.

"Commander Dax reports that we've reached the *Kreechta*, Captain," the ensign said. "I have the transport coordinates, and the Ferengi signal that they're ready."

"Very good," Sisko said. "Energize."

The ensign operated the controls and the high-frequency purr of the transporter filled the room. Soft white granules of light gathered on the platform. First the shape and then the substance of Bractor materialized. He was clad in the gray uniform of the Ferengi military; gold circles at the ends of his sleeves testified to his rank.

"DaiMon," Sisko said. "Welcome to the *Defiant.*"

"Captain Sisko." Bractor brought his wrists together in front of him in the conventional Ferengi salutation, his hands apart, his fingers curled. He bowed slightly and stepped from the transporter platform, peering around in a blatantly curious manner; other than Quark, who had once accompanied the *DS9* crew on a trade mission to the Gamma Quadrant, no Ferengi had ever before been aboard *Defiant.* "You have a handsome vessel," Bractor said.

"That's very generous," Sisko said, "considering that you've only seen the inside of a transporter room, and for only a few seconds."

"Yes, well, you'll find that we Ferengi are generous." Bractor started for the doors. When he saw that Sisko was not following him, he asked, "Shall we be going, Captain?"

"Going?" Sisko asked in return. "Going where?"

"I assume that you have suitable a facility in which we can meet."

"Oh, I think we can stay right here." Sisko had been right: Bractor seemed very interested in seeing more of the ship; Sisko was equally as interested in not allowing him access to anything other than this one room. "What I have to say won't take very long." There was only the slightest lag before Bractor turned away from the doors and back toward the captain.

"Very well," Bractor said, evidently shifting his attention with ease. "You said that you have a business proposition for the nagus?"

"Yes, I did say that." Sisko glanced over at the transporter operator. "Ensign, would you excuse us for a moment?"

"Aye-aye, sir." The young officer quickly operated his console, locking it down, then exited the room. In the brief time that the doors were open, Bractor eyed the section of corridor that was visible beyond them.

"Now then," Sisko began, "I have two requests to make of Grand Nagus Zek, as well as a proposition for him."

"First, Captain, perhaps you can tell me why I should deliver this proposition—and these requests—to the nagus."

"Because it will benefit him."

"And what about me?"

"What about you?" Sisko asked, smiling. This was a question he had anticipated. "If you don't return an answer to me from the nagus within three days, I'll have to assume that you chose not to deliver my message. If that happens, I'll have to send it to him over subspace."

"Why don't you just do that now?" Bractor asked, taking a step back toward the transporter platform, as though he was ready to end this meeting and beam back to his ship right now. His impatience was no doubt a result of his appraisal that there would be nothing of value for him in whatever dealings Sisko had with the nagus.

"My reasons are my own," Sisko said. He was not about to reveal that part of his message to the nagus would probably be adjudged by the Federation Council to be a violation of Resolution 49-535 if they ever learned of it. But Sisko was unwilling to allow the Bajorans to suffer further when it might be within his power to prevent it. "When the nagus receives the message directly from me and learns that you refused to bring it to him personally—which I will make sure he does—and when the delay ends up losing him profit, what do you think your fate will be?"

Bractor regarded Sisko for a few moments without saying anything. At first, Sisko was unconcerned, but as the seconds passed, he began to think he might have overplayed his admittedly weak hand.

"What's the proposition?" Bractor asked at last.

"The requests, first," Sisko told him. "As an official representative of the United Federation of Planets, I am asking Grand Nagus Zek to allow food and medical provisions to be carried by Starfleet vessels through the Ferengi blockade to Bajor."

Bractor's eyes widened. He looked as though Sisko had just asked the nagus to renounce all of his material possessions. Still, he made no verbal comment.

"I would also like to request," Sisko continued, "that the nagus delay the completion of the auction for the Ninth Orb until after the matters of contention between the Ferengi and the Bajorans have been resolved."

Bractor shrugged, seemingly unimpressed, but he moved on to the next subject.

"All right," he said. "Now, what's the proposition?"

"I am offering my personal services as a mediator between the Alliance and the Bajoran government to resolve their current set of disputes."

"That really doesn't sound like much of an offer," Bractor remarked. He started gazing about the transporter room again, his focus wandering from the discussion. "The nagus has indicated that he doesn't want to speak to the Bajorans either directly or through an intermediary. He's already turned down several of their attempts to negotiate."

"He has not turned down *my* personal services," Sisko said. "Nor has anybody promised to maximize the nagus's profits within the context of mediation."

"Are *you* promising that?" Bractor wanted to know, returning his attention to Sisko. The notion of maximum profit must have been impossible for him to resist.

"I am." While Sisko was uncertain whether he would be able to fulfill such a promise, he actually believed that it might be possible. Zek would never agree to allow humanitarian aid through the blockade, but if Sisko could simply bring the two factions into a dialogue, he thought he could prompt them toward deescalation. Surely the blockade was costing the Ferengi, and clearly it was costing the Bajorans—and would yet cost them more if it was permitted to continue. Sisko was confident that he could persuade the nagus to lower the blockade, and the first minister to repeal the edict, if he could just bring the matter of the Ninth Orb to even temporary resolution.

"Let me think about that a moment," Bractor said, and he made a show of considering what Sisko had told him: he tilted his head back as though in thought, clasped his hands together behind his back, and began pacing about the room. For all of that, Sisko figured that the daiMon had already made the decision to take the message back to the nagus, and that he was stalling now in the hopes that he might still discover something of value about *Defiant*. As evidence of that, Bractor edged closer and closer to the transporter console. Sisko let him go; the console had been locked down by the young ensign.

Sisko thought now that there was a good chance his plan would work. As a mediator, he believed he would be able to reach an agreement on a price that the Bajorans would be willing to pay for the Orb, but if not, he would effectively side with the nagus. He would argue that, since Zek had possession of the Orb, it therefore belonged to him—at least from a pragmatic standpoint—and that it must be the will of the Prophets that this had happened. He would also rely on the fact that only one of the nine Orbs presently resided on Bajor; the continued absence of the Orb of Wisdom would therefore not be very disruptive to Bajoran spiritual life. He would quote from *When the Prophets Cried* and the ancient tale of the Third Orb—"the Third Tear"—and if necessary, he would use his purported position as the Emissary to convince the Bajorans to relent. The Vedek Assembly would probably support his view, although Kai Winn would fight him. Shakaar, though, was a practical man, and despite his tendency toward action, Sisko thought that the first minister would eventually see the good sense in settling Bajor's differences with the nagus, even at the sacrifice of procuring another Tear of the Prophets at this time.

You probably should have done all of that in the first place, Sisko told himself. Of course, he had not anticipated that either the Bajorans or the Ferengi would proceed on such severe courses. And there had also been the matter of Resolution 49-535; there was *still* the matter of Resolution 49-535. But if something was not done soon, Bajorans would begin dying, a consequence that Sisko was sure had not been an intention of the Federation Council when it had passed the resolution.

A motion caught Sisko's eye, and he looked over to see Bractor attempting to access the transporter console. When nothing happened, the daiMon tried again. Finally, he gave up and walked back toward the platform.

"Very well," he said as he passed Sisko. "I will deliver your message." He climbed up onto the platform.

Sisko walked around the transporter console and unlocked it with touches to the appropriate controls. He worked the console in preparation for beaming Bractor back to his ship.

"DaiMon Bractor," Sisko said. The Ferengi had been studying the platform, and now he looked up. "The nagus and I have a personal relationship." Sisko and Zek had met on a couple of occasions; their interaction had been cordial, defined for Zek, Sisko was sure, by the fact that Sisko maintained some power with respect to the wormhole.

Bractor seemed unimpressed.

"Anything else?" he asked.

"Actually, there is one more thing," Sisko said. "You look awfully familiar to me. Have we met before?"

"No, we haven't," Bractor said. "I'm sure all Ferengi look alike to you."

Sisko could not tell whether or not the daiMon was joking, but he chose to accept the remark in that regard. He swept his hand across the transporter console, and Bractor was gone.

A response came the third day, transmitted directly to the station: "Bractor instructed to ask you to wait for an answer."

Sisko was suspicious. Had the nagus genuinely responded in this manner, or had Bractor chosen not to deliver the message? With few options available to him, and wanting to give this course of action every opportunity to succeed, Sisko opted to wait.

Two days later, another response came. This too was transmitted directly to the station, but it promised something definite: the captain was told to meet DaiMon Bractor once more. This time, Sisko traveled alone to the blockade, in the runabout *Rubicon*.

As Sisko approached *Kreechta* in the small, limited-range starship, the Marauder filled the forward windows. From this vantage, the Ferengi vessel appeared more powerful—more sinister, even—than it had when viewed from the bridge of *Defiant*. Anxious both to complete his business here and to learn the nagus's response, Sisko contacted Bractor and made arrangements for him to transport onto *Rubicon*.

"DaiMon Bractor," Sisko greeted the Ferengi when he stepped from the two-person transporter at the rear of the runabout's cockpit. "How nice to see you again."

"I delivered your message," Bractor said without preamble, an annoyed tone in his voice. Sisko suspected that the Ferengi captain did not appreciate being employed as an envoy when there had been no profit in it for him. "This—" He stepped from the transporter and held up an isolinear optical chip. "—is the nagus's reply." The chip, utilized for data processing and storage, was the Federation counterpart of the Cardassian isolinear rods in use aboard *Deep Space Nine*. It did not surprise Sisko at all to find Federation technology in Ferengi hands; after all, the Alliance had at some point usurped phaser technology for use aboard their Marauders.

"Thank you, DaiMon," Sisko said, stepping forward and taking the chip from Bractor. "I—" Sisko had been about to say *I owe you,* but then realized that perhaps that was not such a wise thing to say to a Ferengi. "I will not forget this," he said instead.

"Wait until you hear the nagus's response," Bractor told him. "You may not wish to thank or remember me."

"Do you know what's on here?" Sisko asked.

"No," Bractor said. "It's been encoded to be accessed only one time, and then it erases itself. But I heard what you asked of the nagus." Saying nothing more, he turned and moved back onto the transporter pad. Sisko took the daiMon's lead and, without saying another word, operated the transporter controls.

After Bractor had beamed back over to *Kreechta,* Sisko moved to the runabout's primary functions console. There, he slipped the isolinear optical chip into an input receptacle. With a mixture of apprehension and hope, he activated playback.

On a viewer above and to the left of the primary console, the image of Grand Nagus Zek appeared. It took less than one minute to completely review the recording, but what the nagus communicated in that short span of time astonished Sisko.

CHAPTER

16

ACROSS THE ROOM, Xillius Vas stuffed the newly lighted cigar into his mouth as he studied the monitor. There were monitors everywhere here, in every wall, from ceiling to floor, from one side to the other. They were arranged in no observable pattern, and all of them were active. Some spewed pictures and sounds, others were alive with words and figures in an array of different languages. It was a kaleidoscope of visual and auditory images, an amalgam of sensory input both more and less than the sum of its constituents: a combination of information surpassing individual facts, and a pollution of knowledge, its meaning removed by its own noise. And all of it was surrounded by the noxious blue smoke emitted by the cigar of Xillius Vas.

Shakaar watched the Yridian. If the natural texture of the skin of his race had not been wizen, Shakaar was certain that Vas's would nevertheless be a mass of wrinkles; the fetid roll of burning tobacco seemed to leave his mouth only when it was exhausted and ready to be replaced by another.

It had not been easy for Shakaar to leave Bajor in this time of need for his people, but it had been his idea to come here once he had learned what Vas had to offer. He was anxious, though, to complete his business and return home. There was nothing illegitimate about the transaction he was making, but the atmosphere of this dark, smoky room, ceaselessly saturated as it was by imported and unfamiliar sights and sounds, lent the circumstances a vulgar air.

"Vas," Shakaar called from where he was sitting at one of several plain tables, this one near the room's only door. Vas was the only other person present at the moment, but Shakaar could easily visualize all of the tables filled with Yridian agents, gathering and collating data in an attempt to satiate their cupidity for marketable information.

"Wait," Vas said without turning from the monitor he was inspecting.

Wait, thought Shakaar. *I've been waiting all day.* His eyes burned from the blue haze suffusing the room, the inside of his nose felt raw from the fetor of the smoke, and he wanted to blame somebody for his discomfort: the Prophets, the Ferengi, even his own people. Starfleet, perhaps; if they had only been willing to accede to his request . . .

But no, even in this one moment, finding a target for his reproach would not have satisfied him. His truest desires were about being back home on Bajor, not in his office, but out on a tract of farmland in Dahkur Province, sans his ministerial responsibilities. Solitude but for a few friends, open land under an open sky . . .

All day, he thought, then dismissed the words in favor of a difficult truth: *I've been waiting all my life.*

It was almost another hour before Xillius Vas pulled himself away from the monitor. When he did, he shuffled over to the table by the door and sat down across from Shakaar.

"You've finally finished?" Shakaar asked.

"Patience, my friend," Vas said in his raspy voice. He spoke, Shakaar thought, with an ingratiating tone that did not at all match his words. "I had to ascertain whether what you sought was available, and whether what you offered was worth the exchange." He paused, evidently wanting to be prompted for the information.

"My patience, 'my friend,' is at an end," Shakaar said. "Tell me what I need to know and let's be done with this."

"I will tell you this," Vas said. "The value of the information you wish to peddle is higher than I had estimated. All we must do now is determine a delivery schedule."

"You know my needs are immediate."

"So you said. There is travel time involved, of course . . . the earliest we could arrive at Bajor would be two and a half days from now."

"You also know that it will be much easier for me to provide the information to you after that time," Shakaar said.

"Yes, but once we satisfy our portion of the bargain, if you renege on yours," Vas warned, pointing a gnarled finger in Shakaar's direction, "you will have a far greater problem on your hands than the Ferengi blockade."

"I understand."

"If you renege for *any* reason," Vas continued, as though Shakaar had said nothing. "If Sisko opposes you—"

"I understand," Shakaar repeated, loudly and firmly. *"Deep Space Nine* is Bajoran property; Captain Sisko will have no choice but to do as I say."

"Very well," Vas said. "Then let us execute the transaction."

Vas turned and retrieved a padd and another small device from a neighboring table. After both Vas and Shakaar had reviewed the language of their agreement on the padd, they each pressed a finger against the input plate of the other device; from each, a microscopic amount of epidermis was taken, from which the device then extracted their DNA code.

That quickly, Shakaar had committed Bajor to a new course of action.

Back in his office, Shakaar found himself inundated by messages left for him in his absence. He had been away from Bajor for less than a day and a half, and yet he had been contacted by nearly a third of the provincial ministers, several vedeks, Kai Winn, Captain Sisko, and a number of other people. Shakaar's trip had been clandestine—he had wished neither to raise hopes prematurely nor to invite debate—and so nobody would have considered routing their communications to the second minister. Shakaar had informed both his assistant and his deputy about his time away from Bajor, and he was pleased to see from Sirsy's report that the second minister had already responded to many of the people who had contacted the office—although not to Kai Winn and not to Captain Sisko.

Shakaar sat down next to the small table in his office into which a comm panel was set. He reviewed the summary of the situation on Bajor prepared by the second minister, then set up an appointment with him for later in the day. Finally, he operated the controls of the comm panel and opened a channel to *Deep Space Nine*. After a moment, the image of Nerys appeared.

"Edon," she said. She smiled when she saw who it was, but her face fell once she had a chance to really look at him. "What's wrong?" she wanted to know. The concern in her voice was obviously personal. After his travels, he realized, he must have appeared haggard.

"I'm fine, Nerys," he told her. "I'm just not getting much sleep. How are you?"

"I'm not sleeping very well these days myself," she said, something the dark areas beneath her eyes had already told him. "Otherwise I'm fine. How are things on Bajor?"

"Deteriorating, but not yet at emergency levels."

"I think Captain Sisko may have some encouraging news," she said.

Kira's smile returned, and in it, Shakaar found an unexpected source of hope. Could Starfleet have reconsidered his request for military aid? Short of the Ferengi relinquishing their stranglehold on the Bajoran trade routes and the nagus's claim to the Ninth Orb, he could not think of a better turn of events.

"Good news would be a welcome change," he said. "Is the captain available?"

"He is for you," Nerys said. "Just a minute." She worked her controls and the Starfleet emblem replaced her on the display. While Shakaar waited, he checked to see when it was that Sisko had tried to reach him; it had only been a few hours ago.

"First minister." Shakaar looked up to see Sisko now on the screen.

"Captain," Shakaar said. "I'm sorry I haven't responded to your message sooner, but things are very hectic at the present time."

"I understand," Sisko said.

"Major Kira said that you might have something good to tell me."

"I do," Sisko said. "I'm not sure I can explain it, but I welcome it. I'm sure you will too."

Perhaps they have *reconsidered,* Shakaar thought. There was still time to cancel his pact with Vas.

"After an appeal from the Federation Council," Sisko declared, "Grand Nagus Zek has consented to allow Starfleet vessels, subject to inspection, to ship humanitarian aid through the Ferengi blockade. Shipments should begin arriving on Bajor within ten days."

Shakaar exhaled slowly and realized he had been holding his breath without being aware of it. He was surprised and pleased, of course: this would save the lives of uncounted Bajorans. And yet he was struck by the hollow feeling that it would not be enough.

"Minister?" On the display, Sisko had his head cocked to one side and was fixing Shakaar with a quizzical look.

"That is good news, Captain," Shakaar said without inflection.

"If you'll pardon my saying so," Sisko said, "you don't seem quite as happy about this as I expected you to be. As I am."

"Yes, I'm very happy about it," Shakaar said. "But this one measure falls far short of solving all of Bajor's problems with the Ferengi."

"That may be true," Sisko agreed, "but it certainly is a significant step toward accommodation."

Accommodation. Shakaar wondered how often he had heard that word in his life, wondered how often the Cardassians had claimed to be seeking *accommodation* with the people of Bajor, when all they had ever really done was rape their world and crush their society. The terms offered by invaders were always terms of surrender.

A susurrant sound awoke Shakaar from his thoughts. He thought at first that it had been his own breathing that had brought him back to the moment, but as he listened, he realized that it had begun to rain outside. The first of the gentle summer storms that would nurture the growing season in this part of Bajor had arrived.

"Captain," Shakaar said, "the humanitarian aid is of enormous importance, and we will welcome it, but Bajor also requires military support—support beyond the limited defense that *Deep Space Nine* offers. We want to resume importing more than just the necessities of food and medicine, and also to renew the export of our own manufactured goods. To do that, the Ferengi blockade must be rendered ineffective; if they will not end it, then we must do so ourselves."

"You know that Starfleet cannot provide such support," Sisko said. "To do so would be tantamount to promoting a war effort. But if you and the nagus would agree to sit down together and talk . . . perhaps I could function as a mediator between the two sides—"

"There will be no talks," Shakaar insisted, "until the Ninth Orb is on its way to Bajor." Thunder resounded in the distance.

"I'm very sorry that you feel that way, Minister," Sisko said. "But there is still time to talk; representatives of the nagus have informed me that the final round of the auction will not be held for at least another month."

Shakaar erupted.

"Why should we negotiate for that which we have a right to?" he yelled, bringing his fist down on the table. "And I'm not just talking about the Orb, but about the right to control our own solar system, and the right to travel freely through open space."

"Minister—"

"Last time that Bajorans attempted to bargain for rights we already possessed by virtue of our own freedom and self-determination, an occupying army nearly destroyed us."

"Minister, you know I sympathize with the long plight the Cardassian Occupation brought to Bajor," Sisko said. "But the Ferengi are not the Cardassians."

"Nor will we give them the opportunity to become them."

"Very well," Sisko said, apparently perceiving Shakaar's resolve. "But my offer to mediate still stands."

"If there's nothing further, Captain," Shakaar said, "I have much to do."

"No, that's all."

"Good day, then." Shakaar touched a comm-panel control and his link to *DS9* was severed.

CHAPTER

17

THE FIRST INDICATION of the invaders came from the subspace relay.

"Kira, are you getting the same readings I am?" Dax asked from her sciences console in Ops.

Sisko had been about to enter his office, but now he stopped. He turned and waited to hear what it was that had provoked Dax's curiosity. He watched as his first officer examined her own console before she responded.

"What are you looking at?" Kira asked, evidently seeing nothing of interest in her display.

"The communications and sensor relay," Dax answered. "It's picking up an unusual warp signature."

"Switching over," Kira said, operating her console.

Among its other functions, the relay—positioned just beyond the mouth of the wormhole in the Gamma Quadrant—continuously transmitted the results of its local sensor scans back through the wormhole to *Deep Space Nine*. If an "unusual warp signature" had been detected, then that might indicate an unknown type of vessel. Sisko walked down to the lower level and over to Kira's station to look at the readings himself.

"I've got it," Kira said as the readout of the relay's output came up on her display. On a graphical representation of the region of space about the relay, a speck of light moving against the stars signified the source of the unusual readings. An inset in the upper right corner of the display showed the warp signature of the unidentified vessel, and another in the lower right showed its configuration, as well as other details that the sensors had gleaned.

"What type of ship is that?" Sisko asked, unfamiliar with the readings. Although he had tried to keep his voice casual, he was not sure if he had succeeded.

"Nothing I'm acquainted with," Dax said.

"Mr. Worf?" Sisko asked. The Klingon was already checking the readings at another console.

"It is reminiscent of a Ferengi Marauder," Worf said, "with its sweeping aft section. . . ."

"That's no Ferengi vessel," Sisko said.

"No," Worf agreed. "The closest design—"

"Dax, do you see that?" Kira interrupted. "Can these readings be accurate?"

Sisko studied Kira's console. The warp signature had multiplied into two warp signatures . . . four . . . eight . . . many more. A cluster of lights now advanced across the display.

"I count at least thirty-five ships," Dax confirmed. "And they're on a direct heading for the wormhole."

"It could be the Dominion," Chief O'Brien suggested at his station.

"It could be, but those aren't Jem'Hadar ships," Sisko said, hoping that the chief's conjecture did not prove to be prophetic. As heavily armed and fortified as *DS9* now was, and as much of a warrior as *Defiant* was, they could not by themselves withstand the onslaught of such a large squadron of Jem'Hadar vessels. And once *DS9* fell, both the wormhole and Bajor would be left virtually undefended. "Whoever they are, they shouldn't be approaching the wormhole unannounced and in such numbers. Hail them, Major."

"Hailing them," Kira replied, her fingers fluttering rapidly across her controls. "There's no response."

"Keep trying," Sisko said. "Dax, how long till they get here?"

"Not long . . . twenty minutes."

"Mr. Worf, how close are the nearest Starfleet vessels?" Sisko asked.

"The *New York* is accompanying the first wave of transports bringing aid to Bajor and will be here in eight days; if needed, it could leave the convoy and reach the station within two. The *Tian An Men* is investigating the Kilandra Cluster, three days away."

"Not much help," Sisko commented, more to himself than to anybody else. "Mr. Worf, crew the *Defiant.*"

"Aye, sir," Worf said. "We will prepare for battle." Worf headed for the turbolift.

"I want you to be prepared for a fight, commander," Sisko called after him, "or for flight."

"Sir," Worf protested, "a Klingon warrior—"

"Yes, yes, I've heard that before," Sisko cut him off. "But if we're completely overmatched, Starfleet cannot afford for the *Defiant* to be either captured or destroyed. Not with the threats of the Dominion and the Borg still looming."

"Yes, sir." Worf entered the lift and ordered it to take him to *Defiant.*

"Captain," Dax said, "what about the Ferengi?"

"The Ferengi?" Kira echoed, clearly surprised at their mention.

"They have at least twenty ships enforcing the blockade," Dax explained.

"Actually, I was considering them myself," Sisko said. "Major, I want to speak with DaiMon Bractor immediately." Sisko headed for his office, already trying to determine what he could possibly say to persuade the Ferengi to protect a Federation crew, aboard a Bajoran installation, from attack.

"Captain Sisko," Bractor intoned, "I do not think you understand the Ferengi very well." His lips approximated a smile around teeth that exploded from his mouth at all angles.

"I thought you told me that the Ferengi were generous,"

Sisko said, realizing immediately that it had been a useless thing to say. He stood before the comm panel in one wall of his office and saw Bractor's smile grow wider.

"Yes, well, not to a fault," the daiMon said. "Although the Ferengi Alliance is presently at peace with the Federation, there is no treaty between our peoples assuring mutual protection. And the state of our relations with Bajor . . ." Bractor laughed heartily; he seemed genuinely amused by the situation.

"I know it must seem preposterous to you, DaiMon," Sisko said, "but you also believed that the Federation request to allow humanitarian aid to Bajor was preposterous, and yet the nagus approved it."

"I do not pretend to understand all of the actions the nagus takes," Bractor allowed, his smile disappearing as his manner quickly became serious. "Or his reasons for those actions."

"But there is profit to be had here," Sisko tempted, hoping that he could logically make the argument he had in mind. It was not always an easy task to reason in such an alien context.

"What profit?" Bractor asked, nibbling at the bait.

"If the Ferengi protect Bajor or *Deep Space Nine*," Sisko contended, "then the Bajorans would be in the Ferengi's debt. Surely, they would then have to lift the ban on Ferengi use of the wormhole, which would reestablish your ability to trade in the Gamma Quadrant and clearly bring a profit. And the blockade would no longer need to be maintained, which would save in resources."

"You actually make a persuasive case, Captain," Bractor responded, "but I know that the nagus would not grant approval for Ferengi ships to protect *Deep Space Nine* and Bajor."

"How can you be so sure?" Sisko asked. "You were wrong about his reaction to my previous requests."

"I can be sure because my orders are quite definitive with respect to such a contingency," Bractor said. "Under no circumstances am I to permit Ferengi ships to defend anything in Bajoran space, including both Bajor and your space station."

How odd that Bractor's orders would be so specific, Sis

thought. But then, the Ferengi were nothing if not thorough when it came to pursuing profit. Sisko considered making a moral appeal, but knew that would be futile.

"Nevertheless," Sisko tried one last time, "I urge you to consult with the nagus on this."

"I'll consider it, Captain," Bractor offered, but it was evident that he intended to do no such thing. Sisko did not even think a bribe would have helped. "Bractor out," the daiMon said, and his image was replaced on the screen with the emblem of the Ferengi Alliance.

Sisko reached up and touched a control, and the comm panel went completely dark. He stood alone in his office for a moment, staring at the empty screen and contemplating what other alternatives were available to him. He was still thinking when Kira called him to Ops.

"Two minutes to the wormhole," Dax announced.

Tension filled Ops. Sisko saw anxiety reflected in the uneasy movements of his crew. The past few weeks had been difficult for them, he knew. Not only had their day-to-day lives been affected by the blockade, but their deep concern for the people of Bajor had been unceasingly tried. Indeed, several members of the Bajoran Militia who worked on *Deep Space Nine* had returned home to be with their families, while those who remained aboard were understandably worried.

"One minute."

"Weapons status?" Sisko wanted to know. He paced along the upper level of Ops.

"Phasers are fully charged," O'Brien reported. "Photon torpedoes are loaded and ready."

"Shields?"

"Up full," said O'Brien.

"What about the *Defiant?*" Sisko asked.

"She's away," reported Kira. "Ready to attack or retreat."

Attack or retreat, Sisko thought. But there was no retreat for the station. There was only negotiation or defense; there was only peace or war.

"The alien ships are entering the wormhole."

"Battle stations," Sisko ordered. He stopped walking and

peered up at the main viewer. On it was an empty starscape, but it was there that the mouth of the wormhole would open. Sisko stared at the image as he and his crew waited. For unmeasured seconds, Ops was silent.

Then: "Reading elevated neutrino levels," Dax said. "The wormhole is opening."

On the viewer, a swirling vortex of vibrant blue appeared as though from nowhere, spinning outward in a radiant spiral. In the eye of the maelstrom, a maw of white light unfolded, revealing the beginning of a tunnel of nearly stellar brightness. Dark objects, too small to identify at this distance, emerged from the cosmic whirlpool in a long group.

And then the entrance to the wormhole collapsed in on itself, light and color shrinking down to a point. The great subspace bridge was gone, but it left behind the objects that had just navigated through it. As the objects drew nearer to the station, they resolved into ships.

Sisko eyed the lead vessel on the viewscreen; it was definitely a design unknown to him. The main body was cylindrical, with rounded ends. Above this sat a small, circular annex, with a diameter no larger than that of the cylinder, possibly a control section. Two warp nacelles projected from the main body of the ship, parallel to it. But the most prominent features of the ship were the two huge structures that obtruded fore and aft from the rounded end of the cylinder; they resembled armor plating, square in shape, but slightly curved, like huge sections cut from the surface of a great sphere.

"They're headed in this direction," Kira said.

"Weapons?" Sisko asked.

"I'm scanning the ships now," Dax said. "I'm reading Klingon-style disruptors—"

"Klingon?" Sisko said with surprise, pulling his gaze from the viewer and looking over at Dax.

"—and Starfleet-style photon torpedoes."

"What?" Sisko could not keep himself from asking. He glanced around Ops and saw that nobody had any answers.

"Benjamin," Dax said, looking up from her console, "their weapons aren't powered up." She checked something, and then added, "I don't read any deflectors operating either."

"So they're not prepared to attack," Sisko concluded. He looked back up at the viewer and regarded the ships once more. "Stay alert," he told his crew, but he felt himself relax a bit. He let his arms down to his sides, unaware until that moment that he had raised one hand in front of him, tensed it into a fist, and wrapped his other hand around it.

"What are those . . . those shieldlike structures?" Kira asked.

"I think they may be just that," Dax speculated. "Physical shields for the ship, to augment or replace deflectors."

"Do they have deflectors?" O'Brien asked.

"Yes, a deflector grid is embedded in each physical shield." Dax examined her readouts. "There's also a sensor array in each. In fact—" Dax worked her controls. "—the sensors are engineered to Cardassian specifications, and the deflectors to Romulan specs."

"Where in the blazes are those ships from?" O'Brien _rted.

"It appears that they're from everywhere," Sisko said. "Are there life signs?"

"Yes," Dax said, "but I'm having trouble getting anything definitive; the sensor arrays in those big shields are scrambling our scans."

"Major, have you been continuing hails?"

"Since our first sensor contact, yes, sir," Kira said. "They're not responding."

Who is this, and what do they want? Sisko raised a hand and rubbed it along the line of his jaw.

"Captain," Dax said, "the ships are passing the station."

"Bajor?" Kira said, her voice filled with dread.

Dax looked up from her console, her expression troubled. She confirmed Kira's fear with a nod.

Sisko did not hesitate.

"Major, get me the first minister right now. Then I want to talk to Bractor again. There must be something I can do to convince him to help."

Kira contacted Bajor and was put through to Shakaar immediately. Within seconds of his order, Sisko was looking at the face of the first minister on the main viewer. It was almost as though Shakaar had been waiting for Sisko to contact him.

"First minister, I'm sorry for the urgency," Sisko said quickly, "but a squadron of thirty-five ships has just passed through the wormhole and is on a direct course to Bajor. Their intentions are unknown, the ships are of a type we've never encountered before."

"The ships are not unknown to me, Captain," Shakaar said. "Nor are the intentions of their crews."

"I don't understand," Sisko said, but he thought he probably did. He hoped he was wrong.

"Bajor has purchased these vessels," Shakaar revealed, "for our defense."

Sisko dropped his head and shook it back and forth in disbelief. Whether Bractor wanted to or not, whether the nagus wanted to or not, the Ferengi Marauders composing the blockade would be battling this squadron of ships soon enough.

CHAPTER
18

ROM WAS COLD.

In the darkness, he reached up and pinched the bottom of his right earlobe. He felt nothing.

Cautiously, he rubbed together the fingers of his raised hand. He heard the noise, but only faintly. Still, that was good. At least he had not completely lost his hearing yet.

He hugged his thin blanket tightly about himself. Then, putting his hand down for a moment to adjust the way in which he was lying, he felt the wood of his bunk; it too was cold. Winter on Bajor. Winter at Gallitep.

As he raised himself onto his side, trying to find a position in which he could get to sleep, the bunk creaked. It was loud enough that he heard it even with his bad ear. Rom stiffened with fear, his entire body tensing. The barracks were monitored, even at night, and for a couple of the jailors, even the slightest infraction of the rules—such as moving around after lights out—was provocation enough to punish the prisoners.

For minutes, Rom remained motionless, alert for the sound of approaching footfalls outside. Even after he was sure nobody was coming, he kept still, afraid that if he

221

moved at all, the bunk would creak again. But soon, his arm began to tremble, what little strength he had left exhausted from the simple effort of propping up his body. As slowly as he could without collapsing, Rom eased himself back down. Thankfully, he was able to do so without making any noise.

Weary though he was, Rom found that he could not fall back to sleep. The cold had woken him, and it was still cold. It had been cold for days. *He* had been cold for days.

Rom opened his eyes and saw nothing, surrounded as he was by the ebon texture of his lightless prison. He listened again for sounds, not beyond the barracks this time, but within it. He picked out the breathing of five . . . six . . . seven . . . all eight of his fellow prisoners. Because of the hearing problem in his one ear, he could not accurately fix the location of each person in the room, but he knew where they were.

The seven other prisoners beside Rom and Quark were all Ferengi. They had already been brought here to Gallitep by the time Rom and his brother had been arrested. Five of them had been captured in their small cargo ship, attempting to make a run into Bajoran space and through the wormhole after the deadline. Their story would have been comic, Rom thought, if not for the dreadful consequences it had wrought. Their ship had lost its engines far from the wormhole, and they had floated in space for a day while laboring to make repairs. They had nearly finished restoring power to their drive when they had been chanced upon by a pair of Bajoran transports. Neither their ship nor the transports had possessed any weapons or defenses to speak of, but the Bajorans had had working engines and tractor beams, and that had been all they had needed. The Ferengi cargo ship had been towed to Bajor and its entire crew arrested.

Both of the other two Ferengi had been on Bajor when they had been discovered and taken into custody. One of them, Cort, had been conducting business on the planet and had not been able to leave before the deadline. The other, Karg, had not even known of the edict—or of Zek's purchase of the Ninth Orb, or of any other detail in this entire episode; he had retired several years ago to Bajor, where he had lived somewhat reclusively in a modest home in the province of Wyntara Mas, painting still lifes and landscapes.

Such an existence, Rom reflected, held great appeal, though he himself had no aptitude for painting. But he was very good with little creatures—*treni* cats and *jebrets,* in particular—and at growing plants of various sorts. He had long hoped that he would someday retire in a fashion similar to that of Karg. Quark had many times spoken of purchasing his own moon and withdrawing to it from his workaday business existence, and he had also frequently implied that he would want Rom to accompany him; he had even gone so far as to offer Rom such hypothetical entice-ments as a room of his own, a garden, and his own private menagerie of small animals. It was to a vision of such a life that Rom often retreated these days—and most especially on those days filled by Colonel Mitra.

As Rom lay huddled in his bunk, the thought of Mitra filled him with a distress he had not felt since . . . well, he had thought never, but perhaps since the time in his youth when Breel had so thoroughly humiliated him. Mitra humil-iated him too, but in an adult manner that struck with a harshness that cut him far more deeply. There was a physical component to the pain as well, significant despite not being directly administered—Rom had to push away thoughts of his ears, his feet, that one section of his lower back—but the healing he would have to do when he got out of here would require far more than just the skills of Dr. Bashir.

If we ever get out of here.

When they had first been brought to the prison camp, there had been no doubts about their eventual departure. They would be held here until they stood trial for having violated the Bajoran edict. They would be found guilty, of course, and serve what would probably be a short term in a jail somewhere on Bajor. Until the trial, they at least had food and shelter—the meals were tasteless and the barracks uncomfortable, but their circumstances were not that bad. The guards were not friendly—the colonel had ordered them not to be—but the prisoners had been treated tolera-bly well. Even Quark's numerous bribery attempts had only been met with disdain, rather than punishment.

And then one day, things had changed. The colonel came by the barracks to inform the prisoners that they were no longer being held for trial. For a fleeting, cruelly hopeful moment, Rom thought that they were being released. Instead, the colonel told them about the blockade, and that as a result, the Ferengi would now be detained as political prisoners until the differences between Bajor and Ferenginar had been resolved. From that day forward, the situation had deteriorated rapidly. It was as though the prisoners had been completely forgotten by the outside world, and left to the mercy of Gallitep and their keepers.

The notion that they would not leave this place was unimaginable to Rom. He clung to the hope that there would eventually be release or escape, tomorrow, or the day after, or the day after that. Without that hope, Rom was sure that he could not have continued: he would just fail to rouse one day when one of the guards arrived at dawn, and if it was not Mitra, then Mitra would be there before long, and he would see Rom hurt, again and again, until Rom was dead—or worse, until he wished for death.

Colonel Mitra was like no other Bajoran Rom had ever met. He was like no other person he had ever met. Rom had known liars and thieves and cheats; he had them in his own family, and he understood them. He had also been acquainted with violent people, murderers even, and he had heard many tales of beings who were altogether evil, and even though malice for its own sake, with no thought of profit or strategic gain, was senseless to him—as it was, he was sure, to most Ferengi—he at least could understand how such people were motivated. But none of these categories could accurately contain the colonel. Rom did not understand why or how, but something was missing from Mitra, some essential quality no man could have lived without, and yet Mitra somehow did. It was a mystery to Rom, but not one for which he sought an answer; he prayed that he never came to understand that which drove—and which failed to drive—his ranking jailer.

How long had they been here now? Rom suddenly wondered in the darkness. At least a month, he was sure, probably two, but beyond that, he had difficulty knowing. The days were interminable, the nights without dimension.

He had made an effort to track the time here when they had first arrived—as any numerically minded Ferengi would—but at some point since then, even this most ingrained of habits had become a forgotten detail, one less connection to his previous life. There would come a time soon, Rom understood, when his thoughts of that previous life would cease being memories and become only illusions instead, sanguine dreams torturous for their inaccessibility.

Life, once filled with promise, was now beginning to be marked by its absence. Rom had wanted to ask the dabo girl Leeta to go out with him, he recalled, trying to envisage *Deep Space Nine* and his life there.

He wanted to watch his son graduate from Starfleet Academy.

He wanted to help his brother achieve the business successes he craved.

He wanted to see his mother again.

He wanted to go home. That, he realized now, more than anything else: he wanted to go home.

So thinking, Rom drifted into a restless sleep.

He felt like he was walking on knives. Pain, metallic in its strength and sharpness and linearity, sliced up his legs from his soles. He was scared to look down, fearful that he would see his shins and calves filled with long, vertical cuts, his skin peeling away and hanging down in strips. His feet were numb.

And still he marched.

There was no choice, really. Sergeant Wyte was running them today. If Rom did not march, he would be beaten and then he would have to march anyway; march, or be dragged.

Rom was positioned toward the head of the line of prisoners; only Cort walked in front of him. Quark was near the back of the line, he thought, although he could not be sure. The prisoners were ordered in a single file and made to face forward, so that there could be no eye contact between them, no opportunity for even modest camaraderie, no chance for one to gain emotional strength from another as they marched. These were Mitra's orders to the four guards who, in addition to Mitra, maintained watch over the nine Ferengi held here, and those rules were rigidly obeyed—in the cases of three of the guards, Rom believed, for fear of reprisal; in Wyte's case, because of the sergeant's conviction that the colonel was a brilliant tactician and leader.

Looking past Cort, Rom saw the barren land within the confines of the prison camp lead up to the tall mesh fence that surrounded it. That fence was electrified, Rom knew: Quark and Kreln—the pilot of the captured Ferengi cargo ship—had tested it a couple of weeks ago in preparation for an attempted escape. Mitra had somehow learned of this, and he had beaten Kreln for the action, in the middle of the barracks, in forced view of the other prisoners. To Kreln's credit, he had claimed to have acted alone, refusing through the entire assault to name Quark as his accomplice. And Quark had not stepped forward, which had earned him the enmity of Kreln and his four shipmates. It was Rom's opinion that Mitra had known of Quark's involvement in the escape planning, had guessed that Quark would not admit it, and then used that knowledge to divide the prisoners.

Both before and after the incident, Quark had tried to plot other escapes, but none had progressed past their planning. As best they could tell, the camp had no transporter and no communications station, and no shuttles ever visited here. Gallitep, for all of its primitive features—even because of them—was a fortress. It was not necessarily that the perimeter could not be breached from within, but if it was, there was nowhere to flee. The remoteness of the prison camp could not have been more effective as a deterrent to escape than if the camp had been enclosed by walls of pure neutronium.

Rom observed that remoteness now as he marched on his aching legs, his unfeeling feet. The bleak, empty landscape stretched away in all directions, providing no break for the winds on this part of Bajor. As winter deepened here, so too did the winds grow stronger. More and more often these days, Rom would lose the feeling in his extremities—his fingers, his toes, his lobes—when they marched. Though the guards had gloves and, Rom presumed, insulated footwear, the prisoners did not; upon arrival here, each had been given a plain brown jumpsuit and basic shoes. Both the clothes and the shoes fit poorly, and neither had ever been mended, no matter their state of disrepair. Kreln's jumpsuit, after his many physical encounters with Sergeant Wyte, hung in virtual tatters about him. Their shoes—

—Rom tripped.

One moment, he had been marching mechanically behind Cort, and the next, he found himself sprawling face-first onto the infertile ground, almost striking the backs of Cort's legs as he went down. He did not know whether he had tripped in a hole, or on a stone, or on his own foot; he had no feeling below his ankles. He had barely been able to raise his arms to cushion his fall.

Cautiously, he lifted his head. He saw Cort's feet, which were now pointed toward him, suddenly back away. A hand grabbed the back of Rom's neck like a vise. He winced as he felt himself being lifted.

"On your feet, you big-eared freak," Wyte snarled. He set Rom down.

Rom crumbled to the ground, landing faceup this time. He had not fallen again intentionally, but he had been powerless to remain standing. He did not know why; his body felt sound, though weak and stung by cold—all but his feet, which he could not feel at all. He tried to raise his head and look at them, but Wyte's two paws shot down and grabbed him by the front of his jumpsuit. Gravity tugged him one way as Wyte tugged him the other. Rom's head lolled back on his neck.

There was a moment were Rom's progress upward stopped. He heard something with his good ear, what sounded like the frenetic scraping of feet in the dry, stony dirt. He thought he heard his brother's voice—*Leave him alone*—and then he was falling again. The back of his head struck the ground, and he fell further, into darkness, not the harsh, uncaring darkness of night at Gallitep, but a velvety and comforting darkness. Rom welcomed it.

When Rom awoke, it was night once more. He was in the barracks, on his bunk, lying on his back. It was evidently before lights-out, because the low-powered lighting panels in the ceiling were still on. Rom had wondered for a while why Colonel Mitra permitted the prisoners this free time together in the barracks, when they could talk and possibly regain some emotional vigor from each other. That is, Rom had wondered until the day Borit—one of Kreln's shipmates; Drayan, Tarken, and Lenk were the other three—had done something wrong and been taken away to spend two days by himself in a small, dark cell; it was then that Rom had realized that Mitra provided this time, the only time the prisoners could interact with each other, so that he could have something to take away from them.

In the dimness, Rom saw Quark leaning over him, looking down at him with what Rom could only characterize as brotherly concern. Quark's face was badly bruised: his left eye was swollen shut, and a long gash slanted across his cheek to the bridge of his nose.

"Brother," Rom rasped, his mouth dry. "What happened?"

"You passed out," Quark told him quietly.

"I mean: What happened to you?"

"Nothing."

"Was it Sergeant Wyte?"

Quark shook his head slowly.

"When you fell, he tried to put you back on your feet, and you fell again." Quark paused. It seemed difficult for him to continue. "He was going to beat you," he said finally. "I couldn't let him."

"So you tried to stop him, and he beat you instead."

Quark shrugged.

"I hate him," he said simply.

"No," Rom said, prompting a puzzled look on his brother's face. Rom was not denying that Wyte was a hateful individual; it was obvious, after all, that he envisioned himself as the protégé of Colonel Mitra. But where Mitra was an enigma, Wyte was eminently solvable: he was a man who had tormented small animals as a boy; he was Breel; he was scared and lonely and reaching for the wrong things to prove his own worth to himself; he was quotidian in every aspect of his life but one: his anger at his own undistinguished life. Rom did not hate him; he pitied him.

"I'm tougher than you," Quark said when Rom did not go on, apparently continuing to explain his actions. "And it's my fault that we're here."

"No," Rom said, even though he agreed that it was

Quark's fault that they were here. But Quark had accepted that responsibility, and Rom had long ago forgiven him for his mistake; Rom always forgave his brother for the mistakes he made.

"Anyway," Quark said, "I figured—"

The sound of the door to the barracks opening on its hinges stopped Quark. His head spun toward the door. Rom lifted himself up onto his elbows and looked as well. When he did so, he saw his own feet for the first time since before he had fallen. His shoes had been removed, but his skin was not visible; all Rom could see was the gritty, burgundy mixture of blood and soil. He abruptly discovered that feeling had partially returned to that part of his body: his feet now felt as if they were burning, although in a distant, almost secondhand way.

Looking past his feet, Rom saw, in one corner of the room, three of the men from the captured cargo ship talking among themselves. The other prisoners were lying quietly in their bunks.

Sergeant Argan was at the door.

"What do you want?" Quark said with undisguised contempt.

To Rom's surprise, Argan held up a pair of shoes.

"I have new shoes for prisoner nine," he said, lifting them even higher. None of the guards were allowed to call any of the prisoners by their names. Argan closed the door and walked over to Rom and Quark. He displayed the shoes again. Unable to prop himself up any longer, Rom eased himself down onto his back.

"Is this a trick?" Quark asked.

"No," Argan said. He stole a backward glance at the door, then turned and spoke directly to Quark. "I convinced Wyte that he'd be in big trouble with the colonel if he found out that he marched prisoner nine—" Argan stopped and peered down at Rom. "—if he ever found out that Wyte marched Rom right through the bottom of his shoes."

He handed the new shoes to Quark, who took them cautiously. Argan bent and picked up what were apparently Rom's old shoes. They looked black to Rom, although he knew that they were tan; then he realized that they were soaked through in his own blood. The soles, Rom saw, were almost entirely gone, and only paper thin where they still existed.

"I'm sorry," Argan said, not looking at Rom or Quark, but staring at the threadbare shoes.

"This *is* a trick," Quark said.

"No," Argan insisted, and Rom found that he believed him. Argan was not Mitra, and he was not Wyte; Argan and the other two guards—Prana and Jessel—had never, to Rom's knowledge, abused any of the prisoners. Of course, before now, neither had they helped any of them.

"We know the barracks is monitored," Quark argued.

"Jessel is monitoring right now; Wyte had to get medical attention after you attacked him." Argan actually smiled.

"What did you do, brother?" Rom asked, his voice weak.

"He jumped on Wyte's back and wrapped his arms around his head," Argan recounted, still smiling. He and Wyte had been the two guards charged with marching the prisoners around today. "He didn't do much damage before I pulled him off, but he did manage to poke Wyte in the eye. We fixed the scratch, but it'll be morning before the swelling goes down."

"For me too," Quark said, touching his fingers to the side of his own injured eye.

"Look," Argan said, again peering back at the door nervously. "This—" He reached behind himself and pulled a small medical kit from the waistband of his pants. "—should help both of you." He looked down at Rom again. "Especially you." To Quark, he said, "Don't do too much cosmetically; your injuries still need to look bad, otherwise Jessel and I'll be in here beside you." He reached into his pocket and pulled out a handful of pills. "These are vitamins; there should be enough for everybody." He gave them to Quark, then checked the door for a third time. "I'll get the medkit when we bring your food later."

"I wouldn't exactly call bread and water 'food,'" Quark said.

"Water sounds pretty good to me right now," Rom said; his mouth was still very dry.

"Okay, I'll be back in about an hour." Argan crossed the barracks quickly, Rom's old shoes gripped in one hand. He opened the door and was gone into the night.

"Well," Quark said, "that was interesting." He opened the medical kit and examined the instruments inside. "Do you know how to use any of these?" he asked Rom. He held the open kit down by the surface of the bunk so that Rom could see it.

"Not really," Rom said, "but the scanner will probably have instructions." Quark pulled the medical scanner out of the kit and turned it on. From what Rom could see, it resembled Starfleet's standard-issue tricorder, with which he knew Quark was familiar. Before long, Quark had found directions for the usage of the medical instruments. After reading them, he began to work on healing Rom's feet, although he took obvious pains not to clean the wounds externally.

Rom watched for some time as Quark tended to him. He was moved by his brother's careful attention. He thought again about the moon Quark hoped someday to purchase, and about how Quark wanted to bring him along to garden and keep animals. Rom's mind filled with images of that dream future. His brother had described those images to Rom many times before, and right now, Rom found that what he wanted was to hear those wonderful descriptions once more.

"Tell me about the *jebrets,* Quark," he said.

231

CHAPTER

19

"YOU'RE GOING to destroy Bajor."

"Obviously I don't think so, Captain," Shakaar said. "We are protecting it, and ultimately, we will save it."

"Save it from what?" Sisko demanded, his voice raised, his tone harsh. "From inconvenience? Maybe some economic hardship? Starfleet will be bringing food and medicine; there will be no famine, no pandemic health crisis."

The two stood facing each other at close range in the first minister's office. Sisko had rushed here upon learning of Bajor's purchase of the thirty-five starships that had passed through the wormhole. It was another violation of the Federation Council's resolution for him to be talking with Shakaar in this manner, he knew, but that was of little importance to him right now. What was important was preventing the destruction of the Bajoran people, and that meant convincing the first minister to abandon the perilous course of action he had chosen to take.

Shakaar backed away from Sisko and moved to the archway leading to the balcony. He lifted an arm, motioning outside with his hand.

"Captain, if you would," he invited. Sisko strode over to

the first minister and faced him once more. "Please," Shakaar said, gesturing again through the doorway with his outstretched hand. After a moment, Sisko walked out onto the balcony, and Shakaar followed.

The day was warm, though the skies were overcast. The air was very still, with a barely perceptible electric taste about it. Sisko could feel that there was a summer storm threatening, and still he found the panorama splendid, even without the beautifying effects of the sun. And the reborn loveliness of Bajor reinforced his belief that its people must not take up arms against the Ferengi.

Although Sisko had seen the devastation that had been visited here during the Occupation, it was in this way—overlooking a lush, natural landscape at the edge of a vital, ancient city—that he most often pictured Bajor. He had come to find this world and its inhabitants captivating and inspiring. Like no place else in his life—not even New Orleans, back on Earth—Sisko felt at home here, among these people.

They have to be protected, Sisko thought. And perhaps right now they most needed to be protected not from an external menace, but from their own determination and the bitter memory of their subjugation.

"It is majestic, isn't it?" Shakaar asked as the two men peered out across the land.

"It is," Sisko agreed. "It would be a shame to lose it."

"You're absolutely right," Shakaar said. "We cannot lose this—" He swung his arm out in an arc, encompassing all that they could see. "—again. Once before, we came frighteningly close to losing this—to losing *everything*—forever."

"Minister," Sisko said, turning to face him, "the situation is different this time. The Ferengi are not attacking Bajor; they're not seeking to annex your world, nor are they likely to do so." The first minister continued to look outward, away from Sisko.

"Just because they have not invaded does not mean that they are not an enemy, that they are not fighting us," Shakaar said. "Their blockade *is* an attack. Their unwillingness to let us purchase the Ninth Orb is an attack."

"The Ferengi have also consented to allow necessities to

be delivered to Bajor," Sisko argued. "They have agreed to weaken their own blockade. If it is an attack, then it's one that no longer threatens the lives or the health of your population."

"The ways in which we choose to live out our existences must not be dictated by others," Shakaar insisted. Now, finally, he turned to face the captain, as though trying to emphasize the importance of what he was about to say. "The Cardassians came here with their arms open, promising friendship and peace, telling us that they wanted to visit Bajor for its natural beauty and its wonderful people. But when they wanted more than we were willing to permit them to have, they claimed our world for themselves and discarded us. And it is a far shorter journey to travel from a blockade to an invasion than it is to travel from peace and friendship to an invasion."

"The Ferengi are not the Cardassians," Sisko said.

"Maybe not," Shakaar granted, "but they are on our doorstep. I have been chosen to lead our people, and I therefore have a responsibility to protect them. I cannot risk letting what happened before happen again." He paused, his gaze becoming unfocused for a moment. "So many horrible things were done to my people and our world," he said, suddenly remote. Slowly, his face twisted into an expression of repugnance and hatred. "Do you know what it's like?" he asked, and then he looked at Sisko again. "I saw it myself. Do you know what it's like to watch your friends suffer mutilations, to watch them perish right in front of you?"

"Perhaps you forget my own history," Sisko said gently. He was sympathetic, but not blindly so. "I know that you're a religious man, so I suspect that you're aware of the major events in the 'Emissary's' life. And so you'll remember when I tell you that I watched the woman I loved more than anything else in this universe die." Sisko stopped, seeing that Shakaar's countenance had softened.

"I'm sorry," the first minister said. "I . . ."

Sisko involuntarily looked away; although he had come to terms in his own life with his wife's death, he was uncomfortable speaking about such a personal matter with someone he was not close to. He realized that there was an important point to be made here, though, and so he returned his gaze to the first minister and pressed on.

"To answer your question," he said, "yes, I do know what it's like to watch a loved one perish right in front of me. I saw my wife's body blown into nothingness by a morally bankrupt enemy. It made me sad, and angry, and full of hate. And in the end, what I learned was: That's no way to live."

"No," Shakaar said. "It isn't. And one way for us to avoid living like that—full of sadness and anger and hatred—is not to live under somebody else's rule, either directly or indirectly. We have to learn from our past."

"But you don't have to live there," Sisko said.

"We must *never* forget the Occupation."

"Of course you mustn't," Sisko concurred. "But as you said, you should learn from it. Grow from it . . . grow *away* from it. If you let what the Cardassians did in the past dictate your actions now, then you're really not free of their influence, are you? In a way, a Cardassian presence will still be occupying Bajor."

"We are under siege," Shakaar said evenly. "We cannot let the Ferengi have these lands." He motioned again to indicate the region surrounding the city. "What would this become? No doubt a marketplace of some sort."

A flurry of motion caught Sisko's eye. He leaned a little to his right to look past Shakaar and saw that a bird had set down on the rectangular, waist-high wall surrounding the balcony. The bird's plumage was predominantly blue, with patches of white on its breast, and a bright-green crest. The first minister followed Sisko's gaze, then turned back around.

"Captain—"

"Minister," Sisko responded. "Bajor is not under siege. At most, you have a political war, maybe a trade war, on your hands. The Ferengi aren't interested in capturing Bajor; all they want is access to the wormhole."

"And all we want is the Orb." Sisko thought that the first minister, despite the obvious sincerity of his views, sounded petulant. Behind Shakaar, the bird hopped along the top of the wall, coming closer to the two men.

"And so you're going to start a war with the Ferengi,"

Sisko said, frustrated, "and that's how they'll come to occupy Bajor. You can't possibly win this fight; those Ferengi Marauders out there—" Sisko pointed up to the sky. "—will destroy your new starships." At the motion, the bird spread its wings and took to the sky, rustling the air as it did so.

"That remains to be seen," Shakaar said.

"Even if your ships are the equal of the Marauders," Sisko said, "or even more powerful, you're still outgunned. Maybe not here at the blockade, but the Ferengi have a fleet which dwarfs your thirty-five-ship squadron. They will crush you, and then they will take both the wormhole and Bajor as the plunder of war."

"We do not intend to start a war," Shakaar said, backing down at least a little bit, Sisko thought, from his militant emotions. "We only want to open our trade routes, and our new vessels will allow us to do that. They were designed as defensive transports, perfect for running the blockade."

"As you said, that remains to be seen. What happens if the Ferengi are able to stop your new ships?" But Sisko already knew the answer to that.

"We will do what we have to do to maintain and protect our sovereignty," Shakaar said.

If Sisko had been concerned that his position as Emissary would unduly influence Shakaar, he clearly need not have been. It was apparent that the first minister—and perhaps most Bajorans—believed it preferable to battle against impossible odds rather than to submit to the will of another. It was a valiant attitude, to be sure, one Sisko even subscribed to himself, but it required moderation in its implementation. There would be no moderation now, though, Sisko saw; the Occupation had changed the Bajorans, driven out their capability for temperance, at least in matters such as these.

"I wish you luck, Minister," Sisko said. "More than that, I wish you peace." He tapped his combadge. "Sisko to *Defiant.*"

"Captain," Shakaar said. "There is another matter I must discuss with you."

"*Defiant* here," came Worf's voice.

"Status," Sisko said. He had been ready to transport

aboard, but now he would wait to see what else Shakaar had to say.

"No change," Worf reported. "All of the ships remain in orbit about Bajor."

"Good," Sisko said, looking questioningly at the first minister. "Stand by. Sisko out."

"The transports need their cargoes loaded before they go anywhere," Shakaar explained.

"I see," said Sisko. "Now, what is this other matter?"

"May we?" Shakaar asked, gesturing toward the doorway.

Sisko nodded, and the first minister walked back inside the office. As Sisko followed, he experienced a presentiment of impending catastrophe.

"Are there more ships coming?" he asked, stopping just inside.

"No," Shakaar said. "We purchased what we could without drawing from the treasury. If our breaking the blockade convinces the nagus to change his mind, we don't expect that he will give us the Orb; we will still have to purchase it, and the price will doubtless be high." The first minister proceeded to the table sitting amid the chairs and the sofa. There, he leaned down and picked up a Bajoran padd.

"If you didn't use the resources of the treasury," Sisko asked, "then how did you buy the ships?"

"We acquired them from the Yridians," Shakaar revealed.

"The Yridians?" As far as Sisko was aware, the Yridians regarded themselves as interstellar dealers of information. To that end, the only items they ever manufactured were related to gathering and storing data; they certainly did not possess the facilities to construct starships.

"You know of their penchant for trading in information?" Shakaar asked, walking back across the office again.

"Yes?"

"It was information we promised to provide in exchange for the transports." Shakaar paused. He seemed uncomfortable. "More precisely," he finally went on, reaching out to hand Sisko the padd, "it was *access* to information. We promised to provide a man named Xillius Vas access to all the data relayed to *Deep Space Nine* through the wormhole."

237

Sisko was thunderstruck. He took the padd and examined it. What appeared to be the beginning of a legal contract showed on the display.

"That data is not yours to sell," Sisko said firmly. "It belongs to Starfleet."

"I disagree, Captain," Shakaar said. "As do Bajor's legal authorities. I'm sure those of the Federation will as well."

"I'm not as sure," Sisko said.

"The data transmitted to *Deep Space Nine* belongs to Starfleet no more than does the space station itself," Shakaar explained. "Further, the data resides in Bajoran space. We therefore have a manifest right to it. We've merely extended that right to another party."

"I'll have to consult with Starfleet Command," Sisko said, knowing that Starfleet would never approve such access.

"Of course," Shakaar said with equanimity. "I expected that to be the case. You have five days from now until Mr. Vas or his representatives arrive to begin monitoring communications from the relay station."

"And if Starfleet refuses to cooperate?" Sisko asked. He held up the padd to return it to Shakaar.

"Please keep it. Review it," Shakaar said. "You'll see that, since we already have the starships, it is now incumbent upon us to complete our part of the bargain. If Starfleet insists on preventing us from doing so, we will have to abrogate their invitation to operate the station."

"Threats?" Sisko asked.

"Not at all, captain," Shakaar said. "We want Starfleet to stay. But it was necessary for us to acquire some defensive military power, and we dealt that which we had. Starfleet's place in the middle of this is unfortunate, but really coincidental."

"Not so coincidental as all that," Sisko said. "Without Starfleet, there would be no sophisticated communications system on *DS9*, and no relay in the Gamma Quadrant. You would not have been able to trade access to this information, because the information itself would not have existed."

"Nor would it have existed had Bajor not invited Starfleet

to operate *DS9,*" Shakaar said. "Captain, we are only doing what we have to do in order to protect ourselves."

"I know you believe that," Sisko said, staring the first minister in the eye. "I only wish you'd stop to see that there are preferable alternatives to the path you've chosen." He tapped his combadge. "Sisko to *Defiant.*"

"*Defiant.* This is Worf."

"One to beam up, Mr. Worf."

Sisko dematerialized.

CHAPTER
20

As Worf LISTENED to Admiral Whatley, something tugged at
his awareness. He glanced across the table at Captain
Sisko—they were the only two in the conference room at
the moment—then back to the wall comm panel, where the
admiral was continuing to talk. Sensing that whatever it was
that was troubling him was important, Worf split his
attention, distractedly following the conversation the two
senior officers were having, and at the same time trying to
locate the source of his vexation.

Captain Sisko had returned from Bajor and briefed his
senior staff on the situation before contacting Starfleet.
Most of the officers—but for Major Kira, whose opinion
seemed to waver—had agreed that First Minister Shakaar
was making a grave error in leading his world to the brink of
battle against a superior force. Personally, Worf held Shakaar and the Bajoran people in very high esteem. He
respected their willingness to fight for that in which they
believed, as well as their strength of character in protecting
and nourishing those beliefs. By his reckoning, they were a
noble people.

Still, that was not to say that Worf approved of the first

minister's choice to peddle the data collected on *DS9* from the Gamma Quadrant. It occurred to him now that such an action was something he would sooner have expected from the unscrupulous Ferengi. But it was something more than just the uncharacteristic behavior of Shakaar, Worf knew, that was concerning him now.

"This places us in a precarious position," Worf heard Admiral Whatley intone. "With the Dominion threat, the uncertainties with the Klingons and the Cardassians, and the obvious importance and value of the wormhole, Starfleet Command—and the Federation Council—wants nothing to jeopardize our presence on *Deep Space Nine*."

"I understand that," Sisko responded, "but if the Yridians are given access to our data, there is no question that they'll sell it. Since some of the data is of strategic import, that could cause us some very serious security problems."

Whatley, a lean, slightly older man whom Worf thought frail-looking, rubbed his chin. He was a good man, but unimaginative; he could produce a cogent argument given all the facts in a situation, but his lack of intuition would not allow him to draw another, less-than-obvious conclusion from those facts. Worf would be very surprised if the admiral was able to add any new perspectives about what they were discussing.

"Mr. Worf," Whatley said at last, "what is your analysis?"

"I believe," Worf answered, "that both problems—being forced to leave *DS9* by the Bajorans if we refuse to comply with the terms of their deal with the Yridians, or being forced to grant the Yridians access to our data—are actually two sides of the same problem."

"Explain that."

"In either case," Worf said, *"Deep Space Nine*—not the Starfleet personnel here, but the actual station—is put at risk. And if the station is at risk, then so is the wormhole and so is Bajor."

"You're telling me that we mustn't select either of our two alternatives," Whatley said.

"Yes, sir," Worf replied.

"Do you have a third suggestion?"

"No," Worf said, and thought: *Leave me alone.* He

needed time to think, not about some hypothetical third option with regard to Shakaar and the data, but about what it was that was nagging at him.

"Captain?" Whatley asked, turning his attention away from Worf and back to Sisko.

"I'm not sure what else we can do," Sisko said. The captain's fingers were drumming quietly on the tabletop, Worf noticed.

"If the only other choice is for Starfleet to abandon *Deep Space Nine*," Whatley decided, "then we'll have to let the Yridians have the data."

"Understood," Sisko said, with obvious reluctance.

"But I want a third alternative before that happens," Whatley said. He did not seem pleased.

"Yes, sir."

"Keep me informed. Whatley out." On the comm panel, the Starfleet emblem replaced the visage of the admiral. The captain turned in his chair and faced Worf.

"The admiral's right," Sisko said. "We need another option; I don't like the idea of our data being on the auction block."

"I suppose," Worf offered, "we could always purchase the data ourselves." The notion of Starfleet having to buy something that was already theirs was appalling to Worf, but the situation was serious enough, he thought, to warrant such a repellent measure.

"I don't think that would do us much good," Sisko said. "I don't believe that exclusivity is an attribute of Yridian information sales."

That was true, Worf realized.

"In the meantime," Sisko went on, shifting the conversation, "we have other concerns. The new Bajoran transports will doubtless be headed out on the trade routes soon. I want you to take the *Defiant* to the blockade and seed the area with long-range sensor buoys. If somebody throws a rock out there, I want to know about it."

"Aye, sir."

As Worf rose from his chair, he saw Sisko reach for a padd sitting on the table. The captain activated the device and began studying its readout. Worf left the conference room and started down the hall for the turbolift, intending to proceed directly to *Defiant.* Before he reached the lift, though, something Sisko had just said juxtaposed itself with another fact, unexpectedly illuminating the source of Worf's disquiet. It was something the captain had mentioned earlier as well, during the briefing he had given upon his return from Bajor, but it was only now that Worf saw its significance. He quickly went back to the conference room.

"Commander?" Sisko asked when Worf reentered the room. The padd was still in his hand.

"Captain, you just said that the starships the Bajorans acquired were transports," Worf said. "I believe you also mentioned that during your briefing." Although Worf offered these as statements, his tone invited a response.

"That's right," Sisko said. "Shakaar called them 'defensive transports,' I assumed because of the added defense supplied by those huge physical shields fore and aft. Is that significant?"

"Perhaps," Worf said. He walked over to the table and sat down in the chair next to the captain. "The first minister also said that the Bajorans purchased the starships from the Yridians."

"Yes."

"But the Yridians do not manufacture vessels of any kind," Worf said.

"No, they don't," Sisko concurred. He put the padd down on the table and leaned forward in his chair, resting his elbows on his knees. "I'd had the same thought myself," he said.

"That would lead us to the conclusion that either the Yridians purchased the ships themselves from another source," Worf reasoned, "or that they merely acted as intermediaries in the deal with the Bajorans."

"That makes sense," Sisko said. He stood up and began pacing the room. His hands were clasped together in front of him, Worf saw, kneading and working against each other, almost as if the captain were trying to physically construct his chain of thought. "It's not likely that they were intermediaries," he continued. "The Bajoran payment of information is a notably Yridian requisite."

"So the Yridians took possession of the ships before selling them to the Bajorans," Worf concluded. "But these are not just any ships; they are transports—*defensive* transports—precisely the type of ships the Bajorans would need to make an attempt to run the Ferengi blockade."

"Yes," Sisko said. "Coincidence?"

"That is what troubles me," Worf said. "Could it possibly be only a coincidence that a faction who does not normally manufacture or sell starships would have starships just when the Bajorans needed them, and that those starships would be perfectly suited to the Bajorans' needs?"

"And not their usual needs, either," Sisko added. He moved over to the outer bulkhead and leaned one hand against the wall; with the other, he massaged his forehead. Finally, he turned back to Worf.

"You think somebody is manipulating events." It was not a question, but Worf nodded his assent. "Trying to instigate a war between the Bajorans and the Ferengi."

"That, but not just that," Worf said. "They are also trying to weaken the defenses of the station, either by driving Starfleet from *DS9* or by forcing us to compromise security by losing control of our data."

"All of which could leave the wormhole undefended."

"The Dominion," Worf said simply. There had long been both implicit and explicit threats of a Dominion incursion into the Alpha Quadrant.

"Maybe," Sisko said. "But the Romulans also covet the wormhole, and they are very fond of deceptions and manipulations such as these."

"That is also true of the Obsidian Order." The highly secretive, covert-operations arm of the Cardassian Union had been weakened considerably a year earlier, ambushed by the Jem'Hadar in the Omarion Nebula, but Worf believed it was only a matter of time until the organization emerged stronger than before.

"You're right," Sisko said, dropping back into his chair. "Even though the military regime on Cardassia has been deposed—perhaps *because* it has been deposed—the Order could be searching for a new path to power. Control of the wormhole—even the reoccupation of Bajor—would certainly be a means to accomplishing that."

"We must learn where the Bajoran transports came

from," Worf suggested. The captain nodded his agreement and activated his combadge.

"Sisko to Constable Odo."

"This is Odo," came the constable's immediate response.

"Meet me in my office in five minutes."

"Yes, sir. Out."

To Worf, Sisko said, "I'm going to have the constable do a little reconnaissance. Right now, your orders stand: I want those sensor buoys positioned along the Bajoran trade routes."

"Aye, sir."

Worf spun sharply on his heel and exited the conference room, not stopping this time until he reached the bridge of *Defiant*.

CHAPTER
21

Shots were fired.

Sisko was in his quarters when Kira contacted him with
the news. It had been less than a day since the defensive
transports had arrived through the wormhole, since he had
ordered Worf to string the long-range sensors near the
blockade, since he had sent Odo to learn the source of the
new Bajoran ships. So far, there had been no word from
the constable. Events were transpiring rapidly now, Sisko
felt, and yet he was not even sure of the true identity of the
enemy they were actually battling—or should be battling.
Hell, he was not even really sure that there was an enemy.
Regardless, he understood that they had to slow the progres-
sion of circumstances before their effects became irrevo-
cable.

"Ops to Captain Sisko," Kira's voice intruded into the
early-morning quiet of his quarters. Jake was in his own
bedroom, still asleep.

"Sisko here."

"Captain," Kira said, "the sensor buoys are picking up
weapons fire."

"Have the crew board the *Defiant*," Sisko responded

without hesitation. The ship, he knew, was at full readiness, maintained that way by Worf in anticipation of the incident now unfolding. "I'll meet you there, Major." He was already racing from his quarters.

"Yes, sir."

Sisko made it to the bridge of *Defiant* within three minutes. Kira had already arrived and was preparing to crew one of the secondary stations. Dax, Worf, and O'Brien were already situated at their customary consoles. Dr. Bashir loitered off to one side and observed the proceedings.

Thirty seconds after Sisko sat down in the command chair, docking clamps had been released and *Defiant* was pulling away from its berth. At the conn, Dax set a course for the source of the weapons fire. The thrum of the ship's engines surrounded them as *Defiant* came about and accelerated to full impulse speed, headed in the direction of the Bajoran trade routes.

"Report," Sisko said when the bustle of the swift departure had subsided. He looked to his first officer.

"Whatever's happening out there," Kira said, "it's happening at the very limit of the buoy's scanning range. The readings are fading in and out, but there's definitely been phaser activity."

"That would be a Marauder," Sisko said, thinking aloud. "With what intensity were the phasers fired?" As far as they knew, none of the attacks so far launched on cargo ships by the Ferengi had been of deadly force, only enough to turn the ships back on their courses. Sisko's concern, though, was that the Bajoran transports would not retreat.

"Again, because of the distance from the buoy, it's difficult to know accurately," Kira said. "But I believe—" Kira operated her console, obviously looking for the answer to Sisko's question. "—ten to twenty percent of normal."

"Sustained?"

"Intermittent."

"Do we know for sure that the Marauder is firing on a Bajoran ship?" Sisko asked.

"We have a pretty good idea," Kira said. "There's at least one of the new ships out there."

A short time later, *Defiant*'s sensor scans provided definite answers.

"I'm reading two of the new Bajoran transports," Worf said, not contradicting Kira, Sisko knew, but adding to her information. "We have passed the buoy and are now within sensor range ourselves."

Sisko gazed at the main viewer. The deep jet of infinity stared back at him, featureless but for the stars. Then, in the distance, a sharp-edged ray of light flashed in the empty desert of space—except that it was not just light, Sisko knew, but phased energy, rectified into a coherent and potentially destructive beam. *Defiant* was too far yet for the combatants to be visible on the viewer.

"The intensity of the phasers is now at forty percent," said Worf.

As *Defiant* drew nearer the scene, the three vessels—the Ferengi Marauder and the two Bajoran transports—finally began to take form on the viewer. Despite their sizable physical shields fore and aft, the transports together were not as large as the Marauder.

"The Bajoran ships don't seem to be affected by the phaser hits," O'Brien reported from his operations console. "They're continuing onward."

"How many people?" Sisko wanted to know.

"Nineteen on one transport . . . eighteen on the other," O'Brien said. After a moment, he added, "Two hundred seventy-one on the Marauder."

Suddenly, a salvo erupted from the Ferengi vessel. The Marauder surged ahead like an uncoiling snake, multiple phaser banks discharging their venom. The transports took strikes all across their forward shields, but the phaser blasts seemed to die there. For an instant, the two smaller ships appeared tethered to the larger one by the beams of light, like marionettes to a puppeteer.

"Those were full phasers," Sisko said, not needing confirmation, but receiving it anyway from Worf. Sisko wanted to order Dax to take *Defiant* in, to protect the Bajoran ships. But Resolution 49-535 demanded that he remain clear of the conflict. This was not the Federation's battle, and he had violated the Council's decree twice already. More than that, if he was to help the Bajorans, then the Ferengi would surely retract their offer to allow humanitarian aid through the blockade, which would in turn demand that somebody—the Bajorans, or more likely, Starfleet—would have to fight to deliver food and medicine to Bajor. The Bajorans were fighting right now, but if they lost this fight, they would still survive, their population would not be starved, its health would not be put in jeopardy.

"The transports' deflectors are down to sixty and fifty-seven percent," Worf said. "They are powering their disruptors."

Sisko felt as though he were watching someone leap to their death. He had granted Shakaar's assertion that the new transports might be able to withstand attack by the Ferengi Marauders, but Sisko had not really believed that possibility to exist; even if the smaller ships were somehow more powerful than the larger one, their crews would be too inexperienced to overcome their more practiced adversary.

And now the Bajorans were going to open fire on that adversary.

Sisko and his crew watched as the two transports broke from each other, moving to either side of the Marauder. To Sisko's surprise, the Ferengi ship did not alter its heading. Then, like drops of colored liquid, electric-blue moments of directed energy slipped from the transports. From each of the four corners of their forward shields, the disruptors flashed toward the Ferengi ship. The eight shots landed all over the great rounded aft section of the Marauder.

"The Ferengi deflectors are intact," Worf said. "They sustained no damage at all."

"None?" Sisko asked. "How is that possible?" Even as superior as he believed the Marauder to be, eight simultaneous disruptor blasts should have had some effect on it, if only a minor decrease in deflector power levels.

"The disruptors the transports are equipped with are of an outmoded design," O'Brien explained, studying his readouts. "They're at least two generations behind those in use now on the Klingon heavies."

On the viewer, phasers burst forth again, this time from the aft of the Marauder as it passed between the two transports. Unlike the previous attack, only one of the transports was targeted. The energy blasts buffeted its rear physical shield, continuing far longer than the previous barrages.

"The transport has lost its deflectors," Worf said.

"The Ferengi are powering up their plasma weapon," O'Brien reported.

"Captain," Kira said, spinning in her chair toward Sisko. Her voice was both urgent and beseeching.

"Hail the Ferengi," Sisko said loudly and quickly, bounding up out of the command chair.

"Hailing them," Worf said, working his instruments.

"What will a plasma strike do to a ship with no deflectors?" Sisko wanted to know.

"It won't be good," O'Brien said quietly.

"What about the physical shields?" Sisko asked, hoping more than believing. "Will they make any difference?"

"Against phasers and photon torpedoes, probably," O'Brien said. "But plasma energy weapons envelop their targets. . . ." The chief considered the possibilities. "At best, they might survive a first strike, if one of their shields can manage to take the entire attack, but the shield itself will definitely be destroyed. They'd never survive a second hit. But they might not even survive a first hit."

"Captain," Kira said again, now coming up out of her seat and taking a step away from her console. "You have to do something. There are nineteen Bajorans on that ship."

"Mr. Worf?" Sisko asked, ignoring the major's plea; he was as aware as she was of the danger to the Bajoran crews.

"No response to our hails," he answered.

Sisko looked at the main viewer. The transports had come back together again, side by side, trying to continue on their way. The Marauder, he saw, was coming about, in pursuit. He stepped over to the conn and leaned in next to Dax.

"Take us in," he said. "Interpose us between the Marauder and the transports." He stood up and turned to address all of his crew. "If the Ferengi fire their plasma weapon, I want the *Defiant* to take the blow. It could be a bumpy ride." Dr. Bashir, silent through all of this, was still very much aware of all that was happening, Sisko saw; he was paying close attention to the captain.

Defiant surged around them, leaping toward the fray.

Major Kira sat back down at her console. She appeared relieved.

Sisko was not. What he was about to do was not only a violation of Resolution 49-353, but likely to cause some very serious problems, for the Bajorans, for the Ferengi, and for the Federation. Perhaps even for the entire Alpha Quadrant, Sisko realized. But he was not going to allow nineteen people—thirty-seven, between the two transports—to be killed when he could prevent that from occurring.

I've already seen too many damn people die in my life without being able to do anything about it, he thought.

Sisko saw on the viewer that the Marauder was almost on top of the transports. He did not know why the Ferengi were waiting to fire—maybe they would destroy only one of the ships, in the belief that the other would then return to Bajor—but it was providing an opportunity for *Defiant* to move into position to protect the weaker ships.

"Moving in," Dax said.

Ahead, on the viewer, there were now only the transports; the Marauder was behind and above *Defiant*. Then, without warning, one of the transports dove away, out from *Defiant*'s protective cover.

"What are they doing?" Kira asked, clearly horrified.

As though in mute response, the other transport slid off in the opposite direction of the first. Just before it left the viewer, its disruptors issued forth once more.

"Both transports are firing," Worf said.

"Let me see," Sisko ordered.

One of the crew—probably Worf, but Sisko did not see who—operated the appropriate controls and the image on the viewer changed, revealing an incredible tableau: the overmatched transports were attacking the Marauder again. The eight disruptor blasts—four from each transport—landed this time on the same spot, near the central, aft section of the Ferengi vessel. The transports fired continuously.

"They're draining their disruptors," O'Brien said. "Their reactors are in danger of going supercritical."

The disruptors ceased, and for a moment, there was peace. Then a fusillade of photon torpedoes emerged from both transports, aimed at the focal point of the disruptor blasts on the Marauder.

Sisko heard Kira say, softly and sadly, "They don't care if they die."

"I'm reading a power surge in the Marauder's plasma weapon," O'Brien said.

"They're going to fire," Worf explained.

"Dax, get to one of the transports and shadow it," Sisko said. "We're going to save at least one of those ships." Dax did not acknowledge verbally, but set to following her orders. Standing over her, Sisko watched her expertly pilot the ship. The transports, though, were flying a randomized, serpentine course, making it virtually impossible for Dax to maneuver *Defiant* into position.

Phasers struck once more from the Marauder, first one transport, then the other.

"Deflectors have failed on the second transport," Worf said.

On the first transport, blackened metal bloomed beneath the phaser onslaught.

"Walk with the Prophets," Kira said quietly, more to herself, Sisko thought, than to her crewmates. She apparently expected the destruction of the transports at any time. So did Sisko.

"I'm reading another power surge in the Marauder," O'Brien said.

Kira dropped her head.

"The plasma weapon is off-line," Worf announced, surprise in his voice.

"No," O'Brien countered. "At least, not off-line on purpose. That's the source of the surge."

"I have it," Worf said, working his console. "It seems to be—"

"The weapon is discharging within the ship," O'Brien said.

"My god," Sisko said, understanding the horrific implications for the Ferengi. "Can we beam the crew off?"

"Negative," Worf reported. "Their deflectors are intact."

"And they're causing a feedback in the plasma emitter," O'Brien added. "There's massive radiation."

"Hail them," Sisko said. "Offer our assistance."

"The warp drive just went down," Kira said.

"No response," Worf said.

"Keep trying."

As Sisko watched the main viewer, he saw the Ferengi vessel die. It had been coasting through space, powered and directed, and then its speed fell off, its attitude skewed, and it became immediately clear that there was no longer anybody at the helm.

The transports had evidently not been prepared for what had happened. As the Marauder began to drift, the port side of the aft section struck one of the smaller ships. But the transport was moving under its own power, and the Ferengi vessel canted off its forward physical shield.

The two transports arced around to their original course. Somehow, they had run the blockade. Once clear of Bajoran space, Sisko knew, they would go to warp, headed for a destination of which he was unaware.

"How bad is it?" Sisko asked.

"Bad," O'Brien said. "The radiation is making it difficult to get readings . . . life-support is fluctuating . . . the warp core assembly's been destroyed; I'm surprised there wasn't a core breach."

"Life signs?"

"I'm having trouble getting a fix," O'Brien said. "We need to compensate for the radiation—"

"I've got it, Chief," Kira said, operating the controls at her console. "Adjusting for the increased levels of—" Kira stopped abruptly. Sisko, still standing beside the conn, swung around to look at her. Her face, he saw, was ashen.

"Major?" he asked. "How many left alive?"

Her eyes looked empty to Sisko when she answered: "None."

CHAPTER

22

THERE WAS SILENCE on the bridge of *Defiant*.

Julian watched as Captain Sisko walked sluggishly back to the command chair and fell into it. Dax turned at her console and watched the captain too. O'Brien, Worf, Kira—their eyes also found their commanding officer and did not leave him. It seemed to Julian that they were all waiting for something, though no order, no word, could mitigate the devastating loss of life they had just witnessed.

Slowly, Julian made his way over to Kira's console. She looked up at him when he approached. The muscles of her face were tensed, he saw, lending her a pained aspect.

"I'd like to see," Julian told her, so quietly that she did not hear him and he had to repeat himself. Kira moved to the side to allow Julian to stand next to her at her station. He leaned in and examined the readouts.

"How did this happen?" Dax asked at last, apparently of everybody.

Or perhaps of nobody, Julian thought. He looked up for a moment and saw the captain shake his head from side to side.

"I thought it was the Bajoran ships that needed protecting," Sisko said. The irony was evidently agonizing for him.

It was agonizing for everybody, Julian thought.

"It should have been that way," the chief offered. "Those transports were not the better of that Marauder."

"I agree," Worf said. "Their choice to bombard the section of the Ferengi vessel that housed the plasma weapon was a wise tactical maneuver, but it should not have worked."

"But it did, Mr. Worf," Sisko said resignedly. "It did."

"But it shouldn't have," Worf reiterated. He stood up and moved from his console over to the captain. "Starfleet has had numerous encounters with this class of Ferengi Marauder over the years. The machinery of their plasma weapon is well shielded; even *Defiant*'s quantum torpedoes should not have been able to accomplish what the outdated weapons of those transports just did."

"And yet they did," Sisko replied, his voice rising in frustration. "How do you explain that?"

"That's just it, sir," the chief said from his console. "We can't."

"So what does that mean?" Sisko demanded.

"It means," Dax said calmly, "that something is wrong." She paused, and Julian suspected that she was searching for a rational theory to expound. Finally, she said, "The Ferengi ship could have been sabotaged."

"Sabotaged?" Sisko asked. "By who? For what purpose?"

"I don't know," Dax said, "but where are the other Marauders from the blockade? Wouldn't you expect a ship in trouble to call for help?"

"Perhaps they didn't realize they were in trouble until it was too late," Sisko hypothesized, but it did not sound to Julian as though he had much confidence in what he was saying.

"Perhaps," Dax said.

"Captain," Julian said.

"Yes, Doctor?"

"I'm not convinced that these sensor readings are entirely accurate," Julian reported. "Major Kira cleaned up the scans considerably, but with this type of radiation, in such concentrated amounts, I think it's possible that we might be missing something."

"Are you suggesting that there might still be people alive aboard that ship?" Sisko wanted to know.

"It's possible," Julian said. "Probably not more than a handful, though, otherwise we would be getting some indication of life over there."

"Do you think anybody could have survived such high doses of radiation?" the chief asked.

"As Mr. Worf indicated, some areas of the ship are better shielded than others," Julian replied. Then, to Sisko, he said, "If there are survivors, they've probably been critically injured, but regardless, they probably wouldn't last very long on that ship, irradiated as it is."

"What do you recommend, Doctor?" Sisko asked. "Even if we could get a fix on their life signs, we couldn't beam them over; their deflectors are still operating."

"I could take a shuttle over," Julian said. "I couldn't board the Marauder because of the radiation, but proximate scans of the ship would tell us for sure whether or not there's anybody left alive. We could breach the deflectors and transport survivors into a quarantine field set up on the shuttle."

The captain took very little time to consider the issue before responding.

"Do it," he said.

Da Vinci slipped from its berth easily and moved out into space.

Unlike most of Starfleet's vessels, *Defiant* did not have a shuttlebay, nor did it carry a fleet of small, short-range craft. *Defiant* had been designed as a battleship, and so, with no cargo- or passenger-related duties in its future, and no scientific mission profiles, it had been reasoned that there would be little or no need for shuttles. *Defiant* had only two, each maintained in its own small, fitted dock on the underside of the vessel.

This was the first time that Julian had been inside one of *Defiant*'s shuttles. He noticed immediately that *da Vinci* was neither as large nor as sophisticated as *Deep Space*

Nine's runabouts. Still, it would suffice in letting him perform his search and—he hoped—rescue.

Chief O'Brien was piloting *da Vinci*. His fingers moved deftly across the flight controls as he brought the shuttle away from *Defiant* and onto a course for the Marauder. Julian sat beside him, configuring the shuttle's sensors for the scan of the Ferengi vessel. Through the forward windows of the shuttle, Julian watched the Ferengi vessel slide into view.

"So," the chief asked, "what do you think the chances are?"

"Of finding anybody alive?" Julian considered this. The levels of radiation that prevented an exhaustive sensor scan also made it unlikely that very many had survived aboard the Marauder. At the same time, the vessel's large size and its many bulkheads and different degrees of shielding made it possible that some small number of people had escaped death. "Maybe five percent," Julian decided. "If we do find anybody over there, though, they're likely to be suffering from serious radiation trauma."

"What a horrible way to go," the chief said.

"It is one of the more gruesome ways," Julian agreed, though somewhat distractedly. "Where are the controls for the emergency transporters?" he asked, having searched a second time across the console without finding them.

"Back there," the chief said, cocking his head toward the rear of the compartment. "On the bulkhead to the aft section."

The shuttle, compact though it was, was divided into two compartments. The rear, Julian discovered when he rose and examined it, contained the emergency transporter. He found the controls and set up a quarantine field to prevent their own exposure to radiation should they transport aboard any survivors.

When he was done, Julian returned to his seat. The Marauder, he saw, had grown larger in the forward windows, dwarfing *da Vinci*. They were close enough now that he could make out the alien-looking markings of the Ferengi language on the hull, arranged in their odd, branching patterns, flowchart-like.

"Matching velocities," the chief said. Since the Ferengi

vessel was drifting, Julian knew, it was necessary to synchronize *da Vinci's* lateral movement as the shuttle approached.

Their plan was to penetrate the deflector shields surrounding the Marauder. They would trace a path along the exterior structure of the vessel, with Julian scanning for signs of life. If they located any, they would transport the survivors into the quarantine field on *da Vinci,* then withdraw from within the Marauder's deflectors and beam the survivors to *Defiant.*

"One hundred meters to the deflectors," the chief announced. The Marauder filled the windows. Julian could not see open space past it. "Fifty . . . twenty-five . . . ten."

There was a slight shimmy as the shuttle contacted the Marauder's deflectors. Julian reached for the controls to initiate the sensor scan. And then, without warning, *da Vinci* was thrown violently, hurtling upward and to port. Julian came out of his chair, flying across the cabin until he struck the port bulkhead. His head hit the ceiling, but only a glancing blow; he absorbed most of the impact with his left shoulder, which he felt give way. He thought he could hear his bones fracture, although that must have been impossible with the many alarms now shrieking their warnings inside the shuttle. The interior lights blinked several times, then went out completely, replaced a moment later by the red hues of the emergency lighting.

Julian's knee twisted as he collapsed onto the floor—striking a chair on the way down, he thought. Later, he would learn that his knee had actually been injured when it had pounded into the chief's head.

Before he passed out, Julian's gaze passed across the forward windows. The Marauder seemed to be moving away from *da Vinci,* although his dimming mind told him that it must really have been the shuttle's own movement which caused this illusion.

But how could the Marauder look so much smaller so quickly? he wondered idly. It was his last thought before his mind faded to blackness.

Dax saw it first.

"It's moving," she said.

On the main viewer, *da Vinci* was approaching the Marauder. The massive Ferengi vessel, only a moment before drifting through space without engine power, had abruptly stopped its unchecked momentum. It turned slowly, as though being directed onto a new course.

"What's happening out there?" Sisko asked.

"I'm not reading any active drive systems," Worf said. "Not even thrusters."

The shuttle, Dax saw, was staying with the larger vessel. Its relative position beside the Marauder was probably being maintained automatically, she guessed, to account for the Marauder's drift. As close as *da Vinci* was now to the Ferengi vessel, Julian and the chief would likely not be able to perceive the new movement because, with respect to the Marauder, their position would not be changing.

"Well, something's going on," Sisko said. "Raise the shuttle."

Before Worf could even respond to the captain, the Marauder started away. The shuttle, partially through the larger ship's deflectors, was pulled along briefly, and then its mass was too much for the deflectors to bear under the Marauder's increasing acceleration. *Da Vinci* sheared off as the Ferengi vessel adjusted its heading. The shuttle tumbled away.

"Dax," Sisko said. He did not have to give the order for her to set *Defiant* in pursuit of the errant shuttle.

"Worf, can you raise them?"

"There is no response," Worf answered.

"*Da Vinci*'s inertial dampers are fluctuating," Kira reported, now stationed at the operations console. "Power is unstable . . . life-support is in and out. . . ."

"I do read two life signs," Worf said.

"Coming up on them," Dax said.

"Tractor beam," Sisko ordered.

"Aye," Worf said, working his controls.

"Get them slowly, Mr. Worf," Sisko said. "We don't want to send the chief and the doctor slamming into a bulkhead."

"Aye."

On the viewer, a thin beam of light-blue energy lanced out from *Defiant* and intersected the toppling shuttle. As Worf increased the intensity of the beam, its color grew more intense, and the shuttle slowed its end-over-end motion. Finally, *da Vinci* was brought to a complete stop.

"Transporter Room One," Sisko called.

"Transporter Room One," came the voice of the young man stationed there. Ensign Phlugg, Dax thought it was.

"Beam Chief O'Brien and Dr. Bashir from the shuttle directly to sickbay," Sisko ordered. "Commander Worf will provide coordinates."

"Yes, sir," Phlugg replied.

Worf operated his tactical console, no doubt transferring the transporter coordinates. Everybody on the bridge watched the image of the snared shuttle on the viewer and waited.

"Transporter Room to Captain Sisko," came Ensign Phlugg's voice after a few seconds. "They're aboard."

"Acknowledged," Sisko said. Then, "Mr. Worf, bring the shuttle aboard."

"Aye, sir." On the viewer, the tractor beam began to reel in *da Vinci*.

"Dax," Sisko said, "once we've retrieved the shuttle, I want to find that Marauder."

Ten minutes later, *da Vinci* had been hauled back aboard, and *Defiant* started in pursuit of the mysterious Ferengi vessel.

When Julian regained consciousness, he was in *Defiant*'s sickbay, being ministered to by nurse Taren, the newest member of his medical staff. The nurse was a tall man, with hair down to his shoulders and with, Julian thought, a surly countenance and a terrible bedside manner.

"Oh, you're awake," the nurse said, with what could only be termed as displeasure.

"Yes, I am," said Julian, and he propped himself up on his elbows. He was lying on a medical diagnostic pallet, and the nurse, standing over him, tried to restrain him with a hand to his chest. He need not have: Julian quickly found that he was not going anywhere; the quick movement ignited a dull ache in his head and a sharper pain in his left shoulder. He lowered himself back down. "What happened?" he groaned.

"What happened," the nurse said, looking down at Julian

with obvious forbearance, "is that you injured yourself in a shuttle mishap. When you were brought in here, you were suffering a mild concussion, a fractured clavicle, and a sprained knee. I have fixed the concussion and the sprain, but I am still working on repairing your shoulder. If you think you can lie still long enough, that is."

"I meant, what happened to the shuttle?"

"I'm a nurse," the man said, "not an engineer."

"How's Miles?" Julian asked.

"If you're referring to the chief engineer, he was a much better patient than you," the nurse said, "because he only woke up after I'd finished working on him."

"You don't have to be so churlish," Julian said.

The nurse looked at him for a moment, then lifted a hypospray from a table beside the pallet.

"When I said you needed to lie still," the nurse said, holding up the hypospray threateningly, "I meant that you needed to be quiet as well. Or do you require sedation?"

Julian considered ordering the nurse out of sickbay, but then decided against doing so; his shoulder was in pain, and he really did require medical attention.

"I'll be quiet," Julian acquiesced.

"Good," the nurse said. He put the hypospray down, picked up another instrument, and began to work on Julian's shoulder.

Dax executed the search protocols not once, but twice. *Defiant* covered a lot of territory, even doubling back on the path the seemingly disabled Marauder had taken to be sure that it had not reversed its heading. They found nothing but the other Ferengi ships that composed the blockade.

Dax had Worf download the logs of the sensor buoys strung along the Bajoran trade routes, but wherever the Marauder had gone had been beyond the range of those scans.

Obviously frustrated by the burgeoning mass of unexplained events, Captain Sisko ordered Dax to set a course for *Defiant* back to *Deep Space Nine*.

CHAPTER
23

EVEN REPLAYED on the small screen of a padd, Sisko found the victory of the Bajoran transports over the Ferengi Marauder larger than life. In the sitting area of his office on *DS9*, he sought to discover some explanation for the unlikely incident. In his hands, the three vessels danced across the display amid columns of text and numbers: velocities, deflector intensities, weapons power levels, and the like. Chief O'Brien had downloaded the pictures and measurements for the captain from *Defiant*'s sensor logs.

Once *Defiant* had returned to the station, Sisko had attempted to contact Bractor aboard *Kreechta* to inform him of the battle and its result, hoping both to assess the potential impact of the Bajoran attack and to ascertain what might have happened to the now-vanished Marauder. More than that, really, Sisko was trying to fit together all the inexplicable pieces of what had recently become a large and confusing puzzle. After what had just occurred out on the Bajoran trade routes, he was becoming fully convinced of Worf's suspicions that some unknown faction was manipulating circumstances.

On the padd, phaser fire streaked through space. Sisko

had reviewed the recording twice already and had just begun to play it through a third time when Major Kira's voice broke the silence in the room.

"Ops to Captain Sisko."

"Sisko here," he returned.

"We're receiving a transmission for you from DaiMon Bractor," Kira informed him.

"Thank you, Major," Sisko said, rising and walking across the office toward the wall-mounted comm panel. "Put it through." As he passed in front of his desk, he put the padd down on it.

On the comm panel, the image of Bractor appeared. The Ferengi captain spoke loudly, with no introductory civilities.

"The nagus agrees to let Bajor receive medicine and food, in spite of our blockade, and this is how he's repaid?"

"Then you know about the encounter with the transports?" Sisko asked. He was surprised; neither *Defiant*'s sensor logs nor those of the buoys had indicated any transmissions to or from the ill-fated Marauder. Sisko had assumed that the individual Ferengi ships constituting the blockade maintained regular contact with each other, and that Bractor would therefore be aware that one of those ships was now a casualty—or at least missing—but he did not understand how Bractor could know specifically about the battle that had been fought.

"Of course we know about the *Neemis*," Bractor said, apparently identifying the ship that the transports had defeated.

"But how do you know about it?" Sisko wanted to know.

"What do you mean?" Bractor asked. He seemed genuinely bewildered by the question. "I was aware of the attack as it happened."

"I see," Sisko said, taking a couple of paces away from the comm panel as he considered that. Out of the corner of his eye, he saw movement; when he looked toward his desk, he saw that the recording of the battle was still playing on the padd. It was possible, Sisko supposed, that the long-range sensors of another Ferengi vessel might have detected the action, but—

"If you knew about it," Sisko asked, "then why didn't any of the ships in the blockade come to the aid of the *Neemis?*"

"A *D'Kora*-class Marauder would not require any assistance to defeat two of those new Bajoran vessels," Bractor said.

"Tell me something then," Sisko said, wondering if perhaps the daiMon had just given something away. "How do you know about Bajor's new ships?"

"You told me about them yourself, when you wanted my help in defending *Deep Space Nine* against them."

"Of course," Sisko said, but he was sure that Bractor was prevaricating in some way. Sisko had talked with him in generalities about the previously unknown ships as they had approached the wormhole in the Gamma Quadrant, but he had not known himself at the time that the ships had been purchased by the Bajorans. Nor had he had any notion of the capabilities of those ships. The daiMon must have had some additional source of information.

"I would have sent another ship to fight," Bractor continued, "if I'd known that the Federation was going to become involved."

Sisko felt a jolt of emotion pulse through him.

"Are you making an accusation, daiMon?" Sisko demanded, stepping back up to the companel.

"Sensor records show the *Defiant* entering the field of battle with the Bajoran vessels," Bractor revealed.

"What sensor records?" Sisko knew that long-range scans would not have been capable of recording the details of the engagement.

"Those from the *Neemis,* of course," Bractor answered, although Sisko did not consider that answer to be a mere matter of course.

"You recovered the ship, then?"

"The handful of survivors did," Bractor replied. "They brought the *Neemis* back to the blockade. A scout ship is taking it under tow back to Ferenginar."

"We read no life signs after the battle," Sisko said. He knew that those readings might not have been accurate— that they obviously had not been accurate—but he wanted to learn as much as could about what had transpired.

"Is that why the survivors reported an attempt to board their ship?" Bractor asked.

"We were searching for survivors," Sisko said, a little more defensively than he had intended.

"I thought you said your scans showed no signs of life aboard the *Neemis,*" Bractor charged.

Sisko laughed. The conversation felt as though it had been scripted. He was being maneuvered, he understood that, but he was not sure why.

"I didn't realize that a ship of dead Ferengi was funny," Bractor said icily.

He plays his part well, thought Sisko. He looked across millions of kilometers of space and tried to appraise the daiMon. Bractor met his gaze.

After a moment, Sisko went over to his desk and retrieved the padd. The end of the battle was nearing on the display, he saw. He froze the picture and moved back to the comm panel.

"Would you like to see the *Defiant's* sensor logs?" he asked, holding the padd up for Bractor to see. "We were unsure of them because of the high levels of radiation; we couldn't tell whether or not there were survivors, but we wanted to rescue any if there were."

"We have our own sensor logs," Bractor told him. "The radiation levels on the *Neemis* damaged them, but when the ship reaches Ferenginar, technicians will attempt to recover all of their data."

"I see."

"I hope that you do, Captain," Bractor said, menace now evident in his voice. "Because if a full review of the logs shows that the *Defiant* was directly involved in the annihilation of more than two hundred and fifty Ferengi, there will be grave consequences."

"I don't like threats, Bractor," Sisko said. "And the logs will demonstrate that the *Defiant* did not fire on the Marauder."

"I hope that turns out to be the case," Bractor said. "But we both know that the sensor logs *will* implicate the Bajorans in the deaths of the *Neemis's* crew; they will have to pay for that." The daiMon gestured to somebody off-screen, and the communication abruptly ended.

For a couple of minutes, Sisko stood and stared at the Ferengi emblem on the comm panel, his hands clasped before his face, his fingers steepled together. So much had happened, he thought; so much was still happening. There must be something here, some underlying pattern or link that bound all of these disparate events together. He was sure of it now, and yet he still could not see it.

Sisko parted his hands, reached over to the comm panel, and deactivated it. Then he tapped his comm badge.

"Sisko to Commander Worf," he said.

"Worf here."

"Commander, I want you to find out all you can about the Ferengi Marauder *Neemis.*"

CHAPTER
24

THERE WAS NO ONE in the hold to see the cargo container melt.

The cube, a meter on each side, was covered in the complex ideogrammatic symbols of the Bajorans: weight, mass, destination, contents. This particular container, like several others about it, was apparently headed for Johnson City on Gamma Hydra IV, carrying a shipment of hand-made Bajoran *Muriniri* dolls. The other cargo that had been loaded into this hold was of a similar nature, all various arts and crafts produced in several different provinces on Bajor.

The container of *Muriniri* dolls had been packed into a shuttle on the planet's surface and carried into orbit, where it had then been conveyed onto one of the transports purchased from the Yridians, which would haul it to its intended destination. The dolls—the entire shipment, in fact—would normally have been loaded onto the ship with the use of a transporter, but since all of the items had been fashioned by hand, it was consequently necessary that they be delivered by hand. In general, when people purchased goods noteworthy because they had been handcrafted, they wanted them to remain handcrafted, not converted into energy and then reconstituted by a transporter into its initial material form; if that were acceptable, then a would-be buyer could simply create such goods by employing a replicator.

Workers had just finished filling this cargo hold, though there were a few other holds on the transport yet to be loaded. When that had been done, the ship's manifest would be verified against the actual shipment, and if the container of *Muriniri* dolls was still here, then it would be found to be the twin of another stored on board. And if that happened, then the true identity of the duplicate container would be revealed.

The tone of the container's olive-green casing shifted, slipped through yellow to a shimmering orange that appeared almost metallic. It lost its solid form, liquefying as though from being heated, flowed with the artificial gravity of the ship down to the decking, and upward, directed, into humanoid form.

Odo did not hesitate, but raced through the hold toward the doors of the turbolift. He softened the soles of his feet as he ran, deadening the sound of his footfalls. His movements were so quiet that they did not even generate echoes.

The lift connected this hold with each of the others, Odo presumed, and with the small crew-and-control section mounted atop the larger cargo section. But it was not the lift in which Odo was interested; it was the computer station situated beside it.

For the moment, though, he ignored the computer. Instead, he pressed his hands against the door, his fingers splayed. Feeling no vibrations, he let his hands go, let them become the essence of what he was. The tips of his fingers rippled radiantly, and downward to his wrists, the effect was the same, that part of his being reverting to its unaltered form. With his changeling flesh, he listened without hearing, felt without touching, sensed what he could sense on the other side of the door.

Odo could tell—from sounds, from vibrations—that the turbolift was not in motion at the moment. Somewhere above, there were voices, but their owners were not moving—at least, not in this direction. Satisfied, he solidified his hands back to humanoid form and turned his attention to the computer.

Fortunately, Odo saw, the station was already operating; he would therefore not alert anybody to his presence by having to activate it. He examined the readout and saw what he quickly ascertained to be the manifest for this hold, displayed in the Bajoran language. He looked at it in a cursory fashion, verified that it was what it appeared to be, and moved on.

He next checked the transport's schedule, determining that the ship would be departing Bajor in less than three hours. Odo did not know exactly what he was searching for—something, anything, that would indicate the actual source of this ship, of all the ships the Bajorans had just purchased—but he knew he would have to search swiftly. He flew inward momentarily and willed two additional digits onto each of his hands, something he often did when his work on a computer or a companel required speed. He could shapeshift more than seven fingers onto each hand, of course, or even a third arm and hand, but he found that it was with this combination that he was most dexterous.

This was the second transport that Odo had infiltrated— well, perhaps *infiltrated* was the wrong word. After all, he had not stolen onto this ship; he had been carried aboard. That he had misrepresented himself—as a container of *Muriniri* dolls—was really irrelevant. Captain Sisko might have had a difficult time justifying Odo's actions, but then the good captain had neither inquired about nor restricted Odo's methods when he had assigned him the task of uncovering the origin of the transports. There was a tacit agreement between the two, Odo believed, allowing the constable a great deal of latitude in the performance of his job. Exploring the computers aboard the transports surely fell within those bounds.

Odo worked the controls, his fourteen digits an exemplar of manual coordination. The constant tapping was the only sound in the cargo hold; it reminded Odo of rainfall, something he had not heard recently, but which he had heard often during his youth at the Bajoran Institute of

Science. Unexpectedly, he felt a sudden stab of emotion, a mixture of reminiscence and loneliness.

Odo's fingers paused for a moment. Absently, he gazed around the hold, and then realized he was making sure that nobody was watching him—not because of his unauthorized presence here, but because he had been embarrassed by his unanticipated feelings. He shook his head once, exasperated with himself, and returned to his work.

Data marched across the computer's readout. Odo looked at the manifests for the other holds, at the crew roster, at the depressurization instructions for certain cargoes, at the deflector specifications. The computer lay open to him. He had learned almost everything he knew about computer operations during his service on *Deep Space Nine*—and Terok Nor—first from the Cardassians, and later from Chief O'Brien. Mostly, he had learned—though he could not conceive of a time when he might admit this aloud—by observing Quark.

For the first time in a while, Odo thought of his former nemesis. After the removal of Quark and Rom from *DS9*, Odo had on several occasions made discreet inquiries regarding their status. He had been startled when he had learned that they would not be standing trial, but would instead be held indefinitely as enemies of the state. Odo had intended to find out where they were jailed, but he had not yet done so. He errantly considered probing the transport's computer for information about Quark, but there was no reason at all to think he would find anything. In fact, Odo was not even sure if he would know how to render Quark's name in the Bajoran language.

Abruptly, Odo's many fingers stopped their frenzied movements across the console of the computer station. An idea had developed in his mind. He rapidly evaluated the path he would have to take through the computer to reach what he wanted to inspect, then just as rapidly executed the commands that would take him down that path.

And there it was, in among the base entries, a clue that pointed to somebody other than the Yridians as the source of the transports. The language in which the computer both accepted input and produced output was Bajoran, but the default language setting had been overridden to effectuate this. The default setting, though, was neither Bajoran nor Yridian. What it was made no immediate sense to Odo, but he had hopes that it was the key Sisko had sent him to find.

CHAPTER
25

"THE KAREMMA?"

Dax's voice was rife with either confusion or disbelief, Sisko could not tell which. He glanced across the conference table at his science officer and thought he saw revealed in her face the qualities that he himself was feeling right now: frustration, impotence, even defeat. How many more events were going to occur for which he and his crew could find no suitable explanation? As the Bajorans hurtled toward a major confrontation with the Ferengi, Sisko feared that his own failure to fully understand everything that was taking place would prevent him from helping Bajor avoid disaster.

"The Karemma," Odo repeated with the verbal equivalent of a shrug. What he had learned aboard the transport apparently did not make sense to him either.

Sisko looked over to Kira and Worf, their reflections inverted in front of them in the black surface of the table. He saw no indication that either officer had formed any reasonable interpretation of Odo's discovery. It seemed that every new piece of information, every new incident, brought with it new mysteries.

"The notion that the Karemma provided ships to the

Bajorans, or even to the Yridians . . ." Sisko's voice trailed off to silence. The conference room seemed to close in on him, stifling him. He would rather have been somewhere else, doing something—anything at all—that would actually have made a difference to the people of Bajor. Here, he felt confined, his actions removed from events, futile. But what else was there to do right now?

"It doesn't fit," Kira said. "As far as we know, the Karemma have no trade agreements with the Yridians, and they certainly don't have any with Bajor."

"Nor do the Karemma manufacture starships," Worf added.

"So if we do assume that it was the Karemma who provided the transports to the Bajorans," Sisko said, exasperated, "then we're left with the same questions as when we assumed that the Yridians were the source of the ships." Sisko was also convinced that Shakaar had not lied to him, and that consequently, the transports *must* have come from the Yridians.

"Maybe we're looking at this backward," Dax suggested. She leaned forward, resting her forearms flat on the surface of the table. "Maybe whoever produced the transports produced them specifically *for* the Karemma."

"The economy of the Karemma is dominated by trade," Sisko said, considering the idea. "Transports would be a commodity they would purchase."

"And that would explain why the default language setting of the computer was theirs," Kira noted.

"All right," Sisko said. He stood up and walked along one side of the table. "But if the ships were built for the Karemma, then why were they given—or sold, or traded—to the Yridians?"

"Because," Dax said slowly, evidently reasoning aloud, "the Yridians have a relationship with Bajor; they could let them know the ships were available, and then get the ships to them. And the Bajorans obviously have something the Yridians want."

"Our data," Odo said.

Sisko reached the other end of the table and stopped. His head had begun to pound, an occurrence he was coming to expect these days.

Is there something here, he wanted to know, *or are we just looking for light in a black hole?*

"What that doesn't tell us," he said, "is why ships manufactured for the Karemma were not sold to the Karemma." He turned toward the table to face his crew. "Can we conclude, though, that somebody—whoever provided the ships to the Yridians so that the Yridians could then sell them to the Bajorans—can we conclude that they are trying to manipulate the Bajorans into a battle with the Ferengi?"

"It looks that way, Benjamin," Dax said, and no one disagreed. "And there could be any number of reasons why: to weaken or destroy Bajor, or *Deep Space Nine,* or even the Ferengi."

"If we're to stop this from happening," Sisko said, "we need to know *who* is behind it."

"It is unlikely that any such plot would be masterminded by the Yridians or the Karemma," Worf declared. "For one thing, neither have the military capability of occupying Bajor or defending the wormhole."

"Then obviously it must be somebody else," Sisko said.

He gazed around at his officers and, from their nods, saw that there was a consensus that some other faction must be responsible. The problem, he knew, was that the potential culprits were plentiful—the Founders, the Klingons, the Cardassians, the Romulans, even the Tholians—but there was no indication whatsoever that any of these were in any manner involved in what had been happening.

Sisko was therefore surprised when, five minutes later, a possible answer arrived with Chief O'Brien.

The doors to the conference room parted and O'Brien entered. He carried a padd in one hand.

"Chief," Sisko greeted him. He was once again seated at the head of the table. "How are you feeling after your tumble through space?"

"Still a little bit like I've been hit in the head by a runabout," O'Brien said, but with a smile that belied any pain he might be feeling. "Of course, it just turned out to be Julian's knee."

"How is the doctor?" Sisko asked.

"Oh, he's fine, though I think both of us might have headaches for a couple of days."

"Try being the captain," Sisko joked. The chief chuckled, and Kira and Dax smiled, Sisko saw, but neither Worf nor Odo changed their dour expressions. "So, you said you'd be late because you were investigating something."

"Yes, sir," O'Brien said, his demeanor immediately becoming professional. "When I was getting checked out in the infirmary and talking with Dr. Bashir, he recalled that he was in the process of activating the sensors aboard the *da Vinci* just as we passed through the Marauder's deflectors."

"When the shuttle was thrown off into space," Kira said.

"Right," the chief confirmed. "So I decided to check the *da Vinci*'s sensor logs—" As he spoke, O'Brien moved to the comm panel set into the wall beside the doors. "—and sure enough, for seventy-one-hundredths of a second before the Marauder moved away, the sensors were functioning." He activated the comm panel with a touch, then worked its controls. Data regarding the Ferengi ship appeared on the display. Sisko stood from his chair and walked over beside the chief to get a better view.

"Are you sure this scan is from the *da Vinci*," Sisko asked after a minute, "and not some jumbled sensor data from the *Defiant?*"

"Positive. After I downloaded the data and saw the results, I went aboard the shuttle and verified it personally. That's where I was just now."

Sisko peered again at the data. For two-thirds of the short scan, the log showed everything they had read aboard *Defiant:* a plasma discharge within the Marauder, a failure of the warp drive, extreme radiation, and no life signs. But there was more. For almost the last twenty hundredths of a second, the log reflected a scan of a starship with most of its systems in nominal condition; only minute, expected levels of radiation; and a crew complement of two hundred seventy-one healthy Ferengi.

"How can that be?" Dax asked after the chief had reviewed the data aloud.

"I can't tell for sure," O'Brien said, "but my best guess is that the first set of readings—the one indicating a wrecked ship—is counterfeit."

"The deflectors," Worf said. He rose from his chair and walked over to the comm panel. He pointed to the latter section of the readings, to a measure of the condition of the deflectors; it was one of the few systems not listed as operating at peak capacity. "When we were scanning from the *Defiant* during the battle, we were surprised that the phaser strikes on the Marauder did not diminish its deflector performance. Here, though—" He tapped a figure listed on the comm panel. "—we see that the deflectors are operating at ninety-one percent of normal. That supports the chief's conclusion that this second set of readings is accurate; our scans did not pick it up, though, because we were being fed false readings."

"It makes sense," Dax offered.

"So the Ferengi wanted us to think the transports had beaten the Marauder and killed its crew?" Kira asked.

"And they left so that the *da Vinci* wouldn't discover the truth," Sisko said. He gestured at the comm panel. "Except they waited a fraction of a second too long."

"But why?" Kira wanted to know.

"Whatever the reason, it must involve profit," Odo said cynically.

"I'm sure it does," Sisko agreed. "And I think the profit might just be the wormhole, and maybe even Bajor itself."

"What?" Kira seemed outraged at the possibility.

"Consider it," Sisko said. He moved over to the table and leaned over it, propping himself on his hands. O'Brien and Worf came over from the comm panel and stood off to either side, watching and listening to him. "The Ferengi staged this battle—" He pointed his thumb back over his shoulder at the readout. "—to make it appear as though the Bajorans were instigating the fighting, not them. *And* they have the crew of the *Defiant* as witnesses to the event."

"So if they choose to," Dax said, "they can use this incident as justification to attack Bajor itself."

"Oh, I think they'll attack," Sisko said, wondering if perhaps this is what this situation had been leading up to all along. "This is the one way the Ferengi believed they could be absolutely sure that the Federation wouldn't defend Bajor: if the Bajorans themselves were the aggressors."

"That also might explain why the nagus consented to

allowing humanitarian aid to be sent to Bajor through the blockade," Odo suggested.

"So that he and the Ferengi could look like the good guys," Kira said disgustedly.

"Well that might explain this, then." The chief took a step toward the table and held the padd he was carrying out to Sisko. "This arrived from Starfleet just before I came down here. It's the report Mr. Worf requested on the Ferengi Marauder *Neemis*." Sisko took the short report and quickly read it.

"What does it say?" Kira asked.

"It says that the starship *Neemis*," Sisko said, looking up from the padd, "is one of Grand Nagus Zek's personal honor guard."

CHAPTER
26

ROM LAY ON the hard surface of his bunk, shivering. He was always cold now, there was no respite from it. And he no longer thought that there ever would be.

Each day, each night, of the past few weeks, the temperature had continued to descend, and the winds had grown so strong that they routinely penetrated the poorly constructed, badly maintained barracks. Snows had buried the brittle land, and daylight hours had grown short beneath a perpetually slate-gray sky—although most days remained emotionally protracted. But as cruel as the Bajoran winter had become, it was not the cold that shook Rom so violently right now; it was fear.

Hugging himself, he rocked back and forth, trying to get warm, yes, but also trying somehow to will to his brother what little strength lingered in his own now-frail body. Quark had been gone for a while, and as his time away from the barracks increased, so too did Rom's conviction that he would never return. Rom attempted to persuade himself that his brother had been placed in the small cell in which one or another of the prisoners were occasionally confined, that he was being punished by separation and isolation for some real or invented violation of the rules, it no longer mattered which. He tried to convince himself of that, but he knew that was not why Wyte had come to take Quark.

What was it? Rom asked himself. *Three hours? Four?* Such measures of time were impossible to reckon anymore; there were only days and nights, marching and recuperation, hunger and scraps, pain and numbness. But sometime today, after the prisoners had come back to the barracks after trudging around the camp through the snow, Wyte had appeared and taken Quark. That was bad, being taken by Wyte, but it was survivable. This time, though, Wyte had said that he was taking Quark to see Colonel Mitra.

Through the duration of Rom's internment in Gallitep, Mitra had never once touched him—had never touched any of the internees, as far as he knew—but the colonel had often directed Wyte to do so. It had not happened immediately upon their arrival here, but only after they had been designated political prisoners, and only after they had been enervated by days—weeks? months?—of physical hardship. It had been then that Mitra had begun having his "sessions" with each of the prisoners. It was, Rom feared, where Quark was now.

During these sessions, the colonel's instructions to Wyte were meticulous, and they bespoke a knowledge of anatomy and torture that was as remarkable for its magnitude as it was for its savagery. The pain Mitra bid Wyte to inflict, layered as it was on top of exhaustion and hunger and despair, was excruciating. But for all of that, it did not last. As with almost anything else, Rom discovered, he could become accustomed to pain—and after a while, nerves became deadened, desensitized to what otherwise would have been mounting agony.

But there was more than mere physical abuse. Colonel Mitra talked, and when he talked, he was no longer a separate person, no longer outside of you. When Mitra talked, he got inside, burrowed his way in, somehow, ferreted about until he unearthed what you had within yourself that could wound and be wounded. Reapplied though they were by another, those reopened wounds carried the torment of self-infliction. Mitra became a bad dream recalling all the ills of life, became a shadow play of personal tragedies once believed outgrown or forgotten. And there was little salve for such anguish, because even when the colonel was gone, what he had said, what he had reminded you of, what he had raised from your depths, was all still there, still true. Whether Mitra had ever lived or not, the memory he had raked from you was still an ugly, extant thing that could eat away who you were. Rom had come to think of Mitra as a devourer of souls, perhaps filling the empty place inside himself, though if so, then never for very long; the colonel's emptiness always reasserted itself. Always.

Rom was deeply worried that Quark was there at present, in the midst of that emptiness.

Be strong, brother, Rom thought. *Be strong.* Because with each session of Mitra's, things got worse. Much worse.

A gale buffeted the barracks, blustered through thin walls and open joints. Rom hugged himself again, his arms and hands encircling his torso. His ribs were easily detectable to his touch; he had lost weight since he had been here, almost to the point of emaciation. So had Quark. So had all of the prisoners. It was remarkable, Rom reflected, that none of them had yet taken ill; he supposed that their relatively good health was probably a result of the vitamins regularly smuggled to them by Argan and Jessel, and the occasional healing afforded them by the medical kit that the two guards brought when things had been particularly bad.

In his time here, the easiest periods for Rom had been when he had been placed in isolation. Except for his concern for his brother, he felt almost at peace then. In his separation from his fellow internees, there was also separation from Mitra and Wyte. Hunger and cold seemed to have no real hold on him in the small, dark cell—not emotionally anyway, though they still had their physical effects. Once, Rom had been confined for three days. When he had been released and taken back to the barracks, his eyes had teared for nearly an hour, no longer acclimated to light after eighty-four hours of darkness. His ears had been ashen from the cold, and Quark had been distressed that he might lose his lobes. But the feeling had come back to both within a day, although the hearing in his right ear had completely gone.

For Rom, though, solitary confinement became grateful solitude, and it was what he found himself wishing for most often these days. That was possible because he now doubted that they would ever leave Gallitep alive. For some reason, official Bajor must have forgotten about their nine Ferengi internees, or they were unaware of the deplorable treatment of them. Quark did not necessarily believe that to be the case, but Rom was sure of it. He knew many Bajorans—he had even met First Minister Shakaar—and he knew of their world and their civilization, and they were not like this, not like Mitra and Wyte. Something had gone wrong. These prisoners were not supposed to be here, at least not like this. This was a mistake. Because they were here, though, under these conditions, it was reasonable to assume that the mistake was unknown outside of Gallitep; consequently, with escape virtually impossible, the only way they would ever leave here would be if they were permitted to leave by those who guarded them—or if they awoke one day, not alive, but in the Divine Treasury, where they would make their eternal reckoning.

Rom and Quark had approached Argan and Jessel several times, soliciting their assistance. Unbeknownst to Quark, Rom had also approached Prana; Quark had not believed Prana to be trustworthy, because the only indication that they had that he was not supportive of Mitra and Wyte was that he did not abuse the prisoners. But neither did Prana ever join with Argan and Jessel to help them.

As it turned out, Rom and Quark learned that the guards were as much prisoners here as the Ferengi. Ordered here by the colonel for a six-month tour of duty, they were not allowed to leave the camp for any reason, at any time. If they chose to desert, they would have before them as impossible a task as the internees had of trying to escape. With no shuttles required to bring in supplies—there were enough provisions to last at least half a year—and no transporters, there was simply no means of leaving the camp, except on foot, and that would have meant almost certain death.

Thus, the only hope Rom and Quark ever had of departing with their lives from Gallitep was no hope at all: Mitra would have to let them go. And of all the things Rom knew in this world and in this life, he was more certain of this than of anything else: Mitra would *never* let them go. Rom did not think that the colonel enjoyed being here; the situation was different from that. Wyte enjoyed being here, base creature that he was, but Mitra . . . Mitra had to be here; as sure as he had to breathe air and take nourishment, he had to be here. He seemed neither happy nor sad about his life here at the camp, nor even really accepting of it; for the colonel, this was simply the way life was.

And that meant that this was the way life was—and would continue to be—for everybody else here at Gallitep.

Rom awoke with a jolt when the door flew open and crashed back against the wall.

Quark, he thought immediately, and then realized that it must be the guards; the prisoners had not yet been given their sustenance—it was impossible to call what they were fed a "meal"—tonight. He looked up from his bunk as the low-powered lighting panels came on overhead. The other prisoners, he saw, were also peering up at the disturbance.

In the doorway stood Sergeant Wyte. A wide smile, though mirthless, nevertheless looked foreign on his face. Quark was not with him. He was alone.

"Well, look, everybody's awake," Wyte said, looking around and laughing heartily, as though he had just said something exceedingly funny.

"Where's my brother?" Rom demanded, not feeling either brave or scared, but resigned to the fact that there was as much chance that Wyte would beat him whether he spoke up or not.

The sergeant bounded across the room, his long strides quickly swallowing up the distance between the door and Rom. Wyte was a large man, not tall, but thick. His head was squarish, set almost flush atop his shoulders, and covered with cropped black hair. The horizontal ridges on the bridge of his Bajoran nose were so full that they were barely distinguishable.

Rom watched, unmoving, as Wyte's trunklike body bore down on him. The powerful sergeant stopped at his bunk, reached down, and yanked him to his feet. The frayed blanket slipped to the floor as though gravity had taken only a passing interest in it.

"You want your brother?" Wyte asked "I'll take you to see your brother."

And Rom suddenly knew, in a flash mixed of intuition and understanding, that Quark was dead. Rom would be led to the guard's barracks, or maybe to Mitra's office, and he would be shown his brother's inert body. Quark's face would be a mass of bloody injuries, or perhaps it would have been something subtler—a misused cardiostimulator or a properly administered neural paralyzer—and Quark would simply appear to be asleep, though with the color drained from his features.

Rom fell through Wyte's hands like water through a sieve. His knees struck the wooden flooring with two quick popping sounds. Wyte reached down right away, grabbed the front of Rom's jumpsuit, and hauled him upward. Rom thought he heard a seam begin to give way, and then he was on his feet once more, his head tilted back and facing up at the sergeant.

"If I have to carry you," Wyte screamed at him, "I'll do it by your neck." Wyte adjusted his hold on Rom, taking him by the back of his jumpsuit with one hand, and by the biceps of his left arm with the other. The sergeant jerked him forward. Rom was almost pulled from his feet, but he managed to keep his balance.

As Wyte loped back toward the still-open door, Rom was forced to vault along beside him. They burst over the threshold and out into the gusting winds of winter. The rectangle of dim light from the barracks behind them failed to penetrate very far into the night, and a dozen paces across the snow-covered grounds, they plunged into uncompromising darkness. If any of Bajor's five moons were overhead, their reflected glow failed to shine through the sky, which had been ceaselessly heavy with cloud cover for weeks now. It was as cold as space.

Rom looked down in an effort to help him keep his footing as Wyte alternately pushed and pulled him on their journey, but he was unable even to see his own feet. He sensed, from changes in the direction of the wind, the shapes of other structures in the camp—more prisoners barracks, housing for the guards, other buildings whose functions were not apparent to Rom because they were not currently being used and he had never been inside them.

Unsure of their direction, Rom glanced up only when the wind broke in front of them. Near at hand, light gleamed through a window almost directly ahead. As they drew even closer, Rom was able to identify details within the field of illumination.

It was Mitra's building.

Although Rom had guessed that this was where he was being taken, his heart seemed to seize up in his chest. This was it: Mitra had killed Quark—or had had Wyte do it—and now he was going to kill Rom. Rom was not necessarily opposed to that idea, he found; he had been moving steadily for days, or longer, toward resignation and even acceptance that this must be the way that this would end. He regretted only that his beloved Moogie would be so hurt by her sons' passing.

At the front of the building, Wyte pushed Rom hard into the wall beside the door. Rom barely felt it. He wondered idly if it was because his body was too cold or too tired, or if maybe his emotions had finally just drained away.

Wyte reached forward and opened the door, then grabbed the front of Rom's jumpsuit with both hands. The sergeant pulled him from the outside wall, and this time, the seams of the jumpsuit did give way, the torso ripping away from the arms where they met at the shoulders. With a look of disgust, Wyte pumped his fists into Rom's chest. Rom went backward through the doorway, his arms flailing as he tried to remain upright. His reflexes had staled during his harsh captivity, though, and he went down hard onto his back.

"Get up," Wyte yelled at him, entering the building after him and kicking Rom's foot with his own. When Rom did not move, Wyte took another step inside and pulled his leg back sharply, aiming it at Rom's midsection. Rom, unable to find either the strength or the will to defend himself, waited for the kick to land. He did not even close his eyes.

"Stop," came a voice from farther inside the building, not loudly, but honed enough to slice through the sound of the wind from outside. To Rom's surprise, Wyte froze in the very act of bringing his foot forward. "You may put your leg down, Sergeant." Wyte did. "And close the door." He did that as well, relegating the gales of the night to a remove.

Rom tilted his head back slightly, the rear portion of his bare skull resting on the floor. He peered farther into the building, down the corridor that led from the entrance hall in which he was lying. A short distance away, a door stood open, a shadowy figure framed in the light that was emanating from the room beyond: Colonel Mitra.

"Prisoner nine," Mitra said, the scorched rasp of his voice never raising above the level of normal speech. "Would you care to join me?"

Rom did not move. He kept his eyes focused on Mitra and did nothing else. There was a shuffling next to him, and he knew that Wyte was arranging himself above Rom so that he could lift him off the floor. Still, Rom did not move.

"Wait," the colonel said, holding up a hand, palm out. The shuffling beside Rom halted. "I believe prisoner nine can manage by himself, given the choice."

Rom had not been presented with many choices during the course of his incarceration, but he had nevertheless learned that it was wise to make them when provided the opportunity. Except that, right now, Rom did not want to enter Mitra's office. About that, though, he knew there was no choice.

He pulled himself up, rising shakily to his feet. He was facing the front door and Sergeant Wyte. Gathering himself, he turned toward the corridor and the waiting silhouette of Mitra . . . except that Mitra was no longer there.

"Go on," Wyte said in low, angry tones behind him. He placed his hand on the back of Rom's head and pushed.

Rom started toward the doorway to Mitra's office, the only source of light in the corridor. Just before he reached the door, he braced himself. He closed his eyes and turned through the doorway into the room.

There was a moment of near-silence—somewhere in the room, a clock ticked—during which Rom anticipated some revelatory sound—words from Mitra, a laugh from Wyte, something—that never came. Surprised, he opened his eyes.

Quark was there, in the center of the room, dead.

His body was slumped in a heavy wooden chair, his arms bound to its arms. His head had fallen forward, his chin resting on his chest. His face looked different than it had this afternoon, but only in degree; for weeks, Quark's features had been in a constantly alternating state of injury and healing. Earlier today, his facial wounds had been on the mend, purplish green contusions fading, the remnants of scrapes and cuts only a suggestion of the wounds that had preceded them. Now, new injuries had been added, and old ones reopened.

Rom felt his own face contort with grief. Tears formed in his eyes.

"Brother," Rom said, more a breath than a spoken word. He sensed the presence of Wyte behind him and felt the sudden, explosive impulse to turn on the vile man, to launch himself at his throat and shred it with his own teeth. It had been the sergeant, of course, who had killed Quark; the colonel would not have deigned to sully himself by actually doing it himself, though he had no doubt choreographed the violence. Rom did not know if he any longer pitied Wyte; he only knew that he hated him.

"Prisoner nine," Mitra said then, "won't you join us?" He acted as though he were inviting people into his home for a drink.

Rom looked to his right, to where Mitra stood behind a desk. The chamber was not large, more like an anteroom than a main office. Behind the desk was the window through which Rom had seen a light shining out into the night as they had approached the building. There were two other doors in the room, both closed at the moment, one in the wall opposite where Rom stood, and one in the wall to his left. The walls and floor were of finished wood, the floor worn bare in places from the tread of many feet across many years.

The chair supporting Quark's body was in the center of the room, facing Mitra's desk. Other than the chair, the desk, and a second chair for Mitra to sit in, the room had no furnishings. The ticking clock sat on the desk next to a metal basin of some sort.

Rom, feeling hollow inside, and aimless, moved farther into the room, toward his brother.

"Sergeant," Mitra said, "would you bring another chair out for prisoner nine?"

Wyte crossed to the opposite side of the room, brushing past Rom quickly and almost knocking him from his feet. He opened the door and went through it. Rom did not peer into the next room, but in other visits here, he had spied what he had thought to be storage cabinets for hardcopy files. After a moment, Wyte emerged with another chair.

"Right here," Mitra said, holding his hand out to indicate the spot directly in front of his desk.

It was only then that Rom noticed the colonel's exposed arm. Rom lifted his gaze to look at Mitra—really look at him—for the first time since he had entered the office. The colonel was bare to the waist. His silvering hair, fastidiously maintained since Rom and Quark had arrived at Gallitep, was disheveled. In his other hand—the one not indicating where Wyte should place the chair—he held a white towel, stained with what appeared to be crimson smudges. And his angular face looked strained, its muscles tensed, his gray eyes—in direct counterpoint to the quality of his voice—wild. Perhaps most surprising of all, a welt had been raised on his otherwise unblemished skin, high on one cheekbone, near the corner of one eye.

Good work, brother, Rom thought. Quark had lost the war against Mitra, but he had captured at least one small victory.

Wyte placed the chair before the colonel's desk, facing it. Rom, with no alternative and no interest in resisting—what point was there?—sat down. Quark's body was now behind him.

"There. Good," Mitra said. Then, to Wyte, he said, "Sergeant, I need another uniform tunic." Wyte grunted his acknowledgment and left the room by the door through which he and Rom had entered. Mitra sat down behind his desk. "Do you know why you're here, prisoner nine?"

Rom considered this for a moment. It was a question he had asked of the universe at large many times since he and his brother had been brought here. Finally, Rom shrugged.

"To die," he said.

Mitra looked at him, blinked.

"No," he told Rom. "You are here to assist me in obtaining what I want."

"You think I'd ever help you?" Rom asked. "You killed my brother, and now you think I'll help you?"

Again, the colonel stared at Rom for a time, before he said, "You Ferengi are such difficult prisoners. In some ways, you are like the Bajorans." Rom did not understand this comment, and his confusion must have shown on his face, because Mitra continued, explaining it. "The Cardassian occupying force found it virtually impossible to defeat the Bajorans. Oh, they pillaged the planet, enslaved and tortured thousands of Bajorans, killed millions, but they could not force them to stop fighting against the Occupation. The Bajoran spirit for independence was a motivation with which the Cardassians could not compete."

Mitra paused, and seemed only then to realize that he was still holding the towel in his hand. He looked to his left—to Rom's right—and tossed the towel into the corner, where a tunic—the one the colonel had earlier stripped off, Rom supposed—was already sitting in a pile. Mitra then moved the metal bowl from the center of the desk off to one side. He folded his hands together atop the desk. Rom found his calmness and control unnerving in view of the mania in his eyes. He again addressed Rom.

"So, the Bajorans were inexpugnable—" Rom did not know what that word meant. "—and so are the Ferengi. Not because of their desire for autonomy, though, but because of their thirst for profit. There is almost nothing I can threaten or offer that can compare with it. Except in your case, prisoner nine. In your case, there is a profit I can offer to you that just might convince you to assist me."

Rom fought the urge to laugh. Boy, did Mitra have the wrong Ferengi.

"First, let me tell you what I want," the colonel went on. "It is very simple, really: the Ninth Orb of the Prophets."

Rom did laugh then, a short yip. He had been unable to stop himself.

"I didn't realize you were such a spiritual man," Rom said.

Mitra's eyes narrowed, their intensity increasing. For an instant, with Wyte gone, Rom thought that the colonel himself would actually strike him. Instead, he continued speaking.

"I *am* a spiritual man," he said. "Which is why I believe that the Ninth Orb of the Prophets should be returned to Bajor."

"I don't have the Orb," Rom said. "You know that."

There was a noise off to one side, and Rom turned in his chair to see Wyte reenter the room. He walked over to the desk and handed a uniform tunic to the colonel, who rose to take it. Mitra said nothing, but pulled the tunic on over his head, then straightened his hair with his hands. Wyte walked around Rom to the other side of the desk, where he leaned against one corner of it.

"You're right, prisoner nine," Mitra said, still standing. "I do know that you don't have the Orb. But that doesn't mean that you can't get it, or that you can't help me get it."

The colonel walked out from behind his desk, to Rom's left. Wyte stood up and backed away to let him pass. Mitra looked down at Rom.

"You believe I killed your brother?" he asked.

Rom turned slightly and tilted his head to the side to peer up at Mitra. Then he nodded in Wyte's direction, though his gaze never left the colonel's face.

"Or told him to," Rom said.

"I see." Mitra said. He walked away from the desk, away from Rom, and Rom had to will himself not to turn, knowing that any movement not specifically commanded by the colonel would probably result in an attack by Wyte. But Mitra must have gestured to the sergeant, because Wyte came over and spun Rom and his chair around so that he was facing his brother. The colonel stood behind Quark.

"I have killed tonight," Mitra said, and it seemed to Rom as though the wildness in the colonel's eyes had somehow spread now to his voice. "Yes, let's be clear about that. I intended to kill, I had reason to kill, and so I killed. Sergeant Wyte did nothing . . . nothing but watch and delight in the pain, in the actual demise, of another. He is a misanthrope."

The last, stray comment startled Rom, and he could not

help glancing over at Wyte. The sergeant appeared surprised too. He turned his head slowly from Rom toward Mitra, a look of confusion surfacing on his face. Rom was not sure whether Wyte did not understand *what* the colonel had said, or *why* it had been said.

"He is a barbarian and a sycophant," Mitra went on. "But he has been useful to me."

Rom said nothing. Although he was facing in his brother's direction, he found that he could not look at the body. His gaze held fast above Quark's head, on the face of Colonel Mitra.

"I killed," Mitra said again, "but this—" He motioned with both of his hands down at Quark's body. "—I would not touch. This is a wretched being—like yourself, prisoner nine—a lowly, vile Ferengi. He—you, your people—do not deserve their world. We will annex it, bring it into the Empire."

The Empire? Rom wondered if he had heard the colonel correctly. *The . . . Bajoran . . . Empire?*

"The richness of your world's resources should be made to serve superior beings," Mitra said.

What was he talking about? Bajor had suffered the depletion of its natural resources during the Cardassian Occupation; was the colonel proposing that the Bajorans should therefore conquer Ferenginar for it what it had offer?

Mitra looked over at Wyte and nodded, then nodded down at Quark's body. Wyte walked over and stood facing Quark, between where Rom was sitting and where Quark's body sat slouched. Rom saw the sergeant's upper body move—his arm drew back and drove forward—and he heard the sound of flesh against flesh. Rom could not actually see the blow, could not see around Wyte, but it was obvious that Quark had been struck in the face.

Rom came up out of his seat, rage filling him, and wrapped his arms around Wyte's massive body. The sergeant shrugged, bringing his elbows up and out, and Rom was sent flying backward, stunned, into his chair.

"Bind him," Rom heard the colonel order.

Wyte was on him quickly, tugging his arms down and securing them to the chair. Rom shook his head to clear it. Before him, movement caught his eye. He focused on it, desperate for it to be his brother, but the body was unmoving. As Rom looked at Quark, though, he saw that color had flashed into his face where he had been struck.

Could that happen if he was dead?

Quark lifted his head and opened his eyes.

"Brother," Rom called out in joy. Rom did not see anything—nothing but Quark, anyway—but Mitra must have signaled to Wyte, because the brute's bare knuckles smashed into the side of Rom's head. It hurt, but Rom did not care. All he could do was stare at his brother—*alive!*—and cry. He could not remember being this happy in a very long time, and maybe even never before now. His sobs were loud in the room.

"Be quiet," the colonel said.

To Rom, his voice had about it the quality of cooking meat. Rom looked up from Quark into Mitra's deep-set eyes, wondering for the first time not just what was happening behind those eyes, but what had happened in front of them.

"This," the colonel said, indicating Quark with a glance, "is what I have to offer you in the way of profit."

"You already said that you know I don't have the Orb," Rom said, choosing his words with care. "And I don't have any idea how to help you get it, but I'll do whatever I can." He had to save his brother's life.

"Very wise, prisoner nine," Mitra said. "Perhaps, though, I can settle for something else from you right now . . . such as the name of the guard who has been providing vitamins to the prisoners."

Rom said nothing.

"Your silence does not . . . profit . . . you at all," the colonel said. "As you are already aware, you will be unable to remain silent once Sergeant Wyte begins his process of coercing you. This is simple information for which I'm asking."

"I . . ." Rom began, and stopped. "I've been stealing the vitamins myself."

"I see," Mitra said. "And how do you accomplish this?"

"I . . . uh . . . sneak out of the barracks at night, sometimes, when everybody's asleep, and I make my way over to the . . . uh . . . the supply. . . ."

"Yes," Mitra said, "the supply." He paused, then walked a half-circle around Quark to stand in front of Rom. "I have been told that Ferengi lack courage, and yet here you are, prisoner nine, before your captor—" Rom found it interesting that the colonel used the singular form of the word. "—bound, facing your own death as well as the death of your dear brother, and you lie to me to protect Sergeants Argan and Jessel."

Rom could not prevent the look of surprise he knew had appeared on his face.

"Oh, yes, I already knew," Mitra told him. "I just wanted to see whether you were brave enough—or foolish enough; is it just foolishness?—to lie to me. I must say, I am amazed." Then, without changing the beat of his speech, he said, "Sergeant Wyte."

Before Rom could prepare himself, Wyte's arm swept around his neck. He felt his eyes widen as he lost the ability to breathe. The colonel stepped away then, leaving Quark in Rom's line of sight. His brother was clearly groggy, unaware of what was going on around him. Then, as quickly as Wyte had begun to choke him, he stopped. Rom gasped for breath, his chest heaving as he swallowed gulps of air. When his breathing returned to normal and he quieted, he heard Mitra's voice from somewhere behind him; it sounded as though he was seated in the chair behind his desk.

"Now then, prisoner nine," he said, "I understand that you are attached—not just in a literal way, as we all are—but in a figurative, in an emotional, way, to your right hand."

Rom looked at Quark. Mitra had obviously extracted personal information from him, including this select tidbit from Rom's youth on Ferenginar. Still, Rom felt nothing but love and affection and sorrow for his brother. This admission—and perhaps others—though it had nothing to do with Quark specifically, must have been very hard on him. How many days, how many weeks, had they been here now? How many hours had Quark suffered through today before Colonel Mitra had been able to dredge such data from him?

A long time ago, memories of the way he had been

manipulated by Breel, of his own impotence in that ancient situation, had brought Rom great pain. Not even so long ago, he admitted to himself. But that had been prior to his internment at Gallitep. Now, the old events and emotions seemed trivial. In a way, Rom realized, Mitra had failed, because the colonel's brutal treatment had served to harden him.

"Go ahead," Rom said quietly. "Take my hand."

Silence. Rom waited.

"I will, I think," Mitra said at last. "I believe I'll have it shipped to Ferenginar. To Moogie."

Rom knew that would kill his mother; she so loved her two boys. Outwardly, though, Rom betrayed nothing.

"I'm sure she'd like to have reminders of her sons," he said. "Why don't you take my heart too?" Rom knew that he was never going to leave Gallitep alive, and doing so had ceased to be important to him. If he could only find some way of saving his brother, then he could simply die and be rid of Mitra and Wyte permanently. But Rom could not conceive of any method for him to get Quark away from here. Perhaps his joy for his brother had been misplaced; perhaps Quark would have been better off if he had already been dead at this point.

"Your heart?" the colonel said, as though musing. "Perhaps. But not yet. And not you, not your hand. I think perhaps . . . one of prisoner eight's ears."

Rom's heart pounded heavily in his chest. *Quark's ear.* The ears, the lobes, were everything to a Ferengi: the most significant parts of their bodies, sense organs, erogenous zones, used as a metaphor for ages about the strength and power of Ferengi males. *Anything,* Rom thought, *anything but the ears.*

"Sergeant," Mitra ordered.

To Rom's right, Wyte moved, again entering the small file room. He returned shortly with a Bajoran phaser pistol in his hand. On the proper setting, Rom knew, it would easily slice through Quark's skin and cartilage.

"No," the colonel said. "Not that way." There came the sound of a chair scraping along the floor as Mitra pushed it back. He entered Rom's peripheral vision, and Rom saw him walk into the file room. He reappeared a moment later. In his hand, he carried a long knife, its blade maybe twenty-five centimeters in length. It was sleek, Rom saw, but for a few dull streaks of crimson here and there. Mitra handed the knife to Wyte, who took it and stuffed the phaser into the waistband of his uniform. The colonel went back behind his desk again, and Rom heard him sit down.

Wyte made his way behind Quark, a villainous smile decorating his face. With one hand, the sergeant pulled Quark's head up and back; with the other, he laid the blade of the knife against the flange of Quark's right ear.

Rom tensed his body. He was going to do something, he had to—

Sudden movement startled him. Quark's head dipped down and his legs thrust onto the floor, sending his chair hurtling backward into Wyte's midsection. Wyte backpedaled uncontrollably, stopping only when he struck the wall.

At the same time, Quark came down on the rear, right leg of the chair and was unable to keep his balance. He went over sideways, landing on his side on the floor, still secured to the chair.

Wyte, shaken, started to come forward from the wall. Rom did not hesitate—he did not know what Mitra was doing behind him, and he was not going to wait to find out. He moved quickly, rocking forward onto his feet and surging ahead across the room. He pounded his head into Wyte's chest. The burly sergeant sailed backward again. This time, his head slammed into the wall with a sickening crack. Rom heard, but did not see, the phaser clatter on the floor.

He spun quickly past Wyte's slumping body, sending his chair crashing into the wall. The old wooden chair burst apart at its joints. Rom's arms came free, though they were both still attached to the splinters that remained of the chair arms. He did not bother with them, but dropped to his knees and hunted for the phaser. Out of the corner of his eye, he saw Mitra coming around the desk at him.

Rom scrambled, moving around on all fours, his eyes darting everywhere—until he saw it, there, the phaser pistol just on the other side of Wyte's sprawling form. Rom dove over the sergeant and grabbed it. He whirled and stood in one motion, sending himself into the far corner of the room.

Mitra was maybe three paces away.

Rom held up the phaser, pointing it at the colonel. Beyond Mitra, Quark was dazedly moving on the floor. Wyte was motionless. Mitra looked at Rom, then in turn at Wyte, at Quark, and finally back at Rom and the phaser.

Mitra smiled, a dead rictus of a smile that reflected the insanity in his eyes.

"Don't come any closer," Rom said.

"Let's see if you really have any courage," Mitra said. He stepped forward, as though Rom's words had been an invitation. "I'm betting that you don't." His voice was not angry or fearful in tone, but merely conversational. "None of you Bajorans do."

Bajorans?

"And even if you do, so what? If you kill me, then somebody will replace me." Rom did not believe that was true; Mitra was acting on his own here, he was sure. "We own this planet," Mitra continued. "It is ours. You and your people are just an inconvenience to us. Although I must say, we do enjoy having you here at Gallitep." He took another step toward Rom.

"Stop or I'll shoot you. I swear I will," Rom said. The phaser shook in his hand.

"That phaser is calibrated to kill," Mitra said. "So go ahead. Shoot, Rom."

Rom should have known better. Even if the phaser had been set to kill, so what? Rom was no killer, but he had been forced into this position; he had to do this in order to save the lives of his brother and the other prisoners, not to mention his own life and maybe even those of the other guards.

Instead, Rom glanced down at the setting on the phaser. Mitra took the final step forward.

Rom raised the phaser higher, closed his eyes, and——

——and Mitra slapped his hands, hard. The phaser arced into the wall and dropped to the floor. It was the first time Rom had ever felt the colonel's touch.

Mitra's hands shot forward and grabbed Rom at the sides of his rib cage. With no time to react, Rom was lifted from the floor and thrown across the room into the far wall. He was unconscious before he hit the floor.

When Rom came to, the first thing he heard was water splashing. The second thing was his brother.

"Are you all right?" Quark asked. His voice sounded thick, as though he were speaking around a mouthful of tube grubs.

"Yes," Rom said, shaking himself awake. He peered around. He was sitting on the floor of Mitra's office, his back to the wall, more or less where he had been thrown by the colonel. Quark was next to him. He tried to move and discovered that both his hands—which were behind his back—and his feet were bound. So were Quark's, he saw.

On the floor in front of Rom, the remnants of the chair he had destroyed were scattered about. The other chair, the one to which Quark had been secured, was farther away, on the other side of the room, on its side, as though it had been thrown there. Between the broken wood and the whole chair, Sergeant Wyte lay where he had fallen. Rom saw that a pool of blood, almost black, had spread beneath his head.

Colonel Mitra was behind his desk, standing over the metal basin. He had removed the tunic that Wyte had brought him; it had been tossed over next to the other one, which was still in a heap in the corner, Rom noted. In one hand, the colonel held a brush of some sort. Methodically, he dipped the brush into the basin, along with something else Rom could not make out but assumed was soap, and then he scrubbed away at his skin. Mitra's hands, arms, and chest, Rom saw with horror, had been scraped raw; the flesh was beginning to ooze blood.

As Mitra cleaned himself—if what he was doing could be called "cleaning"—Rom realized that the colonel was also talking to himself in a constant stream, though so low that Rom, with only one ear functioning, had to struggle to make out any words at all.

". . . lowly Bajorans . . . stop . . . the glory of Cardassia . . . what do they think? . . ."

"He's been like that for an hour," Quark said.

"What's he doing?" Rom wanted to know, unable to pull his gaze away from the bizarre sight.

"I don't know," Quark said, "and I don't care."

"What about us? What are we going to do?"

"I'm certainly open to suggestions," Quark said. "But I think what's going to happen is that he's going to kill us."

Rom looked over again at the colonel.

"I don't know," Rom said. "I don't even think he knows we're here anymore."

"Oh, I know you're here," Mitra said immediately, his voice gaining in volume. He did not look up, but simply continued scrubbing himself. "And when I finish cleaning your vile putrescence from my body, yes, it will be your time. You will die slowly and painfully for your ill-considered attempt to defeat Gul Mitra."

Gul? Rom thought. That was a Cardassian title.

"He's insane," Quark told Rom.

"I am not insane," Mitra said. He put the soap down on his desk and picked up the phaser, which had apparently been lying beside the basin. He waved it in the general direction of Rom and Quark. "You don't know what it's like to run this place . . . to have to deal with inferior creatures like yourself. . . ."

And neither do you, Rom thought. *Not in the way you're talking about.* And then a suspicion came into Rom's mind.

"You were a prisoner here yourself during the Occupation, weren't you, Colonel Mitra?"

Mitra stopped waving the phaser, stopped moving completely. It was as though he were a character in a suspended holosuite program. Then, slowly, deliberately, he put the phaser back down and resumed his scrubbing, though free this time of any commentary.

"We have to do something," Rom whispered to Quark.

"What?" Quark asked. "What do you—"

The door to the corridor started to open. Rom and Quark both looked up, startled. Mitra continued to scrub himself.

Corporal Prana walked into the room, looking ashen and shaky; his eyes were rimmed in red. Rom saw his gaze travel first to the dormant form of Sergeant Wyte, then to Mitra, and lastly to himself and Quark. Rom thought that he should say something, scream to the guard about what had been happening, but he felt powerless to speak. And as Quark had long ago pointed out, they had no idea where

Prana's allegiance actually lay. Besides, the picture before the corporal's eyes spoke for itself.

"Corporal Prana," Mitra said, and Prana turned to his commanding officer. "I'm delighted to see you. We've had a slight problem here." All the while, the colonel continued to scrub himself.

"I see that," Prana said. "What happened to Sergeant Wyte?"

"The prisoners killed him," Mitra said.

"And Jessel and Argan?" Prana asked.

"They killed them too."

Rom shuddered as he realized that the other two guards had been murdered. That must have been what Mitra had meant when he had spoken of having killed tonight.

"Oh," Prana said, glancing down again at Rom and Quark. "What are you doing, sir?" he asked, his eyes still on the internees.

"I am purifying myself once more," Mitra said. "And then I am going to kill the prisoners."

"Uh-huh," Prana said calmly, now looking back up at the colonel. After a moment, he walked over to the desk, bent over, and reached down onto its surface. When he stood up fully again, Rom saw that he had picked up the phaser. Another sidearm, Rom noticed, was already fastened to Prana's uniform at his waist.

"Well, yes, if you want to kill them now, that's fine," Mitra said. "I wanted to do it slowly, but really, I've had enough of them."

Prana turned and faced Rom and Quark. He stood there, looking at the two Ferengi for what seemed to Rom like a very long time.

"Fire, Corporal," Mitra finally said. "Fire."

Prana did.

CHAPTER
27

THE DOOR CHIME SOUNDED just as Sisko was preparing to leave his office. He stepped up to the doors and they opened before him. Odo stood on the other side of the threshold, hands behind his back, head turned and looking back down into Ops.

"Can I help you, Constable?" Sisko asked.

"Oh," Odo said, evidently startled as he spun around to see Sisko right there, at the doors. "Were you going somewhere, Captain?"

"I was thinking about it," Sisko said, "but no." The simulated night was approaching on *Deep Space Nine,* and although he still had work to do, Sisko had indeed been thinking about getting away from his office for a little while. He had been considering asking Dax to take a walk with him so that he could seek her counsel, but that could wait until after he had seen what Odo wanted. "Come in."

Sisko retreated into his office and circled back around his desk. The constable followed him inside, the doors sliding closed behind him. As Sisko sat down, he gestured to a chair on the other side of the desk.

"Have a seat," he invited Odo.

"That's all right," the constable said, remaining on his feet. "This shouldn't take very long."

"All right then," Sisko said. "What can I do for you?"

"Major Kira briefed me about the first minister's reaction to our findings," Odo began.

Earlier today, Sisko had contacted Shakaar to discuss what Chief O'Brien had learned from *da Vinci's* sensor logs. Unexpectedly, the first minister had received the information regarding the possibility of a staged battle out on the trade routes as though it were of no importance. His perspective, he had explained, was that the Ferengi were already acting contrary to the interests of Bajor, and that he expected them to continue to do so. It was therefore of no additional consequence that the Ferengi might have chosen to contrive an incident that would bring the two worlds to the flash point. Shakaar had even concluded that the potential revelation only reinforced his belief that the present course his people were pursuing to militantly defend themselves was the proper one.

"Shakaar's reaction was disappointing," Sisko agreed. "And the Federation Council's wasn't much better." Prior to speaking with the first minister, Sisko had made a report of the situation to Starfleet Command, who had relayed it on to the Council. The opinions of the delegates had presaged those of Shakaar. "I don't know. Maybe the first minister and the Council members are right: if the Ferengi want to force the Bajorans into a fight, and the Bajorans choose to respond, then . . . well, I guess it's not the Federation's business."

"It doesn't sound like you believe that," Odo commented. His hands were clasped behind his back once more, in a rigid, militaristic pose familiar to Sisko.

"That's because I don't believe it," Sisko said. "I feel that there must be some way for us to stop this before lives are lost, before . . ." He did not voice his complete thought.

"Before Bajor faces another occupying force," Odo finished.

"Not an occupying force," Sisko said, and the urge to leave his office suddenly struck him again. Needing at least to move around, he stood up from his chair. "Occupation's not the Ferengi way. But maybe something worse than that."

"Worse?"

"If the Ferengi wage war on the Bajorans, they'll win," Sisko said, coming out from behind his desk and pacing across the room as he spoke. "And if they win, you can bet that they'll keep the wormhole—and probably enact a toll—but that they'll sell Bajor and its moons to whoever offers the most for them."

"That hadn't occurred to me," Odo said. "They could hand Bajor back over to the Cardassians."

"They could hand it over to anybody: the Klingons, the Romulans, the Dominion. . . ." Sisko turned at the far end of the room and peered back at Odo.

"What do you propose to do?" Odo asked.

"I propose nothing," Sisko replied. "If the Bajorans won't listen, if the Federation won't listen, then I don't know who will."

"Perhaps the grand nagus will," Odo suggested.

"I already attempted to change Zek's mind once," Sisko reminded him. He walked back toward the desk, his anxiety pushing him into motion.

"And you were successful," Odo noted. "It was your request that impelled him to allow humanitarian aid to be carried through the blockade."

"That may have been a ploy, as we discussed," Sisko said. He stopped beside Odo. "The aid won't even be here for another week; who knows if the nagus will really allow it all the way to Bajor."

"You also persuaded him to delay the final round of the auction for at least another month."

"I don't think I did," Sisko said. "I think the final round was already scheduled for that time." *The truth is,* he thought, *I haven't changed anybody's mind about anything.*

"Perhaps," Odo admitted. "But actually, it wasn't you who I was thinking should speak with the nagus."

"Then who?" Sisko asked.

"Quark."

"Quark?" Sisko half-leaned, half-sat on the edge of the desk. He had not anticipated such a recommendation from the constable. It had always been Sisko's impression that

Odo had only contempt for Quark. In fact, the constable's well-known and well-honed sense of justice probably would have allowed for nothing less, considering the Ferengi's reputation for circumventing—if not violating—the law.

"I think Quark would be a useful mediator," Odo explained.

"But neither the Bajorans nor the Ferengi are interested in mediation," Sisko said. "That's a road we've already traveled."

"Yes, but not with Quark," Odo countered. "He has a relationship with the nagus."

That was true, Sisko knew, although he was not entirely certain of the nature of that relationship. Still, it was doubtless stronger—positively or negatively—than Sisko's own weak ties with Zek. Absently, he plucked the baseball sitting on his desk from its stand.

"And Quark has intimate, detailed knowledge of both the Ferengi and the Bajorans," Odo continued. "He understands their political circumstances, the things that motivate them, the ways in which they think. It's conceivable that he might succeed in persuading the nagus not just to reinstate the Bajorans in the bidding for the Orb—"

"—which is where this entire situation started," Sisko interjected, reasoning along with Odo.

"—but to actually sell it to them," Odo finished. "Such an action might go a long way in defusing the current tensions."

"It might," Sisko said, though he was far from convinced. He rolled the baseball around in his hands. "But I'm not so sure that the nagus wants these tensions defused."

"That's certainly possible," Odo concurred. "But that means that nothing we do will change the course of events. Does that mean we shouldn't try?" Odo paused as Sisko digested this. "Maybe the recent actions of the nagus have only come as a *re*action to what the Bajorans have done."

"You mean cutting the Ferengi off from the wormhole," Sisko said.

"Yes. And if the nagus can be made to relent on his initial position—excluding the Bajorans from the auction—then surely the Bajorans will rescind their edict."

"And you think Quark can help bring this about?" Sisko

asked. He glanced down at the baseball spinning in his hands; its white leather covering was smooth against his fingers, the two hundred and sixteen raised red stitches that held the ball together providing the only friction.

"I think it's possible," Odo replied.

"I didn't you know you had so much . . ." Sisko searched for another word and could not find one. ". . . respect? . . . for Quark."

"I don't believe I would choose the word *respect*," Odo said. "I *recognize* Quark's abilities. He's a businessman—a good businessman, I think, if not a good Ferengi businessman. Oddly enough, he also abides by at least the letter of our laws."

"I'm surprised to hear you say that," Sisko said. He manipulated the baseball with his right hand—index and middle fingers on top, thumb below—holding it with different grips: four-seam fastball, two-seam fastball, curveball.

"Yes, well, it doesn't mean that I don't think he acts criminally sometimes," Odo equivocated. "But he is persuasive."

"Yes, he is that," Sisko said. Then, with no better options having yet been devised, he told the constable, "I'll consider it."

Odo nodded in his stiffly formal manner, and apparently having made the point he wanted to make, he turned and left the office. Sisko watched him go, thinking that even if this was the alternative with the best possibility of avoiding further hostilities between the Bajorans and the Ferengi, there would still be significant hurdles to overcome: even if they could convince Quark to do this—of which there was no guarantee—Quark was still in jail on Bajor. As least, Sisko thought he was still in jail on Bajor; the truth was, with all that had been happening, he had not thought about Quark in quite some time.

Sisko walked with Dax along the main concourse of the Promenade. Almost all of the shops were dark now, he saw. The Ferengi blockade had been extremely effective in preventing many of the local shopkeepers from receiving the goods they required for the everyday operations of their businesses. Other shops, such as Garak's tailor shop, had shut down because of the corresponding reduction in the consumer traffic on the Promenade.

"I didn't know the Klingon restaurant had closed," Sisko noticed as he and Dax strolled past it.

"A couple of days ago," Dax told him. "The chef had been making do with replicated substitutes for native Klingon foods, but it wasn't the same; you could really taste the difference with a lot of the fare."

"Since there's probably no such thing as a Klingon vegetarian," Sisko joked, "I'll bet you could." Although replicators were often utilized to reproduce foods, they were less effective in mimicking those derived from animate sources.

"I think when he was forced to close," Dax went on, "the chef was considering declaring war on the Ferengi himself."

Sisko laughed.

"Somehow, I don't doubt that," he said. "You know, I think the primary reason Klingons can be so aggressive is that food they eat."

"Oh, it's tasty. You just never had the stomach for it," Dax teased.

"And I never will," Sisko said. "What was that one dish Curzon used to love so much?"

"*Rokeg* blood pie," Dax said. "Delicious."

"I tend to avoid dishes that have the word *blood* in them."

"Well, then I guess you won't want to know what the word *rokeg* means."

Sisko laughed again, harder this time. Dax almost never failed to bolster him when that was what he needed. As they walked along the Promenade, Sisko explained to his old friend the responses he had received from both the Bajorans and the Federation Council regarding the battle possibly staged by the Ferengi. He also spelled out Constable Odo's notions about Quark's ability to help.

"What do you think?" Sisko asked when he had finished telling her everything.

"I think Odo's right," Dax said without hesitation. "Quark knows the players involved, and he can be very persuasive when he wants to be."

"Then you agree that using Quark as a mediator might work?" Sisko said.

"Yes, *I* agree," she said, "but can you be sure that *Quark* will?"

"I know," Sisko admitted. "What profit is there in it for him?"

"It's more than just that," Dax said. "Nobody here did anything to help him when he was faced with losing his business and his home for something he didn't even do."

"I understand that," Sisko said, forcefully enough that he realized he was feeling defensive. "You're right," he told Dax. "Maybe we should've helped him. But the Federation Council wouldn't have allowed it."

"And it won't allow it now," Dax said. "So how do you suggest that we get Quark out of Bajoran custody?"

"I don't suggest that *we* do anything," Sisko told her. "I've already violated Resolution 49-535 informally; I'm not about to do it in a formal context. But I do have somebody else in mind for the job."

CHAPTER
28

KIRA ARRIVED earlier than she needed to, and the officer of the assembly—a small, round, officious man—requested that she wait in an adjoining anteroom until it was time for her to speak. As she sat in one of the half-dozen chairs in the small room, she found that her hands were disagreeably moist, and cold to the touch.

Nerves, she thought, and wondered, *What have I got to be nervous about?*

Although she had never before addressed Bajor's Chamber of Ministers, she had a couple of times spoken to the Vedek Assembly. She had also certainly presented her share of briefings during her tenure on *Deep Space Nine.* It was ridiculous, she told herself, to think that public speaking would cause her such anxiety.

Except that, on those other occasions, the words and ideas she had presented had been her own, and she had believed in them.

Does that mean I don't believe in the Emissary?

That was an uncomfortable notion. Of course, *When the Prophets Cried* and the other sacred writings did not proclaim the Emissary to be infallible, nor did Kira presume him to be so. And yet her respect for the Emissary—and for Captain Sisko, for Benjamin Sisko, the man—was considerable. But what he had asked of her—to petition the Bajoran government for the release of that blackguard Quark—was so difficult for her to understand.

Am I wrong? Perhaps that was the real question she should be asking herself.

Captain Sisko had shown up at her quarters last night, unannounced, and asked if he might speak with her for a few moments. She had initially been delighted that he had called upon her—her reverence for the Emissary really allowed her no other reaction—but she had quickly become disquieted when the conversation had turned to Quark.

She had listened calmly as the captain had outlined his plan, and then she had just as calmly attempted to point out its flaws to him. Even if she was able to convince the Bajoran government to release Quark, what assurance did they have that he would agree to speak with the nagus? After all, he had refused her request to do as much months ago, back when the Bajorans had been eliminated from the auction for the Orb. The captain had argued that they now had something of value to offer Quark in exchange for his cooperation: his freedom. That still did not mean that Quark would be able to accomplish what they would ask of him, Kira had countered. No, Sisko had conceded, but maybe he would be successful, in which case this dangerous situation would be eased, *and* the Ninth Orb might then find its way back to Bajor.

For one of the very few times, Kira had not found the captain's arguments to be very compelling. She had not said so outright, but she was sure that he had known; he was a bright and perceptive man. And of course, he was the Emissary. And on that basis, Kira had acquiesced. She had contacted Shakaar and entreated him to grant her an emergency audience in the Great Assembly, although she had not told him why. He had alerted her this morning that she would be given that audience.

When Kira had informed the captain, he had been pleased. Kira's conscience, though, had demanded that she be honest and forthright with Sisko, and so she had divulged to him her reluctance to perform this task. Further, she had revealed that she was averse to seeing Quark released from jail, and that she was therefore uncertain that she would be able to lobby the Assembly as well as she otherwise might. She also thought it unlikely that the Bajoran leaders would want to set Quark free; although he was currently being held as a political prisoner, it was also true that he had willfully violated the edict, for which crime he had not yet been made to stand trial. Captain Sisko had simply smiled at all of her qualms, accepting them. This was not an order, he told her, but a request, and he had faith in her abilities.

And that was ironic, wasn't it, because that was what this crisis of confidence was all about: faith. Her faith in the Emissary and her faith in herself. But where did self-confidence and self-awareness meet with spirituality? Where did reason and intellect intersect with belief?

Kira was still posing these questions to herself—these and others—when the officer of the Assembly knocked on the door and then entered the anteroom.

"They're ready to hear your petition now," he told her.

Kira stood and followed the officer toward the Great Assembly. Her hands were still icy and damp.

When Kira reached the assembly hall, she found that it was only about half-filled. As she entered at the rear of the semicircular dais, she gazed out over the rising arcs of seats emanating outward from where she stood. The doors at the ends of the three radial aisles leading to the entryways were all closed. There were enough seats here, she knew, to accommodate every member of both the Chamber of Ministers and the Vedek Assembly. Looking out at the people watching her, she recognized a number of faces: Vedeks Pralon and Sorretta, and Minister Hannan, and a few others.

As she approached the front of the rostrum, she saw movement. Seated near the area from which she would make her address were the first minister and the kai. Shakaar was rising from his chair to greet her, she saw. The image of him taking her in his arms flitted momentarily across her mind, and then was gone; she missed him, but her duties took precedence right now.

At the edge of the dais, the first minister held out both of his hands, palms up, in greeting. Kira placed her own hands in his, palms down. She felt the pressure of his fingers as he squeezed gently—*I love you, I miss you, do well,* the touch all at once seemed to say to her—and then he leaned in toward her. For a confusing moment, she thought he was going to kiss her, but then his face was past hers and he was speaking quietly into her ear.

"A lot of the ministers and vedeks felt they couldn't leave their people right now," Shakaar said to her. "The food shortage is more acute in some places than in others. But we do have a quorum."

"Thank you," she said, a bit awkwardly. He began to release her hands and turn away, but she did not let go. When he turned back questioningly, she said, "Really: thank you." She smiled and dropped his hands.

Shakaar walked to the front of the dais and introduced Kira to the assemblage, some of whom knew her, most of whom at least knew *of* her. There was, after all, only one Bajoran liaison to *Deep Space Nine,* only one Bajoran who served as executive officer to the Emissary. Shakaar took his seat beside Winn, and Kira strode forward.

"Good day," she said, making sure her voice was loud enough to carry to everybody present. "Thank you, First Minister. I have come here today to propose a course of action that I think—" She wanted to say *will,* Sisko would have wanted her to say *will,* but she could not bring herself to do so. "—that I think *might* bring an end to our troubles with the Ferengi. It might also bring the Ninth Orb back to Bajor."

A murmur rose in the audience. Kira watched as several people turned to exchange glances with those seated near them. She had apparently gotten their attention.

"There is a man incarcerated on Bajor," Kira continued, and then feeling the need to elaborate, said, "A Ferengi." Suddenly, she had the sense that she had just said something very ugly: *There is a man—no, not a man; a Ferengi—incarcerated on Bajor.* As though Quark were not man, not a person, but a thing, an inferior thing. She had many negative opinions about Quark, but she had not intended to suggest that he was not a person . . . had she? Unnerved, she began to move slowly along the front edge of the rostrum, walking to her left as she resumed.

"This man's name is Quark," she said. "I know him. He lived and worked on *Deep Space Nine,* and when he refused to leave by the deadline specified in the edict expelling all Ferengi from Bajoran space, he was arrested and brought to Bajor by the order of the first minister." She motioned in Shakaar's direction. "This man—Quark—has a relationship with Grand Nagus Zek, and I have reason to think that, in exchange for his freedom from jail, Quark would be willing to try to convince the nagus to allow Bajor to purchase the Orb."

The murmurs now rose, graduating into distinct voices and audible words. Kira glanced back at the first minister and the kai—Kira had drifted from the center of the rostrum almost halfway to its left-hand edge—and she saw that Winn's eyes were downcast, her head shaking slowly back and forth. It was an unambiguous sign, not only of dissent, Kira thought, but of disrespect; Winn was entitled to disagree with Kira's view—or the view she was presenting, anyway—but the kai should have been considerate enough to wait until the appropriate time to express her own opinions. Shakaar, at least, was motionless, his face impassive, although when he and Kira made eye contact, she noticed his eyebrows jump almost imperceptibly; he was letting her know that it would be difficult for her to sell what she was proposing to the ministers and the vedeks— and perhaps even to him.

"What's your reason?" somebody called out from the assemblage. Kira stopped where she was and peered around, attempting to locate the source of the question. As her gaze passed over one man, he stood and gestured to her. "You said that you had reason to think this Ferengi would be willing to help us," he said. "I wanted to know what that reason is."

Did I say that? Kira wondered. *Did I say I had reason to think Quark would help us?* She must have, but she had probably just been employing a figure of speech. Regardless, she realized that the question was a valid one—one she had asked Sisko, and for which she had not received a very convincing answer. So how was she going to persuade these people now?

"I think that, like all Ferengi, Quark is driven by profit," she said, and on the heels of that, thought, *All Ferengi? Rom? Nog?* She pushed the questions aside and continued. "Since Quark can't pursue material gain while he's in jail, I'm sure he would be motivated enough to do as we ask if we promise to let him go."

"That's a reason that he'd want to get out of jail," somebody else said, a woman seated close to the dais, "not a reason to think he'd get the nagus to change his mind."

"Yes, that's right," Kira said, "but I . . ." *I what?* she thought. *I agree with these people.*

Many were now conversing in the audience, no longer content to keep their thoughts to themselves or their voices low. Kira turned to Shakaar—for strength, for a look of support, anything—but he had already perceived that she was in trouble; he was out of his chair and walking toward her. As he crossed the dais, he held up a hand, and some of the talking quieted.

"What is it, Nerys?" Shakaar asked as he reached her.

Kira looked up into his eyes and wanted to tell him, wanted to confess that she was trying to espouse a position in which she did not truly believe. But if this was going to be so difficult, if she was going to be unable to accede to Sisko's request, then why had she agreed to come down here? Why?

The answer, she suddenly discovered, was simple: She had faith.

"Nothing," she told Shakaar. "I'm all right." With a gentle touch to his arm, she pushed him back toward his seat. Kai Winn, Kira saw, was staring at her. Kira turned away from her and strode back to the middle of the rostrum.

"The Emissary asked me to come here today," she announced, and the Great Assembly grew immediately quiet. This was not something Kira was supposed to reveal; it was a violation of the Federation Council's resolution— not for her, since she was not a Federation citizen, but for Captain Sisko. Was she betraying him? No, she decided; it would have been a betrayal if she had come here and failed to make the Emissary's thoughts and feelings understood. Nobody here was going to contact the Federation Council to inform them that Sisko had acted in contravention of their Resolution 49-535; nobody here would want to see the captain disciplined—or in a worst-case scenario, removed from the command of *DS9*—for wanting to help the people of Bajor.

Not even Winn, Kira thought. The kai might not be sure that Sisko was truly the Emissary, but neither was she sure that he was not.

"As I said before, I know Quark myself," Kira continued. "To be honest, I don't trust him. But I do trust the Emissary, and he believes that Quark may be the key to easing our tensions with the Ferengi and to retrieving the Ninth Orb." She paused, wanting everybody to take this in before she went on. She looked out again at individual faces and this time saw pensive expressions on many of them. The word of the Emissary, she knew, was obviously worth considering. The Assembly might not adopt Sisko's plan, but they would deliberate about it.

"Captain Sisko intends to escort Quark to Ferenginar himself," Kira said. "He will see to it that Quark meets with Grand Nagus Zek." And that was it. There was nothing else she could say, no chain of reasoning she could outline, that would carry more weight than the word of the Emissary and his planned involvement to help Bajor. And that was understandable, Kira thought; no living Bajoran had ever been in the presence of the Prophets, or had communicated with them, as Benjamin Sisko had.

And as Quark had.

A chill passed through Kira's body as she recalled the events surrounding the nagus's purchase of the Ninth Orb. Immediately after he had bought it, the nagus had journeyed to the wormhole; he had hoped to use the Orb to contact the aliens within—who, according to the Emissary, did not experience their existence linearly through time. Zek had wanted to be given a glimpse of the future so that he could increase his personal fortune. But when he had come out of the wormhole and visited *DS9,* he had exhibited a profoundly altered personality, one which valued benevolence and philanthropy over materialism. Quark had subsequently taken Zek back into the wormhole, and when they had emerged, the nagus's original personality had been restored. Later, Quark had claimed that when he had returned with Zek to the wormhole—to the Celestial Temple—he had made contact with the aliens who had constructed it and who resided within it, the Prophets. At the time, Kira had quickly and easily dismissed Quark's account as apocryphal, but she wondered now what the repercussions would be if he had been telling the truth. It was yet another question for which she was going to have to seek an answer.

Shakaar was up and standing beside Kira once more, she saw. He was regarding her stoically, and she wished she knew what he was thinking. She doubted that his perspective had been swayed; he seemed confident in the justness of the position he and Kai Winn shared: there would be no diplomatic relations with Ferenginar until the Ninth Orb was on its way back to Bajor. Nevertheless, Kira knew that he would invite a full discussion of the matter with those present in the Assembly; if there was a consensus contrary to his view, then he might be persuaded to act as the captain had suggested.

"Are you finished, Nerys?" Shakaar asked. His tone was neutral, neither supportive nor antagonistic.

"I don't know that I did a very good job of presenting the Emissary's position," Kira admitted, "but I don't think there's anything more I can say."

"All right," he said. "Will you stay while we debate the issue, in case there are questions we need to have answered?"

I have enough questions of my own to answer, Kira thought, but said, "Of course."

"Thank you." Shakaar turned to the assemblage. Kira took a step back as he began to speak, as a sign of respect, so that the focus of the people would be on him. "Major Kira has given us an alter—"

Shakaar clipped his sentence in midword. Kira looked over at him and saw that he was looking elsewhere. She followed his gaze to the back of the hall, to the end of the central aisle. There, the entryway door was just closing; Sirsy, Shakaar's assistant, was rushing toward the dais.

"Excuse me," Shakaar told everybody. He proceeded to one side of the rostrum, where stairs led down to the floor of the assembly hall. Unbidden, Kira followed.

"What is it, Sirsy?" he asked when she met them at the base of the steps.

"You have an urgent message, Minister," Sirsy said, her breathing rapid from her exertion. "It's from Grand Nagus Zek."

CHAPTER 29

Sisko had Major Kira's communication put right through to his office.

"Major, I hadn't expected to hear from you quite so soon," he told his executive officer.

"I wish you weren't hearing from me now," Kira replied.

Her tone—solemn, flat—caused him to gaze at her image on the comm panel more closely. She appeared anxious, and as though she had been under a great strain. Sisko felt a sting of regret that he had asked her to undertake a task she had not felt comfortable performing. But was her anxiety because she had convinced the Assembly of the workability of his plan, or because she had failed to do so?

"Has the Assembly finished hearing you already?" he asked.

"We were interrupted," Kira said.

"Major, are you all right?" Sisko wanted to know. "Where are you?"

"I'm not sure how I'm doing," she said. "I'm in Shakaar's office. He just received a message directly from the nagus." Sisko felt his heart leap in his chest. "Shakaar asked me to contact you; he's already in conference."

"What is it? What's happened?"

"I'll play you the message, Captain," Kira said. "It's brief."

Sisko watched as Kira peered offscreen. He saw her upper arm move as she operated the comm panel in Shakaar's office. After a moment, Kira's image was replaced with that of Grand Nagus Zek. The old Ferengi's face almost seemed to drip from his head, his wrinkled flesh in surrender after years of battling gravity. And yet there was a gleam in the grand nagus's eye, Sisko thought, a hint that he was fully enjoying the business at hand.

"First Minister Shakaar Edon of Bajor," Zek began. Numbers spelling out a stardate ran across the bottom of the screen. "This is Grand Nagus Zek of the Ferengi Alliance. In light of the recent provocations Bajor has made to Ferenginar—including the expulsion of Ferengi nationals from your star system; the closing of your borders and the Gamma Quadrant wormhole to Ferengi nationals; and the brutal attack by two Bajoran starships on a Ferengi starship, causing the loss of all hands, and witnessed by the Starfleet vessel *U.S.S. Defiant*—"

Sisko felt sick at the mention of his ship.

"—I am informing you that as of the current stardate—"

Sisko braced himself, knowing what Zek was going to say before he said it, and hoping that he would say anything else at all.

"—Ferenginar declares war on Bajor."

316

PART III

The 76th Rule

CHAPTER
30

MITRA WAS DEAD.

Quark considered saying the words aloud, thinking that perhaps hearing them spoken might lend them more truth. Instead, he continued to gaze out silently through the window of the guards' barracks. The bleak, boreal landscape looked unforgiving and impossible to survive in—something else Quark desperately wanted to be true right now, even though it would likely relegate him to remaining in Gallitep until the winter had passed.

Mitra is dead, he told himself again.

The truth was, they *thought* he was dead. Hoped, really, because the situation was horrible enough without a madman roaming the camp. But truly, they did not know with certainty.

Wyte, on the other hand, was definitely no longer among the living. Quark himself had felt for, and failed to find, a pulse in the sergeant's body. Quark knew that he should have experienced some sort of sorrow about the death; all life, every life, was sacred—priceless—it was widely held, and he understood that belief and even agreed with it, to some degree anyway. But Wyte had been a detestable man, a

319

cruel savage who had not only tortured Quark and the others, but who had enjoyed doing so. His death was no loss to the universe. No, right or wrong, Quark was not sorry to learn that he was gone.

At the same time, Rom and Corporal Prana had attempted to save Wyte's miserable life. When Rom had sent the brawny sergeant careening into the wall in Mitra's office, Wyte had sustained a serious head injury, and his neck had been broken. By the time Prana had entered the office and shot the colonel with his own phaser—which, they would discover later, had *not* been set to kill—Wyte had also lost a great deal of blood. When they examined him, he appeared to be in a coma.

Quark had gone with Rom and Prana to obtain help for the sergeant. Quark had no particular interest in seeing that Wyte received medical attention, but he elected not to interfere with such efforts either. Before leaving the office and the building, Quark did not think to check Mitra's condition, nor apparently did the other two. Prana's phaser shot had propelled the colonel over backward, the chair behind the desk toppling as he had fallen, hard, to the floor. Mitra had landed with his head canted to one side, and a massive section of flesh seared on his bare chest. Wisps of smoke had actually drifted up from the body. There seemed to be no question that he was dead.

When Quark returned with Rom and Prana to the office after the two had procured a medical kit, both of the bodies were in the same places, in the same positions, in which they had been left. The room was redolent with the scent of charred skin, and Quark was careful to breathe only through his mouth. Rom and Prana began doing whatever they could for Wyte—which proved to be very little. Even if either of them had been trained in medicine, Quark thought, even if Dr. Bashir were here to minister to the sergeant, the nature and extensiveness of Wyte's injuries probably would have rendered it impossible to save him.

As Rom and Prana tended to Wyte, the corporal recounted how he had come to Mitra's office when he had. Neither Quark nor Rom interrupted as Prana revealed another grisly chapter in the history of Gallitep. He had been on sentry duty during the night, he told them—the colonel required that a watch be maintained on the perimeter at all times—and Jessel had been late to relieve him. Because Prana was fighting the flu, Jessel had agreed to take over for him a couple of hours earlier than scheduled. When Jessel did not show up at the appointed time, Prana had felt tired enough to risk Mitra's wrath by leaving his post; the corporal had gone back to the guards' barracks seeking his replacement.

When he arrived there, he said, he found the place dark—which was to be expected, as Jessel, Argan, and Wyte would have gone to sleep by then; Jessel had probably just failed to awaken at the proper time for his sentry assignment. Inside the barracks, there was a strange iron odor, but wanting desperately to sleep himself, Prana ignored it. He made his way over to Jessel's bunk, quietly and in the dark, so that he would not rouse either of the other two guards. Once there, he bent and shook the sergeant, gently at first, and then with more vigor when Jessel did not stir. When Prana at last pulled his hand back, he found it tacky and moist. Fear took hold of him then and he turned on the overhead lighting panels.

The first thing he saw, he told Quark and Rom, was his hand, coated red. Jessel was lying faceup in his bunk, the picture of sleep, but his bedclothes were mantled in blood. Prana glanced over at Argan in his bed and viewed a similar sight.

Prana told Quark and Rom that he doubled over and vomited on the floor then, feeling as though he had been struck in the stomach. His head immediately began pounding, he said. He felt his heart flutter, and for a time, he could not catch his breath.

The corporal paused for a moment in his story, and Quark thought that he might retch again as he relived his horror. Prana's eyes were still bloodshot, Quark saw, his complexion still terribly pale. After taking a couple of deep breaths, though, he was able to resume his tale.

Once his stomach stopped heaving, Prana continued, he stumbled to the bathroom and cleaned himself up, splashing water on his face and leaning heavily on the sink for several minutes. When he was able, he went back into the main room and inspected Jessel's and Argan's bodies; their throats had been sliced open, but not, it appeared, until after they had experienced various other torments. Their postures were obviously unnatural with respect to their injuries; the corpses had clearly been arranged in the bunks, purposefully made to look serene.

Prana did not bother to check the prisoners' barracks; he told Quark and Rom that it never even occurred to him that any of the Ferengi might have been responsible for what had happened to Jessel and Argan. He knew right away that either Mitra or Wyte—and more than likely both—had committed the atrocities. Wyte's conspicuous absence from the scene of the carnage was just one indication of what had occurred. And while Wyte was capable of such brutality, the placement of the bodies on the bunks clearly pointed to Mitra's involvement.

And that had made sense, Prana told them, because he and Jessel and Argan had for weeks been attempting to devise some means for escaping the terror that Gallitep had once again become. Ever since word had arrived—via shuttle, in the last outside communication that had come to the camp—that the prisoners would not stand trial and were to be held indefinitely, Colonel Mitra had descended steadily into madness. Jessel had believed that the colonel himself had been interned at Gallitep during the Occupation—or if not here, then at one of the other camps—and that his complete control over his own set of prisoners, in this setting, had sent him over the edge. Whatever the reasons, the colonel's orders could only have been to detain the Ferengi, not to mistreat—let alone torture—them. Trapped here themselves, the guards—but for Wyte, of course—had conspired to desert Gallitep and bring back help. Clearly, Mitra must somehow have learned of their plotting.

Prana recalled that, as he had stood in the guards' barracks—transformed as they were into a tomb—he had wondered why he had been spared. But then, he was still supposed to be on sentry duty for another few hours, he had realized; obviously, Wyte or Mitra would be coming for him soon enough.

And so, almost in a trance, Prana had forced himself to go

to Mitra's office, where he had shot the colonel with the colonel's own phaser.

As Quark had listened to Prana relate his story, Rom and the corporal had continued to work over the inert form of Sergeant Wyte. When they had done everything they could, Quark—who was not really sure that Rom and Prana had accomplished anything—demanded that they shackle the sergeant's arms and legs, in the unlikely event that he underwent a miraculous recovery. Neither Rom nor Prana thought such a measure was necessary, but it took very little arguing for Quark to convince them to accede to his demand. They used the same security binding that Wyte had used on Quark and Rom.

By this time, dawn had been breaking.

The three men had tramped quietly over to the prisoners' barracks. As they mutely approached the building, Quark realized that he expected to find seven more corpses, and he suspected that Rom and Prana did too. Instead, they discovered the other Ferengi internees alive—weak, cold, and hungry, as they had been almost since the day they had arrived here, but still alive. Quark, Rom, and Prana apprised them of what had happened; nobody seemed surprised.

The first thing they did was to break out food from the supply; none of the prisoners had eaten anything at all for nearly an entire day. Prana opened one of the other guards' barracks—they were better insulated than those to which the internees had been assigned—and then he took Cort and Karg to give him a hand with the food. When they returned, Quark and most of the prisoners began to eat heartily, but then soon quit; they had all been sustained on starvation diets for too long, their stomachs unaccustomed to other than minuscule amounts of food. Quark and Kreln actually got ill. Quark noticed that Rom ate far less than all of the other Ferengi, though, and Prana, doubtless still queasy from all he had witnessed that day, had nothing at all.

At no time, as far as Quark knew, did anybody discuss the sudden shift in the relationship between Corporal Prana and the nine internees. There seemed to be no need. And

whatever bad feelings had existed among the Ferengi themselves—notably between Quark and the five men who had
crewed the captured cargo vessel—evaporated as though
they had never existed, also without anything being said.
What had transpired in the camp during the previous day
bound the survivors of Mitra's insanity together, Quark
figured, in a way that words could not.

After eating, Prana got new jumpsuits and shoes for all
the Ferengi, and then it was decided that all of the internees—but for Quark and Rom, who were exhausted—would
search the camp for a means by which to escape from
Gallitep. Prana, too, would stay behind in the barracks,
needing to rest after his interminable night. The primary
objective of the search would be to locate any kind of
communications equipment. Prana knew of no such matériel, but that did not necessarily mean that it did not exist.
There was some discussion about who they would contact if
such equipment was found, but Rom prompted them to
leave the problem for later.

When Quark fell exhausted into a bunk in the barracks,
he thought his sleep would be fitful, considering everything
that had taken place within the past fourteen hours or so.
He expected a vibrant dream filled with meaning, something he often experienced when his life was in flux. He
discovered otherwise. He rested soundly for six hours and
would have continued, had he not been awakened by Borit.
It was actually several of the Ferengi that were raising the
alarm, but it was Borit's voice Quark first heard.

Their search for communications gear had covered several different buildings. Understandably, though, nobody had
wanted to enter either the first guards' barracks or Mitra's
building. But after hours of futility, it became apparent that
the most likely place they would find anything would be
where the colonel had lived and worked.

Borit told everybody that he had entered the building
cautiously with two of his shipmates, Drayan and Lenk. The
three scoured the entire place, but for Mitra's office and the
two rooms that connected to it. They found nothing that
would be of use to them. Finally, frustration overcame their
apprehension and they made their way to the office.

Borit had been the first one inside. Gazing around, he saw

the colonel's desk, the two overturned chairs—the one behind the desk and the one across the room—the remnants of the chair Rom had shattered against the wall, and the body of Sergeant Wyte. But according to Borit's description, there were two significant differences between the scene they surveyed and the one that Quark, Rom, and Prana had left.

First, a knife—doubtless the one that Wyte had been going to use to slice off Quark's ear—had been driven deep into the sergeant's chest and through his heart.

Second—and it had been this that had caused the Ferengi search party to sound the alert—Mitra had vanished.

Prana quickly checked the phaser with which he had shot the colonel, and which he had brought with him that morning from the office. He was surprised to find that it had not been set specifically to kill, but the discharge from the weapon, fired at such close range, should have been powerful enough to cause death, or minimally, an incapacitating trauma. Of course, they had all learned that Colonel Mitra was an exception to many rules.

All of that had happened two days ago. Quark peered out across the winter wastes and knew that everybody claimed to be certain that Mitra was dead, wherever he was, but the doubt that lingered in the back of Quark's mind was distressing. Still, a thorough exploration of the camp—and especially of Mitra's building—led by Corporal Prana, had turned up no trace of the missing colonel. If he had left the grounds of Gallitep, he would not last long out on the snow-covered tundra; there was nothing to eat out there, and no means of enduring the arctic weather. Coupled with what should have been mortal wounds inflicted on the colonel, Ferengi odds-making left little room for doubt—and yet, Quark was still troubled.

The reinspection of Mitra's building and office—during which Quark had insisted on checking Wyte's inanimate body himself—had revealed no clues of where the colonel might have gone. They had not found his tracks in the snow around the building—or anywhere in the camp—but the grounds had been traveled so extensively since the last snowfall that it might have been possible for Mitra to have walked in existing tracks. And after a few hours, any fresh tracks he might have left would have quickly been covered by the constant winds, which rendered even their own foot trails transitory.

Now, sure that the colonel was dead, but bowing to the fear that he had inspired in them, the ten men agreed to travel through the camp in groups of no less than five. And when they slept, two men would stand guard. Corporal Prana had gathered up and distributed all five of the phasers that he knew were in the camp; they had so far uncovered no other useful weapons.

And so they would continue to hunt for a way out of this place—in vain, at least for now, Quark believed. As he stared out at the vast, empty lands around Gallitep, he knew that the dark winter would hold them here as long as it lasted—and right now, that was fine with him, because the brutality of the season that would keep them here would also see an end to Mitra, if the colonel had somehow managed to survive even this long.

Which was not to say that Quark wanted to stay here; the moment it was possible for them to leave, he would lead the way. Rom had the notion that he might be able to fashion a crude communicator from one of the medical scanners, but Quark was not counting on that to save them. When springtime came—and they had enough food to last the several months until then—it would be possible to walk out of here. Prana put the nearest settlement at about six hundred and fifty kilometers; it would be difficult, but it was possible. Until then, Quark thought, there was really nothing else they could do but shiver and survive.

CHAPTER
31

Sisko abandoned all pretense. He showed up at the office of the first minister and insisted upon waiting until Shakaar returned from a meeting with the defense minister and the ranking leaders of the Bajoran Militia. Sisko was—and would be—violating Resolution 49-535 again, he knew, this time in a much more visible fashion, at least if he was successful. He was far more concerned with another matter, though: saving the people of Bajor from fighting a war they could not possibly win. And he had to act quickly, because he was certain that he would shortly be receiving new orders—orders he probably would not agree with—from Starfleet Command.

The problem is, Sisko thought, *I'm not sure what I can do to prevent this war.* The one idea he had developed—that had, in fact, been suggested to him—was at best speculative. But the more he had considered it, the more attractive it had become to him, and the more he had become convinced that it could work. Now, if he was only able to convince the first minister of that.

Shakaar arrived back in his office within the hour, accompanied by a woman and a man who wore uniforms of the

Bajoran Militia—advisors, Sisko guessed, perhaps helping the first minister formulate a military strategy against the Ferengi. The manners of the two officers were very serious, although they seemed less sure of themselves when they were introduced to the Emissary; Sisko had encountered such behavior many times before.

"Please forgive my unscheduled visit," Sisko said after the civilities had been completed. Shakaar, flanked by the two officers, faced Sisko just inside the doorway.

"Not at all, Captain," the first minister returned. "It's always good to see you. As you can imagine, though, we're extremely busy right now." Shakaar looked at each of the officers—both generals, Sisko saw from the rank pips on their collars—to include them in his statement. "So unless you're here to offer your assistance—which would be most welcome—I'm afraid I'll have to ask if we can meet at some future time."

"It just so happens," Sisko told him, "that I am here to help."

Shakaar's eyebrows flashed upward momentarily; he had evidently not expected such a response. He again glanced at each of the generals in turn; it appeared to Sisko to be more an action born of reflex than any kind of meaningful exchange.

"Really?" Shakaar said. He walked past Sisko and deeper into the office. Halfway across the room, he stopped and turned. "I must say, I thought the Federation was intent on keeping its distance from our troubles with the Ferengi."

"They are," Sisko said. "*We* are. But there is a course of action to be taken that I truly believe can bring this situation to a peaceful resolution."

"Indeed," Shakaar said, sounding intrigued. "We would be interested in such a solution, of course—anything to save Bajoran lives."

"I'm glad to hear you say that, Minister," Sisko said, pacing over to him, "because what I propose is really very simple: You want the Ninth Orb, and I will see that it is brought to Bajor. In exchange, you must rescind the edict barring the Ferengi from your system and the wormhole."

"You'll see that the Orb is brought to Bajor?" Shakaar repeated, his tone reflecting skepticism. "If that were to occur, then yes, I would be perfectly willing to make the concession you mentioned. But forgive me, Captain, if I can't see how you'll be able to make this happen."

"I can do it, but I'll need some assistance," Sisko said. "You have a man in custody named—"

"—Quark," Shakaar finished. Whatever expectation or hope the first minister might have had was gone from his voice now.

"Yes."

"Major Kira already suggested this course of action in the Great Assembly." Shakaar moved over to the sitting area, apparently ready to dismiss Sisko. He gestured to the militia officers, and they walked over and sat down. Shakaar also took a seat.

"She did?" Sisko asked, following the first minister and ignoring his move to end the conversation. For the moment, he also sought to maintain the illusion that he knew nothing of Kira's plea to the leaders of her world. "How was she received?"

"It was difficult to tell," Shakaar answered, looking up at Sisko. "To be honest, I think that some of the governors and some of the vedeks would have supported her plan—*this* plan. I'm not sure that there would have been enough support for it, though, to set it in motion."

"And what about you, Shakaar?" Sisko wanted to know, employing the use of the minister's name to emphasize his earnestness. "Where do you stand?"

"Please understand," Shakaar said, clearly reacting to Sisko's stern demeanor. "I do not wish to lead my people into a war. But at the same time, I cannot allow any faction to dictate any aspect of Bajoran life. You know this; we've been through this."

"The stakes have never been quite this high, though," Sisko said loudly—he was almost yelling at the first minister—but he chose not to moderate his voice level. "This isn't just a blockade anymore, and it's not even just an occupation; the Ferengi are going to send their fleet here. They'll destroy every starship you have, and then they'll conquer your world and dismantle all that your people have rebuilt."

"Captain—"

"And how will your people feel," Sisko continued, talking over the first minister, "when the Ferengi defeat them and take not just their world, but the wormhole—the Celestial Temple—as well?"

"The Vedek Assembly has already considered that," Shakaar said. "We will collapse the entrance to the Celestial Temple before we will allow it to fall into the hands of the Ferengi."

"The Yridians won't be too happy when they discover they won't be able to monitor communications from the Gamma Quadrant after all." Xillius Vas was supposed to arrive at *Deep Space Nine* tomorrow.

"That is now the least of my concerns."

"You sound very sure of yourself," Sisko said.

"I am sure of the course we are taking," Shakaar said. "Bajor must remain free."

"You'd better be sure," Sisko told him, his voice crisp and cool, "because you're going to have to live with the consequences of these actions for the rest of your life."

Understanding that he would make no progress here, that there was no point in saying anything more, Sisko pivoted on his heel and marched out of the office. And all he could think was that he hoped Shakaar lived long enough to regret what he was doing.

"According to the readings from the long-range sensor buoys," Dax reported from her station in Ops, "the Marauders are retreating." There was a note of bewilderment in her tone.

"Not retreating," Sisko said, standing on the lower level and listening as his crew issued their reports. "Regrouping."

"They'll wait for more of their forces to arrive before they launch any offensives," Kira explained. Sisko thought his first officer looked not only anxious, but ill.

"What about the Bajoran ships?" Chief O'Brien asked.

"The two transports that defeated . . . well, that *seemed* to defeat . . . the Marauder have returned to Bajor," Kira said. "Along with the thirty-five new ships, various other, smaller cargo ships are congregating in orbit."

"Cargo ships?" O'Brien blurted. "What good are they going to be against Ferengi Marauders?"

Sisko watched as Kira bowed her head and closed her eyes. She had no answer for the chief.

"We've got an incoming message," Dax announced. She worked her console and then said, grimly, "Benjamin, it's Starfleet Command. Admiral Whatley."

"In my office," Sisko ordered, starting up the stairs to the upper level. He wanted instead to have Dax tell the admiral that he was not available right now, that yes, the captain of course realizes that this must be an important message, but he really cannot speak to you at the present time. That was what he wanted to do, and knew that he could not.

Sisko headed up the steps to his office and through the doors, which parted at his approach. As the doors closed behind him, he asked himself—not for the first time—what more he could have done. He felt that he had been unable to see the big picture in all that had been happening, and in the wake of that failure, that none of his blind efforts to resolve the situation had achieved anything of significance. The most important thing he had done—getting the nagus to allow Starfleet to deliver humanitarian aid to Bajor—had still done nothing to prevent a war from erupting. And the first shipments of that aid had been scheduled to arrive in four days; obviously, that would never happen now.

Sisko sat down at his desk and activated the tabletop comm panel. Admiral Whatley regarded him from his own desk light-years away. He looked extremely tired. That was understandable; once Sisko had informed Command of the Ferengi declaration of war on Bajor, they would have informed the Federation president and the Federation Council. After that, the efforts to determine how to proceed would have been ceaseless and intense.

"Ben," Whatley greeted him. He even sounded tired, Sisko thought, and perhaps dejected as well; Admiral Whatley had been a keen supporter of the campaign to admit Bajor into the Federation. Now, like never before, the possibility of that happening in the near term was about to fade.

"This isn't good news, is it, Admiral?" Sisko asked. He felt so disappointed himself; in the back of his mind, he had harbored the faint hope that the Federation would choose to side with Bajor against Ferenginar. Of course, Sisko had not really wanted that to occur either; he had no desire to see the Federation itself at war.

"I'm afraid it's not," Whatley agreed. "I have the unfortunate task of ordering you to evacuate all Starfleet personnel from *Deep Space Nine* within the next fourteen hours."

"That's not a lot of time," Sisko found himself saying, automatically attempting to stall, in the hope that—

—*That what?* Sisko asked himself. *That the Prophets will suddenly decide to emerge from the wormhole and perform a miracle?*

"Don't tell me that, Ben," Whatley said. "We both know it's not true; you just don't want to leave the station."

"You're right," Sisko admitted, "but it's more than just having to leave *DS9*. I don't want to desert the people of Bajor precisely when they need us the most."

"I know. Believe me, I know. Nobody has championed the cause of Bajor entering the Federation more than I have." The admiral seemed to lose himself in his own thoughts for a moment, gazing briefly into the middle distance, and then he apparently realized with whom he was speaking: Sisko himself was the point man for Bajoran admittance to the Federation. "If only this were happening next year, or the year after," Whatley yearned aloud. "But I guess I don't have to remind you of our responsibilities to the Federation Council."

"No, you don't," Sisko said, a little too sharply. On the comm panel, the admiral stared back at him, brow furrowing. Sisko raised his hands in contrition. "I'm sorry, Admiral, but I live with these people, I work with them. Despite the way they fought the Cardassians, they are not warriors. This shouldn't be happening."

"I feel the same way," Whatley said. "But it is happening, and we have to accept that this is not our fight."

"Is the Council committed to this retreat?" Sisko wanted to know.

"It is, and Starfleet Command concurs. We can't fight a war for Bajor."

"But if we were to remain on the station . . ." Sisko suggested.

"Remain on a *Bajoran* space station?" Whatley asked rhetorically. "Then we would be siding with Bajor, as well as putting our own people in harm's way. And if the Ferengi are victorious, and Starfleet is still a presence on *DS9*, well, the repercussions would be very serious."

"And the wormhole?" Sisko asked. With the threat of a Dominion invasion from the Gamma Quadrant a real possibility, it was critical to maintain a strong military presence at the mouth of the wormhole in the Alpha Quadrant.

"If the Ferengi defeat the Bajorans, then we will have to negotiate with the Alliance about defending the wormhole," Whatley said. "It would be in their own best interests—including their business interests—to see that the wormhole is protected."

"Evidently, the Council and Starfleet have considered everything," Sisko relented.

"We have," Whatley said. "The ships carrying humanitarian aid to Bajor have been ordered to return to the Federation. The *New York*, which was accompanying the convoy, is proceeding directly to *DS9*; it should be there within three hours. All Starfleet personnel currently assigned to the station will be evacuated to the *New York* and transported to Starbase Icarus. The *Defiant* is to report there with your command crew as well, by stardate—"

The admiral specified a stardate, but Sisko did not hear him; he was watching Whatley's image on the comm panel, was seeing his lips move, but the words no longer penetrated past Sisko's own thoughts.

The Defiant . . . *all Starfleet personnel . . . Starbase Icarus . . . by a certain stardate. They're assuring that I'm left with no latitude to operate,* he thought. *They made their decisions, and now they want them implemented.*

"Admiral," Sisko started, his tone beseeching. "I'd like—"

"Ben," Whatley interrupted. His tone was not without compassion, Sisko thought. "It's over."

"Admiral—"

"Whatley out." The image on the comm panel disappeared. Sisko thumbed off the device.

How could I have failed? he asked himself. *Failed so thoroughly?* And then, in a way of thinking that was foreign to him, at least on a conscious level, he thought, *I am the*

Emissary. I'm supposed to save the people of Bajor, not abandon them to the fates of war.

Sisko rose from his chair without knowing exactly where he was going to go or what he was going to do. He stood motionless, the tips of his fingers brushing the top of his desk. In a few minutes, he knew, he would have to replay the communication with Whatley to find out the stardate the admiral had mentioned, as well as anything else he might have missed. And then he would have to give the order to evacuate *Deep Space Nine.*

But not just yet, he decided.

Sisko turned and moved around his chair, right up to the window behind his desk. From the vantage of his office, which sat atop the hub of the space station, he gazed outward, and downward, past the great, outer ring of *DS9.* Also visible from here, to the left and right, were two of the station's three docking pylons, looking like the giant, bare ribs of some long-dead metallic beast.

Beyond the station were the stars, profound in their innumerableness and constancy—or so they seemed. Sisko had discovered some time ago that they no longer held the same fascination for him as when he had been a boy—or even when he had been at the Academy, or aboard *Okinawa* or *Saratoga.* Jennifer had died out there, amid the stars. The universe was a place of wonder, he thought, but it could also be a cold and uninviting place.

Unlike there, he thought, peering at a bluish white mote that hung in the darkness. He stared at that bright spot of light, slightly larger than most of the other spots of light, not because it was actually larger, but because it was so much closer to where Sisko was standing; it was Bajor. Somehow, without his being aware of it at first, Sisko had grown to love that world and its people. He knew that he would one day live there.

At least, he *had* known that. Had known that, one day, he would have a house there and still be within the confines of the Federation. Home had once been New Orleans and then San Francisco on Earth, and then Bradbury Township on Mars, and eventually, home had simply become Jennifer. After that, after he had lost her, there had been no refuge for a long time. He had carried a hollowness around inside of him, not a crippling thing—though nearly so—just a thing that existed, something that had happened, through which he had to live, from which he had to grow. But now, even though he had not quite yet made it there, home was Bajor.

And he thought once again, *How could I have failed?*

CHAPTER
32

CHAPTER

32

IT WAS CORT who turned out to be an engineering genius, not Rom.

It was late afternoon, and the brief appearance that the hibernal Bajoran sun made each day had already passed. The sun had not been visible when it had tracked through the sky in a short arc just above the horizon; only a dull brightening of the murky cloud cover had betrayed its rising at all. Now, as the night readied to devour the fleeting day, the lands surrounding Gallitep had taken on a strange quality: the clouds above had grown indistinguishable from the snow below, the horizon had become invisible, and solid objects no longer generated shadows: whiteout.

In the guards' barracks that Corporal Prana had opened—and which had subsequently become the prisoners' home—Quark lay on one of the bunks, his head propped up on one of his hands. He was observing from a distance Rom's attempts to modify one of the medical scanners so that it could be used, at the very least, to broadcast a distress signal. On a small table next to the one at which Rom was working, Borit and Karg were playing a card game of some sort.

The deck of cards had belonged to Sergeant Jessel, and it had been Prana's idea to retrieve it from the first guards' barracks. The corporal had refused to reenter the building himself, though; the bodies of Argan and Jessel remained as he had found them, laid out in the blood-soaked sheets and blankets of their bunks. That, too, had been Prana's idea, not to disturb the bodies of any of the dead guards—including that of Sergeant Wyte—so that they could eventually be examined by the appropriate authorities. Prana had turned off the heat in those buildings so that the corpses would be preserved by the cold.

As Quark watched Rom work on the other side of the room, with Borit and Karg also in his sight, he wondered idly where the fifth member of their group was. He peered around and located Cort at the very back of the barracks, over in the far corner. Quark could not see what he was doing.

The other five prisoners—Quark considered Corporal Prana to be as much a prisoner now as any of the Ferengi— were out in the camp somewhere, tenaciously pursuing something, anything, that would help to get them away from here. The continued searching of the camp had so far resulted in nothing but frustration, and it was that frustration, Quark knew, that was driving Rom to seek his own solution. Quark viewed his brother's endeavors with a mixture of amusement and anger. Rom's solemn efforts with makeshift tools that were hardly suited to delicate electronics work were frequently very funny; more than once, a tool or a part had been projected halfway across the width of the room. But with each failure, Quark and Rom and everybody else marooned here came no closer to escaping this terrible place.

And then Cort stepped away from his shadowy corner of the barracks and walked over to where Quark was resting. Cradled in both of Cort's hands were the remnants of a dismantled medical scanner, along with some additional materials Quark could not identify.

"I've been successful," Cort announced.

Quark saw Rom stop working and glance over at Cort. Borit and Karg also looked over, Karg's hand freezing in place as he either discarded or drew a card.

"Successful at what?" Quark asked, although he had already surmised what it was that Cort was claiming. Nevertheless, he found himself immediately skeptical, reluctant to believe Cort's assertion for fear of being disappointed. Quark had experienced more than enough of that during these many weeks here—they all had, he supposed.

"I've managed to modify the scanner to send a homing signal," Cort replied. Now Rom put down the tool with which he had been working, rose, and started across the room. Borit and Karg followed along after him.

"A homing signal?" Quark asked, sitting up and dropping his feet over the side of his bunk to the floor. "To send to who?"

"Not to who," Cort said. "To what. My ship."

Rom, Borit, and Karg gathered around, forming a loose semicircle about Cort. Quark noticed that, while Borit's hands were empty, Karg's were not: he was still carrying his cards.

"What ship?" Quark asked at the same time as Borit. Quark stood up now, looking over at his brother as he got to his feet. Rom was staring at the gallimaufry of components that Cort was holding in his hands.

"The shuttle that brought me to Bajor for business," Cort said.

"You expect your shuttle to still be in orbit after so long?" Borit asked incredulously. Judging from his tone, he apparently thought this assumption to be the height of lunacy.

Although he said nothing for the moment, Quark agreed with Borit. There would be no leaving Gallitep yet, he realized. He sank back down onto the edge of his bunk, fighting to maintain control of his emotions.

"My shuttle's not in orbit," Cort said. "It's on the surface of Bajor."

"What is all of that?" Rom asked suddenly, pointing to Cort's handiwork and evidently ignoring the rest of the conversation. "It doesn't look like it's just a scanner."

"It's not," Cort said. "I also used parts from one of the phasers."

"Oh," Rom said. "That was a good idea." Rom moved forward, to get a better view of the jury-rigged homing device, Quark presumed. Cort turned away from him, though, interposing his body between Rom and his work.

Quark found Cort's movement odd; it was not as though he had the need to protect some proprietary technology . . . or was it? Perhaps Cort had crafted his homing instrument in some new fashion that would allow him to market it once they left here. It seemed unlikely, Quark thought, but he had no other explanation for Cort's behavior.

"Can I see what you've done?" Rom persisted. "Maybe we could adapt it to also send out a general distress call."

"No," Cort said simply.

"No?" Quark echoed.

"This will work," Cort insisted.

"Listen," Borit said loudly, and Quark could see that he was getting angry. "It doesn't matter whether your shuttle's in orbit, on the surface, or under the ocean; there's a good chance it's not where you left it." He landed a hand heavily on Cort's shoulder. "You don't think they just forgot about your property once they brought you here, do you?"

"Don't you want to get out of here as soon as possible?" Quark implored Cort.

"Of course," he responded, still keeping his device away from Rom's prying gaze, "but not so that we can be put in some other Bajoran prison camp."

"He's right," Karg said quietly. "If we send out a distress signal and somebody receives it, they'll call in the Bajoran Militia. And when they come get us, no matter what's happened here, they're not just going to let us go."

"Even another prison would be better than staying here," Borit contended, but his voice was not quite as loud as it had previously been. The possibility of being consigned to another prison had evidently rendered him less sure of his argument.

"If this doesn't work," Cort asserted, "if my shuttle doesn't arrive here by tomorrow, then whoever wants to can take this—" He lifted his hands higher for a second, indicating his improvised creation. "—and modify it however they want to."

"That seems fair," Rom said, and shrugged. It was the same nonchalant shrug Quark had been witnessing for decades, but that he had not seen once, he now recalled, in the entire time that he and his brother had been interned on Bajor.

"Your shuttle is automated?" Borit asked. It appeared to Quark that he was attempting to convince himself that Cort's plan was sound, and that it might actually lead to their salvation.

"It has some automated systems," Cort answered, "including flight control, navigation, and retrieval." He paused briefly, and then added, "It should be able to travel here without raising any suspicions."

"You're a smuggler," Quark blurted, looking up at Cort and exclaiming the words as they occurred to him. Cort returned his look and said nothing, and Quark immediately regretted having spoken his thought aloud. Still, he was inwardly pleased with the implications of his realization; he was far more confident in the abilities of a contrabandist to accomplish what was being suggested than in the abilities of just about anybody else.

"I'm a businessman," Cort said at last.

"Of course. I didn't mean . . . it's . . . I . . ." Quark sputtered a few more words without completing a sentence, and then he simply closed his mouth. Later, when Quark discovered what Cort actually did for a living, he would remember this moment, and how well Cort had played it.

A short silence followed. Quark was not sure what everybody else was thinking, but he discovered that he was genuinely beginning to believe that Cort's shuttle might arrive here within a day and provide a means of fleeing from this horrible place.

"Well," Quark said finally, "should we go find the others and let them know we're about to spend our last night in Gallitep?"

Quark heard it first, though only by a matter of seconds. There were quite a few good ears in the barracks, despite the effects of the cold on each of the Ferengi's hearing. Rom and Drayan had suffered the greatest consequences of the winter weather; they had each lost the use of one of their ears, and nobody possessed enough expertise with the medical kits to be able to help them.

The sound that roused Quark—and very quickly, the others—at first resembled a sustained gust of wind. Such winds were hardly uncommon here, and they had often woken Quark during the course of his internment. This time, though, the bay of the wind was accompanied by a low-frequency thrum. To Quark, with his eight years in the Ferengi merchant service, the sound was immediately recognizable: the drive of a shuttle.

Quark threw back the covers and lunged from his bunk. As he scrabbled to locate his shoes, he heard others beginning to move about in the darkened barracks as well. He found his shoes and put them on, then quickly moved to the wall and switched on the overhead lighting panels. All of the Ferengi were awake, including Rom and Drayan, and most were already getting to their feet. Only Prana was still asleep, and as Quark started toward him, the Bajoran rolled over and blinked his eyes blearily open.

"It's the shuttle," Quark said. The corporal rose up on one elbow and gazed around at the commotion, then looked blankly up at Quark. For a long, onerous moment, Quark feared that this was not going to go as easily as he had hoped, that they were going to have to face some very serious trouble after all.

Yesterday, when Prana had learned about Cort's shuttle and its alleged impending arrival, his reaction had been, at least to Quark, unexpected. He told everybody that they could not do this, that they could not simply board a shuttle and leave Bajor; they were prisoners—criminals, he said—and they were still in his charge. He believed that, yes, they would all eventually leave Gallitep, but either by being recovered by the Bajoran Militia, or by finding their way to the nearest settlement once spring came. But Prana stated flatly that he had not anticipated this, which was to his way of thinking an escape, and despite the horrors that the Ferengi had endured here, he was still an officer in Bajor's military, with a responsibility not to allow the internees to break from their captivity.

There was vociferous opposition to the corporal's views, expressed loudest of all by Kreln and Borit. Prana was beset from just about all sides. But Quark—and Rom—said little; although Quark desperately wished to leave here by whatever means possible, it remained fresh in his mind that Prana had saved his and Rom's lives.

Emotions, already tested by recent events, raged. Prana argued with Kreln and Borit and began to defend how he felt. Then, suddenly, he quieted. He needed time to think, he claimed, and without waiting for anybody's reaction, he grabbed his coat and fled the barracks. It was the first time Quark knew of that somebody had been alone somewhere in the camp since Colonel Mitra had ended Sergeant Wyte's life and then gone missing himself.

With thoughts of Mitra coming to mind, a sense of dread developed within Quark, along with a growing certainty that the colonel was not dead. Quark quickly became convinced that Corporal Prana would never come back to the barracks, but would instead be stalked and dispatched by the phantom Mitra. When the corporal ultimately did return safely a couple of hours later, Quark saw from the looks of obvious relief on some of the others' faces that he had not been alone in his fears.

Everybody was also relieved, it turned out, because Prana proceeded to apologize for his earlier outburst. He explained that the time here had been very difficult for him—something that Quark believed required no explanation—and that he had reacted without thinking. But now that he had considered the situation at length, he would willingly support whatever method they could devise for leaving Gallitep, even if that meant leaving Bajor as well.

Now, as Quark peered down at the empty expression on Prana's face, he worried that the corporal had changed his mind again, that he had reverted to the position that his primary role was still that of jailer. But after the corporal blinked a few times and saw everybody moving about, he grinned up at Quark.

"The shuttle," Prana said, with recognition, and he began to climb out of his bunk and put on his shoes.

Quark was relieved. He was also excited in a way that he had not been for a long time. He turned from Prana, ran to the door, and threw it wide. He padded out into the snow—several more centimeters had fallen during the night, and it was still coming down—and tilted his head back and looked skyward. At first, he saw nothing but the snowflakes falling into the thrust of light pouring through the barracks doorway, but then he tuned in to the hum of the shuttle's engines. There, barely discernible, but there, coming to a halt perhaps fifty meters up, directly above the barracks, was the ship. Quark rushed back inside.

"It's here," he told everybody. "Right above us."

They all seemed to move at once, speeding toward the door. As they pounded past Quark and out into the night, he looked for Cort, but he did not see him go past. He glanced around and spotted him in the corner, the homing device held in his cupped hands.

"Cort, your shuttle's here," Quark called to him, thinking that Cort must have been sleepy and that he did not realize what was happening. "Is it going to land?"

Cort looked up then, opening his mouth as if to respond to Quark, but then a familiar whine filled the barracks. As Quark watched, the streaking light of a transporter beam enveloped Cort. In a moment, he was gone.

Quark felt panic clutch at him. He heard the beating of his own heart in his ears. His throat constricted, making it impossible to swallow.

What happened? Quark's mind screamed. Had they done something to Cort, or said something—perhaps Quark's inadvertent remark about his being a smuggler—that had driven him to abandon them all here and make an escape only for himself?

Quark raced back through the open doorway. The others were all there, gathered together with their necks craned upward. Quark peered upward too, expecting to see the shuttle moving away, or to see nothing at all. Instead, the shuttle was just where it had been when he had first seen it moments ago. As he watched—as they all watched—it began to descend.

The group backed up as one as the shuttle neared the ground and finally alighted. The ship, Quark was surprised to see, was of Bajoran design; it was obvious now why Cort had thought that the shuttle could travel across Bajor without eliciting undue attention. Quark wondered if it was stolen, then dismissed the question as unimportant; at this point, the shuttle could have been hijacked from the Klingons and sought by the entire Imperial Fleet and it would have made no difference at all to him.

The main hatch opened. Cort appeared, and gazed out at the assemblage.

"Now boarding," he said with a broad smile.

The shuttle climbed through the atmosphere of Bajor, and relief rushed over Quark like a flood across desolate plains. But even as Gallitep receded below, he knew the memories of what had happened there would not be as accommodating. Without intending to, he touched a hand to his face; since there had been only so much that they had been able to accomplish with the medical kits, there were bruises and cuts on his face—all over his body, in fact—that were still in the process of healing.

Cort's shuttle was fairly small, about the size of the forward compartment of a runabout. It was configured to hold a pair of operators and twice as many passengers, with two seats situated at the forward control panels and four behind. With ten people inside right now, the ride was cramped, though nobody had yet complained. Rom and Karg had been relegated to sitting on the floor—Rom was focused on something in his hands that Quark could not see—while Prana and Drayan had ended up perched on the one-person transporter pad at the rear of the cabin. Cort captained the ship, and Kreln—the pilot of the cargo vessel that had been captured by the Bajorans after the deadline had passed—sat next to him and assisted.

"Power the boosters," Cort told Kreln. "We'll need them to climb into orbit."

"Powering up," Kreln responded, and Quark watched him work the controls. "Nominal," he reported a moment later.

The shuttle was ascending at a steep, though manageable, angle. They had already cleared the cloud layer of Bajor, and the panoply of stars beckoned through the single window in the bow. At this altitude, Bajor's gravitational pull had diminished sufficiently that it was superseded by the artificial-gravity system of the shuttle.

As they continued upward, Corporal Prana asked to be transported down to his home, or at least to his home city. Prior to yesterday, Quark thought, the Ferengi might have permitted him to do so. After Prana's initial disapproval of the prisoners' plan to leave Bajor, though—and despite his later recanting that view—it seemed to Quark that the corporal no longer had everybody's trust. Nobody said as much, but it became obvious to Quark when the consensus was reached that Prana should stay with the Ferengi until they were completely out of the Bajoran system. It must have been obvious to Prana as well, Quark thought. Nevertheless, the corporal accepted the collective decision without argument, perhaps understanding the source of the judgment.

"We're thirty seconds away from the apex of our suborbital course," Kreln announced, intent on the readouts marching across his console.

"Acknowledged," Cort said conversationally. He operated his panel, paused, and then tapped another control. "Firing boosters," he said.

There was a jolt from below as the shuttle's thrusters engaged. The noise level within the cabin swelled significantly. The inertial dampers must not have been functioning at maximum levels, because Quark sensed the increase in their acceleration. A deep, bass vibration also shook the shuttle.

Quark gazed around the cabin. Everybody seemed to him to be relatively comfortable, with the exception of Karg, whose hands were twisting and writhing about each other. Quark guessed that the reclusive painter did not travel much, and so he was probably not accustomed to the sense of speed and the steep angle of takeoff from a planetary surface.

After a short burn, the thrusters cut out. The shuttle steadied in its course, and the cabin quieted.

"Orbit achieved," Kreln said into the silence. "We have—" He stopped abruptly. "What the . . . ?"

Quark peered over at Kreln and saw him staring through the forward window. Quark followed his gaze and saw a small Bajoran freighter. He was confused; it was hardly unexpected to find a native ship in orbit. But then another movement captured his attention, and he saw that there was another ship beyond the freighter . . . and there was a third ship . . . and a fourth.

"How many do you read?" Cort asked, far calmer than Quark now felt.

"Nine in proximity," Kreln answered, "and more further out." His voice did not sound nearly as calm.

Quark and Borit both rose and moved to stand directly in back of Cort and Kreln. Quark heard movement behind him, and he turned to find that Tarken and Lenk had come forward too.

"What are they all doing here?" Borit asked.

"Don't worry," Cort said. "They're not here for us."

"How can you be certain?" Quark wanted to know.

"They're preparing for war," Cort said simply.

"War?" Quark barked. "With who?"

"You didn't think the Alliance would just allow the Bajorans to jail Ferengi citizens, did you?" Cort asked.

Quark considered this and concluded that the Alliance *would* allow such a thing. *Why not?* he thought. *Why would the nagus care?*

"Or let them ban them from using the wormhole?" Cort added.

That made more sense. The value of trade with the Gamma Quadrant might have been worth a fight.

Behind Quark, some of the others were asking questions, wanting to know what Cort knew and how he knew it. It was obvious to Quark, though, that Cort knew nothing for sure, but was simply making guesses about the situation.

"We need to come about," Cort told Kreln, ignoring the questions and concentrating instead on what he was doing. "Set a bearing of one-six-seven mark thirteen."

"This is a small craft," Kreln responded. "I can probably evade—"

"No," Cort said, looking up. "No evasive maneuvers. We're in a Bajoran shuttle; we'll be fine if we don't draw attention to ourselves."

"We're nine *Ferengi* in a Bajoran shuttle," Borit noted.

"We're nine Ferengi and one Bajoran," Prana said from the rear of the cabin.

"Either way, it won't be good for any of us if they scan us," Quark said.

"They have no reason to scan us," Cort maintained, "unless we give them one. Now I need that course change plotted."

Kreln looked a moment longer at Cort, then complied with the order.

"Course plotted and laid in," Kreln said. It had quickly become clear who was in charge.

"Just tell me this shuttle isn't stolen," Quark said.

"No," Cort said, "it isn't." Then: "Coming about, and throttling up to maximum."

As the ship changed course, Quark saw more and more vessels amassed about Bajor, mostly small freighters, a few passenger shuttles, and—

Quark did a double take, but by the time he looked the second time, the ship he thought he had seen was gone from view. Had it been one of those new transports meant to be sold to the Yridians? Quark suddenly felt ill; if the deal had not actually been completed, or if something had gone wrong in his absence—

Am I ruined? he thought. Quark squeezed between Tarken and Lenk and fell back into his seat. It was bad enough that his bar had been stolen from him, that he had been made to endure all that time in Gallitep, that he had been beaten, frozen, and virtually starved, but to lose his liquid assets . . .

"How long will it take us to get out of Bajoran space?" Tarken asked. Cort named a figure. The words drifted to Quark as though from a long distance; he was reeling from the possibility that while he had been interned on Bajor, he had become impoverished.

"It'll take longer than that to leave the system," Kreln said in response to Cort's estimate. "Unless this crate can go twice as fast as this."

"It can't," Cort said, "but we have a shortcut."

"A shortcut?" Lenk asked.

"The wormhole," Cort said.

"But that'll take us past *Deep Space Nine*," Borit complained.

"Starfleet has no reason to stop us," Cort said. "And even

if they did, it would be against the resolution the Federation Council passed; they're not going to get involved in a Ferengi-Bajoran dispute."

"Even if their scans show Ferengi on a Bajoran shuttle?" Lenk asked.

"It won't matter," Quark said automatically. "When we violated the Bajoran edict, Starfleet didn't arrest Rom and me, and when the Bajorans did arrest us, Starfleet didn't stop them."

"Where are we going?" Borit wanted to know.

Oddly enough, Quark realized, they had not discussed what their destination would be once they had left Bajor—though perhaps it was not so odd after all, Quark corrected himself; they had all been so thoroughly focused on escaping from Gallitep that it really had not mattered where they would go. Until Borit asked, Quark had never even considered the issue himself.

"There's a base on the other side of the wormhole in the Gamma Quadrant," Cort revealed. "My friends have a ship there . . . a starship, not a shuttle. I'm sure we can arrange to take everybody wherever they need to go."

"What about me?" Prana asked.

"We'll find a way to get you back to Bajor," Cort replied, "if that's what you want."

"It is," Prana said quietly.

Evidently satisfied with Cort's plan, everybody grew silent. Borit, Tarken, and Lenk returned to their seats. Rom, Quark noticed, was still huddled over something unseen on the floor; he was going to ask his brother what he was doing, but he found that he did not have the strength; the contemplation of his possible financial ruin had left him spent.

Quark looked forward and saw through the bow window that their course appeared clear of any vessels. Somewhere up ahead, he knew, lay the wormhole. That was just as well, he thought. If all of his resources had been depleted, then the best thing for him to do might be to start all over again in another quadrant, ninety-thousand light-years from where people—where his creditors—knew him. Perhaps Cort could use another smuggler in his operation.

So much for ever owning my own moon, Quark thought wistfully.

An explosion rocked the shuttle. Inertial dampers failed. Everybody was thrown about the cabin—everybody but Cort, Quark saw, who was strapped into his pilot's seat. With little room to move, bodies piled into bodies.

"What happened?" somebody yelled. Quark could not tell who it was. The cabin was alive with sound. A conduit had given way somewhere beneath the floor, and a gas of some sort—a coolant, Quark thought—was venting with a deafening hiss into the passenger compartment. The shuttle shook violently.

"There's a crack in one of the drive shells," Cort bellowed above the noise. "We hit a mine."

"We're losing deuterium," Kreln reported after he had climbed back into the navigator's seat.

"What?" Karg screamed right next to Quark. He was obviously scared. So was Quark.

The shuttle bucked, and the mass of bodies surged forward. Quark heard Borit yell something unintelligible. Quark scrambled to his feet—stepping on somebody's arm or leg as he did so—and looked wildly around for Rom. The din was tremendous.

Suddenly, the overhead lighting panels failed. They were replaced a second later by the emergency lights, and an eerie red glow bathed the cabin. An instant after that, the backup also failed, and they were left in almost complete darkness; the only meager illumination came from the control panels.

And then there was a flash of light, and Quark thought that the shuttle was coming apart.

"Brother," he shouted into the darkness.

And then they were gone.

CHAPTER

33

"CAPTAIN, sensors just detected an explosion in nearby space."

No, Sisko thought, instantly imagining that the first shot of the war had been fired. He felt the now-familiar emotions of anger and frustration rise within him, amplified by his impotence to do anything about the source of those feelings.

"An explosion of what, Mr. Worf?" Sisko asked. He sat in the command chair in the center of *Defiant's* bridge, not long after the evacuation of Starfleet personnel from *Deep Space Nine. New York* had departed the station an hour ago with most of the crew. Major Kira had been left in charge of *DS9,* and at least on an interim basis, she had chosen Odo to serve as her executive officer.

"I am getting indications of infernite," Worf said, studying the readouts at the tactical station. "There seem to be at least trace amounts of cabrodine as well."

Infernite and cabrodine, Sisko knew, were chemical explosives, common enough. What they were not were phasers or photon torpedoes, plasma weapons or disruptors. Whatever had happened out there, it had not been one ship firing on another.

"So what blew up?" Sisko asked.

"There's a trail of deuterium leading away from the explosion," Chief O'Brien reported from the operations console. "I think there may be a ship in trouble out there."

"There is," Worf confirmed, working his controls. "By configuration, it is a small Bajoran passenger shuttle."

"Are there any Ferengi ships about?" Sisko asked, wanting to be absolutely certain that his assumption that the war had not yet begun was correct. If *Defiant* was going to take any action at all here, he needed to know that he would not be involving Starfleet in the Bajoran-Ferengi hostilities.

"Negative," Worf said. "There are no other ships in the vicinity."

"The explosion appears to have occurred within one of the shuttle's drive shells," O'Brien observed.

"Hail them," Sisko ordered. "See if they require our assistance."

"Aye, sir." Sisko watched as Worf worked his console, once, twice, three times. "There is no response; they are not receiving us."

"Set a course for them," Sisko said. "Full impulse."

"Aye, sir." At the conn, Dax complied with the order.

"We may not be permitted to get involved in a war," Sisko said, thinking aloud, "but we can at least render aid to a ship in distress."

"Actually, I'm not sure how much distress they're in," O'Brien remarked. "They may be shaken up a bit, but they don't appear to be in any danger of a hull breach or another explosion. Of course, it may take them some time to get anywhere."

"An emergency on a ship that isn't life-threatening for the crew," Sisko mused, managing a quick smile; good news had been infrequent of late. "How refreshing." He saw Dax turn partially toward him with a grin on her face.

"Captain, we are receiving a distress call," Worf said. "It is being broadcast on a Starfleet emergency channel."

"Maybe they've seen us or scanned us," Sisko hypothesized. "Put it on screen."

"There is no visual or aural component to the communication," Worf explained. "The transmission is rendered completely in text."

"That's strange," Sisko noticed. "Maybe their Chambers coil is out."

"Their coil emissions are normal," O'Brien declared.

"They claim to be in danger of a hull breach," Worf said, sounding suspicious. "They are requesting that their ship be evacuated."

"Chief?" Sisko asked.

"Their structural integrity is sound," O'Brien said. "I think they're overreacting."

"It's understandable that they'd be shaken up a bit," Dax said. "An explosion in a small ship like that has got to be pretty frightening."

"It also looks like their inertial dampers are off-line," O'Brien said, relenting a bit, Sisko thought, from his allegation of "overreacting." "They may be shaken literally as well as figuratively."

"Are they reporting any casualties?" Sisko wanted to know.

"No," said Worf.

"We're entering visual range," Dax announced.

"Let's see it," Sisko said.

Worf worked to bring the image up on the main viewer. The starscape shifted and the shuttle appeared in the center of the screen. The small craft wobbled and vibrated as it floated through space, apparently unpowered. Sisko saw that the running lights were off, and he thought that he could make out the dark line of a fissure crawling horizontally along one of the engine shells.

"How are their life signs?" Sisko asked.

"The deuterium stream is making it difficult for the sensors to pick out individual life-forms," Worf said. "But the readings we are getting suggest that there are approximately eight to twelve people on board."

"Eight to twelve?" Dax repeated. "That's got to be cozy."

Not cozy, Sisko thought. *Tremulous and panic-stricken, maybe, but not cozy.* The people on that shuttle, he guessed, were probably fleeing before the battle for their world began.

"Can we get a transporter lock on them?" Sisko asked, calling on the chief's years of experience as a transporter operator.

"Not automatically," O'Brien answered, "but we should be able to perform a wide-band retrieval for all humanoid life."

"Do it," Sisko told O'Brien. "Inform Transporter Room One of the procedure and have the shuttle passengers beamed over."

"Aye, sir." O'Brien set about contacting the operator in the transporter room.

"Dax, once the Bajorans are aboard, I want you to take us back to *Deep Space Nine*," Sisko said. "After Dr. Bashir administers treatment to whoever needs it, we'll transport them to the station and resume our course to Starbase Icarus."

"Aye, sir."

"Mr. Worf, engage the tractor beam; we'll tow the shuttle back to the station for our guests."

"Yes, sir."

And that was all that needed to be done right now. For a few moments, nobody spoke, and the only sounds on the bridge were those of the ship responding to the commands of Sisko's crew.

And then: "Transporter Room One to Captain Sisko," came the voice of the young ensign over the intercom system; Sisko still could not recall his name, although he did recognize his voice.

"Sisko here. What is it, Ensign? Have you got the crew of the shuttle?"

"Oh, we've got them all right," the ensign said. "Sir, I think you'd better get down here."

There were nine Ferengi, one Bajoran, and innumerable questions, both being asked of Sisko and forming in his own mind. But all of those questions would have to be set aside for now; without warning, the opportunity Sisko had been seeking from the Bajoran government had somehow been delivered into his hands, and he was not going to allow any time to pass before he attempted to capitalize on it. Never before had he been so happy to see Quark.

"I want you to assign quarters and escorts to them," Sisko told Lieutenant Robinson, the senior security officer present. He looked past her at the group they had beamed aboard from the troubled shuttle. They all appeared to be in some distress, presumably because of the accident aboard their craft: they stood huddled together in one corner of the transporter room, whispering to each other, their eyes darting about nervously. Their ride must have been rough once the inertial dampers had failed, Sisko decided, because he saw bruises and cuts on every face—although the lone Bajoran among them seemed to have escaped with the fewest injuries, with only a single small cut over his left eye.

"When they're all settled," Sisko continued telling the lieutenant, "accompany each of them, one by one, to sickbay, so that Dr. Bashir can treat them."

"Aye, Captain." Robinson directed both her team—a pair of male ensigns—and the group of shuttle passengers, explaining what they would be doing. The security officers began to lead the ragged Ferengi—and the one Bajoran—away.

"Quark," Sisko called as the transporter-room door opened before the assemblage. The former barkeeper stopped and stepped away from the group; his brother did the same. "I'd like you to stay here for a moment; I want to talk to you." Lieutenant Robinson brought her officers and their charges to a halt.

"I really have nothing to say to you . . . Captain." Out of Quark's mouth, Sisko's rank sounded like an insult. Quark turned his back and rejoined the group—all of them were watching him—and Rom followed.

"I see," Sisko said, bringing his hands together behind his back. He would to have to tread carefully here if there was going to be any chance of eliciting Quark's assistance. "Let me ask again then: Would you please stay here so that you and I can talk?"

Quark froze. The word *please* seemed to have some effect on him, though Sisko could not be sure that it was the effect at which he had been aiming. He saw Quark glance over at Rom.

"Go to sickbay," Quark told his brother. "You really need to have your face worked on."

"Yours isn't looking so good either, brother," Rom returned.

"This face?" Quark asked rhetorically. "Nothing could

destroy the beauty in this face." Then, in gentler tones, and more seriously, he said, "Go ahead, Rom. I'll be there shortly."

It was a moment of tenderness Sisko had never expected to witness. In his experience, Quark's relationship with his brother had been characterized by Quark's continual yelling and his inveterate use of the epithet *you idiot.*

Rom gazed over at Sisko with an expression the captain could not read—was it a warning? an entreaty?—then returned to the rest of the shuttle passengers. Robinson and her security team ushered the group away, and the door slid shut.

"Ensign," Sisko said, addressing the transporter operator, wishing again that he could recall his name. "Would you excuse us?" Sisko remembered his meeting here with Dai-Mon Bractor, and it occurred to him that the transporter room aboard *Defiant* was beginning to feel more like a conference room.

"Yes, sir," the ensign replied. He secured his console and left the room. Quark watched him go, then turned and regarded Sisko.

"I want political asylum for my brother and me," he said.

"Just the two of you?" Sisko asked sarcastically. "What about the rest of your friends?" He spoke as though granting political sanctuary were the simplest task in the universe to perform, thereby implying how problematic it could actually be.

"They can do whatever they want to do, ask for asylum if they want to, I don't care," Quark said, and it was clear from the way he delivered his words that he really did not care. "I'm just asking for Rom and me."

Sisko saw an opening here, but he would still have to be circumspect in his approach. He paced along one wall, away from Quark, as he responded.

"We've spoken before about the Federation Council's resolution with respect to the current troubles between the Bajorans and the Ferengi," Sisko said. "The resolution is still in effect, and I know you understand it." He circled around behind the transporter console and faced Quark across the room.

"Of course I understand it," Quark snapped. "These cuts

and bruises—" He pointed a finger up at his face. "—were given to me by that resolution."

"I'm not sure what that's supposed to mean," Sisko said, a little more dismissive than he had intended. He hesitated and took a moment to look more closely at Quark. He saw that, while one or two of the wounds on his face appeared fresh, others were in various stages of healing; that would indicate that they could not have been caused by the incident aboard the shuttle. And Sisko noticed something else as well: Quark's features were drawn—no, not just drawn; they were *gaunt*. He was wearing a loose-fitting jumpsuit—his jailhouse garb, Sisko assumed—that hid his body, but even so, he seemed to have lost weight during the time he had been away from *Deep Space Nine*. Even through the clothing, Sisko could see a boniness to Quark's shoulders that had not been there before, and the Ferengi's forearms, visible where they emerged from the sleeves of the jumpsuit, appeared painfully thin. Quark had lost *a lot* of weight, Sisko saw now, maybe even to the point of emaciation.

This couldn't have happened on Bajor, Sisko thought. This was not how the Bajorans treated their prisoners—or anybody, for that matter, not even the most violent of convicted criminals. As Sisko peered across the room, Quark looked away; more than that, he shrank back, as though uncomfortable with the captain's scrutiny.

"Do you want to tell me what happened to you?" Sisko asked, striving to temper his attitude.

"Never mind," Quark said, waving away the matter of his injuries. "I'm just saying that I don't care about the resolution. My brother and I are political refugees, we've been jailed for no other reason than because we're Ferengi, and we demand that the Federation provide us protection and immunity from extradition to Bajor."

"You 'demand'?" Sisko repeated. "You break out of jail, abduct a Bajoran national, and steal a Bajoran shuttle—" Quark suddenly raised a hand to his forehead, as though he had just realized something. "—and you have the audacity to make demands?" That fast, Sisko observed, he had reverted to the adversarial pattern typical of his relationship with Quark.

"Are you interested in facts, Captain?" Quark dropped his hand and started across the room toward Sisko. "Or are you going to hide behind Federation sanctimony and blame me one more time for things I didn't do?" He stopped in front of the transporter console and glared up and over it at Sisko.

"What things didn't you do?" Sisko started out from behind the console, and Quark flinched and backed away quickly, almost as though he expected Sisko to strike him.

"Quark—?" Sisko started to ask.

"I didn't kidnap that Bajoran, for one thing," Quark said, ignoring what had just happened.

"Well, that would certainly be easy enough to verify."

"Go ahead and verify it," Quark insisted. "His name is Prana, he's a corporal in the Bajoran Militia, and he came with us willingly. And I don't think the shuttle was stolen either. At least, I was told it wasn't."

"But you did escape from prison."

Quark laughed. Not just a chuckle, but a hearty, full-throated guffaw; the sound, though, was far from jovial. Quark moved away from the captain and around the room in a meandering fashion, his head thrown back and his mouth open wide in a manner approaching hysteria. He climbed onto the transporter platform and dropped down to a sitting position, knees up and leaning his back against the wall.

Sisko watched Quark, and mixed in with the laughter, he thought he saw tears; the Ferengi was breaking down right in front of him. Sisko did not understand even remotely why Quark was behaving this way, except . . . he had seen this type of behavior before, hadn't he? Several times, in fact. It had not always been manifested in just this way, but it was nevertheless recognizable: post-traumatic stress. But what trauma had Quark undergone? The injuries to his face, the loss of weight . . . and again Sisko thought: *This could not have happened on Bajor.*

"Do you want to know where I escaped from?" Quark asked from his sitting position on the transporter platform; he did not look up. Sisko said nothing. "Gallitep."

"What?" Sisko gasped, unable to withhold his reaction. What Quark was saying was unthinkable: the Gallitep forced-labor camp was for all of Bajor a powerful symbol of the pure evil embodied in the Cardassian Occupation. Sisko knew that the camp had not been destroyed, but had been preserved—after a bitter and difficult social debate—as a tribute to the many Bajorans who had lived through the camps, and to the many who had not; it also served as a reminder that such horrors must never be permitted to happen again. For the Bajorans to have reopened the camp, even as a place of simple incarceration—

And then Sisko recalled the injuries—and the remnants of injuries—on the faces of all the Ferengi they had beamed aboard.

No, he told himself. *This could not have been.*

"You heard me," Quark said. "They sent us to the place they hate more than any other." Now he looked up. "So much for the deep spirituality of the Bajoran people."

Sisko was stunned. He walked over to the platform and looked again at Quark. His face was covered with cuts and greenish purple contusions. To his dismay, Sisko now saw a long, thin scar traveling across one cheek to the bridge of Quark's nose. This was impossible.

"I can't believe it," Sisko said. Quark must have heard the anguish in his voice, though, because he did not seem to think that Sisko was questioning his story. "That there would not have been a public outcry when you were taken there—" Sisko stopped then, realizing that, imprisoned in Gallitep or in some other facility, there was no imaginable reason that Quark should have been hurt—and perhaps even starved—the way he had been. And then a terrible question occurred to Sisko: *Why didn't I know about this?* The answer, he found, was even more terrible: he had not thought about Quark much after he had been taken from the station—not until his help had been needed. Sisko bent at the knees and sat down on the transporter platform, across from Quark.

"All right," Sisko said. "Asylum."

"Wonderful," Quark responded. He seemed exhausted. Slowly, he got to his feet and dismounted the platform. As he headed for the door, Sisko called after him.

"Quark."

For the second time, Quark stopped and turned before he reached the door.

"I need your help."

"*You* want *my* help?" Quark said, his voice rising in obvious anger, maybe even in incredulity. "You mean like the way you helped me when I came to you . . . I don't even know how long ago it was, because I've been beaten just about every day since then."

Beaten? Sisko reeled at the thought.

"I'm genuinely sorry about that." It was not enough, Sisko knew, but it was how he truly felt. When this was all over—if it ever was—he pledged to himself that he would learn exactly what had happened to Quark and the others, and he would see those responsible brought to justice.

"You know," Quark began, his voice still loud, "you don't like me, Captain, and Kira doesn't like me, and O'Brien and Bashir and Worf, and none of you even really know me. To you, I'm just a short and greedy Ferengi, or on a good day, when you want my services, I'm a Ferengi bartender. Or I was, anyway. Just because we don't have all the same values doesn't mean that you're right and I'm wrong, or that I'm not a good person. But forget about right and wrong, good and bad; I'm never just Quark to you, just a person. I'm always a member of a people that you never really tried to understand; I'm always a *Ferengi.*"

"And aren't we all just 'hyoo-mons' to you?" Sisko asked, mimicking Quark's derogatory pronunciation of the word *humans.* He understood why Quark had not included Dax in his litany of the people he thought did not like him—she was perhaps the most tolerant person Sisko had ever known—but he was curious at the omission of Odo, whose name he would have expected to head the list.

"Maybe you wouldn't be 'hyoo-mons' if you didn't look down on me from a distance."

"Maybe," Sisko said, rising from the platform. "This is not the first time you've mentioned these types of issues to me."

"No," Quark agreed.

"And it's not the first time I've listened, either. You may be right—" Sisko corrected himself. "You *are* right, at least about some of the things you've said with respect to me; I can't speak for anybody else."

"So what does that mean?"

"It means . . . I don't know what it means," Sisko admitted. "Perhaps I can take you to a baseball game in a holosuite sometime."

"Ugh. How can you watch those holoprograms?" Quark asked. "They are *so* boring."

Sisko welcomed the light chatter, and he supposed that Quark did too; it served to lessen the friction between them.

"Well, something else then. Maybe."

"Yeah. Maybe you'll invite me to a dinner where I don't have to serve."

There was a lull, and it seemed as though the conversation had ended. But it could not end, Sisko knew. Not yet.

"Quark, you and your brother have asylum. I'll grant it to all the Ferengi. I'm not interested in pursuing threats to get your assistance." Sisko knew that threats were often effective with Quark, but he felt it would not be right to employ such tactics, particularly after what had apparently happened at—Sisko still found it hard to believe—Gallitep. "I think you were wronged, and I was wrong not to speak up about it."

Quark's eyes narrowed in what Sisko took to be an appraising look, but the Ferengi said nothing.

"I think I can offer you a better deal than asylum, though. A profitable deal."

Now Quark's eyes widened.

"I'm listening," he said.

"This isn't for me," Sisko said soberly. "It's for the people of Bajor—" Quark began to react, but Sisko held him back by raising both his hands, palms out. "—and the people of Ferenginar." In truth, Sisko had previously only thought of the need to resolve this conflict, to avoid this war, in terms of the consequences that would be spared the Bajorans, and he felt ashamed now as he realized that. He hoped that his narrow focus had been because he had always believed that the Ferengi would win a war with the Bajorans, but even if that was true, the Ferengi would still surely suffer casualties, and one conviction that Sisko held absolutely, applied here, was that the life of a Bajoran was no more or less valuable than the life of a Ferengi.

"What is it you want?" Quark asked.

"It's the same thing it's been all along," Sisko said. "The Orb of the Prophets."

Quark seemed to deflate. This was something he clearly did not want to do.

"Hasn't the nagus sold that thing yet?"

"Apparently not." Which was, Sisko thought, odd. "Quark, the stakes are much higher now: the nagus has declared war on Bajor."

"I know," Quark said, and he appeared to lose himself in thought for a moment.

"You do?"

"Oh, uh, I saw all the ships around Bajor, and I just figured it out." Quark paused, and then said, "Listen, why should I care if the Alliance goes to war with Bajor?"

"Let's think this through," Sisko said. "If you don't help and there is a war, then either Ferenginar will win or Bajor will win."

"I'd put a bet down on the Alliance," Quark commented.

"Let's say the Alliance is victorious. Then the Ferengi will take over *Deep Space Nine*. Do you believe that the nagus will give the bar back to you, or do you think he'd claim it as a war prize and have one of his associates run it for him?" From the expression on Quark's face, Sisko knew that he had correctly surmised the consequences of a Ferengi victory. "And if the unlikely happens and Bajor wins the war, they'll never return your bar to you."

"You have a point," Quark allowed. "But if I agree to help, there's no guarantee that I'll be able to change the nagus's mind."

"If you can't, then I promise that you and Rom will still have asylum," Sisko said. "But if you can persuade the nagus not just to reinstate the Bajorans in the auction, but to sell the Ninth Orb to them, then Shakaar has already told me that he will rescind the edict barring Ferengi from Bajoran space. Starfleet will be able to maintain a presence on the station, and I personally guarantee—*as the Emissary*—that your bar will be given back to you, and you and Rom will be granted amnesty for whatever crimes the Bajorans believe you to have committed."

"Do you even know where the nagus is right now?"

"Intelligence reports put him on Ferenginar."

"I need time to think about this," Quark said, beginning to pace slowly around the room. Considering a business proposition, Quark almost looked like his former, vital self.

"There's no time. The Ferengi fleet will be here soon."

"I have your word?" Quark asked.

"You have my word," Sisko promised. He was not entirely sure how he would be able to fulfill that promise, but he would do everything he possibly could to make it happen.

"What about the resolution?"

"The Council's resolution is a wonderful guideline," Sisko answered carefully. "But it's not appropriate to follow any decision blindly." He paused, and then added, "Isn't there a Rule of Acquisition to cover this?"

"There's a Rule of Acquisition to cover everything," Quark said, "but that doesn't mean one's always got to be applied." And Quark smiled.

CHAPTER
34

QUARK CONSIDERED keeping the scar.

"You're joking, aren't you?" Bashir asked him.

"I don't know," Quark said as he sat down on the edge of a diagnostic bed. "I think maybe it makes me look more . . ."

"Beaten up?" Bashir offered.

"I was going to say 'more dangerous.' Don't you think certain people might be more inclined to do business with me if I looked this way?" There had been no mirrors at Gallitep, and so Quark had not had an opportunity to see the extent of his facial injuries until he had arrived in *Defiant*'s sickbay. Even after having had several days in which to heal, his wounds had still looked awful. Dr. Bashir had now repaired all of the damage to his body and face, with the exception of the scar that climbed across his cheek and over to the top of his nose.

"What I think," Bashir said, "is that people might be even more inclined than ever to run and hide when they see you."

"That's very funny, Doctor," Quark said. "Not as funny as mistaking a preganglionic fiber for a postganglionic nerve, but still very funny." Quark was alluding to the one error that Bashir had made on his Starfleet Medical final exam, an error that had consequently prevented him from being valedictorian of his graduating class. Although this had happened several years ago, Quark was aware that it was something that still rankled the doctor; he certainly complained about it enough.

Bashir put a hand on Quark's head and tilted it uncomfortably backward, then raised a medical device to his face; Quark could just see its handle in his peripheral vision. He heard a hum then, and felt heat on his cheek, and an odd, knitting sensation, as though the cells of his skin were somehow weaving themselves together. After a short time, the doctor turned off the device and examined Quark's face.

"Uh-oh," he said.

"Uh-oh?" Quark asked frantically. He jumped from the diagnostic bed and raced over to a mirror. When he examined his reflection, though, all he saw was his own face, restored to its uninjured form.

"Uh-oh," Bashir said, "now you look just like you used to."

"You really are extremely witty, Doctor," Quark told him. "As witty as a salutatorian can be, anyway."

Bashir smiled and seemed to give in.

"I'm done with him," he told Lieutenant Robinson, who was standing off to one side; she had been assigned to "escort" Quark through the ship. "Please take him away, would you?"

"Certainly, sir," Robinson replied. The security officer walked over to Quark. "Captain Sisko wanted me to accompany you to your assigned quarters," she said.

"And what lovely quarters they are," Quark said derisively. He had traveled once before on *Defiant*, on a trade mission to the Gamma Quadrant, and so he was familiar with the ship's austere accommodations. "Four walls, a floor, a ceiling, and two bunks; what more could I want?" As he spoke, he heard the doors to the sickbay open behind him, and then a swirling, liquid sound, almost inaudible, that he could not mistake. He turned to face Odo.

For a moment, the two men regarded each other silently. The last time Quark had seen Odo was when the constable had helped the Bajorans take him and his brother into custody on *Deep Space Nine*. Quark had understandably felt great animosity toward Odo then, but he discovered now that he had no facility for recalling that emotion.

"You're lucky you weren't assigned to ride on the outside of the ship," the constable said at last, and his reversion to their familiar banter seemed to Quark almost like an apology. In Odo's hands, Quark saw what appeared to be a bundle of clothing.

"Constable," Quark said, "I thought you would be on the station." When Sisko had brought Quark down to sickbay from the transporter room, he had explained the current state of affairs among the Bajorans, the Ferengi, and Starfleet. Because of the declaration of war issued by the nagus, Starfleet had elected to evacuate all of their personnel from the station. Odo was not a member of Starfleet, though, and Quark had simply assumed that he had remained on *DS9*.

"I was there," Odo said, "but somebody's got to look after you on the way to Ferenginar."

Odo must have come aboard, Quark realized, when *Defiant* had briefly returned to the station to disembark Corporal Prana and release the shuttle from the tractor beam. The rest of the Ferengi, as far as Quark knew, would be staying on the ship until after Quark's attempt to persuade the nagus to change his mind about selling the Orb to the Bajorans.

"I guess I can assume that Kira isn't here," Quark observed, "since my lobes are still attached to my head."

"Major Kira is still on the station, yes," Odo confirmed. Then, holding out the bundle he was carrying, he said, "Here. Captain Sisko wanted me to replicate something for you to wear."

Quark was still in one of the ill-fitting jumpsuits from the prison camp. He took the clothing from Odo, separated out the undergarments and shoes, and held up the largest piece of apparel by the shoulders, letting gravity unfold it. It was another jumpsuit, this one Starfleet issue, Quark was sure, but not identifiably so. The one plain advantage that it had over what he was presently wearing was that it appeared to be his size.

"Don't you have anything better? It's not as stylish as what I normally wear," Quark noted.

"As a matter of fact, we don't," replied the constable curtly.

"Well, then I suppose it'll do for now."

"How magnanimous of you," Odo intoned.

"Doctor," Quark called just as Bashir was leaving the room, heading for his office, which adjoined the sickbay. "May I use your office to change my clothes?"

"Oh, by all means," Bashir said. "Anything to hasten your departure." He turned to Odo and the two shared a glance Quark recognized as emblematic of their traditional attitude toward him: smug superiority.

Quark went into the doctor's office and began removing the uncomfortable, oversized jumpsuit. As he did so, he started to feel disoriented. Only a few hours ago, he had been in the most infamous prison camp on Bajor, marooned, and with indeterminate prospects of rescue or escape. And just days before that, he had been on the verge of being executed—deliberately and coldly murdered, really—and that had been preceded by weeks and weeks of physical and mental abuse. Now, he was on a Federation starship on his way to Ferenginar, where he would attempt to change the mind of the grand nagus himself. The sequence of events was dizzying. *Life is an ever-changing jewel,* he thought wryly.

Quark stepped out of the Bajoran jumpsuit and began pulling on the new undergarments. He still could not believe that he had agreed to Sisko's request. The captain was quite a negotiator, Quark had to admit; his dealings had been surprisingly impressive. Quark had never thought *hyoo-mons* capable of such shrewdness. Perhaps that was an example of Quark's own biases; perhaps it was time he examined his views about *hyoo-mons—humans,* he forced himself to think—and others. Such a reevaluation would be especially important if there was any possibility that a human might someday outmaneuver him in a business deal.

Quark finished pulling on the Starfleet jumpsuit—it fit him very well, he was delighted to see—and the shoes, and then returned to the main room of the sickbay. Dr. Bashir was leaning against a wall, looking annoyed as he apparently waited to get into his office. Across the room, Odo was stalking back and forth, also waiting. Lieutenant Robinson was no longer present.

"It's about time," Bashir said when he saw Quark. Then, when he noticed that Quark was empty-handed, he said, "Where are the clothes you were wearing?"

"I left them on the floor in there," Quark said, pointing back into the doctor's office. "I figured you'd know where to dispose of them."

"Of course," Bashir said dryly, rolling his eyes. He quickly left the room.

"What happened to Lieutenant Robinson?" Quark asked Odo.

"I relieved her," the constable said. "According to Captain Sisko, you're my responsibility now."

"Well, then," Quark said brightly, "shall we go?" He walked through the doors and out into the corridor, where he intentionally turned in the wrong direction. He did this automatically, out of a long-standing habit of leading Odo to believe that he was always trying to get away with something. In that manner, with Odo continually preventing him from breaking one rule or another, Quark thought that the constable would be less likely to believe that he was actually able to get away with doing something wrong. It was a theory, anyway.

"This way, Quark," Odo said.

"Certainly," Quark said, and he reversed his course in the corridor.

"You seem to be in a good mood," the constable noticed.

Quark was about to disagree—an automatic reaction for him with Odo—when he realized that the constable was right: he was in a good mood.

Sure, and why not? Quark thought. He had escaped being imprisoned on Bajor, and he was now in a position where he would receive either asylum or amnesty. There was also a chance—a very small chance, but still a chance—that he would be able to get his bar back, and he was also pretty sure now that his liquid assets were still intact.

Quark had inferred that last bit of information from what he had learned from Sisko. Quark had asked about the transport he thought he had seen in orbit about Bajor, and the captain had told him that it was one of a squadron of starships that the Bajorans had purchased. That in itself indicated that the deal Quark had orchestrated months ago had not somehow soured in his absence. When Quark had asked the origin of the ships, Sisko had said that he believed that they had initially come from the Karemma, further evidence that the ship Quark had seen was not one of the ones involved in the deal he had brokered. All of which meant that Quark's accounts were probably just as he had left them before being arrested and taken to Bajor.

"You're right," Quark told Odo. "I am in a good mood. I must be happy to see you."

"Right."

They had come to the doors of a turbolift, which opened at their approach. They entered the lift, and Odo specified the deck to which they were going. The lift ascended.

"So," Odo said, with a practiced air of nonchalance that Quark easily recognized, "do you know what you're going to say to the nagus when we get to Ferenginar?"

Quark looked up at Odo. The question, unexpected as it was, brought Quark to a conclusion he had not previously reached.

"This was your idea, wasn't it?" Quark asked. "You must have been the one to suggest my involvement in this mission." This mission, Quark knew from what Sisko had told him, had not spontaneously developed when he and his fellow internees had been plucked from the dying Bajoran shuttle. The captain had said that he had been attempting to engineer Quark's release from prison *before* the nagus had declared war, *before* Starfleet had been forced to evacuate *Deep Space Nine.* Sisko claimed that he had come to believe that Quark was the best hope of defusing the situation between the Bajorans and the Ferengi. That had seemed odd to Quark, and he understood now that such an important political gambit—using Quark to negotiate peace with the nagus—would not have originated with Sisko or any of the Starfleet personnel; none of them had ever taken him seriously. But Odo . . .

"What difference does it make to you whose idea it was?" Odo asked.

The turbolift doors opened, and Quark and Odo walked

out into another corridor on another deck. The constable's question, Quark thought, was a good one. Why should he care about who had first considered seeking his assistance? Well, actually, the first person had been Kira, but she had been asking him to do something—a favor, really—specifically for her and her people. What was being asked of Quark now was for him to avert a war and perhaps save the quadrant.

"It was you," Quark told Odo. "I know it was you. But why?"

"What do you mean, 'why'? How many reasons could there be?"

"I can think of several," Quark said. Odo stopped before a door, apparently the cabin to which Quark had been assigned. Another security officer, one whom Quark recognized from *DS9*, was standing beside the door. "Did you suggest that I should be the one to talk with the nagus because you thought I'd be successful, or because you wanted to see me fail, maybe even get into trouble with the Ferengi Commerce Authority?"

"That's the problem with always making deals, Quark," Odo said, sighing. "Always trying to take from people as much as you can, and giving as little as possible in return . . . you can be certain of your enemies' identities, but do you know who your friends are?"

Quark found Odo's question cryptic. What did he mean? Surely he was not claiming to be Quark's friend . . . was he?

Before Quark could pursue the issue, the single-paneled door opened. Beyond was the small, stark cabin Quark had expected. Rom stood just inside the doorway; he had obviously been the one to open the door. Quark and Odo both looked at him.

"Brother," Rom said with some urgency, "I need to talk to you." Rom's face was still bruised; he clearly had not been to sickbay yet. He was wearing the same Starfleet jumpsuit that Quark had on, though.

Quark glanced back up at Odo and considered continuing the conversation they had been having. There was no point, he decided. Quark knew Odo well enough to know that the constable would never simply spell out the meanings of what he had said.

Quark started through the doorway, and Rom stepped aside to let him pass. The door slid shut behind him.

"Brother, I need to tell you something," Rom reiterated.

"Why haven't you been to see Dr. Bashir yet?" Quark wanted to know. He sat down on the lower bunk.

"I'm going to go see him in a little while," Rom said. "I just needed to talk to you alone first."

"I really think you should go now," Quark said. "Your face looks even worse than it usually does."

"I think we were set up."

"Set up?" Quark rose from the bunk. "When? By who?"

"By Cort."

This was one of the last names Quark had expected to hear. Prana, he had thought, or perhaps Shakaar or Sisko, even Zek. But Cort?

"Are you out of your mind?" Quark said. "Cort saved us, you idiot."

"I know it doesn't make sense," Rom said. "It seems like he saved us; I'm just not sure how."

"What are you talking about? He made that homing device and brought his shuttle to . . . to the camp." Even though he had spoken the name of the camp aloud to Sisko, Quark discovered that he no longer wished it to pass his lips.

"That's just it," Rom said. "He didn't make a homing device."

"What do you mean?"

"When we got in the shuttle, I found the device he supposedly put together; it was in a closed compartment near the back of the cabin."

"He must have put it there when he transported aboard," Quark said, recalling how he had seen Rom huddled over something on the floor of the shuttle. "What do you mean 'supposedly put together'?"

"I mean, that was no homing device."

"What was it then?"

"It wasn't anything," Rom said. "It was just a mass of parts from a medical scanner and a phaser. They had been connected together, but they didn't make anything that functioned."

"But then how did he call the shuttle?"

"I don't know," Rom said, shrugging his usual shrug. "Maybe he had another homing device, a real one."

"Then why would he pretend to build one? And why wouldn't he have called his shuttle to save us—or at least save himself—much sooner than he did?"

"There's another thing, brother," Rom said. "Don't you think it's a pretty big coincidence that right after we escaped from Bajor—" Quark quickly wondered whether Rom also had an aversion to using the name of the prison camp. "—we were picked up by the *Defiant.*"

Events had transpired so quickly—the flight from Bajor, avoiding the many ships massed in orbit, the explosion aboard the shuttle, and the subsequent rescue by the crew of *Defiant*—that Quark had not really had time to consider everything that had happened. Now that he did, though, he agreed with his brother: there had been several unlikely coincidences. And he also remembered that Cort had seemed to know more than he should have about the situation between Ferenginar and Bajor.

"Are you suggesting that Cort is working with somebody from the station, somebody on the *Defiant?*" It seemed preposterous, a Ferengi working with a trusted Starfleet officer. Then again, Rom had been working for Chief O'Brien before they had been taken to Bajor. Of course, Rom was not a typical Ferengi male. Perhaps Cort was not either.

"I don't know," Rom said. "Maybe somebody from the station."

Who, though? Sisko? Quark considered the possibility, but it did not make sense. If Cort had voluntarily stayed in the camp on Bajor—endured imprisonment by Colonel Mitra and Sergeant Wyte—when he had the capability of calling his shuttle and escaping at any time, then Quark was sure that he would have to have been paid extremely well, and Sisko—any Starfleet officer—would not have been able to do that.

There was somebody who obviously could pay well, though, somebody who was embroiled in the midst of the entire Ferengi-Bajoran situation Grand Nagus Zek. But why would he have wanted to keep the internees in the prison camp for so long? And why would he want them to escape now, and why be picked up by the crew of *Defiant?* And where was the profit for Zek? No, it made no sense for it to be the nagus.

The questions Quark was asking himself had to be asked of whoever it was who had set them up, if indeed they had been set up at all. And all of those questions had one component in common, a single question Quark was suddenly sure lay at the heart of the matter: *Why?*

CHAPTER
35

DEFIANT FLEW AT maximum warp.

On the bridge's main viewer, a tactical display showed the Ferengi armada: scores and scores of ships, arrayed in matrix-like formation, a vast legion of firepower, maneuverability, and defense. Sisko scanned the identifiers on the graphic plot and saw that the advancing fleet was comprised not just of the Marauder heavies, but of many different types of smaller ships as well. It was a force, Sisko decided, that would tax even Starfleet in battle. The meager Bajoran squadrons, even augmented as they were with their new defensive transports, could not hope to withstand the formidable assault the Ferengi were mounting.

"Can you punch us through undetected?" Sisko asked Dax.

"I think so," Dax answered from the conn. "Their grouping is moderately tight, but we should be able to sneak through."

Defiant was traveling cloaked, but passing through an array of so many ships traveling at faster-than-light velocities, it would be a simple matter for *Defiant*'s own warp field to have an observable proximate effect on that of another ship, and the last thing that Sisko wanted was to be observed. They could circumnavigate the armada, of course, but that would necessarily add time to their journey, and right now, the Ferengi fleet was closer to Bajor than *Defiant* was to Ferenginar.

"How large are the interstices?" Sisko asked.

"Not very," Dax replied, examining the readouts both on the main viewer and on her console. "The rows and columns of ships in each layer of the formation are staggered, so we won't be able to take a straight path through them. I'm not sure why, but their ships are only traveling at warp factor five; that should make things at least a little easier."

"Perhaps that's the maximum speed of some of the smaller vessels," Sisko guessed.

"Or they may be conserving power for their attack on Bajor," Worf suggested, ever the warrior.

"We're closing rapidly on them, Captain," O'Brien reported. "We'll be committed to a pass-through in thirty seconds."

"Dax?" Sisko asked. The commander's attention, Sisko saw, was focused on her console, her fingers dancing across her controls in an experienced ballet, her eyes searching the numbers for the answer her captain wanted.

"We can do it," Dax announced, "but we'll have to reduce our speed to warp four-point-five."

"Do it," Sisko ordered.

"Aye," Dax acknowledged, already working her controls.

"Twenty seconds," said O'Brien.

"Mr. Worf, let's see the starscape, superimposed with icons showing the actual positions of the ships," Sisko said.

"Yes, sir." The tactical display on the main viewer was replaced with the image of what lay ahead of *Defiant*. Near the four corners of the screen, small, red symbols overlaid the scene. These represented where the closest Ferengi ships actually were, their locations gleaned from sensor readings. Such information could not be determined from visual observation, since the Ferengi ships were traveling toward *Defiant* at velocities faster than light; by the time the light from those ships reached *Defiant*, the ships themselves would have moved on trillions of kilometers.

"Ten seconds."

As *Defiant* neared the Ferengi ships, the icons representing them on the main viewer grew in size and moved outward toward the edges of the screen. As voices quieted, the sounds of the bridge grew less varied: the ever-present pulse of the warp engines pervaded the still atmosphere, with the rapid-fire quavers of the flight-control console providing punctuation. All eyes but Dax's, Sisko knew, would be on the viewer; she would be studying her instrumentation.

"Here we go," Dax said, almost under her breath.

On the screen, the field of stars whirled clockwise as Dax brought *Defiant* around on its beam, spinning to port. The red symbols representing Ferengi ships shot out of view, replaced by others nearer the center of the screen. *Defiant* dipped downward, and rolled now to starboard, the stars seeming to veer in the opposite directions. The new symbols moved on the screen, grew, vanished, and were replaced by others.

"Steady," Dax said.

Sisko understood that she was speaking to herself as she worked to bring the ship on its serpentine course through the armada. He glanced at Dax and saw her concentration, saw the calm but intense manner of her dexterous movements. There was nobody he would have rather had at the helm; he trusted completely in her abilities.

Sisko looked back up at the viewer and saw the stars sliding to port, and then downward. Despite the inertial dampers, which insured that the physical effects of the ship's motion were not felt by the crew, the frenzied, shifting trajectories of *Defiant* were reflected by the images on the screen, and they were unnerving. Sisko peered down at the deck for a moment to prevent himself from becoming disoriented, then looked back up.

A Ferengi Marauder was directly ahead.

The huge ship dominated the viewer; it must have been only hundreds of meters away. There was no way, no time, to avoid it. Sisko had no chance even to think in words; his heart seemed to stop in his chest as he involuntarily braced for the impact. In an instant, the Marauder had grown to fill the screen.

And then it was gone, replaced by an empty starscape. No icons even adorned the viewer.

"We're through," Dax said, and exhaled mightily. "And they never knew we were there."

The image of the Marauder had been just that: an image, the light that had left that ship some seconds ago, and had only now reached *Defiant*. Sisko had known that, but his reaction had been visceral, not intellectual.

"Good work, old man," Sisko said. Dax turned in her seat and smiled.

"Yes, sir," she said, clearly pleased with her own piloting skills. Sisko returned her smile, and she spun back to her console.

"Bring us back up to maximum warp," Sisko told her. "And head us toward Ferenginar."

The doors parted, and Sisko looked over to see Quark entering the bridge. Odo was beside him. Sisko had called Quark here from his quarters because *Defiant* was nearing Ferenginar.

"Quark," Sisko said. "Are you ready?"

"Does it matter?" Quark asked. He spoke quietly and in a monotone, with little energy.

"Yes," Sisko told him earnestly, locking eyes with him. "It matters a great deal." Quark looked away.

"I'm ready, I'm ready," he said, seeming to dismiss the seriousness of the circumstances.

Sisko considered saying something, maybe even taking Quark off the bridge to speak with him privately, but he doubted that he could tell Quark anything that would genuinely help matters. If Quark was unhappy with respect to what he was about to do, then he probably resented Sisko for having manipulated him into this situation in the first place. Further discussion would likely only exacerbate whatever ill feelings Quark already harbored.

"We are approaching Ferenginar," Dax said from the conn.

"Slow to impulse," Sisko ordered. "Enter into a standard orbit." Sisko had already ordered the ship uncloaked as it had neared the planet.

"Aye," Dax acknowledged.

"Captain, I am picking up readings of two Marauders already in orbit," Worf reported.

"I guess the nagus didn't want to leave the homeworld unprotected," Odo commented.

"Actually, you'll find that there's a third ship in orbit on the other side of the planet," Quark revealed. He walked to the center of the bridge and stood beside where Sisko was seated in the command chair. "They always patrol around Ferenginar."

"Always?" Sisko asked. It seemed unusual to him, and a waste of matériel, for three state-of-the-art starships to be relegated exclusively to routine planetary patrol duty. "That seems extreme."

"Well, they're here for a specific purpose," Quark explained. "They maintain a perimeter just in case somebody the Alliance has done business with isn't satisfied after a deal's been closed."

"Wait a minute," Dax said, spinning around in her chair to face Quark and Sisko. "So these heavily armed Marauder starships comprise the Ferengi's customer-service department?"

"What's a customer-service department?" Quark replied.

Dax snickered at that, her eyebrows rising on her forehead.

"How do we get to the nagus?" Sisko asked.

"First," Quark said, pointing at the main viewer, where one Marauder was visible against the backdrop of Ferenginar, "you'll have to get past them. There'll be some legal requirements they'll want you to stipulate to. It could take some time; it was meant to be an involved process."

Sisko's own eyebrows rose now in undisguised frustration; there was no time for all of this. He looked to Dax for guidance. She just shrugged and turned back to her console.

"Establish a macro-orbit above that of the Ferengi ships," Sisko said. "Mr. Worf, open hailing frequencies. Let's do what we have to do."

"Hailing frequencies are open."

"This is Captain Benjamin Sisko of the Federation starship *Defiant*. We have aboard a Ferengi citizen who requests an immediate audience with the grand nagus."

At once, the picture of the Marauder and the planet on the main viewer was replaced with that of a lone Ferengi.

"This is DaiMon Letek of the Marauder *Preekon,*" the man said. He was wiry and never still, Sisko observed. He moved all over the screen, his arms in constant, frenetic motion. "Captain Sisko, what is the name of the Ferengi citizen you're carrying aboard your vessel?"

"My name is Quark," Quark said before Sisko could answer.

"Will it be possible for Quark to meet with the nagus?" Sisko asked.

"One moment," Letek said, and his image was replaced on the screen with the symbol of the Ferengi Alliance.

"What's going on?" Sisko asked Quark, leaning over toward him on the arm of his chair.

"I don't know," Quark said. "This isn't typically the way this procedure goes."

"No?" Sisko said. "I wonder—"

Letek reappeared on the viewer.

"Captain Sisko, will your vessel remain in orbit while Quark is on the surface of Ferenginar?"

"Yes."

"Do you then agree to release the Ferengi Alliance from all claims of liability to your vessel and its crew arising from your stay within Ferengi space?"

"Standard language," Quark noted for Sisko, sotto voce. "If you don't agree, we'll be escorted out of the system."

"Yes," Sisko told Letek.

"Quark, you have a house on Ferenginar?" Letek wanted to know.

"Yes," Quark answered. "My mother lives there."

"And all of your required insurance policies and riders are current?"

"Yes," Quark said.

"And all of your premiums have been paid?"

"Yes, through the end of the year," Quark responded. "As required."

"One moment," Letek said again, and again the symbol of the Alliance appeared in his place.

"Did you see his bottom row of teeth?" Quark asked, apparently of no one in particular. "They looked horrible."

"I don't know about his teeth, but did Letek look familiar to anyone?" Dax asked, apparently of everybody on the bridge. Sisko peered around and saw O'Brien, Worf, and Odo shaking their heads. Quark shrugged.

"Evidently not," Sisko told Dax. "Did he look familiar to you?"

"I thought so," she said, "but I guess not." She returned her attention to her console. Sisko looked back at Quark.

"What's going on?" he asked.

"I'm not sure," Quark said. "These are standard questions, but the process is usually drawn out and far more detailed."

"Do you think that they're going to allow you to meet with the nagus?" Sisko asked, but Quark did not have an opportunity to respond; Letek reappeared on the viewer.

"Captain Sisko, if you'll lower your deflectors, we will transport Quark to Grand Nagus Zek's estate."

Sisko was surprised at the ease and the alacrity with which they had reached this juncture. He glanced over at Quark and saw what he took to be an expression not just of surprise but of astonishment.

"Captain, I do not recommend lowering the shields," Worf said. "Two of the Marauders are within weapons range, and the Ferengi are not to be trusted."

"How else is Quark supposed to get down to the surface, Commander?" Sisko asked, annoyed at the almost-paranoid concerns of the former security officer.

"Sir, a shuttlecraft—"

"—Would take too much time," Sisko said, his interruption and harsh tone meant to end the discussion. Then, turning to face Quark, he asked him again, "Are you ready?" For an instant, it looked to Sisko as if Quark might respond as he earlier had, asking whether it mattered, but then he seemed to think better of it.

"Yes," Quark said at last. "I'm ready."

"DaiMon Letek," Sisko said, "we appreciate your cooperation and your celerity." Then: "Mr. Worf, lower the deflectors."

"The deflectors are down," Worf replied after operating the appropriate controls.

On the viewer, Letek peered off to the side and appeared

to gesture with one hand, though it was difficult for Sisko to tell because of the daiMon's incessant movement. Sisko looked once more at Quark.

"Good luck," he told him. "And thank you."

Quark opened his mouth, but before he could say anything, the sound of the Ferengi transporter began, and Quark was bathed in the light of the transporter effect. After a moment, he was gone.

"We'll inform you when the nagus is done with Quark," Letek said.

"Thank you," Sisko said.

Letek's image disappeared from the screen. The Alliance symbol showed briefly, and then it was replaced by the view from *Defiant* of the *Preekon* orbiting Ferenginar.

"Deflectors are back up," Worf said.

The bridge grew silent. The seriousness of the situation permeated Sisko's thoughts, and probably everybody else's as well, he supposed. The fate of Bajor and Ferenginar, even the futures of the officers aboard *Defiant*, were now contingent upon the outcome of Quark's meeting with Zek.

And so, unable to do anything else, Sisko and his crew settled in to wait.

CHAPTER
36

QUARK MATERIALIZED in the personal transporter room of
the grand nagus. Or at least, in *one* of his personal
transporter rooms. Quark had no idea how many such
facilities Zek had, but from what he knew to be the
tremendous size of his palace, there might well have been
more than one.

There were two men in the room when Quark materialized. One was operating the transporter console, and the
other was standing off to the side. It was the second one who
approached Quark.

"Welcome to the home of Grand Nagus Zek, Quark," the
man said, and then added a variation of the customary
Ferengi greeting. "His house is his house." He brought his
hands together at the wrists and bowed slightly.

"As are its contents," Quark responded in the traditional
way. He stepped down from the transporter platform, and
out of habit, he reached for a slip of gold-pressed latinum
to pay for his entry. He quickly realized, though, that he
was not wearing his own clothing; not only did he not have
any latinum, he did not even have any pockets in which to
keep it.

"Please," the man said, seeing Quark fumbling. He held out a small banking device. The man was smooth; Quark had not seen from where the man had produced the device. Grateful for the privilege of not having to pay in currency, Quark reach out and touched his thumb to the sensor plate; the slip of latinum would automatically be transferred from Quark's accounts into those of Zek.

"My name is Corlan," the man said. "I am one of the grand nagus's personal assistants." As if by magic, the banking device had vanished from Corlan's hands. Quark assumed that he had secreted it away somewhere on his person, but he had done so imperceptibly.

Quickly, Corlan took Quark through the routine of waiving his rights to make claims of liability against Zek while he was in the nagus's home. Quark had done this so many times before in his life—not in Zek's palace, of course, he had never been in Zek's palace, but elsewhere—that he was able to examine his surroundings while providing Corlan with the appropriate responses.

The room Quark was in was small, but aside from the technological appurtenances—the transporter console and the four-person platform—it was elegantly appointed. The floor was of polished stone, with an intricate, interlocking pattern inlaid into it; as Quark looked at it more closely, he realized that the design was a repetition of Zek's name spelled out in the beautiful, branching style so unique to the written Ferengi language. Each of the walls to Quark's right and left were covered entirely by a hanging tapestry; one depicted the writing of the Rules of Acquisition by the very first nagus, Gint, while the other was a listing of the rules themselves. In the wall opposite Quark, behind the transporter operator, a large picture window looked out onto a fabulous Ferenginar landscape—fabulous not least of all because it sat beneath a cloudless sky and a golden sun. Quark was dazzled.

"So," Corlan said when he had finished divesting Quark of most of his personal rights, "the grand nagus has left orders to bring you to the Chamber of the Sun."

The Chamber of the Sun? Quark thought, and then concluded that could not have been right. Corlan must have said, "The Chamber of the *Sum*"; that made more sense.

"The nagus will meet you there," Corlan continued. "The Chamber of the Sun is one of his favorite rooms."

Quark heard the repeated designation and he glanced again at the window behind the transporter console. For anyone on Ferenginar to denote anything *of the sun* was preposterous; the planet was widely known for its perpetual and uniformly ugly climate. In both hemispheres, on every continent, and in every sea, there was usually no respite throughout the year from one form or another of poor weather: dark skies, rain, snow, tornadoes, hurricanes, tidal waves, any number of meteorological afflictions. For the nagus to have a Chamber of the Sun, for him even to have a large window like the one here in the transporter room, was the height, Quark thought, of bravado. Of course, there would be those few days—such as today, apparently— when the sky would clear and Zek would be able to luxuriate in it like no one else in the world.

Corlan led Quark out of the transporter room through a beautiful set of double doors which opened outward at their approach. The doors were a lustrous pearl-gray color, with a texture that appeared soft to the eye, suggesting platinum, Quark thought, or perhaps rodinium. They curved up from the sides and met in a point at their apexes.

Outside the doors, they stepped into an extremely tall, enormously long hall. Doors such as the ones through which they had just passed lined both sides of the hall, and they were interspersed with series of long, thin tapestries hanging down to the floor from near the arched ceiling. On the floor itself, a plush, gold rug ran the length of the hall.

Corlan turned to their left, starting toward the far end of the hall, and Quark followed. When they had both stepped onto the rug, though, Corlan stopped walking. Quark did so as well.

"Since we have to go almost to the end," Corlan explained, gesturing in the direction they were headed, "let's not walk." For an additional few seconds, nothing happened, and then the rug began to move. No, not the rug, Quark saw when he looked down, but a moving walkway of some sort beneath it. The rug was evidently a holographic image. As Quark watched, his feet seemed to swim through the projected golden weave.

As they traveled down the hall, Quark peered at the tapestries. They depicted renowned moments in Ferengi history: the opening of the Sacred Marketplace, the founding of the First Bank of Ferenginar, the discovery of latinum in Terekol Chasm, the accessions of the grand naguses—including Zek himself. Quark found the display inspiring.

Approximately two-thirds of the way down the corridor, Corlan began walking forward. Quark followed, and the walkway beneath them stopped moving. Corlan left the rug and proceeded to a set of doors on the right side of the hall. Again, the doors parted at their approach, this time swinging inward.

"Grand Nagus Zek will be with you shortly," Corlan told Quark, motioning him inside.

Quark moved forward into a chamber far larger than the transporter room. The doors automatically closed behind him. The chamber was as tall as the hall was, and it was at least big enough, Quark estimated, to comfortably contain *Defiant* within it. It was as elegant and impressive as anything he had seen to this point, and more so. The floor was a latticework of different light-hued woods, regal furniture was placed purposefully about, and artwork adorned the walls. The most impressive feature of the room, though, was the far wall, which was composed entirely of a transparent material. Outside this magnificent window, as with the one in the transporter room, lay a beautiful landscape beneath a rare, clear Ferengi day. The brilliant rays of the sun shone in great, angled beams into the chamber.

It's no wonder the nagus wanted to meet in here, Quark thought. *This place is amazing.* It was such a dramatic display of personal wealth that Quark was . . . well, envious. The place could rightly have been called *The Chamber of the Sum,* as it was manifest testimony to the mammoth, unerring financial instincts of the holder of the Ferengi Alliance's highest office.

Quark strode across the length of the chamber to the great window. He had so rarely seen such lovely weather on his homeworld that he was anxious to take in the view now. As he got very near the window, though, something did not seem quite right to him. He brought his face right up to the transparent surface. He could not tell, but he thought that it might be—

"It's a holographic projection," said a scratchy, high-pitched voice from behind him.

He turned and faced Grand Nagus Zek. Quark had been so overwhelmed by the sight of the great window and the radiant sunshine streaking through it that he had not heard the nagus enter the chamber.

"But on nice days, this—" Zek took one ancient, twisted hand from the haft of his walking stick and waved it in an arc to take in the whole wall. "—actually can be made transparent."

"The weather is bad?" Quark asked, finding himself unaccountably disappointed.

"It's *pradooshing* out right now," Zek said. There were one hundred seventy-eight different words for *rain* in the Ferengi language; *pradooshing* referred to long, slim drops falling constantly at a slight angle.

Almost as an afterthought, Zek slid his hands from the knob of his cane and down its twisted shaft; he pushed the cane forward, offering the knob that had been fashioned in his own image from gold-pressed latinum. Quark dropped to one knee and kissed the top of the cane.

"Come," Zek said as Quark rose to his feet. "This way." The nagus shuffled his ancient body along one side of the room until he reached a large, ornamented chair, much like a throne. Zek sat down in it and motioned for Quark to sit across from him, on a bench that sat away from the wall and faced the thronelike chair.

As Quark sat down, he made an effort to moderate the overpowering feelings of reverence and wonder he was feeling being both in the presence of the grand nagus and in this spectacular showplace. As he did so, he recalled his errant speculation that Zek might have played some role in his incarceration—or at least in the escape engineered by Cort. Such thoughts seemed ludicrous now, even in the face of Quark's suspicions about having been so quickly and easily granted an audience with the nagus; Zek's great wealth and his obviously brilliant business talents seemed wholly incompatible with anything he might hope to gain from Quark.

"So," the nagus said, "why have you come to see me? Are you going to offer me a great deal on vole-belly futures?" Zek laughed, a knowing sort of cackle.

"No," Quark said, "I—"

—I what? I think that the greatest businessman in the quadrant—probably in the galaxy—made a mistake? In his cabin aboard *Defiant,* Quark had determined and then rehearsed what it was he would say to the nagus. He had gone over it so many times, repeated it to himself with such increasing conviction, that he had actually come to believe that he might be able to convince Zek of the truth of his position, and even persuade him to act as Sisko wanted. Now, such thoughts seemed like nothing more than chimeras.

"Yes?" Zek coaxed.

"I—" Quark started again, and stopped. But there was no point in not forging ahead through his prepared argument, was there? He was here, sitting before the grand nagus, and there was no prospect of some other rational line of reasoning that he could present occurring to him right now. "I wanted to talk to you about a decision you made." Quark's voice was timorous.

"I see," Zek said, regarding Quark in a manner with which Quark was not very comfortable. "You think that I made a *bad* decision. Perhaps you think I made a *mistake.*"

"No, Nagus," Quark said quickly, even though that was precisely what he had been trying to say. "No, I . . . I—"

Zek laughed heartily. To Quark, he sounded insane. Quark fancied that he could feel himself withering where he sat.

"Don't you know that I make mistakes all the time?" the nagus said at last. It was perhaps the last thing that Quark had expected to hear. He just stared at the nagus. "Well, not all the time. But I do make them. I did not acquire all of this—" Zek's hands parted and lifted slightly, indicating, Quark thought, their surroundings, the chamber, the palace, and the surrounding estate. "—because I don't make mistakes; I acquired it because I recognize my mistakes and capitalize on them."

Quark felt his mouth drop open as he peered at the nagus.

This was not how he had anticipated that this meeting would go.

"So tell me, Quark," Zek urged, "what mistake did I make?"

"Well," Quark began slowly, still reluctant to say that the grand nagus had erred—especially since he did not necessarily believe that himself. "I think that you should sell the Orb of the Prophets you own to the Bajorans."

"And I have obviously chosen not to," Zek said. "So that must be the error you believe me to have made. Now, tell me why it was an error."

"Because selling the Orb to the Bajorans would bring you more profit than not selling it to them."

"But I can sell the Orb to somebody else," the nagus said, "and still make a sizable profit, maybe not as much, but still a large profit."

"Yes, but it's at the cost of trade with the Gamma Quadrant," Quark argued, "since the Bajorans will no longer allow the Ferengi access to the wormhole." He felt more at ease now that he was discussing actual matters of business

"For which reason," the nagus said, "I have declared war on Bajor. There is no question that we will defeat them—"

"But at what cost?" Quark reiterated. "Even winning a war, ships and lives will be lost."

"Of course, but then the wormhole will be ours, and it is certainly the largest source of profit that's been seen in a long time."

Quark had expected the nagus to make this argument. It was a good one, he thought, but there was a critical component to having control of the wormhole beside profit.

"Whoever owns the wormhole," Quark said, "has to defend the wormhole. Because of its obvious strategic importance, every faction in the Alpha Quadrant wants it: the Klingons, the Romulans, the Cardassians, the Tholians."

"The Federation defends the wormhole now," Zek noted.

"They can do that because they're not interested in making a profit, and they've convinced the Bajorans to allow free access to the wormhole. They also maintain treaties and alliances with many governments that we do not. If we took over, those other powers would be more likely to try to take the wormhole from us than they are to take it from the Federation now."

"That would be particularly true if the Alliance charged for the privilege of using the wormhole," Zek said, apparently agreeing with Quark on this point.

"And there's also the threat posed from the Gamma Quadrant by the Dominion."

"An incursion by the Dominion would be costly," the nagus said. He seemed to be genuinely considering what Quark was saying. It was more remarkable, Quark thought, than the stunning opulence of Zek's home.

The nagus sat for a while without saying anything further. His eyes closed after a time, and Quark wondered whether the old man had perhaps fallen asleep. Quark waited, and began to squirm on the bench as he did so. The longer the silence lasted, the more certain he became that the next time Zek spoke, it would be to censure Quark for his impertinence in second-guessing the business dealings of the grand nagus of the Ferengi Alliance. Quark even worried that he might be fined for his actions.

"Quark," Zek said at last. His eyes were still closed, and so Quark, not expecting the nagus to speak at that moment, was startled. "You have fine business instincts."

"Th—thank you," Quark stammered, surprised. Zek opened his eyes and looked at him.

"And since that is the case, I have to ask myself, what's in this for you?"

Briefly, Quark debated the merits of telling the truth. No useful deceptions came to mind, but it probably did not matter; he suspected that any lie—even any mild prevarication—he told would be immediately unmasked as such by the nagus. Of course, Quark thought, a good liar was most effective when he occasionally mixed the truth in among his canards.

"I'm a fugitive from the Bajorans right now, and I've lost my bar," Quark said. "For talking to you about these matters, Captain Sisko has promised me political asylum if I want it. If you change your mind and sell the Orb to the

Bajorans, he promised me amnesty and the possibility of getting my bar back."

"So it is Captain Sisko who is driving this talk?" the nagus asked. Quark thought initially that it must have been a rhetorical question, primarily because the answer was so obvious—Quark had been brought here, after all, in a Starfleet vessel commanded by Sisko—but when Zek said nothing more, he decided that he should say something.

"Yes," he told the nagus, "although the business reasoning is mine." Quark thought about saying something more, and then did. "There's also the seventy-sixth Rule of Acquisition: Every once in a while, declare peace."

"All right," Zek said. "I'll provide you with a response shortly."

It sounded to Quark as though he was being dismissed, and he thought that the nagus would rise from his chair and leave the chamber. And that would be fine with Quark; at least there was a possibility that the nagus would change his mind, which was, frankly, far more than he had ever anticipated.

Suddenly, Quark noticed movement within his peripheral vision, and at the same time, he heard a footstep. He whirled his head around to see that Corlan had returned. It disturbed Quark that he had not heard his approach.

"This way, Quark," Corlan said. "I'll escort you back to the transporter room."

"Oh," Quark said. He was not just being dismissed, but being asked—or told—to leave. Quark rose and moved to join Corlan.

"Quark," the nagus called querulously.

Quark quickly turned back to the nagus and saw that he was sitting forward in his chair and extending the tip of his walking stick outward. Quark paced over, dipped down onto one knee, and kissed the handle.

"Go," Zek told him.

Quark followed Corlan out of the Chamber of the Sun and back to the transporter room. Within minutes of meeting with the grand nagus, Quark found himself back aboard *Defiant,* with no more idea of what his future held than when he had left the ship.

CHAPTER

37

"THIS IS MY FINAL OFFER, Captain," Zek insisted. "If it is not immediately accepted, then the war with Bajor will proceed."

"I understand, Nagus," Sisko said. "I'll get you that answer—that *agreement*—right away."

Zek ended the transmission.

"Mr. Worf, open a channel to First Minister Shakaar on Bajor," Sisko ordered, rising out of the command chair and bounding over to the tactical station. He felt energized. There was a chance now, a good chance, that the war could be averted; he was sure that Shakaar would consent to the terms of the grand nagus's new proposal.

"Captain, I cannot raise Bajor," Worf reported. "It appears that someone is jamming transmissions either near or within the system."

Of course, thought Sisko. There was a war about to be fought—or already being fought, if the Ferengi armada had arrived at Bajor—and both sides would be attempting to block the other's communications.

"Try to raise the station," Sisko said. "They may be far enough away from Bajor itself that we can still contact them." His thinking was that he could convey the nagus's offer to Kira, and that she could take a runabout to Bajor and deliver it directly to the first minister. As soon as Shakaar accepted Zek's terms, the war would be over.

At his console, Worf worked to get to *Deep Space Nine* through the interference. Sisko watched him go through the same motions several times, then try something else. Finally, he looked up in frustration.

"It's no use," he said.

There was only one alternative then.

"Dax, set a course for Bajor," Sisko said. "Maximum possible speed." Then, addressing O'Brien, he said, "Chief, I want you to get down to engineering and monitor the engines yourself. We need the best possible performance from the *Defiant*."

"That means no cloak," O'Brien said, already on the move from the operations console toward the bridge exit. The power demands of the cloaking device were extreme.

"That's all right. We won't need it," Sisko said. "We won't have to avoid the Ferengi armada this time."

Dax looked up then from the flight-control console.

"Not until we reach Bajor, anyway," she said.

Sisko acknowledged Odo and the other security guard, then reached up and touched the door chime. He expected to hear somebody call to tell him to come in, but instead, the door slid open. Rom stood just inside, Sisko saw, and behind him, the cabin was dark. Rom stepped out into the corridor and the door closed. Sisko's first thought was that Quark must be up to something, and that Rom must be trying to prevent Sisko from seeing what that was.

"Quark's asleep," Rom said.

It was the truth, Sisko realized as he peered down at Rom, who looked extremely tired himself. After all that Quark had done and all that he had been through—the meeting with Zek, the explosion aboard the shuttle, the flight from Bajor, and his experiences at Gallitep—he must have been exhausted. Sisko felt abashed at having such instant distrust for Quark so soon after he had perhaps assisted in averting a Ferengi-Bajoran war. Yes, Quark's own self-interests had been at stake too, doubtless providing additional motivation, but he had nevertheless done what Sisko had requested of him; it would be, at best, ungrateful for Sisko not to recognize that. In fact, that was why he had come down here from the bridge: to inform Quark of the nagus's offer, and to thank him for his role in making it happen.

Instead, Sisko settled for telling Rom that his brother might have helped to bring about peace between Ferenginar and Bajor, and that he had just wanted to personally express his appreciation to Quark. Rom, in his humble manner, thanked Sisko and said that he would pass the message on to his brother when he awoke.

"You seem tired too," Sisko observed.

"I am," Rom said, "but I've been having a little trouble sleeping."

"Why is that?"

"Oh, I don't know," Rom said. "You know . . . what happened in . . . well, down on Bajor, I suppose."

"Actually, I don't know," Sisko said. "Not entirely. Quark only told me that you were interned at Gallitep—" Rom reacted physically to the name of the prison camp, cringing noticeably. "—and that you were treated very badly. He didn't provide many details."

"Well," Rom said, and he did not really seem to know what to say. "It was pretty bad."

"Do you want to talk about it?" Sisko asked. "I want to make sure others never go through what you went through."

Rom looked up to his right and then to his left, at Odo and the other security guard. Sisko immediately recognized Rom's reticence to talk in front of too many people.

"Come on," Sisko said. "We'll go to my quarters, where we can speak privately."

Rom did not say anything, but he followed Sisko to his cabin. There, quietly and visibly anguished, Rom told Sisko about Gallitep, and Sergeant Wyte, and Colonel Mitra, and the very worst days of his life.

Defiant slowed to impulse as it neared the field of battle.

"Communications are still being jammed," Worf reported. Sisko watched as the Klingon virtually assaulted the tactical console. "The sensors are overloading . . . there's just too much out there . . . but . . . the Ferengi *have* reached

Bajor ... there are massive amounts of weapons fire ...
I'll have to narrow scans to get any readings at all."

But Worf need not have said anything, the sensors need
not have provided any information whatsoever; it was all
there, magnified, on the main viewer: the Ferengi armada
swarming the planet, the overwhelmed Bajoran forces di-
viding and attacking where they could, varicolored light
streaking through the night as ships sent their destructive
power hurtling toward each other.

"Damn," Sisko said before he even knew he had opened
his mouth. He was up out of the command chair, stalking
anxiously about the bridge. "Get us there, Dax. Bring us in
over the capital city."

"Aye."

"Shall we cloak?" Worf asked.

"No," Sisko said. "Nobody's going to fire on a Federation
starship."

"If somebody believes the *Defiant* is taking sides," Dax
noted as she flew them toward the fighting, "they just might
open fire on us."

Sisko considered this. It was a valid point; *Defiant* would
be swooping quickly into the middle of things, but—

"No," he decided. "We'd have to uncloak anyway for
transport, and it would be far more provocative if we
suddenly appeared in the heat of battle."

There was a tense pause as *Defiant* approached Bajor.
Sisko felt so anxious that he would have gotten behind the
ship and pushed if it would have helped; anything to reach
Bajor, to reach Shakaar, to end this as soon as possible.

"We'll be there in about two minutes, Benjamin," Dax
reported, seeming to read his thoughts.

"Sisko to Transporter Room One," Sisko said. The communications monitor on the bridge automatically opened a
channel.

"Transporter Room One," the young ensign stationed
there responded. "Ensign Phlugg."

Phlugg, Sisko thought; that was the ensign's name that he
had not been able to remember.

"Ensign, we're within two minutes of Bajor," Sisko said.
"Are you ready?"

"Yes, sir."

"Keep this channel open."

Sisko's plan was simple. With ship-to-surface communications still impossible, he would have to deliver the nagus's offer to Shakaar in person. Dax would bring *Defiant* within transporter range of Bajor, Worf would lower the deflectors, and Ensign Phlugg would beam Sisko directly from the bridge down to the first minister's office in the capital city. Shakaar would probably not be there, of course, but since communications would likely still be possible on the surface of Bajor, via ground relays, Sisko would bring a portable, high-powered communicator with him—he wore the small, boxlike device attached to his uniform at his waist right now—with which he should be able to contact the first minister wherever he was on the planet.

"One minute," Dax said.

On the viewer, several ships swept into and out of view, weapons blazing. Dax steered *Defiant* through the melee, down toward Bajor. She counted out the seconds at thirty and twenty and ten, and then by ones down toward zero.

"Energize," Sisko ordered as Dax reached *one*.

The whine of the transporter rose in Sisko's ears, and soft, white light spilled across his vision. After a span of time that could not arbitrarily be defined, his sight cleared. He was still on the Bridge of *Defiant*.

"Sisko to Phlugg," he said immediately. "I'm still here. What happened?"

"Captain—"

Suddenly, *Defiant* was rocked—by a phaser blast or a disruptor bolt, it was difficult to know which. The ship shook violently and Sisko was pitched to the floor, the inertial dampers unable to compensate for motion of the ship induced by an outside source. He pulled himself to his feet and headed for the tactical station.

"Damage report," he said.

"Minimal."

"Was that intentional?" Sisko wanted to know.

"I do not know," Worf said, clearly struggling to get whatever information he could from the sensor readouts. "It was a phaser shot from one of the small Bajoran freighters, so I suspect it was accidental."

That followed, Sisko thought. Few Bajorans would have fired purposely on the Emissary's ship.

"Transporter Room One to the bridge," came Ensign Phlugg's voice. "There's some sort of interference within the atmosphere of the planet inhibiting transport."

"Acknowledged," Sisko said. "Worf?"

"Narrowing the scope of our scans," Worf said, operating his console. "There appear to be several shuttles ringing the planet within the atmosphere. They are creating a deflector-like network of interference all across Bajor."

"Can we get below it?" Dax asked. Though it was not what the ship had been designed to do, *Defiant* could enter the Bajoran atmosphere. Depending on how close to the surface of the planet the interference grid was, they could dive below it in order to use the transporter.

"Negative," Worf said. "The network is also being generated from ground stations."

"Can we punch a hole in it?" Sisko asked, already realizing that they would not be able to act quickly in this regard without possibly endangering the lives of Bajorans either in the shuttles or at the ground stations.

"Eventually," Worf confirmed, "but any safe solution would take time."

"We don't have time," Sisko said. He started for the doors. "Worf, you have the bridge," he said, transferring command. "I'm taking *da Vinci.*"

"Captain, I should——" Worf began, but Sisko cut him off.

"Take *Defiant* out of danger and monitor communications from the surface. I'll get a message to you as soon as I can."

"Benjamin," Dax said, in an imploring tone that made Sisko think that she would try to stop him from taking the shuttle, or try to convince him to allow her to pilot the virtually defenseless craft down to Bajor. Instead, she simply said, "Good luck."

And then Sisko was through the doors, on his way to leaving the most powerful vessel in Starfleet, which was now useless to him.

* * *

Da Vinci eased from the safety of its dock aboard *Defiant* and into a maelstrom. There were ships everywhere, in continuous motion, and an incessant barrage of weaponry streaking through space—a light show that might have been beautiful had it not been carrying along with it the potential of destruction and death.

To Sisko, the combat above—and for—Bajor seemed fiercer now, eyed through the forward windows of the shuttle, rather than on the main viewer on the bridge of *Defiant.* The dangers it evinced were more immediate and more uncaring in a very personal way; Sisko felt like a random element here, an insignificant observer whose life could not even be counted as a casualty for either side if that life was lost. And with all of the firepower massed about Bajor, he knew that the shuttle could easily become an unintended target.

Sisko sat at the main console of *da Vinci* and performed a close-range sensor scan aft of the shuttle; *Defiant,* as he had ordered, had already moved away. He opened a channel to the ship, but he was nevertheless able to make contact. Expecting the same result, he nevertheless attempted to raise the first minister on Bajor; that transmission was also jammed.

Sisko hove *da Vinci* around to starboard. The great arc of Bajor's horizon curved upward before him, and two of the planet's moons hung suspended above it. A third moon was just visible beyond the planet, off to the right, as though just peeking at the raging conflict—or perhaps trying to hide from it. In the foreground, a freighter sped from the blue-and-white backdrop of Bajor, upward and away to port. Farther off, ships too far away to recognize teemed about each other like mosquitoes in a Louisiana bayou.

The sudden memory of Sisko's onetime home brought with it a surge of melancholy. The emotion was at first disconcerting because he had not thought of New Orleans as home in a very long time. He then realized, though, that the pensive sadness he was experiencing was not for the place of his birth, but for the place he now thought of as home—the place that now floated below him like the grail of an itinerant voyager of the spaceways.

Sisko dipped the bow of *da Vinci* down. Because Dax had brought *Defiant* in directly above the capital, Sisko calculated a spiral descent, with the city as the center point of the corkscrew path that the shuttle would describe. He entered the course into the navigational computer, verified it, and executed *da Vinci*'s entrance into the maneuver.

The shuttle breached the top of Bajor's atmosphere smoothly, but as it flew downward and the air density increased, Sisko became aware of a slight tremble developing. The inertial dampers of the small craft struggled against the movements caused by the intensifying friction as *da Vinci* descended. Sisko began to notice the cant of the shuttle toward starboard as it wheeled downward, the force of Bajor's gravitational pull growing stronger than the artificial gravity within the cabin. He moved his right foot out away from himself and braced it against the floor so that he would not slide from his chair.

When Sisko was thrown into the port bulkhead, his first, instinctive reaction was that the shuttle had struck something. That was certainly possible, considering the large number of ships flying around, he thought an instant later, but it was also more likely that something had struck the shuttle. He crawled back into his seat, bracing himself once more with an outstretched leg. *Da Vinci* was no longer merely trembling, but shaking strongly, making it difficult to consult the readouts. Sisko dropped his hands to the console and gripped it tightly in an effort to steady his gaze. He was able to see enough details clearly to know that the shuttle had been hit by a powerful phaser blast. The damage was bad, but not *that* bad: the deuterium flow regulator within one of the two drive shells had been fused open, but he could land with just one engine functioning. He shut down the disabled drive, removing the threat of an overload. Sisko felt an immediate drop in the forward component of the shuttle's velocity, and a corresponding increase in the downward component.

It was unclear from the readings who had fired on *da Vinci,* but Sisko hoped that it had been the Ferengi; traveling down to the planet, he would become less of a target to those ships in orbit. More than likely, though, it had been the Bajorans, shooting from the surface at a small ship attempting to penetrate their defenses. At this altitude, the forces on the ground would not be able to visually identify *da Vinci* as a Starfleet vessel, and Sisko could not mask the shuttle as being one of the Bajorans' because he did not know by what means they had chosen to distinguish their ships—a laser beacon tuned to a special frequency, or a specific movement in flight, or the like. If it had been the Bajorans that had shot at the shuttle, though, Sisko was likely to be facing a difficult approach to the surface.

Sisko pulled *da Vinci's* nose up slightly, slowing its downward speed. He tried again to open communications—with Shakaar or anybody else on Bajor—and was again unsuccessful.

A brilliant shaft of light screamed past the windows, only narrowly missing the shuttle, and Sisko knew what was going to happen: *da Vinci* was going to be shot down. As quickly as he could, he plotted a new course. He knew that no matter what evasive action he took, it would be only luck that would allow the relatively slow-moving shuttle to avoid the phaser blasts before it could land. Still, he did not want the debris of the shuttle's wreckage to rain down on the capital and its inhabitants. Sisko entered the new course along with automatic landing instructions, and then implemented them. *Da Vinci* moved off on a tangent from its previous winding route. If he could just clear the outskirts of the city and bring the shuttle over the surrounding areas, there would be nothing but undeveloped wilderness below him.

Sisko checked his altitude, then got up from his chair and staggered through the shuddering cabin to the bulkhead located amidship, beyond which sat the aft compartment and the emergency transporter. He worked the transporter controls mounted on the wall, entering coordinates for the first minister's office. Then he went back to the front of the shuttle.

Leaning against the main console and peering through the windows, he saw through a break in the clouds that he was still over the capital, but its outermost border was rapidly approaching. Sisko waited for seconds that seemed to elongate painfully. The bosky reach stretching out away from the city grew closer by degrees, and finally, he was there.

Sisko raced back through the cabin—stumbling once,

almost losing his footing—and into the aft compartment. He stepped onto the emergency transporter.

"Computer, energize transporter," he yelled, and only now did he consciously realize how loud it was within the shuttle. The phaser strike that had fused the deuterium regulator must also have compromised the noise-suppression plating. Whatever the cause of the thunderous sound, Sisko could not hear the transporter as it engaged, but the hazy, white light of the effect filled his sight. After an indefinable interval, it cleared.

Sisko was still on the shuttle.

He was not low enough, he realized. The interference the Bajorans were running to prohibit transport to the planet was closer to the surface than *da Vinci* was.

Sisko moved quickly, leaping from the aft compartment and back to the transporter controls. If *Defiant* had not moved out of range, he could beam back to the ship—

That was when the next phaser blast hammered into *da Vinci*. The bow of the shuttle pitched violently downward. Sisko was thrown the length of the forward cabin and against the windows. He had an impression of color and movement—green, blue, white, ground, sky, clouds—and then he was hurtling in another direction as a third phaser shot landed.

The shuttle rolled to port and continued rolling, the bow angled steeply down. Sisko landed again and again, on the floor, the wall, the ceiling, the floor, his head tucked beneath the encircling grasp of his arms. *Da Vinci*'s descent was no longer powered by its drive, he knew, but by gravity.

Perceiving time now as an enemy, Sisko pulled an arm away from his head and reached out for something, anything, that he could grab on to in order to stop being thrown about the cabin. His fingers found brief purchase somewhere and were jerked away. He grabbed again, missed, and then found the side of a console. He held it fast, reached out with his other hand, and got a second hold.

Sisko looked up. He was lying on a wall of the shuttle, facing aft; ahead of him was the threshold between the forward and aft compartments. He did not hesitate, did not brace himself or gather his energy, he just moved, pulling himself along the edge of the console, hand over hand, the shuttle spinning madly and him with it. His gaze held fast on the bulkhead as he pulled himself along, one hand, then another, until at last he sent his fingers into the aft compartment and around the edge of the bulkhead. With prodigious effort, he pulled himself bodily through the opening and out of the forward cabin. The rush of air around the shuttle was heavy now. He crawled onto the emergency transporter and screamed.

"Computer, energize transporter."

Again, Sisko could not hear sound of the transporter, but satiny, white motes danced before his eyes. Through the motes, for an instant, he could make out the windows at the other end of the shuttle, and past the windows, there was only ground.

Da Vinci slammed into Bajor.

Sisko materialized on the floor in Shakaar's office. His breathing came in great gasps. He tried to rise, still aware of why he was here, but the violent movement of the shuttle had disoriented him and he collapsed back onto the floor.

When finally his breathing had calmed and his head had stopped spinning, he rose. He was alone. He had to locate Shakaar.

The shuttle and its communication system were gone, but there was the high-powered communicator that he had earlier affixed to the waist of his uniform. He reached for the device.

It was gone.

For a few seconds, panic gripped Sisko. He felt like letting himself fall back down onto the floor.

Stop it, he told himself. *Think.*

And he did. As quickly as he could, Sisko made his way to the first minister's comm panel and activated it. He opened a general channel, broadcasting to anyone who was out there.

"First Minister Shakaar, this is—" Sisko briefly considered saying "the Emissary," but did not. "—Captain Sisko. I must speak with you immediately. I'm in your office on Bajor."

He waited. There was no response.

"First Minister Shakaar," he repeated, his voice filled

with the urgency of his task. "This is Captain Sisko. I have to speak with you right away. I'm in—"

This time, Sisko heard the whine of the transporter before it took him.

He materialized on a platform in an operations center. People where in constant motion here, ironically reminiscent of the ships waging war far above them.

A woman dressed in the uniform of the Bajoran Militia—all the people here wore such uniforms, Sisko saw—stepped up to the platform to greet him. She seemed to know him, and he realized that he had met her in Shakaar's office the last time he had been on Bajor. He did not remember her name.

"Captain Sisko," she said. "Are you all right?" She glanced up to the side of his head.

Sisko automatically raised a hand to his head, touched it, and examined his fingers; they were covered with blood.

"I'm fine," he said, not really caring right now whether he was or not. "I need to talk to Shakaar."

"The first minister is waiting for you in—"

Sisko was striding across the room in the direction the woman had looked even before she had finished speaking. He passed through a doorway and found the first minister studying a console with two other militia officers.

"Shakaar," Sisko said.

"Captain," Shakaar said, and then repeated it with concern when he looked up at Sisko and saw his injuries. "What happened?"

"It doesn't matter," Sisko said. "I have an offer from Grand Nagus Zek to end the fighting."

"Tell me."

"Zek is willing to do away with the auction completely if you'll rescind your edict and meet his price for the Orb: Bajor's last bid, plus the thirty-five new transports you acquired from the Yridians."

Shakaar regarded Sisko for what seemed like a very long time, and then he looked away. When too much time had passed, Sisko opened his mouth to say something—or yell something—but it was then that the first minister turned back to him and gave him an answer.

"Bajor accepts the terms."

CODA

The 34th Rule

CHAPTER
38

TWO THINGS BOTHERED QUARK. Well, many more things than that bothered him, but as he sat working at the comm panel in his quarters, there were two things in particular that he could not get out of his mind.

One of those things was Cort; there were just too many suspicious events surrounding the businessman—or smuggler, or whatever he was. The more Quark considered Rom's conviction that Cort had somehow set them up, the more he became inclined to believe it as well. Rom was an idiot for the most part, that was true, but not when it came to engineering matters; inexplicably, Rom knew and understood such things. And so when he maintained that the homing device Cort claimed to have constructed had not really been a homing device—had in fact been useless—Quark figured that he was probably correct. The questions now, as when Rom had first mentioned this aboard *Defiant*, were: Why would Cort lie about such a thing, and if he had, then how had he managed to contact the shuttle in which they had subsequently fled?

Quark glanced down at the status monitor on the screen and saw that his latest series of queries was still pending. It had been like that since his return a week ago to *Deep Space Nine*, his tedious searches for information about Cort consuming great chunks of time. Well, actually, Quark had only begun trying to learn about Cort in the last three days. He had spent his first two days back on the station split between sickbay and his quarters, between Dr. Bashir's final ministrations and his own efforts to push away all thoughts—including those of Cort—even remotely related to his time at Gallitep. And during the next couple of days, after the Bajorans had exonerated him of all charges and returned his bar to him, he had focused upon reopening his business.

Gallitep had stayed with him, though, not even allowing him to sleep through a single night. His days were long and sometimes difficult because of his continual fatigue; he was exhausted now, even though it was before midnight. Quark understood that he would have to deal with the nonphysical wounds he had endured, and one way to do that, he had finally decided, was to try to determine why things had happened the way they had. Unfortunately, his quest for information about Cort had so far proven fruitless.

Out of frustration, Quark stabbed at a control with one finger. The comm panel squeaked electronically at him, digitally chastising him for trying to interrupt his own instructions. Quark barked back at the machine— "Bah!"—then got up and walked across his quarters to the replicator.

"Archerian slug wine," Quark ordered. A delicate, thin-stemmed glass materialized on the replicator pad, filled with a yellowish brown liquid. He took it and sipped; not as good as the real thing from Archer IV, of course, not as thick or as pulpy, but considering what he had been drinking—and not drinking—during the past few months, it would do.

Quark thought again about the homing device Cort had pretended to fabricate, and again he asked himself why. The answer that seemed most likely to be true was that Cort had done it in order to hide the fact that he already possessed such a device and had failed to use it for the length of their captivity—that is, while all of the prisoners were starved and beaten, and while four other people lost their lives.

That would also explain how Cort had contacted his shuttle, but it raised another question as well: Why would Cort be willing to remain imprisoned under such horrific conditions when he need not have done so? Quark knew of only one rational motivation: Profit. *Huge* profit. But who could have provided Cort with that profit, and again: *Why?*

The more Quark learned, it seemed, the more new questions arose. Except that he really was not learning anything, was he? No, he was simply reviewing those things he already knew and then interpreting them in one fashion or another.

The comm panel beeped. Quark gazed across the room and saw a small lattice of Ferengi text at the top of the display. He drank once more from the glass of wine—a gulp this time, instead of a sip—and then put it back down on the replicator pad. He strode over to read the contents of the comm panel, expecting to be disappointed. Quark had pored over a substantial number of Ferengi documents in the past three days—medical records, ship schedules, law-enforcement reports, personnel files, whatever he could locate—and yet he had found Cort's name listed nowhere. That in itself was suspicious; there was far less information available about Cort than there should have been.

Which was ironic, Quark thought, since Cort himself had known more than he should have. Most notably, as they had made their escape from Bajor, Cort had told everybody that Ferenginar and Bajor were preparing for war. He had then implied that he had inferred this, but from the way he had spoken—confidently and without hesitation—it seemed to Quark that he had *known*. But having been imprisoned for so long, there was no way that he should have been able to know such a thing. And when Cort was then explicitly questioned about how he knew what he did, he simply ignored those questions and remained intent on piloting the shuttle.

Piloting it toward Defiant, Quark thought. Rom was probably right about that too, that it had been Cort's doing. Quark agreed now that it was an unbelievable coincidence that the shuttle had suffered engine problems so close to the Federation starship, and just as the starship was departing the Bajoran system.

Reaching the comm panel, Quark eyed the brief message displayed there: SEARCH SUBJECT NOT FOUND. He was not surprised. He leaned over the controls and tapped in a command; a list of news-service directories he had earlier compiled blossomed on the screen. Quark quickly programmed a new search algorithm and set it executing.

"Computer," he said, moving away from the comm panel. "When the search is complete, don't notify me audibly."

"Oral notification canceled," the computer confirmed.

Quark headed for his bedroom. It was late, he was weary, and this search would take some time. He would check the results in the morning.

Colonel Mitra slipped silently into the room, negotiating the raised threshold of the doorway as though he had been here a thousand times before. Of course, the space station had been designed and built by Cardassians, and Mitra was very conversant with Cardassians and their ways of life.

And their ways of death.

Mitra smiled as the door slid shut behind him. He waited a moment for his eyes to adjust to the dimness. The only source of illumination in the room was a comm-panel screen, which bathed the surroundings in a faint, eerie glow.

When he could see well enough, Mitra peered about until he spotted the only other door. It stood open, and it would, he knew, lead into the bedroom. Quickly, he started across the room, as quiet as the void. As he passed by the comm panel, he stopped and examined the display; a data search was in progress, he saw. Most of the screen was dark, in fact, and in it, he spied the waxen image of his face. For long seconds, he studied his reflection. It could no longer be said that his features were strong or hard or chiseled; his eyes were still cold—perhaps they had survived the raw days and nights of the Gallitep winter because of their coldness—but his face was otherwise a lifeless, twisted thing. His skin was more than ashen; it was translucent. Blue veins were visible just below the surface, and the surface itself was no longer smooth: gouges in his sunken cheeks marked the places where flesh had died and fallen away, and where his nose had been, a dark, craggy pit now sat.

Mitra stared at himself in the dark display. He watched as his hand reached beneath his tunic and withdrew a long knife. And once more, he smiled, a misshapen rictus of soullessness. It was time.

In three strides, he was at the bedroom door. He stepped boldly through it, no longer caring to be quiet. No, now he wanted to be heard, wanted to be seen. He wanted to be feared.

This room was even darker than the main room, but Mitra's eyes had acclimated now, and he could see the small figure with the large head lying in the bed. Quark was asleep, on his back, a dry, rasping sort of snore issuing from his open mouth.

The colonel reached for the manual controls mounted on the wall beside the door. The overhead lighting panels gradually came on, brightening the room noticeably, but not blindingly. Quark did not stir.

Mitra walked to the bed and looked down at his prey. It had cost the colonel a torturous effort to hunt this far, but already he knew it had been worth it. It was a rule of nature that only the strong should survive; the weak must perish.

Mitra adjusted his grip on the knife. Using what remained of his hands—the cold had killed the tips of his fingers, the dead tissue falling away to expose the bone beneath—he planted the haft deeply into one of his palms, his wasted digits curling tightly around it. He bent down and eased the blade below the wide, circular expanse of Quark's left ear, and brought it up gently so that the sleek metal rested against the alien's flesh. He put his other arm out straight and down, his palm hovering just above Quark's chest.

"Prisoner eight," Mitra said. Although he spoke in a normal tone, his voice seemed loud in the stillness of the night.

Quark's eyes began to flutter open, but then flew wide as he saw somebody above him. He began to rise, but Mitra shoved down hard with his palm, pinning the alien to the mattress and making him a true prisoner once more.

Quark screamed, a shrill, piercing shriek that filled his quarters, but did not penetrate the walls.

Mitra let his weight down onto his arm, and the screaming stopped. Quark struggled to say something, but the only word that passed his lips was "Colonel."

"Address me as Gul."

"Gul Mitra," Quark said, an obvious, desperate attempt at pacification.

"Commander of Gallitep," Mitra said, as though announcing his accomplishments. "The *Butcher* of Gallitep." He jerked his arm backward, dragging the edge of the knife up and through the cartilage of Quark's ear. The Ferengi howled, his flesh parting easily, blood splattering from the wound onto the sheets. Mitra took his hand from Quark's chest, grabbed his ear, and pulled as the blade sliced through Quark's anatomy. Finally, he held up his trophy for his prey to see.

Quark screamed and screamed, bolting up in bed, his hands rushing to the gaping hole in the side of his head. Instead, what he felt was the mass of his ear, whole and uninjured. One hand automatically went to his other ear, and found it also in good condition.

Only a dream, Quark thought. His heart felt as though it might leap from his chest at any time, and his breathing came in great, gasping gulps. *Mitra is dead,* he told himself. *It was only a dream.* Like all the others he had been having since he had returned to *Deep Space Nine,* and like all those he knew he would be having for some time to come.

Quark threw back the bedclothes—he brushed his hands across the sheet by his pillows, feeling vainly for blood in the darkened room—and got up. Knowing that sleep had deserted him for the night, he went back to the main room and his search for sense in an irrational universe.

As Quark worked at the comm panel, he idly reached up and rubbed his earlobe. It was wonderful, he thought, to be out of the awful cold. The feeling in his ears had fully returned while he had been on *Defiant,* during its trip from Ferenginar back to Bajor. Rom's hearing had been another matter; it had taken almost the entire week since *Defiant* had come back to *DS9* for Dr. Bashir to restore his aural capacity fully, but he had at last been able to do so. Rom, of course, had been overjoyed. When Quark had last seen his brother, Rom had been reveling in his revived hearing by listening to—

There it was. The results of Quark's latest search had come back positive: one match for the name Cort in the database he had been accessing, a repository for official informational releases within the Ferengi Alliance. Quark quickly operated the comm panel and called up the specified document. It turned out to be a three-year-old announcement of new appointees in several areas of the Ferengi government. Cort was listed toward the end of perhaps two dozen names. There was also a picture of all of the appointees, which Quark enhanced in order to confirm that this was the same person; it was.

As Quark perused the article, he recalled how, back on Bajor, he had guessed that Cort was a smuggler. More significantly, he recalled Cort's annoyed reaction, which had seemed to indicate that, yes, he was a smuggler, but that it was not something he wanted known.

Oh, he was good, Quark thought. *Very good.* According to the announcement, Cort's duty with the Ferengi government was as a personal assistant to the grand nagus.

And that brought Quark foursquare to the other thing that had been troubling him: Zek himself. If Cort had been paid a large sum to do the things that Quark now suspected him to have done, then the nagus was an obvious potential source for such a payment. What was not obvious was why Zek would have wanted Cort to do those things.

Quark operated the comm panel and brought up notes he had prepared yesterday. In his search for answers, he had reviewed again and again his conversation with the nagus on Ferenginar, with the eventual result being these notes: a transcription, as best as he could remember, of what had been said. From those efforts, something improper had emerged, something Quark thought he should have recognized when it had happened. During his attempt to change the nagus's mind, Quark had asserted that selling the Ninth Orb to the Bajorans would ultimately be more profitable than selling it some other buyer. Zek had replied that selling the Orb to somebody other than the Bajorans would bring him a large profit, maybe not as much, but still a large profit.

Maybe not as much.

That phrase suggested that the nagus had known—even forgetting about sustaining Ferengi access to the wormhole and trade with the Gamma Quadrant—that he could profit most by selling the Orb to the Bajorans. So why hadn't he done so in the first place?

Perhaps that was the problem, it now occurred to Quark. Maybe the nagus had blundered in his handling of the auction for the Orb—maybe he had not thought that the Bajorans would close the wormhole to the Ferengi, or maybe he had simply expelled them from the auction mistakenly. Then, to avoid public concern about his abilities—which could have threatened his position—he had contrived this means to make the sale to the Bajorans.

When Quark thought through this scenario, though, it seemed preposterous. Zek pays Cort to get arrested and then remain interned on Bajor until a specific time—either predetermined or somehow signaled to Cort in the prison camp. At that specific time, Cort calls his shuttle and helps the prisoners escape. He then steers them almost directly to *Defiant*, where he fakes an accident, both to cover his actions and to gain Sisko's attention.

And then what? Quark asked himself. Could the nagus have known that Sisko would bring Quark to Ferenginar? Was Zek's intention to pretend that Quark had changed his mind about selling the Orb to the Bajorans? It was too convoluted a scheme just for the purpose of allowing the nagus to save face, Quark thought. He concluded that it could not have been what had actually transpired.

Quark looked back at the comm panel. He would have to seek additional clues if he was ever going to be able to solve these nagging inconsistencies that plagued him. But he could not do that right now. He was tired of all this, and he suddenly had the uneasy feeling that he might not be ready for the answers that he would find. Because after everything was taken into consideration, there were two things Quark was sure of: When all of this had started, the nagus had failed to sell the Orb to the Bajorans, and when it had ended, he *had* sold the Orb to the Bajorans. And what that indicated to Quark was that Grand Nagus Zek was losing his touch. It was unthinkable, it was profane, and it was not what Quark wanted to believe about the man after whom he had patterned his own business life.

Disgusted and sad, Quark switched off the comm panel. *No,* he thought. *I don't really want to know what happened.*

CHAPTER
39

SISKO THUMBED OFF the comm panel, his subspace conference with Admiral Whatley and several other flag officers from Starfleet Command finally over. Today had been easy, reporting the contents of the letter he had just received from First Minister Shakaar. Earlier in the week, Sisko had been dressed down for disobeying direct orders and violating the Federation Council's resolution, and then lauded for those same actions. In the end, the balance had tipped in his favor; this was why he had been stationed at *Deep Space Nine* in the first place.

Sisko picked up a padd from his desk and read through the first minister's letter a second time. He was satisfied—more than that, he was pleased—with its content. Shakaar had elected to do all the right things, and he had done those things quickly.

Although the edict barring Ferengi from Bajoran space had been rescinded immediately upon the delivery of the Ninth Orb to Bajor, the first minister had asked that the nine prisoners who had escaped their internment be returned to his world for an inquiry into their treatment in prison and their illegal flight. The Ferengi had refused to go back to Bajor, though, and Shakaar had agreed, at Sisko's request, to allow them to stay on *Deep Space Nine* until the inquiry had concluded.

According to Shakaar's letter, that inquiry was still continuing—it had only been a week since the Bajorans had agreed to the nagus's terms—but only with respect to the mistakes that the Bajorans had made. After just two days of investigation, largely thanks to the testimony of Corporal Prana, the nine Ferengi had been provided full pardons for any crimes they were alleged to have committed during the time stretching from the deadline specified in the edict to the final agreement between Bajor and Ferenginar; that included both violating the edict and breaking from jail. Additionally, all property seized in support of the edict had been immediately returned: the cargo ship in which Kreln, Borit, Drayan, Tarken, and Lenk had been captured; Karg's home in the province of Wyntara Mas; Cort's shuttle, which had turned out not to be stolen; and Quark's bar. Each of the Ferengi—including Cort, who had proceeded to have his shuttle repaired—had quickly departed the station after that. Each of the Ferengi had departed, that is, but for Quark and Rom.

Shakaar also wrote that the Bajorans were still trying to determine how Colonel Mitra had managed to reopen and resupply Gallitep. While the colonel had been charged with the responsibility of interning the Ferengi, they were to have been isolated in another, more hospitable facility. The three members of Mitra's squad who were still alive—Lieutenant Carlien, Sergeant Onial, and Corporal Prana—had all been interrogated, but it was clear that they had also been victims of Mitra's insanity. Regardless of how and why the incidents at Gallitep had occurred, though, the first minister promised that official public apologies would be made to each of the Ferengi, and that counselors would be made available to them so that they could have assistance dealing with the traumas they had undergone.

Finally, the letter confirmed a rumor Sisko had considered too good to be true: the death toll during the war had been zero. More an attempt at a war than an actual war, the fighting had lasted less than two hours. Still, in that time, a large number of people could have been killed. And one of them, Sisko reflected, thinking of his near-fatal shuttle trip down to Bajor, could easily have been him.

Sisko completed reading the letter for the second time, and then started to study the document Shakaar had given to him before the war had started. As he did so, the door signal chimed.

"Come in." The doors parted and Quark entered the office. He approached Sisko's desk.

"You asked to see me, Captain?" Quark said.

"Yes, I did. Please have a seat." Sisko outlined for Quark everything contained in the first minister's letter—everything but the report that Colonel Mitra's body had not yet been located, and Quark conspicuously did not ask about that. In particular, Sisko wanted Quark to know about the counselors the Bajorans would be providing. Quark, perhaps predictably, affirmed that he would decline such services, but allowed that they would probably be good for Rom.

"Well, that's it," Sisko said when he had finished. He rose, somewhat formally; he had not had much opportunity to speak with Quark in the past week, and he wanted now to convey his appreciation in an appropriate manner. "Thank you for what you did," Sisko said. Quark got up from his seat and faced Sisko across the desk. "I know that you didn't want to talk to the nagus, and that you had your own reasons for doing so, but it was nevertheless very important. And the fact that you were able to change Zek's mind . . . well, you probably saved tens of thousands of lives, maybe more."

"Yes, well, I don't how to respond to that," Quark said, rather flatly, Sisko thought. "You're welcome, I guess." Quark turned and headed for the doors, which opened before him.

"Quark," Sisko called after him. Quark stopped and turned around. "Is everything all right?"

Quark hesitated for a moment, and Sisko was struck by an impression of Quark that he had never had before, one of uncertainty and even sadness. He thought that Quark was going to leave without saying anything more, but instead,

Quark stepped back into the office. The doors closed behind him.

"I don't think I did—" Quark stopped and began again. "I think . . . I think that the nagus might be losing his abilities as a financial tactician."

"Really?" Sisko said. He had come to a similar opinion— how could the Ferengi ultimately have benefited from a war with Bajor, and how could they have maintained control of the wormhole?—but he was surprised both that Quark felt the same way, and that he was willing to admit it. "What are your reasons?"

"Because the Bajorans' bid in the auction for the Orb was a high one," Quark revealed. "Perhaps the highest of all the bids."

"How do you know that?" Sisko leaned forward, his palms flat on his desk.

"I inferred it from something the nagus said when I spoke with him on Ferenginar."

"But then why would the nagus have denied the Bajorans a chance to bid in the final round of the auction?" Sisko asked. "Even I know enough about business to know that you accept the highest bid. Isn't that the entire reason for having an auction?"

"As I said, I think that the nagus may be losing his business skills."

"I think that's an understatement," Sisko said. "Ejecting the Bajorans from the auction didn't just mean a smaller profit for him. It forced the Bajorans to cut the Ferengi off from the wormhole, which resulted in the Ferengi blockade, and in the eventual arming of Bajor by the Yridians. The nagus's poor business practices could have resulted—"

"Hold it," Quark interrupted. He took a step closer to Sisko, hands raised and index fingers extended, as if he were trying to point to something Sisko had said. "I thought you told me that the Bajorans got those new starships from the Karemma."

"No," Sisko said, trying to recall exactly what he had related to Quark about the defensive transports that Bajor had acquired. "I think you asked about the *origin* of those ships, which is what I told you. We believe that they were first owned by the Karemma." Sisko explained why they believed this, telling him they had learned that the default settings of the ships' computers were defined in the language of the Karemma. "Anyway, the starships were actually sold to the Bajorans by the Yridians. And now they belong to the Ferengi." Sisko enumerated Zek's terms for the sale of the Orb.

Quark stepped up to the desk and fell into one of the chairs sitting before it. In rapid succession, he appeared stunned, and then ill, and finally as though he had experienced a revelation.

"What is it?" Sisko wanted to know.

"Captain," Quark said, *"I* was the one who negotiated the sale of those starships *to* the Yridians. Do you remember that great deal that I made a few months ago?" Sisko shook his head. "That was the deal."

"You arranged the transaction between the Karemma and the Yridians?"

"No," Quark said. "I sold those starships to the Yridians *from the Ferengi."*

"What?" Sisko sat down too.

"When I saw one of those ships when we were escaping from Bajor, I thought it was a Ferengi ship, and that somehow the deal had soured while I was in jail. But then you told me it was a Bajoran ship, and that they had gotten it from the Karemma, so I realized that it wasn't one of the ships in my deal." Quark paused, putting it all together. "It all makes sense now," Quark said. "It was all for greater profits."

"Whose profits?" But Sisko knew: Zek's.

Together, he and Quark traced their way through the maze of the nagus's great scheme. Zek had intentionally expelled the Bajorans from the auction, expecting that they would react by closing the wormhole to the Ferengi. That action had given the nagus sufficient cause to blockade Bajor.

"It's so easy to see now that the blockade was a ruse," Sisko told Quark. "I couldn't figure out why the nagus would execute a blockade, and then allow food and medicine through it." Quark had been imprisoned when that had happened, and so he had not known about it. "It was because the nagus had no real interest in hurting the Bajoran people."

"No," Quark agreed. "He wouldn't have wanted to hurt them. If he had, then the Bajorans might never have allowed the Ferengi to use the wormhole ever again, even if the Orb was eventually given to Bajor."

"It would be difficult for the Bajorans to forgive what they would have viewed as murder." Sisko then explained to Quark how Shakaar had purchased the thirty-five starships from the Yridians. The nagus had doubtless made sure when he sold the ships to the Yridians that they knew the Bajorans would shortly be looking to arm themselves, and he would have played upon the Yridians' thirst for salable information by suggesting this means of gaining access to *DS9*'s Gamma Quadrant data. Sisko then told Quark about the staged encounter between the Bajoran ships and the Marauder, and how Zek had used that as cause to declare war.

"What I don't understand is how could the nagus be sure that I would bring you to Bajor?" Sisko said. "After all, you were in prison."

"I'm sure that if you hadn't brought me to Bajor, or hadn't appeared there yourself, then the nagus would have implemented some contingency plan," Quark said. "Somehow, he would have made that final offer to the Bajorans."

"But why did the nagus do all of this?" Sisko asked. "What could have been worth all of these machinations?"

"Thirty-five brand-new starships," Quark said. "Well, thirty-five slightly used starships. The nagus sold those same ships to the Yridians for a huge profit—I know, because I received a percentage of it for brokering the deal—and now he's going to sell those same thirty-five starships to the Karemma."

"That's who they were built for in the first place," Sisko said, realizing now that Dax had been right, that the computer defaults aboard the ships had been configured, not *by* the Karemma, but *for* them. Sisko felt his jaw drop.

"It's genius," Quark said.

"So all of this, everything, was simply so the nagus could make greater profits?"

"And the Yridians now have an information pipeline into *Deep Space Nine* and the Gamma Quadrant," Quark noted. "With his ties to the Yridians, I'm sure the nagus will also be able to take advantage of that arrangement. The thirty-fourth Rule of Acquisition really applies here: War is good for business." Quark shook his head back in forth, in admiration, Sisko thought. "It's astounding . . . the complexities . . . every detail so perfectly timed and worked out . . . and the nagus ended up with everything he wanted."

"Maybe not everything," Sisko said. He reached across the desk and handed Quark a padd. On it was a copy of the document Sisko had been reading.

"What's this?"

"It's the contract between the Yridians and the Bajorans permitting the Yridians access to the data from our communications relay in the Gamma Quadrant," Sisko explained. "The Yridians have been on the station for a week now, monitoring the relay. I want to find some way of allowing the Bajorans to fulfill the letter of this contract without our having to compromise our data." Sisko paused, and then said, "I thought you might be able to help."

"Let me take a look," Quark said. He spent a short time reading the document. After he had done so, Sisko watched him go back over it, apparently searching for something specific.

"Simplicity itself, Captain," Quark said at last. "This contract states that the Bajorans must allow the Yridians to monitor all transmissions from the Gamma Quadrant relay to the station, but it does not demand that the Yridians *understand* those transmissions."

Sisko understood immediately what Quark was suggesting: "Encryption."

"Exactly."

"You're quite a businessman, Quark," Sisko said. To his surprise, Quark beamed at the compliment.

"Thank you," he said. "It's not a Rule of Acquisition, but it is a business tactic to act the fool; we're not all as dumb as you think we are."

"I'm beginning to realize that," Sisko returned. "Thank you, Quark. For everything."

Quark rose, the meeting clearly at an end. He started for the doors, and for the second time, Sisko called after him.

"Quark," he said. Quark turned back to face him once more. "I'm glad you're back."

Quark tipped his head in acknowledgment, and left.

CHAPTER

40

CHAPTER 40

THE BOLIAN PLACED HIS THUMB on Quark's banking device, completing the transaction.

"I'm sure you'll be very satisfied with it," Quark said. "As Betazoid gift boxes go, this really is one of the finest you'll ever see."

"It better be," the Bolian said. "And it better work."

"Of course it'll work," Quark assured him. "Just program it the way I explained." Betazoid gift boxes were fashioned with a humanoid face on their surface, which in the presence of the gift's recipient would briefly animate and deliver a message.

The Bolian took his hand away from the banking device and picked the gift box up from the bar. He examined his purchase once more, and then, to Quark's horror, he suddenly furrowed his brow.

"What's wrong?" Quark asked, even though he did not really want to know.

"This face," the Bolian said. "It looks a little bit like you."

"What?" Quark was puzzled, because he knew the face was not his; this was a genuine gift box from Betazed, not

422

some counterfeit he had fabricated himself. "The thing doesn't even have any ears."

"You're right," the Bolian said. "Never mind. I must be seeing things." He left the bar with the box.

Quark walked back down to the other end of the bar, where he had left a small knot of listeners in the middle of his telling them the tale of how he had helped to end the Ferengi-Bajoran war. Since he had reopened the bar, many people had wanted to know what had happened to him, and how it was that he had returned to *Deep Space Nine*. In particular, Morn never seemed to tire of asking him questions abut his experiences.

"So, where was I?" Quark said to his audience, which had actually grown, he saw, since he had left a few minutes ago to complete the transaction with the Bolian.

"You were telling us about the nagus's palace," Broc said.

Quark thought about telling Broc to get back to work, but then decided against doing so. He was a Ferengi, and so he would probably appreciate the subtleties of Quark's descriptions more than most of the other people here.

As Quark recounted his arrival at Zek's estate, and his subsequent conversation with the nagus—which he edited in order not to reveal Zek's plan, which might have lessened Quark's efforts in some people's eyes—he privately marveled at the shrewdness and cunning of the nagus. He thought back months ago to when he had believed Zek to be losing his business faculties, only to discover that the nagus had uncovered a flaw in the Bolian Credit Exchange and enacted a bold and brilliant plan; how could Quark have underestimated him again? Actually, Quark realized that the answer was simple: Zek was brilliant.

Quark had not told Sisko about Cort—about his being employed by the nagus, and about how he had made sure that Quark had been delivered into Sisko's hands at just the right time—because Quark had come to understand that he was himself the final payoff in Zek's grand design. The nagus wanted Sisko to believe that Quark had been able to manipulate the Ferengi leader and thereby help defuse a dangerous situation. Sisko might then view Quark in a different light; perhaps Quark might even be able to capture the captain's ear at some point in the future, a circumstance which would doubtless have proven useful to the nagus. And even though Sisko now knew of the nagus's great plan, the captain was still grateful to Quark for what he had done.

Zek, Quark thought, *is a master.*

As Quark finished telling his story, he noticed Major Kira enter the bar. He had not seen her since he had been back on the station, and he was pretty sure that he did not want to see her now. Unfortunately, she headed directly toward him.

"Quark," she said as she reached the bar.

"Major," Quark said. "What can I do for you?"

"You can listen," she said, though without animosity.

"I'm all ears." To Quark's astonishment, Kira smiled, not exactly a warm smile, but one of good humor, he thought.

"I just wanted to tell you that I'm sorry." Quark blinked. He did not know what to say. "I heard about what happened to you on Bajor."

Quark wondered exactly what she had learned, since he and Rom had been circumspect in speaking about their experiences in the prison camp. She had probably only heard a general account of poor conditions and the like, because the Bajorans would not be quick to spell out publicly all of the ugly details. It was possible, though, that Shakaar might have told her more.

"And I also heard about you talking with the nagus to get him to sell us the Orb," Kira continued. "I wanted to say that I was wrong about you in this case, and I wanted to thank you for what you did."

"You're welcome, Major," Quark said, and he could not keep himself from smiling.

"I still don't understand you, or the Ferengi way of life," she went on, "but I guess that's not really a reason to hate you."

"No," Quark agreed. "If it's any consolation, I don't understand you either."

"Of course, that's also not a good reason to like you," she said, but she smiled again as she spoke. Quark smiled back. Kira seemed uncomfortable. She apparently had nothing more to say, because she turned on her heel and strode out of the bar. But the crowd huddled around the serving area, Quark thought, was duly impressed.

Later that night, when he was closing the bar, Quark smiled again when he thought back to the major's visit and to her apology. He had no illusions that he and Kira were now the best of friends—or even the worst of friends—but he recognized that she had at least been big enough to say what she had said in the bar and in front of other people. If nothing else, perhaps it was a starting point for better understanding between the two of them.

Quark finished locking up, and after he had counted and secured the day's receipts, he went to his old familiar place behind the bar and switched on the comm panel there. Easily, as though he had been doing this every night for the past few months, he accessed the financial exchanges and began studying the markets. There was a deal out there waiting for him, he knew. He just had to find it.

The nagus had inspired him. One day, Quark knew, he would own his own moon.

It took patience and experience, he thought, but if you looked in the right places, with the right perspective, it was just possible that the universe actually made sense.

Later that night when he was closing the bar, Grant suppressed a wry laugh. He'd fought back to the major's visit the to her grocery. He had no intuition that he and Kira were now the bad Christian — or ever the worst of drunks — but he recognized that she had at least been big enough to say what she'd said in the bar and in front of other people. If nothing else, perhaps it was a starting point for better understanding between the two of them.

Grant finished locking up, and after he had counted and sorted the day's receipts, he went to his old familiar place behind the bar, and watched the same scene period there. Easily, as though he had been doing this every night for the past few months, he noticed the line-up of empty glasses and began studying the numbers. There was a knock out there waiting for him. He knew the trail had gone cold.

The news had inspired him: One day, Grant knew, he would own his own motel.

It took patience and experience — he thought, but if you looked at the right faces, with the right perspective, it was just possible that the universe actually made sense.

Star Trek: Deep Space Nine®

The Search • Diane Carey
Warped • K. W. Jeter
The Way of the Warrior • Diane Carey
Star Trek: Klingon • Dean W. Smith & Kristine K. Rusch
Trials and Tribble-ations • Diane Carey
Far Beyond the Stars • Steve Barnes
The 34th Rule • Armin Shimerman & David R. George III

Star Trek®: Voyager™

Flashback • Diane Carey
Mosaic • Jeri Taylor
The Black Shore • Greg Cox

#1 *Caretaker* • L. A. Graf
#2 *The Escape* • Dean W. Smith & Kristine K. Rusch
#3 *Ragnarok* • Nathan Archer
#4 *Violations* • Susan Wright
#5 *Incident at Arbuk* • John Gregory Betancourt
#6 *The Murdered Sun* • Christie Golden
#7 *Ghost of a Chance* • Mark A. Garland & Charles G.
    McGraw
#8 *Cybersong* • S. N. Lewitt
#9 *Invasion #4: The Final Fury* • Dafydd ab Hugh
#10 *Bless the Beasts* • Karen Haber
#11 *The Garden* • Melissa Scott
#12 *Chrysalis* • David Niall Wilson
#13 *The Black Shore* • Greg Cox
#14 *Marooned* • Christie Golden
#15 *Echoes* • Dean W. Smith & Kristine K. Rusch
#16 *Seven of Nine* • Christie Golden

Star Trek®: New Frontier

#1 *House of Cards* • Peter David
#2 *Into the Void* • Peter David
#3 *The Two-Front War* • Peter David
#4 *End Game* • Peter David
#5 *Martyr* • Peter David
#6 *Fire on High* • Peter David

Star Trek®: Day of Honor

Book One: *Ancient Blood* • Diane Carey
Book Two: *Armageddon Sky* • L. A. Graf
Book Three: *Her Klingon Soul* • Michael Jan Friedman
Book Four: *Treaty's Law* • Dean W. Smith & Kristine K. Rusch

Star Trek®: The Captain's Table

Star Trek®: The Dominion War

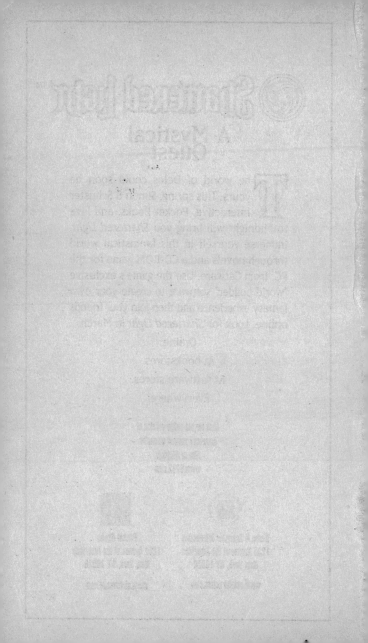